DATE DUE		

Green Centuries

Southern Classics Series

M. E. Bradford, Editor

Southern Classics Series

M. E. Bradford, Series Editor

Green Centuries

CAROLINE GORDON

with a preface by Thomas H. Landess

The long man strode apart.
In green no soul was found,
In that green savage clime
Such ignorance of time.
JOHN PEALE BISHOP

J. S. Sanders & Company
NASHVILLE

Library of Congress Catalog Card Number:
91-67521

ISBN: 1-879941-05-8

Published in the United States by
J. S. Sanders & Company
P. O. Box 50331
Nashville, Tennessee 37205

Distributed to the trade by
National Book Network
4720-A Boston Way
Lanham, Maryland 20706

1992 printing
Manufactured in the United States of America

To Maxwell Perkins

Preface

Caroline Gordon spent most of her adult life trying to steal time to write. Like many serious novelists, she taught in college creative writing programs, where she read and criticized the work of students, attended innumerable faculty functions, and tried to avoid entangling campus politics. She once called poet Wallace Stevens "something of a monster," because he pursued a career as an insurance executive. Had she really understood the no-nonsense world of business, she might have found it less distracting and more conducive to writing than the academy.

But in addition to her teaching, she had other pressing responsibilities. She was a wife and mother; and she devoted much of her creative energy to her husband, Allen Tate, and their daughter. Allen was a chore from the beginning. A charmingly self-indulgent man, he was always preoccupied with his own career, with the pursuit of his numerous literary friendships, and with other women. He was also hospitable to a fault. As a consequence, the Tate household was forever crowded with guests, including some destined to be among the most formidable literary figures of the age—Robert Lowell, Hart Crane, Mark Van Doren, Delmore Schwartz, Andrew Lytle, Malcolm Cowley, Arthur Mizener, and Robert Penn Warren, to name but a few.

With this succession of non-paying boarders, the novelist was forever stretching meals, monitoring sleeping arrangements, and patching up quarrels (when she wasn't starting them herself). Small wonder that it took her some three years to write *Green*

Centuries, which many critics believe is her finest novel. She started work on the book in 1938, when she and Allen were teaching at Greensboro, North Carolina, and she finished it at Princeton in 1941. During this period, she had to deal with the usual distractions: house guests, Allen's writer's block, and academic society. She complained to Muriel Cowley:

> Must get back to my Indians. I plan to kill off twenty six of them today but alas, I will have to stop the bloody work at four o'clock to go and pour tea at a ladies' gathering. The faculty ladies here are all great organizers—and callers. If they know who you are they call on you because they like to call on writers. If they don't know who you are they call more than ever to console you for being so obscure.

Green Centuries was indeed about Indians in a time when they were less fashionable as literary subjects than they are today. To most Americans of the 1940s, "the only good Indian was a dead Indian," or else one attending a mission school on the reservation. Yet in her extensive research on frontier life, Miss Gordon discovered that the Cherokees of that period were more civilized than the white invaders and more refined in their sensibilities. She saw in their society, soon to be destroyed, a beautifully ordered world of ceremony and ritual in which the basic activities of life were given form and transcendent meaning. Miss Gordon grasped what few people of that period understood: that the civilization of the Cherokees was as finely structured and as sensitive to life as a spider web.

Against this highly sophisticated and orderly community, she juxtaposes the coarsening freedom of the white pioneers, who, as they moved westward, shed the vestiges of their Christian European heritage and reverted to their basic instincts for self-gratification. The principal white characters in *Green Centuries*, though by no means two-dimensional villains, find it difficult to maintain their full humanity as they confront the seductive freedom of the American frontier. Unlike the Cherokees, whose every action is invested with transcendent meaning by a traditional society, the frontier folk are often bestial in the pursuit of basic needs and self-centered in their relationships with one another. Theirs is a nightmare vision of liberty grown renegade and insatiable, a world in which the strongest ego prevails.

Though this summary may sound like a 1990s fictional stereotype of the historic confrontation between the noble Indian and the wicked European settler, Miss Gordon's narrative is considerably more complicated and infinitely more credible. In the first place, she does not regard white European civilization as rapacious and barbaric. Her white characters run into spiritual difficulty on the frontier because they lose sight of their religious and cultural heritage in the vast wilderness. Released from biblical and communal controls, they are less human than their Indian counterparts; but the culture from which they come is presented, however implicitly, as good rather than evil.

In the second place, the Cherokee nation is neither oversimplified nor sentimentalized. Miss Gordon's Indians are not noble savages, instinctively virtuous because they still remain in a state of nature. Like the white characters, the Cherokees are fallible creatures living in a fallen world. If they behave better than the European pioneers who threaten and eventually destroy them, it is not because they are innately good but because they act within the rigid confines of convention and tribal law. As human beings, they are no less cruel or lust-driven than their white counterparts. They simply deal in a more orderly fashion with their failings.

In reading *Green Centuries*, one must remember that it was written at a time when the historical works of Frederick Jackson Turner and Henry Nash Smith were quite the rage among liberal intellectuals, who saw in the frontier experience "the crucible of democracy." In the wilderness of the New World, they argued, the white settlers found both freedom and equality. No one was judged by birth or riches but by the ability to survive and prevail. (You survived the rigors of nature and you prevailed over the Indian.) And you were at liberty to become whatever you wished. In Absolute Nature, these social critics maintained, you found Absolute Freedom. (And that's how the New Deal began.)

Miss Gordon, who had probably read more of the primary documents from this early period than all but a handful of historians, believed that such a view was not only simplistic, but wrong-headed. And her novel is based on an entirely different understanding of the early history of the nation—an essentially conservative Christian perspective.

In *Green Centuries* we see no awakening political consciousness, no Whitmanesque celebration of equality and self. Miss Gordon's protagonist, Orion Outlaw, cares less about democracy than he does about survival and appetite. He is so infatuated with his own independence that he rejects the very circumstances in which political activity must take place. Thus politics, which is by definition a communal preoccupation, is for him an entanglement to be avoided. In fact, he flees into the wilderness precisely because he does not want to accept the responsibilities of living in society.

It would be wrong, however, to suggest that *Green Centuries* is about history or political philosophy or anything so abstract. It is a novel rather than a romance, and it is about people rather than ideas. Orion Outlaw is a tragic figure who exemplifies great virtues and possesses great flaws. Like his classical namesake, he is the ultimate hunter, accompanied only by his dog, Sirius, forever pursuing the kill. Yet Orion is not the simple and unchanging character of myth, but a highly complicated man who comes to a tragic awareness of his flaws only after he has destroyed all possibility of leading the good life.

True to the name Outlaw, which is what the MacGregors called themselves after the failure of the Jacobite cause, he flees all authority to seek the wilderness, leaving behind a community where life is still reverenced, where customs and manners are still observed, where courtship is still ritualized in dances and games, and where marriage is still the norm. Orion takes with him Cassy, the daughter of an Anglican clergyman. They have already become lovers; and though the opportunity presents itself at a later time, they choose not to marry.

The relationship between Orion and Cassy is the primary focus of Miss Gordon's narrative—the initial joy of being together, the raising of a family, the prosperity that comes from hard work. Indeed, for awhile it seems as if the frontier is fully capable of producing the kind of independence that Orion seeks and Cassy is content to accept.

However, their relationship cannot survive the rigors of the wilderness and Orion's desire to move ever westward. Daniel Boone, a friend and neighbor for awhile, epitomizes the free spirit of the pioneer—Boone, who abandons his homestead and moves on when stability and order begin to trouble his spirit, fetching along his long-suffering but compliant wife. Far from presenting him as heroic, Miss Gordon renders Boone as a flawed man who represents the worst impulses of the age. Cassy tries to thwart Orion's desire to follow Boone's example; but eventually her efforts prove unsuccessful. The dangerous life they have chosen ends tragically in alienation and death.

In contrast to Orion and Cassy, Miss Gordon gives the reader Archy Outlaw, Orion's brother, and Archy's Cherokee wife, Monon. Though initially a far less formidable figure than Orion, Archy chooses a better path to follow and in the end achieves a peace and maturity that Orion never approaches. The victim of a hunting accident, Archy is discovered by Indian warriors, who take him back to their village and later initiate him into the tribe.

There he learns the customs and beliefs of the Cherokee nation and becomes a hunter, taking the name of Bear Killer. It is through Archy's eyes that we understand the orderly world of the Cherokees, where virtually every action is a ritual invested with religious significance, from the hunting of wild game to the sexual union of man and woman.

In tracing Archy's assimilation into the Cherokee nation, Miss Gordon is able to present dramatic contrasts between life in a traditional society and the life of the frontier. When Orion is tempted by the wife of a neighbor, his betrayal of Cassy is selfish and perfunctory, an act of pure lust unchecked by convention or conscience. On the other hand, in the Cherokee nation, on one

night during a special harvest festival, women are permitted to
choose any man for a sexual partner, regardless of marital status.
One act is an exemplum of unchecked lust. The other is a con-
trolled exercise of sexual desire.

Likewise, hunting and warfare are nothing more than brutal
and dehumanizing slaughter to Orion and his fellow frontiers-
men. One white man, Joe Hubbard, tells casually of ambushing a
Cherokee brave, wounding him, dragging him three miles at the
end of a rope, and then skinning him to make a saddle. To
Hubbard, the Indian is no more than an animal. And to Orion
they become something even lower in the order of nature. Miss
Gordon describes him on a field after battle, surveying the corpses
of slain Cherokees.

> He started running and suddenly it was like some day in summer,
> when going into the field, he would find a melon that had not been
> there the day before and then another and then another, and
> would run from row to row, counting the long, dark shapes. So
> now he ran over the field and the bodies he came on were to him
> like the fruit he had been used to number on that summer day.

In this beautifully crafted passage, Miss Gordon shows Orion's
understanding of the slain warriors as no more than vegetables
ripening in a field, the lowest form of living thing. As the scene
closes, he stands in a puddle of blood laughing. "We let it out of
'em, didn't we?" he cries. "We let it out of 'em!"

Among Archy Outlaw's Cherokees, however, a deep reverence
for life informs the principal masculine pursuits of hunting and
warfare. Both activities are governed by rigid rules that prescribe
respect for prey and enemy. Hunters pay solemn tribute to the
animals they have killed, and warriors treat their fallen adver-
saries with dignity. As Andrew Lytle has written of Miss Gordon's Indians, "Their warfare did not evince a destructive
instinct. It was a religious rite, and therefore a social rite, which
submerged the end of fighting which is death beneath the ritual
practice of it."

It is important to remember that the contrast between frontier life and life among the Cherokees is revealed not through discursive passages or interior monologues, but through the action of the novel, which seems to develop naturally and inevitably, without suffering from thematic manipulation by the author. In fact, so skillfully did Miss Gordon disguise her thematic intent that an old friend, John Crowe Ransom, thought she had surrendered to naturalism.

Green Centuries may well be Caroline Gordon's masterpiece. Certainly it is one of the most well-wrought novels to emerge from the so-called Southern renaissance. The intricate structure of parallel actions is handled with discipline and imagination. By the end of the novel, all the loose ends are tied up by invisible hands, and the meaning of the characters is fully realized without compromising their integrity as human beings. As a consequence, *Green Centuries* is both a good yarn and a book of genuine literary significance—the work of a master.

It is also worth noting that Miss Gordon's prose in this novel is more inventive and lyrical than in her earlier works. Rhetorically, she risks more and gains more, without ever falling into the trap of sacrificing her characters or action for a burst of self-conscious poetry. She knew the difference between a poem and a novel. She wrote novels.

These qualities make *Green Centuries* a valuable model for serious students of fiction to analyze and follow. Miss Gordon, a highly conscious artist, works with classical restraint, avoiding tricks and affectations; and for this reason her later works are lessons in how to tell a story simply and dramatically, while at the same time pushing the art of fiction beyond conventional boundaries.

Of course, consummate artistry doesn't always please the public or pay the bills. The Tates had hoped to live for awhile on the royalties from *Green Centuries*, and their expectations were by no means unrealistic. *None Shall Look Back*, an earlier novel with an historical setting, had sold more than 10,000 copies, enough to support the author and her family for a year. *Green Centuries*, in many ways a superior work, might well have done better. Unfortunately, it sold so poorly that royalties failed to pay back the publisher's advance.

Clearly, the period in which the action was set did not appeal to audiences in the early 1940s. *None Shall Look Back*, a contemporary of *Gone With the Wind*, was about the War Between the States—a perennially popular subject of fiction and history. The pioneer experience had already provided a number of novelists with romantic subject matter, but apparently the public was weary of the period, particularly when treated in realistic terms. In *Close Connections*, a recent biography of Miss Gordon, Ann Waldron reports that *Green Centuries* was rejected by at least one Hollywood producer because it belonged to "the coonskin cap group." Had she chosen to write about ladies and gentlemen in white wigs, she might have fared better. Indeed, Frederick Lewis Allen wrote to her about the book, expressing the snobbery of the current literati: "We can't get much interested in 'Hit war' people."

Miss Gordon was extremely depressed by the experience and wrote to a friend, "My book was a complete failure, financially, didn't even pay back its advance. . . . It was poor timing, of course—people are tired of pioneer stories, and I think that in a way it is a hard book to read, but I had expected it to do better than it did."

Her disappointment turned to bitterness when she went into Scribner's book store, saw *Saratoga Trunk*, a popular potboiler, on prominent display, and looked in vain for her own novel. She wrote indignantly to Mark Van Doren: "I could not find my book anywhere so asked a clerk if he had a book called *Green Centuries*. He led me to a table, piled high with garden books and so help me God proffered me a herb manual."

More than thirty years later, when she was serving as Professor of Creative Writing at the University of Dallas, she still lamented the failure of *Green Centuries* to receive the popular audience she felt it deserved. She saw a copy of the paperback in a Salvation Army thrift shop and came away haunted by the sight.

"I find it heartbreaking to see novels in second-hand book-stores," she said. "They're like old friends who have been abandoned by their families."

Yet *Green Centuries* has seldom been out of print for long; and critical articles increase with every passing year, assessments that are invariably laudatory. Though the novel was once rejected by the public, it now promises to have a longer life than the bestsellers of 1941, most of them written by people of lesser talent and integrity. Indeed, it is now recognized as one of the enduring works of the Southern renaissance.

In a dry season, when novelists of literary merit are few and when critics no longer demand or even understand genuine craftsmanship, it is time to take a second look at Caroline Gordon's work in general, and *Green Centuries* in particular. She was a writer who understood the full potential of the novel and was able to break new ground, both in technique and in subject matter.

Yet, unlike some innovators, her narratives have always been available to the general reader. Though a literary figure of historical significance, she is primarily a first-rate story teller and a shrewd student of the human heart. In addition, she touches on the immutable truths of human experience and reminds us of the perennial need for community, rituals, and a religious vision to give form and meaning to life. These truths remain essential to the survival of a people, whether in pioneer days, when Americans had yet to discover a national identity, or in the last decade of the twentieth century, when we have all but forgotten who we once were. Caroline Gordon is one of a handful of writers who can help us remember, and for this reason alone it is important that she be read.

Falls Church, Virginia   THOMAS LANDESS

PART ONE

"I think it time to remove when I can no longer fall a tree for fuel so that its top will lie within a few yards of my cabin."

DANIEL BOONE

CHAPTER 1

RION AND ARCHY had been in the west field all morning, gathering corn. It was time to knock off for dinner. Rion had just climbed up on the high wagon seat, ready to drive the load to the barn when he saw the stranger come up over the rise and start down the road.

He was alone and footing it faster than men usually did when they came down that road. Rion wondered which one of the neighbors was in such a hurry and said to Archy, "Who's that?"

Archy came around to the side of the wagon just as the pack horse straggled in sight. "It's a peddler," he said.

"I wish he hadn't come at dinner time, "Rion said, "Ma didn't leave but one pie. . . . Hand me them lines."

He took the lines that Archy handed up to him but he did not speak to the horses and he let the lines fall slack across his knee while he watched the tall figure moving on towards them.

The road the stranger was travelling was called the Trading Path and it had been a road long before Rion's father had built his house there on the knoll by the river. The traders came down this road on their way to South Carolina and usually stopped at the house. There was not much difference between those who paid cut money for their dinner and those who asked for a hand-out of bacon and greens at the back door. Greasy vagabonds all and yet Rion never saw one stop at the gate but that a strange feeling, a feeling that he never had at any other time, came over him. He had this feeling now and he thought as he gazed past the man's moving head to where the road wound out of sight between two low hills that it was not the traders themselves but the road they came. He never looked up that road without wondering how it would be to start out and keep going till you reached Pennsylvania. That was where most of the traders came from. You might go on farther than that. There was a trader came through once who said the road went on through Pennsylvania into far northern countries where there was snow all the year around and all the bears were white.

The pack horse was at the fence, thrusting his lean neck through the rails to get at the corn. The stranger came up behind him. A tall, grey-eyed fellow in deerskin. He put his foot on the bottom rail and looked first at Rion and then at Archy who had climbed up beside Rion.

"You boys make this crop yourself?" he asked.

"I don't know who'd a helped us," Rion said. He reached around behind him and got several ears of corn and tossed them over the fence. The horse gave a startled whinny as if he could not believe his good fortune then bared his yellow teeth and bit into an ear. Rion watched the flecks of greenish slobber falling from his mouth and his eyes went to the swollen stomach and sunken flank.

"He's been on grass a long time, ain't he?" he said.

"Grazes all night long every night of his life" the stranger said.

He had his leg up and was straddling the top rail and now he was over and walking down the rows. He stopped near a tall stalk, plucked an ear and husked it carefully, then shelled a few grains into his hand. "Good corn," he said as he dropped them on the ground. "Good corn as I've seen along my way."

"Where'd you come from?" Archy asked.

"Paxtang." He looked over the field to the line of trees that marked the river. "That the Yadkin?"

The boys nodded.

"Then this must be Trading Ford?"

"That's right," Rion said. "Salisbury ain't but four miles. . . . But you might as well stop at the house and git your dinner."

The stranger looked over at the knoll where the Outlaw house stood in its grove of trees. "I'll do that," he said, "Is there a road to get up there?"

"Just keep along the fence," Rion told him, "and you'll see where the road branches off."

He put his hand up to his shoulder and took it down quickly and looked at Archy. His blacksnake whip had been coiled about his neck all morning. He had not felt it go and yet there it was in Archy's hand.

Archy grinned. "Le' me drive."

"All right," Rion said and sat silent while Archy cracked the whip over the horses until he got them into a gallop. He turned the wagon around, dexterously Rion had to admit, and still keeping the horse at a gallop, drove out of the field.

"You could a backed easier" Rion said when they were on the road to the house.

"I like to see how short I can turn 'em" Archy said.

Rion glanced behind him. The stranger had come to the end of the fence and was starting up the road to the house. "Paxtang?" Rion said, "Wasn't that where Daniel was, with Braddock?"

"I reckon so. . . . Ain't he a funny-looking fellow, Rion?"

"He don't look no worse than the rest of them."

They were on top of the knoll, passing along the paling fence that enclosed the small front yard. A few late wall flowers were still blooming against the palings. Beyond them the weathered logs of the house showed grey through the drooping boughs of the mulberry tree. They passed the tree and came in full view of the house. It looked like an old woman asleep in the sunshine, with the two front doors—it was a double log house—closed and latched. Bolted on the inside too, no doubt. Well, that was wise, with people like this peddler here roaming the country.

They were at the lot gate. Rion jumped down and opened it, then waited while the wagon and then the peddler and his nag passed through. Archy turned the wagon around as soon as he got inside the lot, and backed it up against the runway of the barn.

The stranger stood there, smiling, as if admiring Archy's skill.

Rion looked at the horse's sides showing dark with sweat under the heavy pack. "You better take that pack off and water him, hadn't you?" he said and motioned to where the watering trough stood in the shade of a big chestnut tree.

The stranger flung the pack to the ground and led the horse over to the trough. Archy was unhitching Bald and Gal. As soon as they were free of their gear they made for the trough too. The three horses stood in the shade drinking while the bright water spilled over the green lip of the old trough and dropped down into the little stream that had run there from that same trough ever since Rion could remember.

The stranger watched them a minute. His eyes went to the sluice that brought the water down from the spring on the hillside. "That's a nice thing now," he said, "You make it?"

"Naw," Rion said. "It was here when I come."

Archy laughed and ducking down behind the stranger's back winked at Rion.

Rion looked at Archy, noticing how long the lashes were that fringed his brown eyes. And the eyes themselves might have belonged to one of the heifers out there in the pasture, so large they were and with that same liquid sheen.

He glanced down at his own muscular arms. Archy was too thin for a boy of fifteen. He, Rion, had been twenty pounds heavier when he was Archy's age and he had been only fourteen when he put Tom Allsop on his back at a muster day wrestling. Archy had turned fifteen three months ago but Allsop or any of the Salisbury bullies could take him in their two hands and break him like a rotten stick.

"Still," he thought, "they ain't going to want to. Not when he gives you that look, like a heifer begging for shelled corn . . ." Aloud he said "Come on. Less eat before we unload."

They crossed the lot and entered the back yard. It was unenclosed, yet one entering it had the feeling that he was in an enclosure. That was because of the three big chestnut trees whose boughs, interlacing high over the house, kept the place in shade all summer. The leaves on these trees were still green although the ground beneath them was drifted thick with the yellowish, half-open burrs. The peddler stooped and picked up a burr, slipped the shining brown nut out and bit into it, and threw it from him.

"You ain't had a real frost down here yet?"

"One light one," Rion said. "Brought these burrs down night before last."

They were at the back door. The old stag hound, lying in the one spot of sunshine that fell there, thumped his tail at them. "Get out of the way, Roane," Rion said.

They stepped up over the worn doorstone into the kitchen. As always it seemed dark after the open light of the fields, and chill although a few embers from the morning's fire still glowed on the hearth.

Archy went straight to the oven and pulled the door down. "There's the pie," he said, "and there's sweet potatoes too."

"Go down in the cellar and get the milk," Rion told him.

He walked over to the hearth and lifted the lid from the big iron pot. "There's squirrel stew here," he said. "Want some?"

The stranger was standing in the middle of the floor, his light-colored eyes roving around as if everything he saw was strange to him. "I ain't a caring" he said politely.

Rion filled three plates with stew and brought them to the table. Archy came back with a pitcher in the crook of each arm and a plate of butter in one hand and a cheese in the other. "I'm snaggle toothed and double jointed," he said. "Gi' me room."

The stranger had already finished his helping of stew and was presenting his plate for potatoes and ham. "You boys live here by yourself?" he asked.

"No," Rion said, "The folks are all away at a funeral."

The stranger peeled his sweet potato and ate it in two bites. "You have it mighty nice now," he said, "good garden and everything. . . . Old man work you very hard?"

"I wouldn't want to eat my bread in idleness," Rion said, "whether it was the old man's or anybody else's. I get off to the woods two, three times a week."

The stranger looked over to where the autumn landscape showed dimly through the small glass panes of the room's one window. "I don't reckon there's much game around here" he said.

"There ain't no buffalo left," Rion said, "but there's plenty of deer and elk."

"I ain't ever even seen a buffalo," Archy said musingly.

"They was run out of the country before you was born," the stranger said. He laughed. "I've seen three, four hundred grazing in one place like cattle, and deer and elk mixed in with them."

Rion did not like to give the man the lie at his own table so he said only: "And where was that?"

The stranger looked up at the window again, his grey eyes blank as if they gazed inward on the scene he described. "It was a long way from here," he said, his tone tinged with melancholy. "A long way from here."

Archy got up and brought the apple pie still warm from the oven. Rion cut it into halves. "You can have my share," he said, "Least if you like apple pie."

The man's big, loose lips curled in a smile. "I ain't got nothing against it," he said.

Archy was through his pie, bolting it like he did everything else. Rion cut himself a piece of cheese and ate it, then got up from the table. The stranger got up too, holding what was left of his pie in his hand. "You boys got it mighty nice here," he said again.

He leaned over and took a piece of cheese in his other hand and began walking about the room. He came to the door which led into the chamber and paused. "You got another room in there?"

"It's the old folks' room," Rion said and followed the man across the threshold. The outside shutter had been swung to and the room had only the light that came from the kitchen. The peddler looked over in the corner where the bed stood, high with its feather mattress and quilts. He laughed suddenly. "Lord, I ain't ever slept in a bed like that. . . . Where you boys sleep?"

Archy had come in and was standing beside them. "In the loft," he said, "and it's hot in the summer, I tell you."

The stranger jerked his head up as if the leather collar of his shirt was chafing him. "I couldn't stand it," he said, "I tried it one night. In Philadelphia. Had to go out and lay on the ground before day come."

He went over to the dresser. One of Sarah Outlaw's caps was lying there, its pale colored ribbons dangling down over the dark wood. He took it up and twirled it on his thumb. "Women's gear," he said, "I got some in my pack. Ought to have more, I reckon, but I hate to fool with the stuff. '*Master Findley*,' his voice suddenly went high and mincing, '*I ain't plumb sure I want the pink ribbons. Maybe I better take the blue.*'" He spat on to the floor as if to clear his mouth of the sound. "I'd rather trade with the Indians any day. . . . How about the Catawbas? I thought I might trade with them some on the way to Charleston. Only I ain't got much goods left. I stopped three weeks in one of them Cherokee towns and they about cleaned me out. They treat you fine in them towns. They's one of them chiefs, 'the Little Carpenter' they call him, thinks the world of me. Has me set right on the mat beside him. He ain't no common Indian, that fellow. He's been to London to see the King. He told me . . ." He stopped talking, as if from politeness, realizing that he was speaking of matters with which his listeners could not be acquainted.

Rion stood silent, watching the dust motes dance in the shaft of light from the kitchen. He raised his head and glanced about the room, his nostrils widening. It was musty in here. They needn't have fastened everything up so tight even if they were going away for the day.

"Let's go outdoors," he said.

They went out into the back yard. There had been a little wind in the morning but it had died down. Here under the trees it was still and warm, as if winter was never coming.

Archy threw himself down in the strip of sunshine next to the house, his head pillowed on Roane's fat side. The old dog groaned under the weight but did not move.

"That hound any good?" the peddler asked.

"He's done blunted his nose laying by the fire so much," Rion said, "and the women keep him too fat. Archy's worse'n any of 'em. Feeds him at the table."

The stranger shook his head disapprovingly. "I never had much use for a dog. Nine times out of ten they're more trouble than they're worth. . . . Well, I better be starting."

"No hurry," Rion said. "The sun's high yet."

He walked over to where the skin of the deer he had shot two days before hung over a limb, drying. He pinched the skin between his thumb and finger. It felt dry enough. He took it down and laid it on the saw-horse table that stood under the tree. The deer's liver and brains were soaking in water in a green bark trough. He plunged his hand into the tepid water and taking up a mass of the stuff kneaded it to a fine paste which he began working into the hairy skin. Archy came over after a little and began helping him. Rion was careful to see that the liver and brains were mixed in equal proportions.

"If you don't it'll spot. I don't much like to use liver nohow."

The stranger laughed. "Man, you're as particular as an Indian!"

He went into the house, got a coal from the fire to light his pipe and sat down on the door step.

"I knew a fellow was like you once. Man, he had to have everything just right! Still, if I'm taking to the woods I'd as soon go with that fellow as any man I know."

The brothers were silent, bent over their work. The stranger talked on, almost as if to himself: ". . . There's a lot of difference in folks. Indians as well as whites. Now you take up where I been. It ain't so much the French egging 'em on. It's the Indians themselves. These Indians down this way seems like all they want is to be let alone but up there in the Six Nations they study war. Man, I've seen a Shawnee war belt thick as you are and twice as long. . . ."

"Where are them Six Nations?" Rion asked.

"Well, they move around the way Indians do but they mostly stay around the lakes. The Lenni-Lenape say they came from a river they call the Delaware. Make all the other Indians call 'em 'Grandfather.' Except the Mohawks. Them devils are haughty. They just say 'Uncle' when they meet a Lenape."

Archy laughed out. "I wouldn't call no Indian 'Uncle' or 'Grandfather' either."

"You would if they started working on you. A fellow I knew on the Kentuck told me. . . ."

Rion looked up. "*Kentuck?*" he said.

The man nodded. "The Six Nations had 'em a town on the river there. Me and another fellow built us a cabin and started trading. We done pretty well till one night a party of Canadian Indians come in. One of them chiefs reached over the counter and sunk his tomahawk in Joe's head. Split it, just like you split that deer's skull to get the brains out. I went through the back door and Tom Lowry was right after me. The Indians in the store didn't pay any attention but there was a bunch of Indians outside took up the trail and chased us to the river. . . ."

"Did you get away?" Archy had let his end of the hide fall to the ground. His eyes were fixed on the stranger's face.

"We got across, if you could call it that. Tom took cold in his lungs and died of it. I never took no harm except losing my money belt. Scraped it off, I reckon, on one of them ice cakes." He shook his head. "I had ten angels in that belt. More money than I ever had before or since."

Rion eyed him steadily for a moment. His clothing was worn through in several places. His coonskin cap was so dirty that it left a sooty mark on his forehead. His face was tallow pale. Of course that came from being in the woods so much but the hollows in his cheeks looked like he'd gone hungry. He did not believe that the man had ever had ten angels in a belt or anywhere else. And as for his big talk of trading, Rion had seen his pack where he had flung it down there by the trough. The usual peddler's pack containing nothing more valuable than pins and needles with maybe a few gew-gaws for the women.

He bent again to his work but the stranger's words still sounded in his ears. *Kentuck!* He had not thought about it for three years. It was three years ago that his friend, Daniel, had gone off soldiering to come back with tales of a wonderful land that the Indians called Kentuck. He looked up. There was a rift in the trees there to the left. Pilot Knob was a faint blue shadow on the horizon but beyond the Knob there were mountains twice as high. Daniel said that Kentuck lay right beyond those mountains, those mountains that on fair days you could almost see from this house! While Daniel was off with Braddock he had met a man who said there was a gap in those mountains: Kit Gist. He had been through the gap once; he didn't know whether he could find it again. Three years ago, in October, 1766, Daniel and Rion had set out to find that gap. They had spent the better part of a month working through laurel thickets then finally gave up and climbed the mountains. The country on the other side was no different from this. They went down into a valley that was all laurel thicket and worked east for a while, but they had Daniel's little nine year old boy, Jamie, along—they couldn't range forever; so they settled down to trap beaver. They had made that trip and got nothing for it but some prime beaver skins. He, Rion, had come to wonder if there was such a land as Kentuck—it might be just a tall tale of Kit Gist's—but Daniel still studied about it and said there must be some way of getting there.

The stranger was speaking again. "I started down here from Fort Pitt with this pack, thinking to make my way. I'm looking for a man I used to soldier with. Name's Boone. Daniel Boone."

Rion stared, amazed to hear on the man's lips the name of his companion on that long hunt.

Archy laughed. "Rion can tell you where to find *him*."

The stranger stood up. "Is it far?"

"It's about fifty miles," Rion said, "I reckon you can find it." He glanced up at the sun. "But it'll take you two days to get there. You better spend the night here and start early in the morning."

The stranger shook his head. "Naw, I'll start right now. Do I cross the river?"

Rion stood there looking at him. "You cross the river, all right," he said, "then there's three or four creeks you have to cross before you get into that country. . . ." He suddenly jerked the hide away from Archy, rolled it into a firm ball and laid it back on the table. "Leave it laying like that tonight," he said. "Tomorrow you can hang it on a limb."

He started for the house. In a few minutes he came back with his rifle in his hand.

"Where you going?" Archy said.

Rion jerked his thumb towards the stranger. "To Daniel's," he said, "with him."

CHAPTER 2

DARK CAUGHT them ten or fifteen miles from home, near the house of some people Rion knew. They spent the night with them, then set out for the Upper Forks as soon as it was light. They made thirty miles that day. As they went along the country got wilder. The last half was rough going, through thick woods. It was sun-down when they came out on the banks of Bear creek, opposite a high, rocky bluff.

Rion stopped and pointed across the water. "Here we are."

The stranger looked at the steep bluff, at the swift flowing stream. "If the old fox has got his hole here I don't see it."

Rion laughed, knowing that Daniel's house stood back from the brow, in a hollow, with woods around it so thick that the light from the window would not show.

The stranger was walking along the bank. There had been a heavy rain three days ago and the creek was still up. In the fading light the water looked black and deeper than it really was. "Do we have to swim for it?" he asked.

"There's a ford," Rion said and started down the bank. The horse had found some cane and wanted to stay on that side. They drove him through and then drove him on up the bank till they came in sight of the path that led up the side of the bluff. The stranger took the pack off and slung it over his shoulders.

"Ain't you going to hobble him?" Rion asked.

The stranger shook his head and they started up the bluffside. Rion went first. The stranger, laden with the heavy pack, followed slowly. He was winded at last. Rion could hear him puffing as he climbed. "Ain't it just like Daniel to have his house on top of the highest hill in the country?" he asked.

"It ain't much farther now," Rion told him.

A big boulder jutted out into the path. They climbed around it and could see the light from the cabin window. There was a sudden rustle in the leaves above them. Rion caught a glimpse of something white. He put his hand out quickly, caught at the boy's ankles and missed them. "Israel, go tell your Pa you got company for supper," he called.

The feet pattered on ahead. Suddenly a shaft of light fell across the path. The cabin door was open. A boy's figure could be seen slipping over the threshold but no one else was visible.

They came up on to level ground and straightened up. Rion called out: "Daniel! Daniel Boone!"

There was the sound of steps inside the cabin. A woman was standing in the doorway holding a baby in her arms. Rion took off his hat and stepped into the light. "Orion Outlaw," he said, "Mistress Rebecca. And here's a stranger strayed from the Path."

Rebecca stepped aside to let the two men enter the cabin. A short, dark woman who grew stouter as she approached middle age. She laughed good naturedly as Rion deposited on the table the turkey he had shot on the way. "And did you have to bring your meat with you?" she asked.

Israel and the four little girls had retreated to the far corner of the room as the visitors entered and now came stealing back. Rion ran at them and caught the three-year-old Lavinia out from their midst and swung her high over his head. "This is my girl," he said, "I ain't got no use for the rest of 'em."

The peddler was bowing before Rebecca. "John Findley, Madam. An old comrade-in-arms of your husband's. At your service."

Rion, putting Lavinia down, watched Mistress Boone to see how she took the stranger's flourishes. She inclined her head briefly in answer to his salutation but the expression of her plain, dark face did not alter. "Indeed?" she said indifferently, "That will have been when Daniel went with Braddock. Will you draw to the fire?"

The stranger was already establishing himself in the chimney corner, on the big bulls'-hide stool that was Daniel's favorite. "And where is himself?" he asked.

"He and Jamie went down to the run just before dark to see if maybe they could surprise a deer," Rebecca said. She shifted the baby to her hip, advanced to the fire and with the shovel raked some fresh embers out around the trivet. "And how does Mistress Outlaw?" she asked of Rion.

He grinned. "She's in a great way with the new flax. Archy and

I took to the woods the other day. We feared she'd have us spinning before it was over."

Rebecca Boone, still stooping, turned her broad face that was flushed by the heat towards him. "And why not. Ye've as much strength in your finger as the bit woman has in her whole body."

"Don't take strength to spin, takes sleight." Rion, still grinning watched her move back from the fire. He liked Rebecca Bryan. She was plain and dark like all the Bryans but there was humour in her. And she was a good wife to Daniel—the kind, except for her plainness, that he would like to have if he ever took a wife. Daniel could go off on a hunt and stay six months. She'd have nothing to say about it when he got back. The women in his own family were not like that. His mother worried if he stayed out in the woods a single night and his sisters, Jane and Betsy, were almost as bad, wanting to know where he was going every time he stepped out of the house.

The back door opened. Boone entered, followed by Jamie. A man of medium height, sparely built, with the hunter's pale face and forward slanting walk. He halted at the door to put his rifle in its rack then came to the fire. "And how are you, Rion?" he said.

The stranger was up off the stool. "Daniel, my boy. Don't you know me?"

Boone stopped halfway across the room. His grey eyes sharpened under the black brows. He drew a long breath. "John Findley. By all the Powers!"

The two men stood in the middle of the floor. They looked into each other's eyes, grasped each other's hands. Finally Findley's hand fell away. He set his left hand on Boone's shoulder, gave Boone a little push. "Man, I thought you was killed with Braddock!"

Boone looked around at the others. "This fellow was alongside of me when I went with Braddock," he said.

Findley laughed. "We started out together but we war'n't together when the Blues all come crowding back down the road. Man, I've often wondered what become of you. You was caught in the press, war'n't you?"

"I got away, to Gist's place on Laurel Mountain." He shook his head. "That's the last time I try fighting with red-coats."

"A red-coat ain't hardly human," Findley agreed, "He don't live for nothing but to draw his pay and drink it up."

Rebecca had been moving about behind them. "Will ye come to supper?" she asked.

They turned to the table. There was vension and turkey and dried peas and greens and preserves made from wild plums to be eaten with journey cake and there was a great pitcher of buttermilk and one of sweet milk. Rebecca Boone had one of the finest cows in the country. Rion as he ate watched the stranger. John Findley ate as heartily here as he had eaten at Rion's house, of both flesh and fowl, of preserves, of dried peas. When everybody else had finished he poured himself another glass of buttermilk. " 'Tis as good as ale, ma'am," he said with a bow to Rebecca.

Rebecca pressed him to have another glass but he declined and approached the fire, loosening his belt.

Daniel told one of the boys to bring in a fresh log, then said that he would go himself in order to pick one that was properly seasoned. Rion felt he needed air, so he walked out with him. It was a fine night, dark but with the stars showing. Rion looked up until he had located the constellation, Orion. He often looked for it since the time Frank Dawson had told him that he took his name from it. The young schoolmaster had come to stand in the doorway as he was leaving one evening, had dropped his hand on his shoulder.

"Look! Orion, the mighty hunter. The finest constellation in the heavens. . . ."

Daniel had found his back log and was moving towards the house. Rion picked up a turn of wood and followed him. They went slowly, savoring the air which was balmier than it had been last night.

"Reckon that fellow's horse'll be all right down there on the bank?" Rion asked.

"Yes," Boone said in a voice which was surprisingly deep for so slightly built a man. "But there ain't much cane left down there now. My horses have about cleaned it up."

They walked on in silence. Rion was thinking about the stranger, John Findley. A blatherskite and by his own account a vagrant, yet Daniel seemed to think a lot of him. He wondered how that could be, seeing that Daniel was the kind of man he was and Findley the kind he was. He looked over at Daniel's head, bright just then in the light from the doorway. Rion, observing his high forehead and big Roman nose, thought as he had often thought before that Daniel was a fine looking fellow. When you came down to it he was one of the finest fellows in the whole country. Of course some people said he was shiftless. That was because he never made much crop and was always going off on long hunts, leaving his womenfolks to get along as best they could. But he was acknowledged to be the best shot and the best trapper in Rowan county and when you said that about a man you said something. He had taught Rion how to trap beaver. Rub a twig with their own musk and the beaver would swim up to smell it, holding their forepaws under their chins and three times out of five catch a paw in the trap. He, Rion, had learned most of the woodcraft he knew from Daniel. Daniel had begun taking him out in the woods when he wasn't much bigger than Jamie here. Daniel had always seemed to think a lot of them. But this stranger with the blatherskite tongue, Daniel thought a lot of him too. . . .

Daniel was speaking, almost as if he had read Rion's thoughts. "That John Findley, he's a wild, roaming sort of fellow but he's got a power of knowledge."

Rion laughed to cover his hurt. "Them traders! To hear 'em talk they ain't anything they can't do."

Daniel did not seem to have heard. "There ain't any man I'd rather have with me in the woods," he said.

Rion did not answer. They entered the house.

The big iron pot in which the venison had been cooked had been washed and drawn to one side. Rebecca gathered the little girls about her and sat down on the bench. Lavinia came and sat in the stranger's lap. She seemed to have taken a fancy to the fellow. Findley was laughing and fooling with her but the minute Daniel came in he forgot all about the child.

"How long you been living here?" he asked.

"Two or three years," Boone told him, "I thought once of removing to Florida. I took a trip there in '65, I and seven others. Lawyer Henderson in Salisbury furnished us. He'd a fancy to know what the country was like."

"But you didn't settle?"

Rebecca leaned forward from her corner. "There's nought there but sand. Judge Henderson would be furnishing Daniel if he'd remove there and take others with him but I told him he'd have no heart to live in a country where there's no game nor grass."

"Aye," Boone said, "It's no place for a man to live." He turned to Jamie. "Boy, fetch me my gun and while you're up bring the jug."

The boy handed the rifle to his father, then passed the jug of brandy around. Findley took a swig that was equal to another man's two.

Daniel had taken a cloth down from the mantel and with wood ashes and water was polishing the barrel of his gun. After a moment he looked up at Findley. "Mind the tales Kit Gist used to tell of that gap in the Ouasioto mountains?"

"Aye."

"I tried to find it year before last." He jerked his head towards Rion. "Took this boy here with me."

"And what did you find?"

"We couldn't find the gap but we got across the mountains—by the hardest way. Crossed two big rivers and a sight of branches, then found a buffalo trace and followed it. . . ."

Findley interrupted him. "It was the Warriors' Path! Them devils go back and forth along it all the time."

Boone shook his head. "It war'n't Kentuck. It was a rough country, all grown over with laurel. Plenty of game, though. We did a good business trapping. Made us a camp on one of them creeks and took beaver. . . ."

Findley suddenly put the child out of his lap. He leaned forward, his hands on his spread knees.

"I been there, Daniel."

"Been where?"

"Kentuck."

Daniel stopped polishing his gun barrel. He sat there looking down at it for a second, then he called to Jamie: "Put it in the rack, Boy." He turned back to Findley. "Well?"

Findley stood up. He looked down on them. "It ain't like no land you ever saw before." He made a sweeping gesture. "I stood there —it's high land—and it was open all around me. Open and covered with white clover. Stretches level right up to the bank of the river."

"What river is that?"

"A big river, blue as your eyes. The French call it 'La Belle Riviere,' means beautiful river. Man, you ain't seen anything till you've seen that river! I've stood there at the falls and seen wild duck and geese crowd up so thick they'd swim over the cataract and stun themselves on the rocks. A man could go below in a canoe and pick up as many as he wanted." He lifted his hand again then let it fall as if he despaired of describing what he'd seen. "And buffalo! Man, I've walked up on a herd that stretched farther than the eye could see. They was tame too. Bulls and cows and calves and elk and deer mixed with them, all cavorting around them salt licks. You can't name any game you won't find on them levels."

"He told me about that yesterday but I didn't believe him," Rion muttered.

A muscle in Boone's cheek jerked. "How in Creation did you get there?"

Findley sat down. "I went in with General Forbes, when he took Fort Duquesne. But I didn't stay long. There was a fellow named Jennings wanted to go down the river. Had seven bateaux full of goods. Me and Tom Lowry went with him. We come down the river and we saw that country and we didn't want to go on, Tom and me. But Jennings was bound to go on, to the Mississippi. We'd fallen in with some Indians who told us the Six Nations had a big town over on a river they called the Kentuck. We bought some of Jennings' goods—paid high for 'em too—built us a cabin and started trading. We were doing a good business till a party of Canadian Indians come in one night and started a rukus. They took two traders off with them and one trader was killed. Tom and me got away by swimming the river. There war'n't nothing to do then but work our way back to the settlements."

"But you saw the country whilst you was there?" Boone asked.

Findley laughed. "Know that big place Gist used to talk about, where all them big bones was?"

"I mind it," Daniels said.

"I been there. The biggest lick I ever seen, only the bones ain't the bones of no game I ever seen. Why, one of them thigh bones'd do for the ridge pole of a tent. And there was one skull I used to set on and my legs'd dangle."

He got up and reached for the jug. Rebecca looked at his long legs and laughed. He cocked an eye at her as he threw the jug up in the crook of his elbow. "Fact, ma'am," he said solemnly.

Rion took the jug from him as he was about to set it down. "I'll have another drink on that. You mean there's game in that country with bones as big as all that?"

Findley shook his head. "I never seen no game like that but I seen the bones, sure as I'm sitting here. . . . Gi' me back that jug, Boy. I'll just put a little one on top of its pappy."

"What about that gap in the mountains?" Boone said suddenly.

Findley became excited again. "I come mighty near getting there too. The head Indian of that party I travelled with, he said we was on the Warriors' Path. I asked him if we'd come to a gap in the big mountains if we kept on and he said we would. I asked too many questions, I reckon, for all of a sudden they got suspicious and I couldn't get any more out of 'em. About that time nothing would do 'em but to turn back. I'd a gone on by myself but I was short of powder. . . ."

Outdoors some small animal was running across the clearing. They could hear the quick pad of its feet and then there was silence except for the steaming of the kettle. Jemima, sitting on the floor, leaning against her father's leg, had been listening as hard as any of them but now she gave a sigh and got up and crossed over to her mother. Rebecca gathered her on to her lap and looking away from the men into the fire sang to her softly.

Daniel raised his head. His grey eyes fixed Findley's face. "Where you going when you leave here?"

"I was figuring on working on through to Charleston."

"How'd you like to start out from here and try to find that gap?"

"The best in the world. . . . You got any money?"

Boone shook his head. "Couldn't satisfy the sheriff last time he was here. But Judge Henderson over in Salisbury, I believe he'd furnish us if I put it to him right."

"I'll help you put it to him," Findley said and gave his wild Irish laugh.

"No . . . he might not believe you. But he'll believe me, in reason."

"How come this lawyer Henderson is always furnishing you with money to move around the country?"

"He wants to get hold of a big tract of land," Boone said, "Get hold of a big tract and sell it off to settlers."

"Like the Loyal Land Company, eh?"

Boone nodded. "Will you go?"

"Aye," Findley said, "We'll find that gap. Sure as my name is John."

Rion had been gazing steadily into the fire while they made their plans. Suddenly he felt Boone standing beside him and then his hand on his shoulder. "We'll take this boy," Boone said, "He was with me the first time. I've three horses. He can ride one of 'em. . . . If Lawyer Henderson falls in with the scheme at all he'll furnish us, maybe hire some camp keepers. William Holden'd be a good man for that. . . . John Stuart'll want to go and you couldn't have a better man and maybe my brother Squire'll go too. . . . Court's meeting now. We might ride in to Salisbury tomorrow and talk to the judge. . . ."

Rebecca got awkwardly to her feet, still holding the sleeping child. " 'Twill be daylight and time to start if you keep on talking," she said tartly. She turned to her oldest son. "Jamie get them two buffalo skins off the peg so John Findley and Rion can bed down here before the fire."

The family was scattering, Daniel and his wife to their bed in the corner, the girls to the trundle bed, the boys up the ladder to the loft, Jamie had brought the buffalo robes and dropped them in a heap at Rion's feet. He stood gazing down at them. One of the hides was worn slick. Daniel had told him once that he had shot the beast fifteen years ago, over near Pilot Knob. Buffalo were gone from the Yadkin long before that. He, Rion, had never had a shot at a buffalo but great herds of them still roved over Kentuck. . . . Deer too, elk, antelope, wild geese, turkeys, all the game a man could think of. . . .

He had drunk too much of that brandy. He would have to go outside before he went to sleep. Findley was already making for the door. Rion followed him. Findley stopped like a dog at the first bush. Rion went around the side of the cabin. When he had eased himself he walked off a little way, stopped and looked up at the sky.

Mist was rising from the river. The stars were not as bright as they had been a few hours ago. But he could still pick out Orion, the Mighty Hunter. Frank had pointed out to him how the hunter stands, facing the bull, his shoulders marked by two bright stars, the lion skin in his left hand, the club in his right. "His belt, consisting of three stars of the second magnitude, points obliquely down towards Sirius. From the belt hangs the sword, composed of three smaller stars lying north and south. A magnificent white star is there in the left foot. He has no right foot, or if he has it is hidden behind Lepus. . . ."

The brandy still warmed Rion's brain. Standing there alone he laughed. It seemed to him that the Mighty Hunter had come down from the sky. Yes, he, Orion was the mighty hunter, the lion skin in his left hand, the club in his right. But the right foot was not hidden behind Lepus. He could feel it a part of his own body, gigantic, powerful. He glanced up at the sky again. He could take his bearings from the north star and start from here on his giant feet. Due west he'd go, past Pilot Mountain, through the gap Findley talked of, on, on until he stood on the great, level meadow. . . .

Someone called from the house. He was back on the Yadkin. Behind him the cabin was warm with firelight and people moving about. In front of him the pine trees dropped away to the river, mist swirling about their tops. You could not see Pilot Knob but it was there on the horizon and beyond it Stone Mountain. They had turned him back once, those mountains, but this time he would find the way through them. He raised his hand, the fingers clenched. He cried out:

"I'll hunt over that meadow. Before I'm done I'll hunt over that meadow!"

CHAPTER 3

RION TOOK leave of the Boones the next morning and set out for the Yadkin. He got a ride in a gig for part of the way and at sun-down was within ten miles of home. He spent the night at a neighbor's house, slipped out before the family was awake and was on the road again while it was still dark.

At day-break he came to the river, forded it and started across the meadow. As he came up the slope the branches of the mulberry tree sprang out black against the yellow square of the window: the family was up and about their work.

He heard voices in the back and went around to the stable lot. A lantern had been set on a stump near the runway. Archy was hitching the team by its light. As Rion approached his father came out of the run-way carrying a sack of wheat. Rion stepped up, took it from him and hove it into the wagon.

Malcolm Outlaw grunted as Rion took the heavy sack from him, then stood, his body bent forward from the waist, his hands clasped behind him, watching Rion as he briskly loaded five more sacks into the wagon.

"Seven, eight, nine. . . . That's all. . . . So you decided to come, did you?"

"I didn't figure to stay away more'n two nights," Rion told him. He was respectful to his father but he had not stood in awe of him since the day three years ago, when he had wrestled with the old man and put him on his back. Malcolm Outlaw knew this. He was severe with Archy but made no attempt to control Rion beyond exacting from him the amount of labor that he considered his due as a parent.

Archy ducked under the near horse and came up with the belly band in his hand. The horse swelled up as he tried to cinch it. Rion took the strap from him and fastened it. When he had finished he stood for a second, leaning his head against the horse's side so that his face was hidden from his father.

23

"Did you tend to my skin?" he asked in a low voice.

"I hung it up like you said and I got Betsy to help me saw on it some," Archy answered in the same low tone.

Rion moved away while Archy was hitching the horses to a limb and followed his father into the house.

It was still grey outside but the kitchen was as light as day. Fresh logs had just been laid on and the chimney was roaring with the flames. A round bed of glowing coals had been raked to one side of the hearth. Betsy knelt there, cooking journey cakes on a griddle. In another griddle set on a trivet venison collops were broiling.

A small, grey-haired woman moved about the table, setting out plates and bowls. She put down the plate she held and came over to Rion and laid her hand on his arm.

"Why'n't you come home last night?"

He looked down into her blue eyes and patted her shoulder with one hand while the other was unfastening her clasping fingers. "I went to Boone's," he said, "I couldn't make it back any sooner."

A hoarse laugh came from the chimney corner. "It's a wonder you got back this soon," a voice said.

Rion did not glance in the direction from which the voice came. He never looked directly at his sister, Jane, if he could help it. It was not that the sight of her deformity shocked him. The accident which had come near costing her her life had happened long ago. He could not remember the time when she had not been the same dwarfish creature that she was now. But her temper got shorter as she grew older. Nowadays she rarely spoke to him except to criticize something he had done. Rion, like the other children, had been trained to make allowances for Jane. He received her gibes in silence and avoided her as much as he could.

He went to the hearth and began to dry his wet leggings. Betsy saw the steam rising from them and laughed. "Looks like you swum the creek instead of fording it."

"I come through in a hurry," Rion said, "I was afraid they'd get off to town without me."

She shook back the black cloud of her hair and rose, shielding one crimson cheek with her hand. "Here's your meat," she said and set the pan of venison on the table.

Malcolm Outlaw took his place at the head of the table. He was a tall man—taller even than Rion—with a shock of snow-white hair.

His heavy, jutting eyebrows were still black, his beard only a little grizzled. His eyes had once been almost black but were faded now to the purplish brown that one sees in the eyes of the very old. It always surprised Rion to look into his father's eyes. It seemed that they ought to be darker than they were. And yet they had always looked like this as far back as he could remember.

Jane limped over from her corner and Archy took the place next to Rion. Mrs. Outlaw came last, bearing a jar of freshly opened preserves. She sat down at the foot of the table but Betsy stood to wait on the others.

Malcolm Outlaw bent his head and mumbled the grace he always said before meat; he helped himself liberally from the pan which his daughter had set before him and pushed it towards Rion.

Betsy brought hot cakes and Mrs. Outlaw handed from one to the other a plate containing a small pat of butter. "Eat it up," she urged, "We're going to churn today."

"That ain't no reason for eating up all the butter you got now," Malcolm said. He did not look at his wife as he spoke and he spoke almost mechanically, between mouthfuls.

Jane finished eating first and sat with her thin hands clasped in front of her. "What's going on at Boone's?" she asked in the voice that was always a little hoarse.

Rion looked up and saw—as if for the first time—the great purplish scar that covered all one cheek and ran down her neck. "She looks like a buzzard," he thought, "a nesting buzzard. She does, for a fact."

He felt a desire to talk of what was in his mind. He laid down his knife. "That fellow I took up there is the beatenest that ever I saw. Been all the way to Canada. . . ."

"What's he come here for?"

"To find Daniel, I reckon. They used to soldier together."

"A vagrant like that'd be just the fellow for Daniel," Jane said. "He'll be jaunting off with him. They say he can't stay home two months running."

"I reckon he'll go if he's a mind to. He's a man grown."

She gave her hoarse laugh. "I don't see how Rebecca makes out to feed all them children with him away all the time."

Rion looked at her. She looked back at him. A spark grew and flamed in her dull eye. Rion looked away, remembering something he had not thought of in a long time. He, Rion, was responsible for Jane's being like she was. She had been two years old when the accident happened. Betsy was a babe in arms, Archy not yet born. He himself was four years old. He could not remember the incident and yet he had the picture of it in his mind. That was from his mother's story, told always in the same words:

". . . Hog killing time. We was rendering lard in the big kettle right at the back doorstep. Josepha Rogers was here with her children. There was a parcel of you playing around. Jane was the littlest, still crawling. . . ." She always stopped there. When they pressed her for more details she would say only: "I was in the house when the kettle turned over." Or: "It was that rock wasn't steady under it." And once: "It was my fault. I ought to have latched every one of you young ones in the house. . . ."

Rion as a small child could see the whole thing. There were the two figures: the baby, crawling with ant-like steadiness over the hard-baked ground and the little boy who ran up and with a careless hand tilted the big pot until the boiling lard foamed over its lip. He could not see the little boy after that or the baby. When he had asked his mother which of the Rogers boys it was, Joe or Cephas, she had looked at him strangely. "I never did know," she said, "There was a parcel of children." When he stared at her she went on to speak rapidly of the confusion there had been in the house. "When there's a parcel of children you can't tell. You can't tell *which* one did it." He had known then that it was he and not Cephas or Joe who had tilted the pot. That was a long time ago. His chief emotion at the time had been wonder about the boy's face. Why was it that he had always seen Cephas and not himself?

Malcolm Outlaw was standing up. "Y'all quit your squabbling. It'll be daylight before we get started to town."

His wife brought his great coat from the peg. He put it on and tied a woolen muffler about his neck although the day promised to be fair. Rion and Archy followed him outdoors.

Rion stood on the threshold, settling his cap on his head. Before him stretched the meadow, hoar with the light frost that had fallen last night. Zigzagging across it was the red ribbon of the Trader's Path. It was only two days ago that he had been gathering corn in the field over there and had looked up to see John Findley coming down the Path.

His father and Archy were already in the wagon. He ran out and straddled the line pole.

The wagon jolted down the slope. Archy was sitting on top of the sacks and the extra place on the driver's seat was vacant. Malcolm Outlaw turned and motioned Rion to it. Rion refused it with an absent-minded nod. He was still thinking about Jane. "She hates me," he thought, "she just naturally hates me." But you could not blame her for that. Sitting there, his legs swinging to the motion of the wagon, he pondered on the moral consequences of his act. Killing a person outright was kinder than disfiguring her for life. He had been guilty of something very like murder. Would he be punished for it in the hereafter? It didn't seem right that he should be; he had committed the sin when he was an unknowing child and yet sin was sin. In the Bible innocent persons, men, women and children, suckling babes were put to the sword for crimes they had not committed. "It don't seem right," he muttered, "There's no justice in it."

He decided that he was incapable of judgment on such a matter. He would have to consult someone who was more learned in doctrine than he himself was. The putting away of the problem lightened his spirits. As they jolted along he looked about him, noting with a professional eye the extent of damage done by the frost. It had been heavier than he thought. The blades of wild hay had been whitened clear down to their roots. And in the woods the beech and oak and hickory leaves would be wilted to a sodden carpet. Scent would lie well. It was a shame to have to be going to town on such a morning.

They were coming to the river. The Yadkin was deep along here. This was the only ford within two or three miles and it was tricky. A hole there between the island and the bank big enough for the boys to swim in. His father, years ago, had driven stakes in to mark the ford. He said that he was tired of sitting on his front doorstep and hearing the traders yell that they were drowning. A trader had been drowned here, before the stakes were driven in. His body had washed up on the Jersey flats. They had brought it back here to the island to bury. A heap of stones had marked the grave but boys, rocking each other in and out of the swimming hole, had long ago scattered the stones. He, Rion, knew the island as well as anybody and he would be hard put to find the place now.

They were at the river bank. The horses took the gravelly incline with a rush and were in the water. Malcolm Outlaw would not let them stop till they had gone in breast deep. They lowered their heads then and drank. Rion had jumped up into the wagon when they entered the water and now he sat down on a sack of wheat. They were passing the island. It came to a point here. The beach was shelving sand, fluted by the recent high water. Farther back the reeds began. The banks of the island were covered with them but in the middle of the island were as tall trees as you'd find anywhere: beech and sycamore and ash and elm and gum.

The reeds parted and a swan came out. It looked at them for a moment out of its cold black eye then waddled past to launch itself on the stream.

Archy picked up Rion's gun where it lay in the wagon bed, shot at the bird and missed it. He was disappointed— Mama gave him a pint of cream for every swan he killed—and as was often the case with Archy, he was ready with an excuse. "Swan's fast," he said, "fast as greased lightning."

Rion laughed. "He is, compared to you."

He watched the bird make off down the stream. A swan was a pretty sight sailing along like that. But swans were mean. He'd seen them in mating season, standing up tall as a man and one would stun the other with a blow of his wing and then tramp him and tear the vitals out of him.

The swan went out of sight behind some reeds. There was not a living thing to be seen on the river now and no sound except the water rushing against the rocks. On a still night you could hear that sound up at the house. He had been hearing it ever since he was born. When he slept away from home he always felt a little uneasy at first, until he realized what it was he was missing. Malcolm Outlaw said that when he first came to live on the Yadkin years ago it had been deeper. And the trees along the bank, he said, were the tallest he'd seen anywhere, A lot of those trees had been cut down—some to make the beams in the house—but there was a wide fringe left on each side of the stream. Rion looked down to where the river made a bend. A strange thought came to him. Suppose a man came up the road into this valley for the first time, came around that bend in the Path and stopped in that grove of hickories and looked down over the fields to the river. Would it strike him as a good place to settle? He decided that it would, if the fellow knew good land when he saw it.

Their own bottom, just visible between gaps in the trees, lay as nicely as any land around here. When you got back from the river the land was more broken, of course, but it was all good land.

Malcolm Outlaw slapped the line over the black horse's rump. Both horses raised their heads reluctantly and as the line came down again stepped forward into shallower water.

They came up the slope and on to the road which wound along the river bank towards Salisbury.

Their first stop was at the schoolhouse. It stood in a field that had belonged to one of the Craiges but had been abandoned years ago. The house itself had been erected only the previous year. Malcolm Outlaw and Rion had been among the neighbors who had rolled and squared the logs.

As they approached the small log building Malcolm Outlaw pulled his horses up. He did not notice that Archy had already dropped over the wagon side and was running up the path. He sat gazing at the cabin.

"I wish I had them logs down on the ground again. There's one of them joists is sagging."

Rion was watching the man who had passed Archy on the path and was now coming towards them.

Francis Dawson was twenty-two years old, four years older than Rion but he was not as well set up. His shoulders already had what in time would be called a scholar's slouch. His thin, brown hair was always ruffled as if he had just run his hand through it. He was wrapped today in an old matchcoat that had belonged to a larger man. He shivered and the end of his fine nose was reddened by the wind as he came up to the wagon and stood, resting one foot on the hub of a wheel.

"Well, Master Outlaw, on your way to Salisbury?"

Malcolm took his eyes from the logs of the cabin. "Aye. Selling some wheat. I have to satisfy the sheriff."

Dawson laughed. "I've the advantage of you there."

Malcolm groaned. "There's times I think I'll sell every acre and take to the woods." He turned around and brought his hand down on a sack of wheat. "Nine of 'em and 'twill take near all for the tax. Maybe a shilling or so left over to buy salt. Maybe not even that."

Frank Dawson's expression changed. His face took on an eager look that Rion had never seen on it before. He opened his lips and seemed about to say something but he closed them and looked away over the field. When he spoke Rion had the feeling that he was not saying what had been in his mind a moment before.

"Aye, we're tax-ridden. No question. Unless," he laughed again, "you're like me and have no land and no gear."

Rion looked at the young schoolmaster and then back at his father. Malcolm was leaning a little forward as if better to hear what Dawson was saying. He was always like that when he was talking to the schoolmaster and if Dawson came to the house he would rise and go to the door himself and bow as he let him in.

Frank Dawson's standing in the neighborhood did not call for such respect. He was only an old field schoolmaster with hardly a whole shirt to his back. And his presence was not one to awe a body. He was too thin and too low-voiced. It was the learning that Malcolm Outlaw bowed to. He maintained that a man with learning was twice the man that he was without it. Once when Rion was younger he had told him how in the old country a man on the scaffold condemned to be hanged, drawn and quartered could save himself by calling for the Book and reading even as much as a line in it.

"Ye see there's need for learning."

Rion and Betsy had laughed. "There'd be few left in Rowan county if men were hanged, drawn and quartered because they did not know their A B Abs" Betsy told him impudently.

Their father had flown into a rage at that and it was the next week he had arranged that Rion should go to young Dawson on rainy afternoons or in whatever time he could spare from the farm work.

Although Rion had been studying with Francis for a year in his leisure time he had not got through the primer. He wondered if Frank would take this occasion to report to his father and he hoped that he would. The truth would have to out some time. The sooner the better. He would never learn to read. It was too tiresome a business with all there was going on to interest a man. No rhyme nor reason to it either. But it was a wonder how Frank loved it. He would take a book to the field and read in it when he halted the horse at the end of a row and on a rainy day he could sit indoors for hours at a time, reading, as patient as a hunter at a deer stand.

Malcolm was chirruping to the horses. Rion moved up on the seat beside him. Frank took his foot off the hub. He looked at Rion. "Going to the infare tonight?"

"Aye."

"Betsy and Jenny going with you?"

"They can go along with me if they've a mind to," Rion said and grinned. "I don't know that anybody else has bespoke their company."

Francis smiled. "Well, since you've two women on your hands already you'll not mind a third. Cassy has a notion to go. You can pick her up when you drive by here, can't you, and no extra trouble?"

"No trouble at all," Rion said.

Malcolm Outlaw waited until they were out of the schoolmaster's hearing, then he said: "You'll not drive my horses by for her. They'll be tired, time they've gone to Salisbury and back."

"We'll walk then," Rion said shortly.

Malcolm was silent a moment then he asked "Where's the infare at?"

"Lovelatty's Kate is marrying John Weill."

Malcolm gave a high chuckle. "I thought Kate was *your* jularkey."

"She was," Rion said, "but she ain't—now. She and John have been going together for three months."

Malcolm chuckled again. "Let *him* cut you out! He's slow as molasses in December."

"Slow as he is he was too fast for me," Rion said. He spoke composedly, looking his father straight in the eye. The old man was in one of his cross-grained moods today. Nothing could please him. But he was barking up the wrong tree if he thought he could hack him with talk of Kate Lovelatty.

Three months was not such a long time, in one way and yet in another it was as long as a lifetime. He did not know how it had happened. He had picked the quarrel with her, over something that might not amount to anything. That time he got there late and John Weill was leaving. Something, the tone of John's voice or the way he looked at Kate when he was saying goodbye, had made him suspicious. He began to remember things: one other time he'd found them in a room by themselves, not saying anything, just standing there, close together. He ought not to have spoken. He hadn't anything to go on, really. But he taxed her with it. She denied it, but once he'd let the thing come out in the open he couldn't believe her.

But they'd still be going together or on the point of marrying if it hadn't been for Kate. She was quick on the up-take. She wasn't going to sit around waiting for nobody. After dinner that last day she made him come down in the ravine with her. That sycamore ravine! He could see it now. He sitting on a log and she not beside him like always but over on that big rock by the spring, talking, not looking at him but straight ahead, like there was something up the ravine she'd never seen before and all the time one of her hands kept reaching down to pluck spearmint up by the roots.

"Stop!" he said, "You've done already rooted up a whole planta-tion."

She laughed and put her hands in her lap but the next minute was at it again. ". . . And if we was to marry I don't think we'd get along so good." All of a sudden—and that was queer because he hadn't really thought things out—he knew he was going to hold her to that. He stood up. "If that's the way you feel we better be getting back to the house." She took her breath in quick at that but she was game. "That's right," she said and they went up the path together as cool as cucumbers and hadn't spoken a word to each other from that day to this. . . .

They were passing the log cabin in which Frank Dawson lived with his sister. It stood in a clearing surrounded by weathering stumps. The ground in front of the doorstep had been swept so clear of pine needles that it showed red. A box in which a trailing vine grew had been propped against one of the windows.

He remembered the day that cabin was building. And he remem-bered the day the Dawsons moved into it, the Reverend tall and plump and dignified and always smelling of brandy; Frank, looking then just about like he did now; and the girl, Jocasta. The Outlaws had killed a hog the night before. His mother had sent him, a boy of fifteen, over with a basket of spare ribs and chitterlings.

The Reverend had opened the door to him and then had called Jocasta—little, blackhaired thing she was, no bigger than a minute, but she was doing the housekeeping. She stood there and looked down at the meat and didn't know what it was. Rion told her it was mountain oysters. "How'd you get oysters so far from the sea?" she asked.

The Outlaws had split their sides laughing over that. "Aye," Malcolm Outlaw said, "gentle folks. I know 'em. Don't know a hog's ribs from his hams till they get on the table. They'll draw up then, same as anybody else."

His father had not liked the Reverend Dawson when he was alive. But that was because he was Church of England—sent over here right after the Act for the Establishment of an Orthodox Clergy. There had been a big to-do over the provisions of the Act. The minister of St. Luke's Parish was to receive a stated salary of one hundred and thirty pounds, and fees for every marriage performed in the parish, whether or not he performed it, and in addition to all this he was to have the free use of a mansion house and a glebe of at least two hundred acres.

The mansion house was required to be thirty-eight feet long and eighteen feet wide and was to be accompanied with a kitchen, a barn, a dairy and other out-buildings.

Malcolm Outlaw and his neighbor, Andrew Wallace, used to sit around the fire at night, talking about the provisions of the Act. They expected to be taxed for all this Anglican finery. "Thirty-eight feet long," Andrew Wallace would say. "Does the man want a palace, like Tryon's?" And Malcolm said that he could not see how any minister had use for two hundred acres of land.

They had wasted their breath. The Reverend Edward Dawson had lived in the small cabin which Rion and his father had just passed. The glebe of two hundred acres had dwindled to the old field in which Francis taught school and a ten-acre field not much better. The kitchen, dairy and barn had never existed save in the provisions of the Act. The Reverend Dawson himself had died of apoplexy before he had lived in the cabin a year. Dropped dead in the midst of a church quarrel.

Frank Dawson and the girl had stayed on there after the minister's death and the next year Frank had opened his school in the old field which was to have been part of the glebe. Half of his scholars came from Presbyterian homes. One of them was Archy Outlaw, the only one of the Outlaws still young enough to attend school. Rion himself went to the Dawsons' cabin two or three times a week but that was at night.

He liked to go there. He supposed that was one reason why he kept on fooling with trying to learn to read. Half the time when he went over there he didn't say any lessons, just sat around the fire and talked. Sometimes Frank would play a tune on his fiddle and the girl would sing, but mostly Frank would be sorting out his dried herbs and pasting them in a ledger he had. The girl never talked much but she was nobody's fool. Pretty, too, now that she'd filled out and grown up to those big eyes—not that he would want to marry her. He had not had anything to do with girls for a long time now, except once or twice when he had gone with the trappers to Ma'am Clara's place down by the creek. But he had not been there since last May. That was because Joe Abbott had told him about getting the bad disease from one of the girls there. He had let those girls alone after that. The truth was he was scared of girls. You got to fooling around with one and the first thing you knew you were hog-tied, with a lot of kids running around the dooryard. And yet if you didn't marry you had to do without women which wasn't in nature or else keep running to whores all the time like the boys in Salisbury did.

It was hard to tell about women. Some people thought that Rebecca Boone was no better than she should be. Said one of her children was by Daniel's brother, Squire. He didn't believe that. If she was a whore Daniel wouldn't think as much of her as he did. He was as crazy about that woman now as if she was a young girl. That time he and Daniel got back from the trip over the mountains! The children were all laughing and excited because their dad was home. Finally they went outdoors. All except Israel. He settled down on the bench, shelling some peas. Daniel spoke to him right sharp. "Can't you find something to do outdoors, Boy?" Rion saw how it was, so he got up and went with him, saying he'd take a look at the horses. He had to laugh, though, at how anxious Daniel was to get them all out of the room.

He wondered what it would be like to come back from a long hunt and have a wife waiting for you. He could see her: standing on the doorstep as you came into the yard, a small girl, light on her feet, with black hair. . . . No, she'd be down in the yard. She'd come up, asking you questions, wanting to help with your pack. You'd hardly answer. You'd take the hand that was fumbling for the pack and pull her on into the house. The door would swing shut. You'd stand there a second in the warm dark, then she'd turn her face towards you. Why, it was the face of the girl in the house they'd just passed, Jocasta Dawson! No matter. She couldn't escape you now. You'd pull her towards the corner whilst you set your gun down and slung your pack to the floor, then you'd draw her to the bed. A high bed with down pillows. She'd lie back against the pillows, looking at you. She'd let you take her clothes off if you wanted to. She'd let you do anything. . . .

He moved on the wagon seat, so roughly that he jostled his father. Malcolm woke from his half doze. "Hey, what's that? What's the matter with you?"

Rion could hardly keep from laughing. "Nothing. I was just thinking about a fellow I know."

"You war'n't thinking no good thoughts of him. You mighty nigh bounced me off the wagon seat. A little more and you'd skeered the horses."

"Well," Rion said, half laughing. "I won't think about him no more. He don't amount to much nohow."

CHAPTER 4

THE ROAD was smoother. They were entering the town. They came
to the courthouse. Malcolm Outlaw drove slowly in order that he
might admire the weather-boarded storey-and-a-half building. It was
still "the new courthouse" to him though it had been built ten years
ago. Before it was built there had been much discussion as to where
it should stand. The court had finally ruled that it should be placed
in a grove of oaks near a famous spring almost in the center of the
town. Rion had heard old hunters complain that the Salisbury folks
had ruined the best deer stand in the country when they built their
courthouse. It had been a good stand, on that high ground, with the
stream handy, but a man might wait there a long time now for a deer.
That plot of ground was the most populous in all Salisbury, with the
gaol and the pillory and stocks near by and the great town well down
in the corner of the lot.

They passed the trader's place, with its vine-covered barracoon
standing back in the center of the lot, and turned down Innes street.
On the corner of Innes, built flush with the street, stood a low, square
brick building. This was the law office of Earl Granville's land
agents. As the Outlaws passed, the door of this building opened, and
a lean, erect man dressed in black came out. He stood a moment,
then started down the street, walking with his head bent and his eyes
fixed on the ground. When he came to the crossing he glanced up.
The wagon was just passing. Malcolm drove past without looking to
right or left, but Rion stared. He had seen this man only once before
and that at a distance but he had heard about him all his life: Edmund
Fanning, clerk of the superior court at Hillsborough and also register.
It was said that he did not scruple to double a tax when it suited him.
He had come into this country a poor man twenty years ago but he
had quickly feathered his nest. He wore lace at his wrists now and
had a fine house in Hillsborough.

Rion felt his gorge rise at the sight of him. Fanning seemed to read
his thoughts. He raised his long, bony chin a little and his face hardened.

36

The wagon passed on. Rion suddenly began singing, softly at first and then letting his voice ring out:

> *When Fanning first to Orange came,*
> *He looked both pale and wan,*
> *An old, patched coat was on his back,*
> *An old mare he rode on. . . .*

Malcolm turned on him furiously. "Boy, where'd you hear a song like that?"

Rion laughed. "They were singing it at Cochranes' the other night. There's one about our clerk, too. But Fanning's a bigger extortioner than our clerk, if I hear right."

"If you hear right?" Malcolm mimicked him in a high, passionate voice. "You let the clerks alone. A man like you, with no learning and no gear. You'll be transported first thing you know."

"A man don't have to have learning or gear to know when he's being cheated. There's ten shillings on my head same as everybody's else, ain't they?"

"I aim to pay it this very day," Malcolm said, "I aim to satisfy the sheriff and the clerk too, before I leave this town."

"Forty bushels of wheat," Rion said, "but that ain't all they get. Bob Hampson was telling me he come in the other day to see about a pair of marriage licenses. Frohock asked him fifteen dollars. Bob he come home and told Ellen Sawyer they'd have to take the short cut though neither of 'em is Methody."

Malcolm looked up quickly. "What you care about a license? You ain't studying about marrying?"

"I ain't studying about marrying but when the time comes I don't want to pay fifteen dollars."

Malcolm laughed shortly. "When the time comes you'll pay what they ask and be glad it ain't more."

They had arrived at the old Dutchman's store. Malcolm got down stiffly and flung the lines over the wagon seat. Rion jumped over the wheel. He stretched himself and stamped his feet to restore circulation, then followed his father into the store. The big log room, heated only by the fire on a small hearth, was cold and smelled of tallow and hides. Old Wagner, wearing a coat made of buffalo hide and a fur cap, sat in a chair beside the fire. There was a pile of pelts beside him. As the Outlaws entered he lifted the top pelt off, fingered the fur, then entered a tally in his greasy account book. Rion went up and stood on the hearth with his back to the small blaze. He looked down at the old man. "Mangy looking lot o' pelts," he said.

Old Wagner tilted his head and peered at Rion out of a sharp blue eye. Then his gaze went to the father. He half rose, then sinking back, motioned to a vacant chair on the other side of the hearth.

"And how are things out Trading Ford way, Master Outlaw?" he asked politely.

"Andrew Wallance has the bloody flux," Malcolm said as he sat down. "Saving him, all the neighbors are well."

"And yourself?" The German asked, eyeing the powerful, bent frame.

"I have rheumatism, but that's common with me at this season."

The old German contorted his shoulders under the heavy coat. "There's a spot in mine own back that's never easy, from November to May."

"It's this room," Rion told him. "Cold as one of our barns." He turned to the fireplace. "If you hadn't been so stingy when you were building your chimney you'd had a better draft and enough hearth to hold a fire."

Old Jacob's eye sparkled. "I didn't have a smart young man to advise me," he said primly.

Rion laughed. "The more pity!" He raised his head and drew his breath in sharply as if trying to identify the odors that hung heavy in the room. "I vow, Jacob, I'd be scared to have my meal ground here. I'd be scared it'd taste of skunk."

The old German turned his sparkling eye on the father "*Caveat emptor*," he said, "Not everybody has the keen nose like you, my son."

Malcolm stood up. "I've got a wagonload of wheat outside, Jacob. What's it worth?"

"Five shillings a bushel. One shilling of it in silver."

"You mean we get one shilling and take the rest in salt?" Rion demanded.

"Salt or hides or sugar," the German said. He waved his hand about the big room. "You may take your choice of any of the merchandise on my shelves."

Malcolm stood with his head bent down, figuring. He looked up. "I'll take salt," he said. "Let's see. I've got forty bushels out there.

That'll give me forty shillings in silver. . . . It's enough to satisfy the sheriff."

Jacob waited a moment as if to make sure that his customer would not change his mind. He drew out his purse and counted the forty shillings out into Malcolm's hand. When he had done that he reached behind the counter and pulled up a stone jug. He took three glasses down from a shelf and poured them full of brandy. "Sit down and warm yourself, Master Outlaw. The young man and I'll load the salt."

He drank his brandy off and started for the back of the store. Rion followed him to where the oaken hogshead of salt stood. The old man tapped one with his finger. Rion up-ended it with a heave of his powerful shoulders, then getting behind it rolled it the length of the store. Malcolm, meanwhile, had come out and had backed the team up to the door and let down the end board. Jacob laid two stout planks on the end of the wagon and Rion, putting all his weight into it, pushed the hogshead up the plankway.

Jacob stood back, watching him. "I had stout shoulders too when I was a young man."

Rion up on the wagon seat now grinned and patted his pocket.

"Ach! I am forgetting!" The old German came up to the side of the wagon and put several pieces of silver into Rion's palm.

"What's that for?" Malcolm asked.

Rion pocketed the money. "For the hide I sent in the other day by Joe Lovelatty. Prime pelt, war'n't it, Jacob?"

The old man drew the corners of his mouth down. "A prime pelt. Cured a bit soft, maybe."

Rion put his thumb to his nose. "Old Man, you never saw the day you could turn out a pelt like that."

The old man cackled and turned back into the store.

"What you always getting his back up for?" Malcolm asked as they drove off.

"I don't know. Makes me mad to think of him sitting there all day long on his tail, making profit on every hide I bring in."

"Well, somebody's got to handle 'em. And Jacob's got the name of being honest. . . . Five shillings, and only one of it in silver! Do you suppose he'd have paid more if I'd bargained with him?"

Rion shook his head. "Jacob'll give as much as any of 'em. Only he don't bargain."

Malcolm pulled the horses up before the rack on the courthouse lot. "I'll go in now and pay the tax. You coming with me?"

"I'll wait for you across the street," Rion said.

He went into the ordinary. Tom Beard and some other young men from the Trading Ford neighborhood were there, drinking. He joined them. There were no other customers except two men who sat in a corner with their backs turned to the others.

Tom Beard punched Rion in the ribs and pointed to the larger of the two men. "Know who that is?"

Rion shook his head.

"It's Harmon Husbands."

Rion stared at the broad grey-clad back. Harmon Husbands was a Quaker, the owner of large tracts of land on Deep river. But he sided with the poor and was said to be a leader of the "Regulators," a band of men organized secretly to protest illegal taxes.

The other man turned around: Rednap Howell, an old field schoolmaster, a friend of Frank Dawson's. They got up. The Quaker flung some silver down on the counter and marched out without looking to right or left. Howell nodded to the young men from Trading Ford and followed him.

"Wonder what they're up to?" Rion said and added with a wink, "I'm a mind to join the Regulators."

The others laughed out and Tom Beard whispered, "Here's your chance."

Rednap Howell had turned back and was beckoning to Rion: "Could I see you a minute?"

Rion got up and went outside where the two men were standing. Howell presented him to the Quaker who eyed him a moment in silence, lips compressed, then asked if he would deliver a letter to Francis Dawson.

"Aye," Rion said and took the letter, staring meanwhile at the ruddy face out of which two large blue eyes looked so calmly. The Quaker didn't look like a fighter and yet there was a hard set to the fleshy chin. "I reckon he'd fight if he had to," Rion thought and thrust the letter into his pocket.

"There's your father," Howell said, "Will he be having a pint of Jacob's ale?"

Rion shook his head. "He'll be wanting to get home."

He bade them goodbye and hurried out to join his father. "Come on, come on," Malcolm said impatiently, "It'll be dark before we get started."

"It won't if you'll let me handle the team," Rion told him and made him move over so that he could sit on the right. He cracked the whip over his head and chirruped to the horses in a way that caused them to break immediately into a gallop. They rattled down Corbin street and were about to turn the corner which would take them by a short cut to the river road when Rion pulled up and sat with his head cocked on one side.

"I hear music."

"That ain't anything to make a fuss about. Let's get on home."

But Rion sat silent, listening. "By Job, it's a parade," he said suddenly and before his father could interfere he had backed the wagon and was headed back towards the center of the town. The streets were lined with people. As Rion halted his wagon they were falling back to make way for the parade which had just reached the corner.

The musicians came first, a drummer and three fifers. They were playing: "The Bonny Banks of Aden." Behind them walked a dozen men and women. They were dressed in stout new garments and they were laughing and clapping their hands. Capering beside them were four negro children in clean shifts of red stroud cloth. One of these little negroes ran hand in hand with a handsome young negro man. This young man seemed intoxicated by the music. Every now and then he let go his partner's hand and running out to the side of the group turned cart-wheels, coming up each time with a smile and a bow for the onlookers.

"Look at that one," Rion said. "I'd like to have *him*."

"You can't have none of them," Malcolm said. "They're taking them west."

Rion nodded and ran his eye down the line to where a stout, red-faced man rode on a grey horse. "It's Dunc Kerr's outfit," he said. "Lord, he's got a bunch of 'em. Look at them wagons."

Behind the trader came three wagons. Their contents were invisible, for each wagon bed had a cover of stout cloth stretched tent-wise over arched saplings.

The shouts and laughter of the crowd died down at the sight of these wagons. The musicians noticed the lull and redoubled their efforts. The drum sent forth a great roll of sound and the fifers burst into a new tune, but a voice from the crowd sounded above the music:

"Old Dunc Kerr he carry me away,
Whar I be next New Year's Day?"

Malcolm looked at the grey, covered wagons. He groaned. "Lord help the poor cattle!"

Rion was eyeing the crowd which was already dispersing. "Them niggers ain't cast down. Didn't you see 'em dancing and carrying on?"

"The ones inside them wagons couldn't do no dancing," Malcolm said. "They're laying there packed in straw, three deep, and handcuffed. They tell me Kerr had a hard time with the last lot he took west. That's why he had the drum corps this time."

"Well, I reckon he has to put handcuffs on 'em if they won't go willing," Rion said.

Malcolm did not answer for a moment; then he said sadly, "It ain't right to put chains on a man, even a blackamoor."

"Naw, it ain't right to put chains on a man," Rion agreed, "but a nigger ain't hardly a man."

He watched the top of the last wagon fade into the grey of the twilight. West, his father had said. West. Those niggers were going the same road that he himself longed to travel. But they were going chained, packed in straw, like hogs to market. He swelled with a sense of his own freedom. He, too, would go west when the time came. But he would go walking upright on his own two legs and when he got there he would move about free as air, doing service to no man.

CHAPTER 5

WHEN THEY came to the Dawson clearing, Rion sat down on a stump. "You girls go on up to the house and get her. I'll set here and rest." They started up the path but he called them back. "Here, take this letter to Frank. I clean forgot I had it till this minute."

Betsy came back and got the letter, then ran on and caught up with Jane. Rion watched them until they were out of sight among the trees. He wished now that he had gone with them. He would like to see Frank Dawson's face when he was handed that letter. Was it from Rednap Howell or was it from Harmon Husbands himself? Frank might have dealings with Howell, seeing that they were both schoolmasters, but if he was mixed up with Husbands it could mean only one thing: he was a Regulator or getting ready to be one. What would a timid fellow like Frank be doing with that wild crowd?

Jocasta Dawson must have been ready on the dot, for here the girls were coming back. She was walking between them in that long, dark cloak she had brought from the old country. She had a pretty walk, like a deer stepping out from cover.

He stood up. "Come on. Let's get going."

He walked out briskly and the girls followed. They went through the woods. It was dark as pitch. The girls kept close to him. Once Betsy stumbled. "Hell's Fire!" she said. "Looks like Dad would a let us had the horses tonight."

"Y'ought not to cuss like that," Rion said. He slowed his pace a little. "I knew all the time war'n't no chance of the horses tonight. He told me when we was on the way to town."

"They war'n't tired," Betsy said. "Had three or four hours to rest after they got back from town. I told him so too."

"Well, you wasted your breath. Ain't no use arguing with him."

"Naw, a person gets old he gets cross-grained."

"He ain't so old," Rion said absently. He wondered how old his father really was. He doubted if even his mother knew. Malcolm Outlaw had been a man grown when he came to America and he had

43

married comparatively late in life. Rion knew that he had landed at Charleston and had gone out from there trading with the Sapona Indians. Beyond that he knew little of his father's life before he came to live on the Yadkin.

A memory arose from his childhood: he and Archy playing under the china-berry tree—he must have been six or seven years old—and a stranger coming up the path. A thin, brown-haired fellow with a pack on his back. He came up to where Malcolm Outlaw was sitting on the doorstep, dropped his pack to the ground, looked down at him, and smiled. "A time I've had, finding you!" he said.

Rion always remembered that moment. It was the first time he had ever seen a grown person afraid. He and Archy had both been staring at the stranger, but they looked up at their father quickly when they heard the sound of his voice, harsher than they had ever heard it before and with a catch in the breath:

"My name is *Outlaw*. Have you any business with me?"

The stranger laughed. "A night's lodging, Master *Outlaw*," and he picked up his pack and followed Malcolm into the house.

Rion could not remember how long he had stayed but he did remember how he talked around the fire at night, about the Lost Tribes of Israel. The Indians, he said, were the descendants of the Lost Tribes of Israel and he told how the Chickasaw Indians he lived among still carried the Ark of the Covenant into battle. Years later Rion had told his friend, the old Sapona chief, what the man had said. The chief laughed. "We are not Jews. We are Saponas. And we are not lost. Who ever heard of a Sapona losing his way?"

Rion remembered the day the man left. They had all gathered in the dooryard to watch him go down the path—he was going back to live among the Indians, Rion's mother said. He had turned back from the gate: "I hope our next meeting will not be so many years apart, Master Outlaw."

Malcolm had replied that such things were in God's hands, and when the man was out of sight he swore and turned back into the house. His wife cried out and ran after him. The door shut behind her. For half an hour afterwards the children still playing in the yard could hear their voices from the house, the woman weeping softly, the man cursing or talking in a harsh monotone.

The mysterious stranger had never come again and there had been no more talk of him, but Rion wondered now about that long-ago visit. Why had his father been so displeased at seeing the man and why if they were old friends had the stranger made such a point of calling his father "Master Outlaw"? He decided that his father had not always been called Outlaw, that he had changed his name. Had he committed some crime, perhaps killed a man, here or in the old country?

He tried to imagine his father's killing a man but he was not able to visualize such a scene and his curiosity died in a faint wonder. If his father's name was not Outlaw then he, Rion, had been called by the wrong name all his life. He wondered what his real name was.

The Dawson girl spoke up: "How far is it to Lovelattys'?"

"Three miles," he said. "Three miles there and three miles back."

"Maybe we'll get a ride back," Jenny said.

"Maybe, but don't count on it." He struck himself on the breast. "Look at me. I was walking along this same road at sun-up this morning and here I am, footing it back soon as the sun goes down. Fourteen miles I walked already today and yesterday it must have been more like thirty."

Jocasta Dawson had come up beside him. She turned her white face up to his. "Aren't you tired?"

"Naw, I ain't tired. I could walk all night. Dance, too, if I had to."

"I don't reckon you'll have heart for dancing tonight," Jenny said.

He ignored her. He walked closer to Jocasta, put out his hand to help her over a rough place in the road. "I ain't never been to say right down tired in my life," he said. "Yes, I was once. In the full of the moon. I went out at moon-rise, hunting, and come back at sun-up. We was doing fall plowing. I followed the plow all day and that night there was a jollification at Robinsons' and Joe Lovelatty and I went. Walked every step of the way. Least I walked back as far as Lovelattys'. I stopped there, I did, and I says, 'Joe, I'm going to have to spend the night with you. I don't know what is the matter but one of my legs is trembling so I can't hardly make it stay in the road.' Joe, he nearly died laughing. 'You durn fool,' he says. 'It's give down on you. That's what it is. You must have walked all of fifty miles today.'"

"And had you?" Jocasta asked.

"Must have, not counting the dancing."

Betsy had come up with them. "I mind that night," she said. "In November and the moon was full. Like it is tonight."

"It was a pretty night," Rion said. "Something like this. A pretty night you can walk and not feel it."

"I feel it," Jenny said. "I'm worried already. Let's sit down and rest."

The girls found a log and the three sat down on it. Cassy turned her head to stare up through the trees. "Oughtn't the moon to be up?"

"It'll be up in a few minutes," Rion told her. "It'll come up right there, due east," and he pointed to a tall tulip poplar on her left.

He took up his stand before the girls, leaning against a pine, with his arms crossed on his breast. He was thinking of the different ways a man could walk the same road. He and Kate had come along this same road the night of that play party Betsy was talking about. They had sat down on this log the girls were sitting on. It was the first night Kate had ever let him kiss her or cuddle her up much. Well, he'd got about as far with her that night as he'd ever got. Kate was a girl knew her own mind. You could go just so far with her and no farther. It used to pretty near kill him but he was glad of it now. But he'd come near marrying her. That day, down in the ravine, when she said, "If that's the way you feel we better be going back to the house. . . ." She'd stood up when she said that but it was not like she wanted to, it was like she was doing something somebody had told her to do. And then he heard her suck her breath in and she looked at him, just once. Her eyes so blue and that surprised look in them! But he looked away and the next minute she'd said, "That's right," and they were walking back to the house. . . .

Betsy stood up. "We better go. They'll have the wedding supper before we get there."

"Yes," he said, "we better be getting along."

They walked on. Another quarter of a mile took them out of the woods. A broad meadow lay before them. At the top of its slope the Lovelatty house sat in a grove of china-berry trees. From where they stood they could see the lights from the candles shining through the trees and could hear the shouting and going on.

They found the path through the tall grass, followed it to its end, then started up the wagon road that led between scraggly china-berry bushes to the top of the hill. The lights from the house beat on the road and speckled the bushes. Half-way up Betsy turned.

"Somebody's coming!"

"It's the wedding party," Jenny said.

Rion heard the beat of horses' hooves; they must be just at the foot of the hill. "Get off the road," he said. "Don't stand here and let 'em run over you."

The girls rushed off into the bushes. He followed them. "Come on," he said. "Ain't no use standing still. They'll catch up with you." But they stood there, goggling, and after he had walked on a little way he, too, stopped under a dogwood tree.

The riders were in sight now, eight or ten horses, every one carrying double. John Weill's grey a little in the lead, as should be, Nate Goodman's black horse crowding him a little and Jim Arrand on the other side on a horse he must have borrowed. Those fool girls were yelling and shouting from the bushes. Somebody had stopped but the grey horse kept right on.

They were opposite the dogwood tree now. John Weill, looking straight ahead, Kate riding pillion. Her arms were around John's waist and he had one of her hands caught up in his, with the reins. Her face was turned in Rion's direction but he couldn't tell whether or not she had seen him, there in the shade of the tree. . . . The girls were back on the road but he waited until the last horse was past before he stepped out from the bushes. Jenny was still yelling and carrying on. "There goes the bride and groom!"

Dust was in his nostrils. His teeth gritted on it. He swallowed. Lord God! If he'd only had the sense to borrow a horse! Kate had sent him word to come to the infare and he was coming, but he needn't have come on foot with a pack of women at his heels, like somebody's old uncle.

"Come on! Come on!" The girls were running, trying to get to the top of the hill in time to see the wedding party dismount.

"Come on!" he cried and putting his arm around Cassy Dawson's waist hustled her along so fast that she was lifted off her feet for a few paces. She fell over against him, then she was on her feet again and drawing away from him. His arm fell from about her waist. He stopped and looked down at her. "Don't you want to walk with me?" he asked before he knew what he was saying.

She stopped too, stock still in the middle of the road. She turned her face up to his. The light from the house was on them now. He could see her black lashes shining in it. He had thought a minute ago that she was mad at him, but she wasn't mad, she was smiling. "I'll walk with you," she said, "but I won't run."

He took her arm and walked beside her to the house, slowly this
time and with his head bent down as if he were listening to catch
every word she said. "Yes, I never seen so many dips a-burning at
one time. . . . But Kate, she's making a good match. Jim Lovelatty
can afford to give her a good send-off. . . ." No, that was the wrong
tack. Why was he always going on about what a good match John
was? This girl would be thinking his heart was broke. She was looking up at him again, the light shining on those black lashes. "Kate's
too fair," he said abruptly. "I like a dark girl."

She broke away from him, laughing. They were in the yard now.
Hard to get up to the doorstep, there were so many people. Old
Jim Lovelatty up there, grinning like a possum, with his hand stuck
out to everybody. He pushed through the crowd on the porch and
on into the hall. Just as full in here, but a path was opening up to
where Kate and John were backed up against a window, side by side.
She had on a dress of Irish linen. John's hair had so much bear's
grease on it that it shone. He moved up to them. He shook hands.
"I'm sorry I wasn't at the church to see the knot tied." A voice from
the crowd: "She's tied, though, ain't she, John?" John's teeth white in
his brown face. "Yeah, she's tied, all right."

People were moving on through the hall into the chamber where
the supper was laid out. Two trestle tables put end to end and dishes
set out the length of them. Kate's sister, Rhea, was coming towards
him with a platter full of pie. He shook his head. "Naw, I'll get to
the fixings later." He got a trencher and worked his way down the
table to where Joe Lovelatty stood before a great heap of roast beef.
"They ain't no tenderloin here," Joe said. "Come out where they
roasted the beef and we'll get us some tenderloin." "Wait till I get
me something to work on," Rion told him. He put a turkey drum-
stick on his plate, together with some slices of the breast, then lifted
the top crust of a big pasty. "What kind of meat's in there?" "Young
broilers," Joe said. "They ain't worth fooling with, to my notion."
"Well, I'll try some. . . . What about partridges? Ain't you got no
partridges?" "Plenty," Joe said and waved his hand to the other end
of the table. Rion went around and helped himself to three partridges.
He came on Rhea again with her platter and took a slice of sweet
potato pie and an apple tart. "I ain't got no business fooling with
these yet but I'll take 'em along," he said and followed Joe through the
crowd and out into the yard.

The ox had been roasted whole over a slow fire. Out under the trees fifteen or twenty men were moving about in the red glow that came from the pit. One quarter of the ox still lay on a trestle table at the end of the pit. Ed Lovelatty was carving it. Rion and Joe hunted around till they found a strip of tenderloin. Joe thought his wasn't done enough and wrapped it around a ramrod and held it over the coals. Rion began eating: turkey first, then the pasty and the partridges until finally he came to the tenderloin, cold now but good eating at any time. He had finished his meat and was beginning on the pie when he saw John Weill coming through the crowd from the house, a half empty plate in his hand. He came and stood by Rion. "Getting enough?" he asked. "I ain't got there yet," Rion said, "but I aim to." He had finished his pie and was deliberating whether he should go back to the house for a helping from a deep dish custard that he had noticed there or should eat a piece of the beef liver that somebody was broiling on the coals when he noticed that some of the younger boys had cleared a ring and were wrestling. Archy was fool enough to try to take a fall out of Jacob Franck. Jacob put him on his back twice, then when he came up threw him over his head. Archy got up, grinning and rubbing the back of his neck, and came over to where John and Rion were standing. "I ain't heavy enough for Jacob," he said.

"You ain't heavy in the upper storey," Rion said. "There was one time when you could a got a headlock and another time when you could a used 'the Blacksnake' on him but naw, you had to let him get a headlock on you and all he had to do then was throw you over his head. If I was you I wouldn't try to wrestle any more, least till I got dry behind the ears."

John laughed. "You're mighty hard on the boy. . . . Remember that time Peter Arrand put you on your back at the Muster Day?"

Rion looked at him. John's head was too long and narrow in his opinion and there was something about the cut of his mouth that he had never liked. Still, he could see how a woman could think him handsome. It was those black eyes and that black hair that he kept plastered down with bear's grease till you'd have thought him an otter if you met him in the water. He saw now how it could be—he had never really believed it till this minute. Kate *had* preferred John to him. It was she who had made the choice after all. She and John had probably laughed at him many a time behind his back. A red-headed man was never much to look at. People were always making jokes about him. They would joke him to his face if they were not feared to.

He moved nearer to John. "You weigh about as much as Peter Arrand," he said. "Would you like to try it?"

John looked surprised. He hesitated a moment, then went over and set his plate down on the end of the table. "All right," he said and took off his shirt and stood there in his new black breeches.

"You going to wrestle in them?" Rion asked.

"Naw," somebody cried. "He ought not to spoil them wedding breeches," and somebody else took a breech clout down from where it was hanging on a tree and brought it to John. He stepped out of his breeches and put it on, then looked at Rion who had stripped off his shirt but had not removed his breeches. Rion shook his head. "Naw," he said insolently. "I don't aim to even get 'em dusty."

He walked over and suddenly rubbed John's nose with the palm of his hand. John jumped back. Rion ducked and butted him in the chest, then before John could recover from the blow grabbed his right wrist, twisted it behind his back, and with his other arm pulled his head over his shoulder and slowly lifted him and threw him over his head. The fall knocked the wind out of him. Rion was straddling him before he could get it back. He put his two hands on John's shoulders and pressed until he could feel the shoulder blades grinding into the dust. "Got enough?" he asked.

"Naw," John said and then he looked past Rion's shoulder and his face changed. "Let me up, Outlaw," he said.

Rion let him up. John walked off towards the house. Rion watched him go. "Well, I guess he had enough," he remarked.

"He was feared the women was coming out," Lovelatty said. "Somebody told them you all was fighting."

"We war'n't fighting," Rion said shortly. "We was wrestling."

He walked beside Ed to the house. John had stopped on the porch. Rion stepped past him into the hall. The dining room was empty, except for some girls who were clearing the tables. People had all gone across the hall, to the chamber where the musicians were tuning up. Rion did not feel like dancing so he went out on the porch. A few men were there, talking, but they soon drifted into the house. Courting couples began to come out. After a while Rion went back into the house and stood against the wall, watching the dancers. They

were "caging the bird." It was Cassy Dawson on the chair. Somebody had taken a tallow dip from the wall and handed it to her. She
took it and raising it high over her head turned slowly around. Her
shadow was there on the wall behind her turning too, the ruffles on
her cap pointed like the petals of some big flower. She was facing
the crowd now but shyly, looking off over their heads as if they
weren't there. The song was nearing its end. She lowered her head
and, smiling now that it was over, got down from the chair. Rion
watched her face as it went past him, the eyes wide open, the lips
still holding their faint smile. He turned away into the crowd
thinking that he had seen her look just that same way some time or
other, then smiling himself as he realized that it was in his daydream
when she had been lying back on the pillow waiting for him.

He suddenly had the feeling that somebody was looking at him
and turned his head. From across the room Kate was staring at him,
her head tilted to one side, her eyes burning blue and narrowed, like
she was trying all the time she was looking at him to make up her
mind about something.

"*She thinks I still want her. She thinks that's why I wrestled
John.*"

He laughed, out loud, so that anybody standing near him could
have heard, then he walked across the floor to where she was standing. "Ain't I going to get a dance with the bride?" he asked and
bowed before her.

"I'm partnered already," she said in a cold tone.

He walked away. Jocasta Dawson had left her partner of the
dance before and was coming towards him. He stopped her. "You
ain't forgot you were dancing this one with me, Miss Cassy?"

She looked surprised but only for a minute, then she laughed.
"It would have been mighty bad if I'd forgot it."

"It certainly would," Rion said. He took her arm. "Come on,"
he said. "Let's stand over here. They ain't ready yet."

She came obediently and stood beside him. He kept hold of her
wrist. The flesh was cool and soft to the touch. It seemed only a veil
for the wrist bone that sprang out so sharply on the slender arm.
Absent-mindedly, as they stood there watching the dancers form, he
kept pressing her wrist, exploring with the tips of his fingers the delicate coupling of the bones, marvelling as he had sometimes marvelled
in the woods over the intricate workings of muscle and bone and

sinew. Suddenly he felt the fragile ball roll in its socket as she flexed her hand and raised it. He let it go with a smile. "You've got bird bones," he said and took her hand again. "See how easy this wrist'd snap?"

She turned her head towards him quickly, then she was looking away. He ought not to have said that about snapping her wrist. She'd given him that quick look just then, trying to make up her mind why he'd said a thing like that. He had never noticed her eyes before, grey eyes, black in the middle but the ball of the eye clear grey, like water in a deep spring when sunlight hits it. But she was too pale. . . .

"They're forming for the reel," she said in a low voice.

"Well, come on then," he said and led her out on the floor.

CHAPTER 6

THE MUSIC had stopped. The musicians had gone outside to cool off but there were a few people still left in the room. Rion and Jocasta had sat down in an open window after the last dance and were still sitting there, talking sometimes but mostly watching the crowd. She had been drinking punch and held a half-empty horn in her hand. There was a jug of rum on the floor outside the window. Rion reached down now, pulled the jug up and took a drink. As he leaned back to set it down his hand brushed against the girl's hand that was lying on the window seat between them. She moved her hand, turned her head a little and smiled, then faced the company again. Rion straightened up. His breath was coming hard and the blood had risen in his face. Just that touch of her hand had brought back all the thoughts he had had of her the other day. He sat perfectly still, looking straight before him, until his excitement had died away, then he realized that she was turned a little away from him, looking at somebody across the room. On an impulse he could not control he leaned out and with his eyes followed the delicate curve of her cheek to where the flesh seemed stretched tight over the prominent cheek bone. A spot of color glowed there, as bright as if it had been painted. It faded suddenly, then as suddenly deepened. Rion watched it, fascinated. He had thought of her as pale. That was because the color was not in the grain of the flesh as in most women but came and went as it was doing now.

She turned her head again, then jumped to her feet. "Where are all the girls?"

He looked around and noticed that there were only old people left in the room. "They've gone to dress the bride," he said, "but there's plenty of them for that. You don't have to go."

But she was already up and out into the hall and then he heard her running down the front steps.

He got up and went out on the porch. Some old folks were sitting around there but the boys were all down in the yard under the oak tree. He started down the steps, then stopped. "I better get me a drink before I go down there," he said aloud and walked to the shelf and got himself a drink from one of the jugs there, then went down the path towards the oak tree. The way seemed longer than usual. He stopped halfway and stood staring across the field where he could see a light shining. That was in the new cabin. The girls had taken the bride over there and were getting her ready for the groom. He wondered whether Jocasta had caught up with the rest or whether she had had to run all the way over in the dark.

Under the tree the boys had closed in on the groom. Joe Lovelatty set his jug down, squared himself, and tightened his belt. "Well, boys, here goes!" They were rushing John Weill, had him up in the air, every man catching on to him where he could. John was game, not making a sound even when they held him upside down, like a sack of salt.

They didn't like that. "He ain't in good spirits," Tom Beard said. "Le's toss him awhile."

John had got away from them and was off for the cabin. He'd make it. He was a fast runner. . . . No, he had the door swung to and would have had it barred in another minute but they were too quick for him. They were bringing him out in the yard. Somebody had torn a blanket from the bed.

Rion pounded down the path after the others, then leaned against a tree to get his breath back and watched them toss John in the blanket. He was laughing when he went up but he couldn't help making a face each time he came down. "He's feared," somebody called. "Feared of what the bride'll say when she sees her blanket split." "Hen-pecked already," somebody else called out.

The blanket had split: John's right foot had gone right through it. "We better put him to bed," Joe said. "We don't want to wear him out. He's got the night ahead of him."

John was staggering forward, drunk from the tossing but keeping a smiling face.

"I wouldn't laugh," Rion thought, "I'd tell 'em to get to hell."

They were surging towards the cabin again. Joe was calling to the girls up in the loft. "Y'all ready? We got a poor fellow here all wore out, wants to go to bed."

Rion left the yard and followed the others into the house. They had John in the middle of the floor and after they had torn his clothes off they put his night shirt on him. A man looked like a fool standing there in a night shirt with everybody gaping at him. Rion clapped his hands to his ears. Lord God, what screeching! The man next to Rion sang out "Flesh alive and tear it!" then, "They're bringing the bride down." The girls were tumbling down the steps from the loft, pulling the bride after them. Her blue bed gown was torn in one place and her long yellow hair had come out of its plait and was all about her face but she was smiling.

"She didn't put up much fight," Rion said.

The man next to him didn't say anything.

"I ain't goin' to have no infare when I get married," Rion said.

The man leered at him drunkenly. "It ain't but once in a lifetime."

"Maybe not," Rion said, "but once'd be too much for me."

He stepped aside as a crowd of girls bore down on him. Kate in the midst of them, laughing and yelling as hard as the others. He looked her right in the eye but she didn't see him; her eyes were glassy. The men were dragging the groom forward. They'd have them in bed here before everybody in a minute. Well, it probably wasn't the first time. He stepped suddenly to the mantel and blew both candles out. "Get out of here," he shouted. "Get out! You done worried this couple long enough."

Joe Lovelatty was beside him in the dark, breathing hard. "That's right . . . my own sister . . . done worried 'em enough." He and Rion locked arms and began pushing and shoving everybody before them. The girls were the worst. One little devil scratched Rion's cheek. He pinioned her arms and threw her before him out of the house and onto the ground.

Inside the house the bride was still shrieking, then the door swung shut. They heard the bolt being shot. Rion wiped the sweat from his face. "Let's go home," he said.

The girls went scuttling off down the path. Joe and some of the other boys ran and caught up with them. Tom Beard and Bill Johnson and one or two others didn't have any girls. They walked on slowly. Rion caught up a lantern and followed them. Every now and then somebody laughed though there was nothing to laugh for now, the shouting was all over. Bill Johnson clapped Rion on the back. "Y'ought not to have wrestled John on his wedding night," he said. "Poor fellow'll have enough wrestling to do before the night's over."

"I'll take his place," Tom Beard put in, "any time he gets tired."

Bill Johnson had walked on a little way but he turned around to Rion. "You're willing to take his place, too, ain't you, Outlaw?"

"I sure am," Rion said. "Any time. Day or night. All he's got to do is call on me."

A laugh went up. An undersized fellow from the Bethabara community walked up beside Rion. "You used to go with her some, didn't you?"

Rion stopped. He held his lantern up and in its light peered down into the man's face. "How'd you happen to git so far from home?" he asked.

The little man stared back at him truculently, then as Rion made no move walked on without saying anything.

The others moved on faster. Rion was now the last of the line. He held the lantern out, swinging it punctiliously in a wide arc so that the light would fall far ahead of him on the path.

Tom Beard had his jug with him. They were stopping to take another drink. When Rion stopped he held the lantern out stiffly with his arm extended its whole length. Tom laughed. "Thinks he's a post," he said.

Rion set the lantern down carefully. He took a deep drink from the jug. "I ain't drunk," he thought, "I'm the only one that ain't drunk." He looked up at the sky. The stars were fiery tonight. Like candles. Like a million candles in a big room. And the meadow was like a room, only higher up than he had thought it. He started on again, putting his feet down carefully, swinging the lantern in a wider arc. He wished that they could stay here in the meadow with the stars burning down on them. It was like Ma'am Clara's place some nights. Tallow dips flaring everywhere and you would see faces coming at you and then they would go away before you knew what was being said. . . . One face he had seen across a table, a trapper with a slow voice and a wry mouth, one corner of that mouth lifted higher than the other as he told his tale. . . . Rion stopped suddenly, set his lantern down. "I'll tell you a tale," he shouted.

They had stopped and were coming back. He considered whether he should sit down, but nobody else had sat down so he remained standing. "It's about some pigeons," he said, "some pigeons I seen the other night."

"Where was they?" a voice asked.

"Out at the barn. I was out at the barn, feeding, and I seen 'em coming. A flight of them. They was one in the lead prettier'n the rest. I said to myself, 'I'll git her' and I stuck out my hand." He thrust his hand out and toppled over on the grass.

Bill Johnson laughed and helped Tom Beard set him on his feet. "Go on," he said.

Rion stood up as straight as he could, facing Bill. "I kept a-grabbing at that bird," he said, "but I never caught her."

Bill laughed again. "I heard you say you never caught her."

Rion continued to look at Bill. Bill's eyes had been right before him a minute ago but now they seemed to be getting farther away. Mere points of light they were now. With an effort he fixed his gaze on them.

"No," he said, "I never caught her. All I ever got was three little pieces of tail."

There was silence, then somebody laughed, then somebody else. Tom Beard was slower catching on than the others. When he did catch on, he sprawled on the ground, he laughed so hard.

Bill Johnson was beside Rion. He walked on a little way, then he said, "It's a good thing Joe ain't here."

Rion stopped. "What you talking about?"

"Joe Lovelatty. He's little but he's full of fire."

Rion stepped out of the path and faced Bill. He put his hands up. "Well, what of it? You think I said anything against any of the Lovelattys?"

Bill looked right back at him. "I ain't heard you name a Lovelatty this night," he said and walked on, and after a second, Rion let his hands drop and followed him.

They came to the house. Old Jim and Mistress Lovelatty came out to say goodnight. The old folks were all gone by this time. The boys went around in front and began saddling up. Bill Johnson got up into his wagon. It was already loaded with young people. He must have asked to take Betsy home earlier in the evening for there she was on the seat beside him big as life and Jenny down in the straw with the others. Betsy saw Rion and called out, "Ain't you coming? There's room for both of you in here."

Rion shook his head. "No, I'd rather walk." He waved his hand at the young people in the wagon. "Go on. Y'all be long enough getting home as 't is."

Betsy stuck out her tongue at him. Bill had sat quiet there on the seat while Betsy was talking, but now he cracked his whip over the oxen and the wagon rattled off down the hill.

Rion turned back into the yard. "I'd a gone," he said, "if it had been anybody but Bill Johnson."

"What's the matter with Bill Johnson?" a voice asked.

He turned around. Cassy Dawson was standing there by the crape myrtle bush. He had been talking to himself when he said that, thinking that he was alone. "Room for both of you," Betsy had said. She meant him and Cassy. Well, here she was beside him.

He stepped up and took her arm. "Come on," he said. "I know a short cut home."

They went back through the side yard and took a path that slanted down the side of the hill. They walked slowly. Rion kept his head bent down. It felt clear as a bell now. He was trying to remember some of the things that had happened in the last hour and he remembered standing in the meadow and telling the story and he remembered what Bill had said: "I ain't heard you name a Lovelatty this night." He had been about to fight Bill but at that he let his hands fall. There seemed nothing else to do. Now he wondered. Had there been an emphasis on *name*? Did Bill mean that he, Rion, had talked about the Lovelattys behind their backs but wasn't man enough to name them?

They came to a stile. The girl had pulled her arm away and was hopping over, light as a bird. He jumped flat-footed and landed beside her. They stood there, side by side, in the tall grass. He raised his head and looked at the sky.

"Ain't it a pretty night?"

"Yes," she said.

They walked on. He took her arm again, bent over her. "You have a good time?" he asked.

"Yes," she said and laughed suddenly.

He laughed too. "I had a good time. Least I reckon I had a good time. There was one spell there I was hitting the jug so hard I didn't know whether I was coming or going."

They had come to where a big pokeberry bush grew out in the path. Instead of keeping with him she deliberately detached her arm from his grasp and walked on the other side of it.

He went up to her and took her arm again. "What did you do that for?"

She stopped and looked at him. "You needn't be making up to me now," she said in a cold tone. "The party's over."

He laughed. "Well, I swan!" he said. "You think I been hanging around you all evening just to spite Kate?"

She raised her head and looked at him. "I don't think anything about you," she said, "and I don't care who you spite."

"Well, I swan!" he said again.

They were in the woods now. As light as day almost but the leaves on the trees looked black and the tree trunks were black except where the moonlight hit them. Once he thought he heard something moving on the right and slowed his steps to listen. The girl walked on ahead and did not wait for him.

She was opposite the log where they had sat down on the way over. He ran and caught up with her. "Let's sit down," he said. "Let's sit down here and rest awhile."

She took a few steps as if she were going on by herself, then whatever it was moved again off in the woods and she suddenly turned back to the log and sat down beside him. They sat in silence. Off in the woods the game kept moving. A herd of deer most likely; he could hear the leaves rustling and a down twig crackling.

He looked up at the sky. Through a break in the trees he could see the moon, red as blood and as big as a wash tub. A harvest moon. It reminded him of nights he had been down in the ravine with Kate. He didn't want Kate—John was welcome to her—but he wished now that he hadn't told that story. They would think he meant Kate whether he did or not. You ought not to say anything about a woman, no matter how much she roiled you. One way it looked like you couldn't get ahead of a woman, with the devious ways they all had. Another way they were as harmless as deer; anybody could stand up and shoot 'em down. Kate or no other girl could get back at a story like that. He sighed.

"I always heard a red moon was a bad sign for folks in love. . . . But I ain't in love. . . . Are you?"

She did not answer.

"I believe you are," he said.

She sat looking straight ahead like he wasn't there, humming a tune.

"I always heard it warn't polite to sing in company."

She stopped humming.

"I reckon you think I don't hardly count as company."

She turned at that and looked at him. Her eyes were hard. One corner of her mouth lifted, as if she were about to laugh but she didn't. She stood up. "Let's go," she said and started on.

He took two steps and caught up with her. He set his hand on her shoulder and turned her about so that she faced him. With his other hand he took hold of her chin. "What makes you treat me like this?" he said.

He saw her eyeballs flash as she turned her head sharply away. "No, you don't," she said and struck at him, but he held her arms down and kissed her, hard, on the mouth. When he let her go she struck him again, digging her nails into his cheek. Then he heard her feet clatter on the path and he laughed as he put his hand up to his cheek and took the fingers away wet.

"That's the second time tonight I been clawed," he said. "The first time it didn't draw blood."

CHAPTER 7

YOUNG JUDGE HENDERSON sat down at the table. He picked up a quill and wrote something in a big book which was open before him. He looked up at the man from Bethabara. "Well, Master Rogan, I believe that concludes our business."

The man had drawn a leather purse from inside his shirt. "Yes sir, that's the sum, to the round pence. I'm glad to get my money and glad to get it without no court trial." He dropped the coins— twenty shillings—into the purse, drew the string and slipped the purse back under his shirt. He glanced at Daniel Boone who, with his back turned towards them, stood looking out of the window. His mouth took on a sullen slant. "Man has to be careful who gets in his debt these days," he said.

Boone turned around, so quickly that his wool hat fell off the back of his head. He took a step towards the man then stopped and eyed him. "Are you satisfied?" he asked. "Now that you got your money are you satisfied?"

The man took a quick step backwards. "Oh, I'm satisfied. Long as I got my money I got no complaints. 'Course I'd a rather had it last year and without no trial. . . ."

Judge Henderson looked up from his book. His eyes sharpened, his handsome, well-fleshed face grew hard. "There's been no trial," he said, "The matter has been adjusted, to the satisfaction of both parties. Why don't you go on home, Fred Rogan? Daniel Boone and I have business to attend to."

The man took up his hat and left. Judge Henderson said, "Whew!" and laughed out of the side of his mouth. His face changed. His blue eyes became cloudy and speculative. He rose and began walking around the room, his hands in his breeches pockets, his body bent a little at the waist so that his long lawyer's coat tails stood out behind him like a turkey's fan.

Daniel took a few steps away from the desk. Findley was over in the corner before a shelf of law books. He had taken one down and was holding it open, making out he could read. He turned around and gave Daniel a quick look. Daniel did not see him. He was looking out of the window. There was an expression on his face that Rion knew well. A kind of wooden look. The fox had not gone to earth yet but he might at any minute.

Rion sat there studying the floor. He realized that Henderson had stopped in front of him.

"Well, Master Outlaw—the name is Outlaw, isn't it?—these are marvelous tales Master Findley here tells of the land over the mountains."

"My name's Outlaw," Rion said. He looked at Findley. "I ain't ever heard him tell anything I knew war'n't so."

The lawyer laughed and walked back towards the desk. He stopped beside it, picked up a quill and taking out his knife began sharpening it. He had an honest kind of face for a lawyer and people said his word was good, though when he was on the bench he'd grind a poor man down like all the rest of the courthouse crowd.

Rion shifted his body in his chair, trying by the movement to conceal the sound of his own harsh breathing which, it seemed to him, must fill the room. He had hardly got his breath back yet. He had come in to town on foot at a fast clip an hour ago. Frank Dawson had come by the house early in the morning to tell him that Daniel Boone was being sued in Salisbury court that day by Fred Rogan, for a debt of four years' standing. He had started right off for town when he heard that. Just as he was going out of the door Jenny had called after him: one of Daniel's neighbors had been by three days ago with a message. Daniel's horse, Old Blue, was dead of colic. Daniel wanted Rion to come up there. "I plumb forgot it till this minute," she said, and then she laughed. "Well, it ain't your horse anyway."

He had not stopped to argue the matter with her. He didn't trust himself to be around her for a while. He didn't believe that she had forgotten the message. She had kept it from him purposefully, out of that spirit of meanness that cropped up in her ever so often. She needn't pretend that the horse's death was nothing to him. She knew that he had been counting on riding that horse west. She knew, too, that he'd have a hard time finding another horse—Daniel Boone was probably the only man in Rowan that'd lend him a horse or trust him for a horse to go on such a trip.

Judge Henderson had finished sharpening his quill. He put it from him suddenly and, as if he had been waiting only to finish it, called out: "Daniel, will you step here a minute?"

Daniel came over to the desk. The lawyer sat down, then reached out and with his foot pushed a chair up beside his own. He was turning over some pages in his ledger now.

" 'Twas fifty pounds for the Florida trip, war'n't it?"

"Aye," Boone said.

"And another ten pounds in November when you got back. And in January of the next year I took over your account with Wagner."

"Aye," Boone said.

The door opened softly and John Stuart, Daniel's brother-in-law, came in and took his stand against the wall. He cut as strange a figure as Rion himself must cut in a lawyer's office: a tall, powerful fellow, with hair as black as an Indian's and eyes that might have been an Indian's looking out of a long, pale face. Daniel had said from the start that he was taking Stuart with him. Rion didn't blame him. Stuart was a good man to have in the wood. The other fellows—William Holden, William Neeley and James Cooley—didn't amount to much but they were going as camp keepers. All they'd have to do was shoot for the pot. . . .

Lawyer Henderson was still sitting behind the desk, his chair tilted back, his eyes studying the opposite wall. Daniel Boone's eyes were bent on the open ledger. Suddenly, as if he could no longer bear to look at the figures that represented his debts, he stood up.

The front legs of Henderson's chair hit the floor. Almost in the same movement he leaned forward, pulled out a drawer in the desk. "Well, Daniel. . . ."

He was taking gold sovereigns out of the drawer and counting them out on top of the desk. He was advancing Daniel money besides paying the debts he was being sued for!

Then it was all settled. They would make the trip.

Rion got up and started for the door. Boone turned around. "Where you going?"

Rion stared at him and said, "Jacob's. I got a little business with Jacob."

The door shut behind him. He was out of the room and on the street. There was no one in sight. He stood there, thinking of the trip and for a minute it was like he was going with them. . . . *Three, four hundred buffalo grazing in one place, and deer and elk mixed*

*with them. . . . High land and open all around, open and covered
with white clover. . . .* There never had been anything like it,
never would be. But he was not going. . . .

Ben Cochrane was coming towards him. He didn't feel like
talking to him. Where was it he had told Daniel he was going?
Jacob's. He had said he was going over to see Jacob on business. He
began walking slowly up the street, then suddenly broke into a run.
Jacob! Jacob was the very man. Why hadn't he thought of him
before?

He ran half the way to Jacob's place, then at the bottom of the
hill slowed up. It wouldn't do to get there out of breath. He'd need
all the breath he had to persuade Jacob. He must put up a good talk,
not let him think it was some scheme that had just come into his
head.

Jacob was in the back of the store, sorting feathers. He looked
up as Rion entered. "And what can I do for you, Master Outlaw?"

"Nothing particularly," Rion said and took a seat on a low chair
that was drawn up facing the counter. Jacob turned back to his
sorting. There were three big sacks of feathers before him. He shook
feathers from one of the sacks out on to a sheet that he had spread
on the counter and began picking dark feathers out from among the
light. He moaned. "Sally Rogers wants three pence the pound and
she has put the turkey feathers in with the goose!"

Rion laughed. "Everybody ain't as finical as you, Old Son."

Jacob turned suddenly. He fixed Rion with his sunken eye.
"What is it you want? A smart young fellow like you didn't come
here just to keep the old man company."

Rion tilted his chair back and put his feet on the counter. "You're
a cute old fox. . . . How'd you like to put up some money against
the next skins I bring you?"

Jacob drew a rasping breath. "How much?"

"Five pounds. I want to buy a horse."

Jacob was eyeing him suspiciously. "Malcolm Outlaw has two
good horses. Can't they do your fall plowing?"

Rion laughed. "I don't want the horse to plow. I want him to
ride off on a trip, with Daniel Boone and another fellow, into a country that nobody ain't ever been into before. God, Jacob! There's
buffalo in there still and deer and elk and beaver thick as rats. I'll
bring back enough skins to make both our fortunes."

A little point of light grew and danced in Jacob's sunken eye, while Rion watched; then it died. He picked up a sack of feathers and began tying it up with a hemp rope. "Bring 'em all back on my horse, will you?" he said.

Rion had stood up when he began talking and now he came a little nearer to the old man. "Call him your horse till I unload the skins here at your door." He snapped his fingers. "Why, Man, what's a horse? You furnish me five pounds. I can get a good horse for that and I'll bring him back loaded. I'll let you have the bucks for two and a half each though they're worth more than that. Say I bring back fifty hides. There's your horse back and over. If you want me to I'll throw in three prime beaver. . . ."

Jacob slowly shook his head. "You might not bring nothing back. You might not come back yourself."

"Well, Boone and Stuart'd bring my skins back to you."

"Where's Daniel Boone get the money for such a long hunt?"

"Judge Henderson's furnishing him, and Stuart too."

Jacob laughed. "Daniel Boone had better take to the woods. He's being sued for debt on every hand. And Dick Henderson's a rich young man and a justice. I'm only a poor merchant. *Nein!* A crazy scheme. I'll have nothing to do with it."

Rion bent over so that his face was on a level with the old man's. "I'll write you a paper making over my share of the land, if I don't come back before the year's out."

"What land?"

"The land I'll get from my father," Rion said in a low, trembling voice.

Jacob plunged his hand into another sack and brought it up full of feathers. He cackled out. "Malcolm Outlaw'd never sign such a paper. And how do I know that your father'll die before you do? How do I know he won't cut you off before he dies, a wild, young fellow like you?"

Rion looked down at the grey old hand that held the white feathers. "I'm a good mind to crack your skull, you old polecat!"

Jacob shrank back. He called out loudly: "Elsa! Elsa!"

The side door opened. Mrs. Wagner's round face appeared in the opening.

Jacob raised a shaking hand. "Young Master Outlaw is threatening me. Says he'll crack my skull. You be witness, Elsa."

She looked at Rion out of china blue eyes. She smiled. "You'll stay to dinner, Master Outlaw? Pudding and noodles."

"I'm much obliged to you," Rion said, "but I got to be starting home."

He went down the long room between the hogsheads and casks and branches of drying ginseng and stepped out onto the street. It had seemed like late afternoon in there but out here on the street it was still full noon. He blinked in the bright sun, put his hand up over his eyes and drew it down over his mouth where muscles about his lips were still jerking. It came to him suddenly what his father had done in the old country: he had killed a man. He, Rion, had been as near as nothing to strangling old Jacob in there. He could still feel a twitching in the fingers that had wanted to close on the wrinkled neck.

"Damned old polecat!" he muttered and drew a deep, retching breath.

Down the road three tall men were moving towards him. Findley was in the middle, talking. ". . . that Henderson, he's a sharp fellow. And he's got others behind him. What's to hinder them from buying up that whole country? And we'd each get a share. We'd be rich as Creeses. . . ."

They came up to Rion and stopped. Rion jerked his finger over his shoulder. "I been trying to raise the money for a horse. That damned old polecat in there wouldn't give up a penny. Says I might die in the woods and he not get his money back."

John Stuart had been standing with his black eyes still fixed on Findley's face. He laughed suddenly. "Everybody's got to die sometime."

Findley laughed too. "I'd as soon die in the woods as here in this town." He looked around him. "I don't mind coming in to town on a spree but I can't stand 'em day in, day out. They stink so. . . ."

Rion was watching Daniel who had been standing all this time studying the ground. He raised his head and Rion saw in his eyes that bold, dreaming look that he knew so well. "If Old Blue hadn't a died. . . ." he was saying.

Rion did not answer. Daniel looked away, then after a moment: "How about going as a camp keeper? You wouldn't need a horse so much then."

"I guess you better let Holden and Neeley take care of that," Rion said. He did not try to keep the bitterness out of his voice.

Daniel stared at him and for a second his dreaming look went away as he seemed about to say something else, but Findley clapped him on the shoulder. "Daniel, what say we start for the Forks? We got a lot of things to see to."

Boone slowly took his eyes away from Rion's face. "I reckon we had better be getting along," he said.

"I reckon you had," Rion said and stood there and watched them walk off together.

CHAPTER 8

AFTER BOONE and the others had left him Rion walked on down the street to Franck's ordinary. Tom Beard was there with another man from the Trading Ford neighborhood. Rion took what silver he had in his pocket and ordered up a dinner of bacon and greens with a bowl of arrack punch. Before they had finished Joe Lovelatty came in and ordered another bowl of punch. They stayed there, drinking, until past noon. At one o'clock Tom got up to go. When Rion tried to follow him his legs were unsteady, and Jacob Franck, coming in just then, put his hand under his arm and guided him to the back door and turned him out into the yard where a heap of hay was piled up against the fence. Rion lay down in the shade of a sycamore tree and slept. When he woke the western sun was in his face.

He got to his feet and ducked his head in the horse trough, then started for home without going back into the tavern. There was no travel on the road that day, and he walked the four miles without getting a lift. At four o'clock he came to the Dawson clearing.

He had intended to go straight home but he wanted a drink of water, so he turned in at the gate. The front door was latched but the shutters had not been drawn. He stood there on the path and helloed. Nobody answered and after a minute he started around to the back.

Jocasta Dawson was coming towards him on the path, in a blue dress, with some bleached cloth piled up on her arm.

"I heard you calling," she said, "I didn't know whether to answer."

He smiled. "Thought I might be a vagrant? . . . Well, you'll give me a drink of water, won't you?"

She took the gourd down from the wall and walked beside him up the grassy slope to the spring.

"Where's Frank?" he asked.

"Gone to town. I thought you might have seen him."

"Naw," he said absently, "I didn't see him. I had some business to 'tend to and when that was finished I come on home."

68

They had arrived at the spring: a small pool bubbling out from between two leaning rocks. He looked at it with disfavor, remembering the spring at home, walled up almost as high as a man's head. "Frank ought to dig this out," he said. "If he won't do it I'll come over here and fix it for you some time. Dig it out and wall it up and cut all this brush away." He glanced up at a dogwood tree that spread its branches over the water.

She shook her head. "In the spring that tree has big white flowers on it."

He laughed. "I never heard anybody call an old dogwood blossom a flower. Anyway, you don't want it dropping leaves in your water."

He bent over and dipped up a gourd full of water. She said she would not drink, so he drank the full gourd and then drank another. The water was as cold as the water at home but he fancied that it had a bitter taste from the leaves. "Frank ought to dig this out," he said again.

She was sitting down on a bull-hide stool that was propped against a tree. He dropped down beside her on the grass. He had been all right when he was walking along the road though hot as the devil, but when he had bent over to drink he had felt as if the top of his head might drop off into the spring.

The girl smoothed her sewing out on her lap, then took it up again. "I bring my work out here," she said. "It's cooler than it is in the house."

"It's sure hot on the road," he said, "but it's hot everywhere. Seems more like July than April."

"Yes," she said, "it's right warm for the time of year."

His eyes went past her, to the paling fence that Frank had put around the clearing. On the other side of that fence the woods began. You could follow that path that wound between the tree trunks a way, then get your bearings and strike west. In an hour's time you'd be in the Dunn's mountain country. It was hot here in the settlements but over in the deep woods it would be as cool as if it were still spring. You could look down at noon and see dew sparkling, on fallen leaves, on spider webs. You could hunt all day and not feel it in air like that. . . .

He glanced at the girl. Her head was bent down over her sewing. She had the blackest hair he'd ever seen, but you could see a line of white in the middle where it was parted. She looked cool, sitting there in the blue dress, but she was feeling the heat too. The flesh about her eyelids was frail and shone a little, the way a flower that's been touched by a hand does just before it wilts.

You wouldn't think to see her sitting there so calm that the other night she'd scratched his face hard enough to draw blood. He'd hardly said a word to her since then and he wondered if she was still mad at him. A rhyme came into his head:

> "*And sew a fine seam,*
>   *And feast upon strawberries, sugar and cream. . . .*"

He leaned forward. "You like strawberries?"

She nodded.

"I know a place where you can pick strawberries till the world looks level."

She was looking up. "Is it on Craige's creek? I found some there the other day."

He shook his head. "No, it's on a stream flows into Craige's. I don't think anybody knows about this bed but me. Least I never saw anybody there."

She stood up and put down her sewing. "I'll be right back," she said. She went into the house and came back with a bucket.

When they went through the gap they were in the woods. They followed the path a little way then struck off to the woods and walked a mile before they came to a valley covered with second growth with a stream flowing through it. There was one place where there were no trees at all. Strawberries grew there on the wide banks.

The girl was looking at a ruined chimney that showed over a wild plum thicket. "I didn't know there was a house anywhere in these woods."

Rion laughed. "Women'll live on a place half a lifetime and not know what's on it. My mother was out hunting greens the other day and come on a spring on our place she said she didn't know was there."

The girl was going over to look at the chimney. It was old and crumbly. There was a hearthstone at the foot of it, up-tilted by frost and thaws. That was all there was left of the house, not a log left, not a shingle, nothing to show that people had ever lived there. She looked at the hearthstone and the ghostly occupants came stealing out of the woods and ranged themselves about it in a circle, rocking.

"Who was it lived here?" she asked.

"It's Craige's land. I don't know whose cabin it was. But you can see there was clearing done here. That's how the strawberries happen to grow so fine. They don't grow but on cleared land."

She took the bucket and they got down on their knees and started picking the berries. They filled the bucket in no time. Then they started eating. After a while Rion got to his feet.

"There's a waterfall up the stream. Want to see it?"

She hesitated. "Isn't it 'most milking time?"

"Oh, come on," he said and she set the bucket down at the foot of a tree and followed him.

For a while they walked in the sunlight on wide, level banks but as they approached the headwaters of the little stream the way grew rough. The trees closed in, growing down to the stream's edge in some places. The stream was narrower now and flowed over rock ledges. Rion took the girl's hand. "We'll have to go in the bed of the creek but you don't need to get your feet wet if you'll step on the rocks."

They made their way on upstream, stepping from rock to rock, and came to a place where they had to bend nearly double to get through, the hemlock branches came down so low. The banks along here were covered with hemlock needles where ferns weren't growing. Partridge berry and moss ran over the rocks. There was a sharp fragrance in the air.

"What's that smells so good" the girl asked.

"Spearmint," he said, and broke off a leaf and bruised it for her.

They stood together on the big rock. As she made to leave her foot slipped and she went down into the little pool at the side of the rock. He helped her up and they went on. He went first, pushing the hemlock branches aside. Sometimes she was right behind him. Sometimes she was off on the other side of the stream.

When they came out into an open place they looked down into another green tunnel like the one they had just come through, and Rion straightened up. He felt a little confused, a little light-headed. That was because it was so cool and dim in here. No, it was because he knew what was going to happen. He could have this girl if he wanted her. A minute ago when she had fallen to her knees on the rocks and he was helping her up he had set his open palm against her side and then had let his hand linger, feeling the warm softness through the heavy folds of cloth. She turned and looked at him, her eyes not as they had been before, but heavy, with the lids drooping; then as he made no move she drew away, stepping to the other side of the stream.

She was coming towards him now, her head was bent down but in a minute she would be looking up. Her eyes would be heavy again. She was stepping up on the rock beside him. He reached out and took her in his arms. "Let's go over there," he whispered. "Let's go over there and rest."

CHAPTER 9

THE DOOR closed behind Frank. Jocasta left her wheel and came and stood on the hearth. She had been spinning and her fingers were stiff, from cold as much as fatigue. She held them to the fire but got little warmth. Frank had forgotten to bring in a log before he left and there was only a bed of embers on the hearth. She went out into the lean-to and finding a log that was small enough for her to carry brought it in and laid it on the coals. She stood back. When the flames began to lick up over its sides she turned away. The corners of her lips lifted in a smile. "He's gone," she thought, "I'm by myself."

She had not slept well the night before. It had been hard to lie in bed listening to Frank's breathing from the other corner. The moon was up and the curtained recess in which she slept was full of light. When she was sure that Frank was asleep she had propped herself on her pillows to look out at a big beech tree that stood close to that east window, and she imagined herself going to the door, drawing the bolt and slipping out into the night. She would stand there under the tree a while, then she would walk about among the other trees and she might even go a little way into the grove. She grew restless at the thought and had to admonish herself to lie quiet. Frank was asleep now but he would start up at the slightest noise: he would want to know if she had lost her wits, going out to wander in the woods in the dead of night.

She laughed to herself, thinking that perhaps she had lost her wits, and then her breath started coming and going quickly as it had done yesterday and she had to lie back, flat in the bed, her hands clenched on each side of her, her eyes fixed on the beam over her head.

She fell asleep towards day-break but woke almost as soon as it was light. This waking was different from any she had ever known. Yes, she was hard to rouse of mornings and would lie in bed as long as Francis would let her, pretending that she was waiting for the fire to come up but really enjoying the warmth of the bed. This morning

73

she had waked as light and quick as a fox in its lair and was up and dressed before Francis turned to call her.

He had been surprised. "Why, lass, I never saw you so brisk before of a morning."

She replied that there was a great deal to do that day and she was anxious to be at it. When he asked what unusual task was forward she could not think of anything to say, except that she planned to do a good day's spinning and wanted to get the morning's tasks out of the way.

After breakfast she cleared things away so rapidly that Francis said she would be at her spinning before it was good light.

She laughed and then was silent, hearing her own voice high and thin, with a note of excitement in it. Frank looked at her. She looked back and had been dismayed to find the muscles about her mouth quivering. She caught—or thought she caught—him looking at her curiously while she was sweeping the room and putting the side meat on to boil. She got through those tasks as quickly as she could and then went to sit at her spinning wheel. The monotonous hum steadied her so that she was able to look up at him calmly from time to time as he moved about the room, searching for the horn book, getting his matchcoat down from its peg. It seemed a long time before he finished his preparations and stood in the doorway. And even then he had turned back, to give her a message for Rednap Howell in case he should call by this morning.

"How could he?" she asked irritably. " 'Tis a school day and he the master."

Francis turned around and looked at her. "Aye," he said. " 'Tis a school day. Still he might come."

She was alone in the room. She had spun on for a few minutes after he left, unable to realize that she was at last alone. After a little she got up and washed her greens and put them on to boil with the meat. "I must not neglect my tasks," she thought and straightened up and looked about her. The floor was swept, the table pushed back, with the bench ranged alongside it and the two chairs in their places before the fire. She had clayed the hearth day before yesterday. She raised her eyes to the east wall where the shelves that held her provisions had been tidied the same day. The whole room was in order and so was the lean-to beyond it and her dinner was already in the pot cooking. She was tired of spinning and she tried to think of some household task that might occupy her and remembered that Frank had rent a hole in the leg of his breeches, climbing a fence. She got the breeches and, threading with homespun thread the needle that Sarah Outlaw had given her, sat down on a stool by the window. The hole was three-cornered and tedious to mend. She rested her needle to look about the room. It seemed dark with the door shut. She wondered suddenly what the weather was like outside. Then her eyes fell on a little basket that Betsy Outlaw had brought to the house the day before.

She leaned over and picked up the basket. It contained iris roots which Mistress Outlaw had promised for her father's grave. She decided that she would set them out now.

She was walking along the path to the church, carrying the basket in one hand and a spade in the other.

The path led past the schoolhouse. As she walked under the window a boy leaned out. His eyes were a clear brown, fringed with darker lashes. They looked into hers for a moment, then looked away, up the path that she was treading. Archy Outlaw, Rion's younger brother. She wondered when the children had recess and walked faster so that she might be out of the way before they poured out of the schoolhouse.

The path turned into the wagon road. She followed the wagon road for a few hundred yards and came to the log building which in her father's time had been an Anglican church but was now a Presbyterian meeting house. It stood in the corner of an old field. The land had been abandoned many years before. Pines had grown up over the field, some of them as high as a man's head and mingled with them were sweet gums and tulip trees; and the church itself stood in a grove of young dogwood.

Jocasta passed the church and entered the graveyard where it lay in a hollow partly enclosed by a wall of rough stone. The Presbyterians had never found time to complete the wall but they had expended some labor on the plot itself. It was covered with broom sedge and the drying stalks of last year's wild asters but no trees had been allowed to grow in the enclosure except one young dogwood that had come up near the wall.

Edward Dawson had been the first person to be buried here. His grave was in the angle of the wall. A few feet away were other mounds: three of the Lovelatty children, a young girl who had died last fall of disease of the lungs, an old man named Hampton who had asked shelter of the Outlaws one night and had been found dead on the hearth the next morning.

Jocasta passed these mounds and stood at the foot of her father's grave. It, too, was covered with sedge. Out of the sedge rose the skeleton stalk of a wild aster. In summer its purple flowers had seemed to be placed there for ornament but the winter frosts had reduced even that woody stalk and it bent double now to mingle its dank seed pods with the grasses.

Jocasta decided that she would plant her iris in the place where the aster had flowered. She set her basket and trowel down and began pulling up bunches of the sedge grass. But the roots held fast and the tough grasses hurt her fingers. She had to take the spade and dig the roots out, cluster by cluster. At the end of half an hour she had cleared only a small, shallow place at the foot of the grave. She stepped back and looked at it, frowning. Then she remembered that Sarah Outlaw had said that iris should always have its roots exposed. "It's tough," she had said. "Just give it a chance to stick its roots in and hit'll take hold."

Cassy thrust the roots into the cleared dirt and covered them with what little earth she had been able to shake from the roots of the sedge grass. Then, out of breath and hot, she sat down to rest in the shelter of the wall.

She sat there for a long time, her lip caught between her teeth, a hand pressed across her eyes. She was recalling the happenings of yesterday, from the time that she saw Rion standing there on the path to the moment when she had gone with him over to the bank. Hemlock needles covered all that bank. She could feel them now, cool and slick between her fingers. She could hear Rion's voice. "Cassy," he had said as he bent over. "Cassy!" She could see his face as it had lingered over hers, the dark eyes seeming even as they looked into hers to plunge past her. She could re-live all the sensations of yesterday but she could not now call up the emotions that had accompanied them. One moment she had had no intention of surrendering herself to the man and the next moment she surrendered.

She groaned, took her hand away from her eyes and stared before her. A hundred yards away the graveyard ended and the forest began. She got up now and walked slowly into the forest. She looked about her as if she were visiting the spot for the first time. Here was no little growth of pine and dogwood and sweet gum, such as one found in old fields, but forest trees. They went up straight and tall: oak and ash and hickory and beech and maple. She remembered that a wild turkey sitting on a lower bough of one of these trees had been out of range of Rion's gun and she gazed at the great, blackish trunks driving one after another into the upper air and thought that even in summer under their airy, insubstantial crowns of leaves they would still stand black and lost.

When she had first walked into the woods she had been conscious of the trees going past, one after another, but now she began to notice even more than the tree trunks the light in which she moved. This light, filtered down through the high, remote boughs, was dim and faintly greenish but the green was no color of spring. She was moving in the kind of light that might fill a cave.

She walked on, gazing about her with quick eyes, thinking how it would be to keep walking between these black trunks in this strange light. And then it came to her that this light would never change. It stretched on and on. It covered the whole land. She had already gone too far; the whole land was a cave, a cave in which she was about to be lost.

Her breath came fast. She turned and walked back the way she had come, slowly at first and without ever looking over her shoulder. Then she saw the sky bright at the edge of the woods and she was running, dodging between the tree trunks until she emerged into the open field.

She stopped to get her breath, then walked on until she came to the graveyard where her father was buried. His mound was longer than any of the others. Edward Dawson in life had been well over six feet. Cassy's eyes traced the outline of the mound where it swelled up through the grass. Then she moved nearer and stood gazing down on it. The mound was covered with the wild grass but here and there red earth showed through. She bent her head, gazing, as if the red, grass-covered earth were a veil which could be pierced by sight. And then it seemed to her that she could see into the bottom of the grave and could see the bones that were lying there, and she turned away and flung herself down on the slope near the wall. Lying there, face down, her eyes shut and her face pressed into the dry grass, she tried to call up her father's face but it did not come before her and after a little she opened her eyes and raised herself on her elbow. All about her the wiry grasses that had been borne down by her body were springing up. An insect was crawling along the stalk of one that was rising beside the wall. With a kind of despairing idleness she watched it crawl up the feathery grass tip and then transfer itself to the stone.

The stone was covered with moss which appeared to be composed of small green ferns. She brushed the tears from her eyes and leaned closer to examine them. Moss like this grew in a corner of the wall at Temple Guiting. There was a big larch tree near that wall, a seat fixed under it where Frank used to sit to study. After Frank went off to college she and Matty brought their dolls there. They were playing there the day her father came to take her away from that place. She had not seen him for a long time. She was not sure it was he until she heard the little fat man who was with him call him by name and heard him answer. "Aye, the boy's a sizar at Christ college. The girl must be ten years old. . . ." And then he had come through the gate and had stood staring at the two little girls. The fat man laughed. "It's a wise father knows his own child," and he slapped himself on the leg. Her father had kept his gaze on them. Then he said, "Cassy!" and she left the seat and walked over to him, not knowing whether he would kiss her or not. . . . When he stooped and caught her up and her eyes went shut and her half open mouth was pressed against the black wool of his coat she remembered that a long time ago he used to do that. But it was before she came to live at Mistress Slaughter's. And he had not been fat then and his eyes were not blood-shot and he had not the little red veins in his cheeks.

The fat man had sat down on the bench. Her father had sat down, too, drawing her towards him so that she stood at his knee. He turned to Matty: "Lass, run to the house and tell thy mother the parson is come."

Matty ran off. But she had had to stand there, her legs touching his knee, one of her hands still held in his. He asked her questions. She must have answered them. And then the door of the house opened and Mistress Slaughter came out. Her cap was on crooked. Her face was red. That was because she had been crying all morning. Her father had his head turned. He was watching Mistress Slaughter walk towards them along the path between the Canterbury bells and the fox-gloves. Suddenly she forgot that she was afraid of him. She wanted him to know what she knew. She pulled her hand away and went and stood on his other side, next to the fat man. She bent her head down until she could see the grey hair curling about the heavy, red lobe of her father's ear. "She *steals*." Her father jerked his head up quickly. "How now, Lass?" She bent closer, whispering. "Up at the Hall. She was laundering and they missed some forks and sent down for them. She won't give them up but I know where they are." Her father turned about on the seat. "Where?" he whispered. "In her work basket, slipped into a stocking. She made out that she was darning when the man came and she kept the forks in her hand all the time he was looking for them." Her father's eyes had held hers for a moment. "Art sure, Girl? You're not telling a tale?" She gave him back a straight look. "No. I felt them when she wasn't in the room."

He stood up. He went to meet Mistress Slaughter. They stood on the path, talking. When she crept near to listen he sent her into the house. And then Mistress Slaughter came in, crying more than ever, and told her to pack her things. Matty helped her put them in the big red box. She had not known till the stagecoach stopped at the foot of the lane that they were going to London. And she had not known till she met Frank in London that they were going on a ship to America. . . .

She looked up at the sun and calculated that it was eleven o'clock. In a few minutes the children would be coming out of school for their noon recess. She took her spade and basket and hurried along the road, passed the schoolhouse and turned off on the path that led to her own house. Partridge berries covered all the ground along here. You could hardly see the vines for the red berries—partridges would have plenty to eat this year. A red-bud bough, its red blossoms hardly withered yet, lay across the path. Rion had reached up over his head to pull it off as they walked along here yesterday. Only yesterday. She stopped still on the path. Her hands went out in a despairing gesture, then fell at her sides. He could not love her. It was she who had begun it, she who had made the first move. At the infare. People had been laughing at him all evening behind his back and she herself had scorned him for the attentions he was paying her out of pique, then at the end of the evening, when she was about to get up into the wagon with the others she had looked over and had seen him standing at the gate alone. He had the same surprised look on his face that he had when they stopped in front of the Lovelatty house and he had asked her if she didn't want to walk with him. She had gone over to stand beside him. The others probably thought that he had asked for her company home. He himself probably thought that he had— he had been drunk all evening—but she knew that she came of her own accord, because she could not bear to see him standing there alone. Then, in the woods coming home, it was she who had provoked him. He would not have kissed her if she had not provoked him. He might never have noticed her. Yes, it was she who began it. . . .

She moved faster as her thoughts darted before her. She would not see him again. She would not go to his house. Honest Betsy! She would pick a quarrel with her. . . . Sarah Outlaw would be distressed, might even censure her own children. But she herself would stand firm and in the end Sarah would say that all English had strange ways. . . . As for Rion she would see him once, once only to explain to him that he must stay away from her house. He might even have to quarrel with Frank. . . . She emerged from the woods and came in sight of the house. A man was standing on the doorstep. Rion Outlaw. He heard her footsteps and turned around. His eyes looked out at her darkly from under his fur cap, the lids fell. He gave a quick shake of the head and started forward, then stopped. Her eyes fixing his face, she moved slowly towards him over the hard beaten ground. A few more steps and she would be on the doorstep beside him. Another second and the door would have closed behind them. She would be in his arms.

CHAPTER 10

As soon as supper was over Rion went up into the loft and changed from his leather shirt to one of bleached homespun that his mother had made him on his seventeenth birthday. When he came downstairs it was dark. No candles had been lit in the chamber but Jane over by the window caught the gleam of his light shirt and challenged him. "Where you going?"

Rion crossed the room and took down from the mantel a book that Frank Dawson had lent him months before. "I'm going to take this home." He laughed. "Frank allowed that I could spell it out if I wanted to but I've had it here two months now and I ain't spelled e'er word yct."

"Naw, and you ain't going to," Jenny said.

"You ain't such a scholar yourself," Rion remarked.

"I can spell every word in the horn book and that's more'n you'll do if you live to be a hundred," Jenny retorted.

Rion, without answering, moved towards the front door. Archy, coming in, collided with him. "You say you going to Dawsons'?" Archy asked when he got his breath back.

Rion thought fast. "I'm going to take his book home but I don't know as I'm going to stop. I'm minded to go on to Beards'."

"Then I ain't going with you," Archy said.

"You can come or not just as you're a mind to," Rion told him and walked out the door and down the path as fast as his feet would carry him. He did not slow his pace until he had crossed the meadow and was at the ford. He stopped there, took off his moccasins, rolled up his breeches legs and waded across. As he sat down on a log to slip his moccasins on again he drew a deep breath. He had stayed away from the Dawsons last night but all hell fire, he told himself, would not have kept him away tonight. But it was a wonder the stories a man had to tell and the excuses he had to make before he could stroll across the fields to a neighbor's house. He didn't mind

Jenny so much. She was always that way but it had been ticklish when Archy wanted to go. He still had Frank to deal with and he didn't know how he'd manage him.

In the Dawson house Cassy and Frank sat beside the single candle that burned on the table. She was sewing and Frank had his dried herbs spread out before him. Frank knew Rion's step and called 'Come in' before he even looked up. Cassy half rose, then sank back on her stool and went on sewing. Rion did not know until he had drawn the three-legged stool up into the circle of light, nearer to Cassy than to Frank, that she had not spoken. He wondered if Frank had noticed that. He looked over at Frank, who had gone back to sorting his dried herbs. He must say something quick but he didn't know what it would be. When he heard his own voice it was harsher than he had intended. "Don't you ever get tired fooling with them things?"

Frank smiled and reached down among the plants and held up one whose leaves shot out star-shaped from a squat stem. "Know what this is?"

Rion shook his head.

"*Prenanthes Serpentaria* of the tribe of *Chichoriaeccae*. I found it this afternoon over near the creek."

Rion took the plant from him. "Hah," he said suddenly, "rattlesnake root. See the rattles?"

Cassy leaned forward. "Has it really got rattles?"

"Surest thing you know," Rion said and gave the plant into her hand so that she might examine the tuberous root.

Frank looked amused. "Is it really an antidote to the rattlesnake bite?"

"I don't know," Rion said, "but I'll tell you what I saw once. I saw a dog that had it powdered on his nose tromple all over a big rattler."

"And did the snake not strike?"

"No, he just tried to get away. Turned his head away from the dog, he did, like it made him sick at the stomach to even smell it."

"Have you ever seen it given as an antidote when a person has already been bitten?"

Rion shook his head. "No, they say it works by sweating. Sweats you nigh to death if you got the poison in you but don't bother you at all unless you been bitten."

Frank nodded. "The Indians use it, I know. There are many medicinal plants in their pharmacopoeia. I wish I had more knowledge of them."

"You ought to go live with them a while," Rion said and laughed. He glanced at Cassy. He had hardly seen her face since he came in. She had not looked up but that one time. He did not dare to try to make her look up but he could not sit there and not look at her. He kept his eyes fastened on her hands as they moved over her sewing. She had on her blue gown tonight, the sleeves pushed up over her elbow, the arms white against the blue of the gown, the flesh tender. The delicate tendon in her under-arm stood out when she flung back her hand. There was a blue vein running diagonally across it.

She raised her head and her eyes met his, then she looked down at her work. Suddenly she let it fall in her lap. "Frank, I forgot to stop up my chickens!"

"It's so warm tonight it won't hurt," Frank said.

She got up. "It's warm now but the dew's cold. You let little chickens drag around after the hen two or three mornings and there's no strength left in them."

"I'll do it in a minute," Frank said absently.

But she was already at the door. Rion got up and followed her. "I'll do it," he said, "providing you'll stand by and tell me where to put the boards."

They went out into the lean-to and through its open door on to the back porch. Rion put his hand back and pushed the door to behind them. Then he took her in his arms. "Ain't there somewhere we can go?" he whispered.

She drew away from him. "We better stay here. I don't know but Frank suspects something."

She stepped down off the porch. He followed her. He looked overhead. The sky was deep tonight but it still held some blue, so much blue that it made the stars look yellow. She was down in the corner of the yard, bending over one of the triangular doll-like huts. He took the board from her and fitted it into the groove that would hold it suspended, then went to the next coop and the next until all the hens with young chickens were fastened up. When he had finished he went to her, kissed her, put his arm about her and taking her hand slipped it inside his shirt. They stood there, his arm about her waist, her hand pressed against his fast-beating heart. In the woods a sweet-smelling shrub was in bloom. All the yard smelled of it. He looked up again. When he had looked overhead before he had not seen the new moon that hung over the woods. He put his free hand under her chin and turned her face up so that she might see it too. "It's too pretty a night to stay in," he said.

She started. "We'll have to go in. We been out long enough now."

"Let's go the long way then," he said.

They walked around the corner of the house, and before they came into the light from the window Rion drew her back into the shadow of the beech tree. He slipped his hands down inside the bosom of her gown, over her breasts till they came to where her waist curved in. He remembered that the first time he had ever held her he had only set his hand against her waist. Standing in front of her, pressing his hands tight against her smooth sides he shook her body to and fro as a man might clasp a sapling and shake it. "Love me?" he asked. She did not answer, only pressed closer to him. As their bodies touched throughout their length, he felt desire shake him, so suddenly that it was as if his body had received a blow. Still keeping one hand inside her dress he gestured with the other to the edge of the yard where the shadows were deep. "Let's go over there," he said. "Just a minute. Frank won't notice." She was about to answer and then he felt the muscles over her ribs contracting as she drew a sharp breath. He let her go. "What's the matter?" he whispered.

"I saw somebody step up in the yard," she whispered back.

They sprang apart. Jocasta stepped out from the shadow of the beech tree and walked slowly around to the front yard. Rion followed her. In the light from the doorway a short, thick-set man was seen moving up the path. He stopped when he saw them. He took off his hat. "Good evening to you, Mistress Jocasta."

"Good evening to you, Rednap Howell," Jocasta said.

They were full in the light from the doorway now. Howell put out his hand to Rion. He smiled. "And to you, Mister Outlaw, whom I saw last at Franck's ordinary. I make no doubt that you delivered my letter?"

"Aye," Rion said.

They went into the house. Frank looked up, surprised. "Why, Howell, what brings you here?"

The chunky, red-headed schoolmaster was evidently as much at home at the Dawsons, as Rion himself was. He drew a chair up for himself, and before he answered Frank's question he laughed and asked Jocasta why she didn't light another candle. "Why," he added to Frank, "Master Sampson Job was bringing a load of wool to Salisbury market and as 'twas a Friday and no school on Monday— a plague of measles is on my pupils—I told Master Sampson I'd make one of his flock." He looked down and plucked a strand of wool from his black coat. "We started long before sun. 'Twas chill then. I got me down under the wool, so deep I was ready to baa. When I got out at Salisbury in broad day and saw people glancing at me I thought that the wolf might better have come in his own clothing." And he picked another grey fleck from his sleeve.

Jocasta got up and brought the jug of rum and set out three horns. Howell emptied his quickly. When Frank pushed the jug towards him again he shook his head. "No, I must be on my way in a few minutes."

"Where are you bound?" Frank asked him.

"To Michael Braun's. I was bid there some weeks ago to a jollification but my duties did not permit. I thought that so long as I was in the neighborhood I'd stop and pay my respects to Mistress Braun."

"Hadn't you better stop the night here and pay your respects in the morning?" Frank asked.

He shook his head. "No. I'll get there before bedtime. And if the beds are all occupied I'll sleep in the hay. I've a little business to talk over with Master Braun," his sandy eyebrows went up a little, "a little business of a horse."

Rion remembered the letter Howell had given him to deliver to Frank. He had heard about Howell since that day. He was thought to be the head and front of the Regulators, second only to Husbands, some people said. Rion eyed the schoolmaster now, thinking that he was cut out for a leader. He was powerfully built, short but broad in the shoulders, with arms that were longer than those of the ordinary man. He was not handsome. His face was almost as red as his hair, the skin coarse and a little pitted by smallpox, but he had a fine nose and a sparkling blue eye. Like Rion he wore his hair long and turned up in a club at the back. It was tied with a velvet ribbon, a piece of finery that did not consort with his ill-fitting homespun small clothes and black coat.

Frank had gone back to his work and seemed to be paying his friend little attention, but Rion felt that there was plenty they could talk about if no one else were present. Howell looked up. His broad mouth widened still further in a smile.

"I saw a sight yesterday," he said. "Daniel Boone and a party came through Hillsborough. Setting off for the west, they said."

Rion said nothing.

"How many were there?" Frank asked.

"Eight. Daniel and Squire and that stranger that's been at Daniel's all winter and John Stuart and James Cooley and William Holden and William Neeley."

"Your arithmetic's in error," Jocasta said. "You name seven only."

"There was another. Daniel's old Cuff decided to go at the last minute and nothing could stop him."

" 'Twas a mistake," Rion said. "Were I going into Indian country I'd ne'er take a dog to give alarm."

"You're right," Howell said. "Cuff has a bay as deep as Gabriel's horn. But they'll leave him at some settler's cabin before they strike Indian country."

Frank looked over at Rion. "At one time you thought of going with them, did you not?"

"I figured on it some," Rion said, "but I couldn't get hold of a horse."

"You did right to stay at home," Howell said. "There's enough trouble in the country without running off to the woods to look for it." He got up. His eyes met Rion's and for a second it seemed as if he might say something else, but he turned to Jocasta, said, "Goodnight, Lass," and moved towards the door.

Frank pushed away the basket that held his plants and rose too. "I'll walk a piece with you," he said.

Rion sat with head a little bent and eyes fixed on the floor until he heard Frank's and Howell's boots strike on the stone doorstep. He looked up at Jocasta whose eyes were on the door. Suddenly she leaped up and ran outside. Frank was halfway down the path with Howell. She called after him. "Frank, will you be going as far as Robinsons'?"

Frank turned around. "Maybe. What do you want there?"

She came back into the house, ran over to the chest, stooped down and took something from it, then was up again. Rion heard her outside. "Will you give this dress pattern to Dolly? I heard her saying she'd be cutting a gown this week."

Rion got up and walked over to the hearth and stood with his back to the room, looking down into the empty fireplace. When he heard her step behind him he turned around. "How'd you think of that?"

"I had to think of something that would keep him away from the house," she said.

"It'll be an hour," he said. "It'll take him a good half-hour to get to Robinson's."

"And they'll walk slow, talking."

He put his arm about her shoulders. "Let's go outside," he whispered.

They went out the front door and around to the beech tree where they had been standing when Howell came up the path. Rion motioned to a clump of fig trees in the back yard. "Let's go back there," he said. "If anybody comes we're out here seeing what got in the hen house."

She laughed and followed him to the far side of the fig bushes. There was some wild grass growing between the bushes and the fence. They sat down. Cassy turned around and peered between the palings. "I feel like somebody might come up the meadow this way," she said.

"They couldn't see us if they did," Rion said.

He took her hand in his and put his other arm about her and drew her to him. She came willingly but her body remained taut in his clasp and after a second he let her go. She seemed unaware that he had released her.

"What's the matter?" Rion asked in a low voice.

She turned to him. "You wanted to go with them, didn't you?"

"Go with who?" he asked.

"Daniel Boone and those men."

"Yes," he said, "I did figure some on going."

She put her hand up suddenly and touched his face. "I can't stand for you not to go," she whispered.

"It don't make no difference," he said.

She did not answer. He sat looking down at his own hands set side by side on his knees. A minute ago it was all he could do to wait until Frank was off the place, but now desire had left him. She had taken it away with her words. "I can't stand for you not to go." It was as if she wanted to go herself. It was as if they were one person, wanting the same thing. No, it was because she cared more for him than she did for herself. Nobody else had ever felt that way about him. His mother would let herself be cut in pieces for him but she'd be the same way about any of her children. Archy looked up to him and tried to do everything the way he did but Archy was just a shirt-tail boy. When he was grown they might not be so close. No, he never had had, maybe never would have a friend like this girl. He might have a better lover but he'd never find anybody who'd feel the same way about him, for a woman, he saw now, could love you mighty hard without thinking more of you than she did of herself. Most women were like that. They'd love you up to a certain point and then it was everybody for himself and the devil take the hindmost. But this girl, why it was like she was a part of himself. And he himself was a different man from the one who had sat there beside her a moment ago. He shivered slightly. If he had gone west they would not be sitting here like this. He reached over and laid his hand on hers. "I couldn't stand to go west," he said. "I couldn't stand to go anywhere away from you."

CHAPTER 11

IT WAS DARK when Rion rode up from the river on to the big road. As he waited he heard nothing but wood noises and the call of a swan on the river. Then hoof-beats sounded from far down the road. Rion rode Bald off into the woods a little way and dismounted; he hitched him to a sapling and came back and slipped in among some hazel bushes.

The riders came on at a trot: Frank Dawson and Rednap Howell. As they came abreast of the hazel bushes Rednap spoke. "I hope the woman won't fail us."

"Her husband'll make her come," Frank said, "I saw Barton Sprang yesterday. He's with us, if any man is."

Rion stepped out from behind the bushes. "I ain't so sure," he called out.

Both men checked their horses. "Who's that?" Rednap cried. "What do you want?"

"It's the Outlaw boy," Frank said. He came riding back down the road. "What were you hiding in those bushes for, Rion?"

"I war'n't," Rion said, "I was just sitting here, waiting for you two."

Rednap Howell came up to them. "You picked a poor place to wait, friend. We might have shot you for a robber."

"Then you'd a had me to bury," Rion said. He went nearer and caught hold of Smiler's mane. "This Sprang, now," he said, "you sure you ain't made a mistake, letting him in?"

"Why?" Howell asked sharply. "Do you know anything against him?"

Frank laughed. "Don't pay any attention to him, Rednap. He doesn't know anything about Sprang. He's just trying to find out where the meeting is. . . . He's been at me for a week to tell him."

"Well, why don't you? I'm as good a man as Sprang any day."

"Well, why don't you, Frank?" Rednap said.

"He's the son of my neighbor. I'd as lieve he weren't mixed up in it."

89

Rednap laughed at last. "There's plenty of your neighbor's will be there tonight. . . . You got anything against this boy?"

"No," Frank said. "He's hard-headed but he's honest." He suddenly wheeled his horse and made off down the road. "Come on," he called over his shoulder, "we're going to be late."

Rednap laughed and bent down and whispered to Rion. "It's at Matthew Braun's. Walk right in the front door just like you were visiting."

He was off after Frank. Rion got his horse, mounted and caught up with them on the edge of the Braun clearing.

Matthew Braun was not long from the old country. A skilled mason, he had been three years building himself a house. But it was built to last, out of rock that he had blasted out of his stony fields. A tall house of three storeys, the handsomest for miles around.

Howell and Frank rode into the woods a little way and hitched their horses. Rion dismounted near them. "Hear that music!" he said.

Howell laughed. "They told me there was going to be ring games here tonight."

They started for the house. Rednap, who was first, rapped loudly. After a moment the door opened. Matthew Braun stood there.

"Come in," he said heartily. "Come in, neighbors."

They stepped in. He shut the door behind them.

Mistress Braun sat beside the fire. The four children were in the middle of the floor, going round and round, the old grandmother, so bent that she was no taller than a child, in the midst of them. A black-haired boy over in the corner was making the music. As the visitors entered he raised his bow and struck into "Money Musk." The grandmother seized a child by the shoulders and made her stand still but when she tried to range the other children they broke away, giggling and stamping. The grandmother groaned. "Nicht so. So," and she pulled up her skirts and took a few steps on her crooked old legs.

Rednap Howell laughed and started over to join the dance but Braun caught him by the arm. "They're waiting for you downstairs."

They went into the lean-to adjoining the kitchen. There was no fire there, nothing except crocks of milk set to ripen. Matthew stooped and pulled up a trap door. They went down a flight of wooden steps, and were in the cellar.

There was a table over near the wall with a single candle upon it.

A man sat behind the table, his head bent down, writing: the Quaker, Harmon Husbands, from Deep River.

Howell went up and began talking to him. Frank and Rion sat down on some upturned wine casks. There were other people sitting near them. Rion recognized in the dim light the faces of several older men of the neighborhood and there were half a dozen young fellows whom he knew, among them Bill Alexander and the two White boys and Ben Cochrane.

Nobody spoke to him and he looked about him in wonder. He had been in this cellar two years before when the house was building. It had been a small room then, just big enough to hold roots and a few casks of wine. But since then they had dug it out, beyond the house, far into the side of the hill. He stared, trying to see where the glistening walls stopped. Something that he had thought a man's shoulder moved and he saw that it was a horse's rump.

He laughed. "By Job! Do they stable their horses in here?"

"Some of them come in this way," Frank said in a low voice. "It don't do to have too many horses hitched around here at once."

"And do they keep that racket going upstairs every night?"

"Long as they can get anybody to dance."

Rion was going over to examine the end of the long room when he saw that two people had moved up out of the shadows and were standing in front of the table. The woman turned her head: Rhoda Sprang from the Bethabara neighborhood. The man standing beside her was her husband, Barton Sprang.

The Quaker was asking where they lived and writing their answers down.

"You say it was Tom Bannerman who came to your house?"

"Yes, sir."

"Did you see him?"

"No sir, but my wife did," the man said, moving a little away from his wife.

"And will you tell me what happened during the time your husband was away, Mistress Sprang?"

Her "Yes sir" was so low that it had to be repeated. Rednap patted her on the shoulder. "Don't be afraid. Go on, Mistress Sprang."

"He asked me for the tax and I didn't have it. Told him I couldn't get it till we sheared the sheep."

"Yes," Rednap said, "What did he do then?"

"He tore my gown off'n me. Seized it by the bosom and ripped it down, then told me to go spin another."

"I'd a split his head for him," a man standing near Rion muttered. Rednap turned around. He raised his hand. "Neighbors!" He turned back to Rhoda Sprang. "Did he ask you for more than the lawful tax, Mistress Sprang?"

"A shilling extra."

The Quaker's big head was suddenly thrust into the circle of light. Rion studied his face. He had a cold kind of eye. Sometimes that meant that a man would fight. Sometimes it meant that he didn't care about anything enough to fight for it.

But a man had to fight, one way or another, for everything he got. This Sprang now, he ought to have gone right over to Tom Bannerman's and beat him half to death. That would cure him of robbing people quicker than all this talk. They were going at it the wrong way, writing things down on foolscap. But what could you expect when you had a meeting run by two schoolmasters and a Quaker?

Rednap was turning around, beckoning. Frank touched Rion's arm.

"What you want?" Rion whispered.

"Come on," Frank said. "They'll swear you in now."

Rion got up and walked with Frank towards the table. Another man was standing there. Tom Beard. He grinned at Rion, then reached out and laid his hand on the book that Rednap was pushing forward. Rion laid his hand beside Tom's and they repeated the words that Rednap lined out for them:

I do solemnly swear that if any sheriff, county officer or any other person shall attempt to collect taxes unlawfully levied or make distress on any of the goods and chattels or other estate of any person sworn therein . . .

A long oath. Rion drew a deep breath in the middle of it. The Quaker looked up. Rion stared into his blue eyes and continued:

I do further promise and swear that if, in case this, our scheme should be broken or otherwise fail, and should any of our company be put to expense or any confinement, that I will bear an equal share

*in paying and making up said loss to the sufferer. All these things I
do promise and swear to perform, and hereby subscribe my name. ...*

Husbands looked away. Rednap had stopped reading. Rion and
Tom took their hands from the Bible. Rednap was spreading a roll
of foolscap out on the table. It was almost covered with names. He
was putting two more at the foot:

THOMAS BEARD
ORION OUTLAW

Rion reflected that he could have written his name himself. Still
it looked more clerkly that way. He took the quill that Rednap
handed him and made his mark.

There was a commotion over near the door. Somebody had come
from above and was talking to Rednap Howell. He was coming back
towards the table.

"Mistress Braun was walking around in the yard a minute ago and
three men rode past the house."

Husbands stood up. "Put out the light."

The room was suddenly in darkness. Men were grunting and
pushing as they made for the door. Rednap's voice came, steady and
low. "Don't everybody try to go out the same way."

Rion was about to start for the ladder when he felt Frank touch
his arm. "You can go out the back if you want," Frank whispered.
"I'll be along in a minute."

Rion could see a square of grey light on the far wall. It was
blacked out as a man led his horse through the opening. There were
two horsemen left when Rion got there. The last one waited until
Rion had got through and then slid a door into place and piled an
armful of brush against it before he mounted his horse and rode off.

Rion was standing alone in a sumac thicket that they had let grow
up in the back yard. He made his way as quietly as he could through
the sumac bushes and cut across the clearing to the place where he
had left Bald. Frank was not there yet. He got behind a tree trunk
and waited for him.

In the house lights showed and fiddle music was still going, but
all the men must be out of the house by this time. Tom Beard, Ben
Cochrane, Otis James. There must have been a dozen men there

tonight besides the half dozen he had recognized. He had wanted to be a Regulator and now he had taken the oath and was a member of the band. But it was not like he had thought it would be. A lot of men meeting in a dark room and taking down somebody's testimony so that the Quaker could bring it up in court. He had thought that they meant to fight the sheriffs. And the clerks, the clerks of the courts! The Hillsborough clerk, Edmund Fanning, had been tried for extortion the other day, tried and acquitted, when everybody knew that he made every man who came to him pay whatever tax it suited him to name. He himself was too young to have had much court business but he had seen enough. Fanning or no other clerk should take money out of his pocket, not if he had to hang for it.

Frank was suddenly there on the other side of Bald. They mounted and rode out of the clearing. Neither spoke until they had left the big road and turned into the short cut through Shipman's woods. Rion rode up close to Frank.

"How'd you ever get into this business?" he asked.

Frank sighed. "I've no gear but I wear a head on my shoulders like any other man."

Rion laughed. "It was Rednap Howell got you into it. But he's a wild fellow. Make us a better leader than yon Quaker in my opinion."

"You're a fool," Frank said, "and you'll hang somebody yet with your loose talk."

Rion did not say anything. He knew that he ought not to be mentioning Howell's or anybody else's name here on the big road —no telling who might be spying from the bushes. He looked over at Frank, slumped in his saddle, a shapeless bulk in his old cloak and round hat. "I don't like him as well as I used to," he thought. "It's because I've done him wrong. You don't like anybody much after you've done 'em wrong."

They rode in silence. It must be well past midnight by this time. He had told Jocasta that he would not be there till after midnight. She slept in the loft now. The window by her bed was unshuttered, and the big beech thrust its branches right up to that window. She could slip out and swing down on the branches.

She could move soft as a cat. Three nights ago he had come up to the house in the pitch dark, by way of the meadow, and then had slipped across the clearing from tree to tree and had stood looking at the house, wondering if maybe he dared go up and throw a pebble at her shutter. He had decided that she couldn't get out and was turning to go when suddenly she stood beside him, one hand on his arm, the other clapped over his mouth. He could feel her laughter as he drew her away through the trees. All the way she kept on laughing.

They went always to the same place in the meadow. It had been a rabbit warren but the forms were gone now, the grass all pressed down where their two bodies had lain. Every night before he left that place he kicked the grass up and then stooped and with his hands made two or three forms. But you could probably tell that somebody had been lying there if you looked close. They would have to get another place. One was as good as another these dark nights but when the moon was full you could see the meadow from the house.

Cassy wanted him to come sleep in the loft where she slept now, said that Frank never went up there from one year's time to another, and if he did she could always stop him at the head of the ladder, tell him she was changing her clothes. The loft would be safer than outdoors for there was always the danger that Frank might call her some night when she was out of the house. He would like not to have to get up and go. He would like to sleep there by her all night. But he did not like going up into the loft. He didn't like the idea of being caught in Frank Dawson's or any other man's house. . . .

Frank was nodding in his saddle. Rion rode closer to him. "Wake up," he said in a low voice, "you'll fall off and break your neck."

Frank roused himself, yawning. "The last mile is always the longest."

"Yes," Rion said, "it's about a mile now."

If only Frank wasn't with him. Then he could gallop all the way. It would be a long time before he and Cassy could be together. She had said that she would not try to get out until Frank had been in bed a while, said she would tiptoe to the head of the ladder and listen for his breathing. But Frank might want to sit and talk or he might be wakeful after he got in bed. She might have to wait another hour before it was safe to come. . . . He had told her to go to the head of the ladder and listen for Frank's breathing but now he did not see how he could wait. A desire to utter her name came over him. He rode closer to Frank.

"Does Cassy know about this business?"

"She knows where I go," Frank said in a low voice, "but she's safe. Safer than some of the men we've got. She's not like most women."

Rion did not answer. Frank talked on. "She's old for her age. I reckon it's having her mother die so young. That ages a girl."

"How old is she?" Rion asked.

"Sixteen. No, seventeen. She'll be seventeen in October. What's that they say? October's child is born to woe. . . ."

"I don't take stock in them old rhymes," Rion said.

"No more do I. Now I was born in May. Supposed to be lucky. And a more unlucky fellow never lived."

"What makes you think you're so unlucky?" Rion asked.

"I never thought to be teaching an old field school."

"What did you think you'd be doing?" Rion asked curiously.

"There was a time when I thought I would make my mark in the world. That was before I was up at the university."

"Didn't they treat you well?"

Frank laughed. "I was a pensioner and ate broken victuals. But that was to be expected. But I had no chance of a fellowship even if I had taken a good degree. Our county was already in possession of one."

"Wouldn't they give two?"

"Not at a small college like Christ's. . . . I might have been entered at some other college if my father had freed his head of the fumes of brandy long enough to consider the matter."

"Well, I wouldn't worry about it now," Rion said.

His own thoughts went back to Jocasta. He had never asked her her age. He had never given it a thought. Sixteen was young to be doing what she was doing, coming to meet him at night, laughing like a child. An orphan who had never had a mother to guide her. He ought to break things off, meet her one more time and tell her they'd have to stop. He'd have to try to make her see it. He ought to tell her when she came out tonight—he ought not to have anything to do with her, send her right back into the house. He tried to imagine how it would be and it was as if he had her there in his arms in the dark. She had a way of reaching up suddenly and drawing his face down to hers and then kissing him till she was out of breath, little, soft kisses, all over his face, his eyelids, his cheeks, his nose, his ears.

He looked over at Frank. "I can't do it," he thought, "I can't do it and there ain't no other man could unless it was a dried up schoolmaster like Frank."

CHAPTER 12

At two o'clock Jocasta stepped to the door and seeing the Outlaw girls coming up the path went to meet them. Jenny carried the patchwork in a big roll and Betsy had a split basket on her arm. "It's blackeyed peas," she said. "Ma was bound you all didn't have any."

"We haven't," Cassy said, "and I'm glad to get 'em." She took the basket from Betsy and would have taken the quilt scraps too but Jenny held on to them. The three girls entered the house.

Betsy turned up the hem of her skirt and mopped her forehead. "I vow, but it's hot coming across them fields! . . . Let's take our sewing out in the yard. Lot cooler under the trees."

Jenny shook her head. "No, I want to lay the quilt pattern out on the bed."

"I let a jug of metheglin down in the spring this morning," Cassy told Betsy. "That'll cool you off."

When she returned with the jug the two sisters had laid the rolls of quilting out on the bed. "Get your strips," Jenny said, "I want to see how it looks."

Cassy took the long roll of quilting from her work basket and laid it in the empty place. Then she poured three bowls of metheglin. The girls stood, bowls in hand, sipping and looking down at their handiwork. Jenny tilted her head on one side. There was a smile on her thin face. "It's a pretty pattern now, ain't it? I declare I think it's the prettiest pattern they is."

Cassy looked at the quilt. The three long rolls of unbleached cloth which formed the "backing" were ornamented at intervals by two bright, interlaced disks, "the double wedding rings" from which the pattern took its name. The rings were composed of wedge-shaped scraps of calico in various colors. All the rings were complete, except one which still lacked a small segment.

Jenny was eyeing this ring, frowning. "If that piece was in it'd be ready to quilt."

Betsy snatched up the roll which had the unfinished ring. "Ain't but three scraps to quilt in. I can get that done while you all put the other rolls together." She dragged a stool up to the bed and began sewing in the missing scraps.

Jenny took her roll of backing and her strip of patchwork and went over and sat in the big chair before the empty fireplace.

Cassy dropped down on the chest by the window and turned her eyes to the hearth where red still glowed through the grey ashes. This morning when she had gone out to pick greens the air had been chill. After a half hour in the mustard patch she had been glad to come in to dry her wet feet and skirts at the fire. But the weather had changed and those ashes on the hearth were from another season. She looked about the room. It seemed larger since morning. Chests, chairs and tables seemed to stand farther from each other and in another light, though nothing had been changed except that Frank had pushed the big table farther back from the hearth. It was the air. The room was full of balmy summer air coming in from the open fields. She turned to the window. In the last week the leaves on the maple trees had broadened and had lost their tender, new opened look. It would be full summer soon. She gazed at the maple that stood nearest the house and she wished that its leaves would not grow any fuller and that their green would not deepen. Every year since she could remember she had longed for summer and on some one day of the spring had known a sharp thrust of joy as if the season turned in her very heart. But this year, this year summer must not come so suddenly or go by so fast!

Last night she had slipped out of the house after she was supposed to be in bed and had met Rion down at the edge of the old field. He had made a shelter behind one of the larger pines and within it they had lain together under an old buffalo robe. Seeing it in the mind's eyes she felt the blood rise in her face and neck, and yet it was hard for her to remember what life had been like before she and Rion came together. She was sixteen last fall, a woman grown. She had had dreams from which she woke, burning, to realize only later in the day what it was that had excited her. But she never tried to imagine what it would be like to be taken by a man. She had been too proud. She could wait. She had an idea, too, that for her it would be different from what it would be for the other girls and she had listened indifferently to their talk. Ed Tolefree had tried for a year to wait on her. She had never done anything but laugh at him. She had had other would-be beaux but she had discouraged them. In all her life only one man had ever come near enough to her to make her remember him. That was Tom Beard, one night last spring when Frank was away from home and he had said that he would wait until he came in. They had sat there by the fire a long time until she grew sleepy and got up and went out on the back porch to get a drink of water. She stayed out there till she was chilled through, thinking the fresh air might rouse her. Tom met her on the threshold as she came back into the room. He caught her by the waist and before she knew what he was doing he had run his hand down inside her gown. He was stammering and all the time his hand had kept moving over her breast. She looked into his shining eyes and then she felt the nipples of her breasts standing erect and felt a faintness inside and she put both hands on his chest and exerting all her strength pushed herself away from him. He stood as if he did not know what to do, then laughed and came back to the fire. They talked for a few minutes—neither of them mentioning what had just happened —then Tom got up and said he believed he would not wait for Frank after all. That had been in March. For weeks afterwards when she thought about it she could call up the feeling of Tom's warm hand moving over her cold breast and yet never for an instant had she been in danger of yielding to him. There was a part of her that he could never touch, a part that would always say, "No." But with Rion it was different. He had caressed her once, for his hand set against her side like that had been a caress, and she had come straight into his arms. These last few nights and every night that they had been together had told her that she was right. She wondered what it was drew her to him. It was not pleasure. No, it was not pleasure. It was the desire to belong to him and that desire did not reside only in the parts that were made for love but was in all of her. She could feel it aching in her now. It would carry her through the fields, across the river and up to him before everybody if she would let it. She thought of a story Francis had told her from olden times, of how a queen had her lover's heart roasted and served up to her by her husband and his wicked brother and how when they told her that she had eaten her lover's heart she said only that now she had him within her she was so much the stronger.

She gave a start and thrusting her needle into the cloth began to take rapid stitches. She had been so deep in thought these last few

minutes that it had been as if she were out of the room. She glanced
at the girls furtively. Jenny was sitting back, sorting some scraps that
had been left over. Betsy, crouched on her stool, was piecing up the
last ring. She bent over it as if she were tackling a washing and her
large, work-roughened hands fumbled with every stitch. Jenny was
cleverer with her needle but no wonder. Crippled as she was she
couldn't get around to do outside work. Betsy raised her head, smiled
at Cassy, then bent over her work again. Cassy stared at the down-
bent black head. It is a strange thing to have your lover's eyes look
at you out of another head. She had never realized before that Rion
and Betsy had the same eyes. You would expect Rion's to be blue,
with his red hair, but they were brown, not brown, really, but red, a
shining, dark red like a piece of old cherry wood that's had beeswax
on it. Betsy's eyes were a truer brown than Rion's but they had the
same glint in them and they both looked at you the same way, a quick,
glancing look like game peering out of a thicket. Betsy was raising
her head again. Cassy looked away, feeling her vitals twist inside her.
If Betsy knew!

A bumblebee zoomed into the room. Betsy got up and drove him
out. She was coming back to her seat. "Cassy, you going to Robinsons' Saturday night?"

"Frank ain't much on dancing," Cassy said. She smiled uncertainly. "And nobody else has asked me to go."

"Bill Johnson's asked me," Betsy said. "You can walk along with
us if you care to. But I expect Rion he'll be going. Least I reckon he
will. He don't seem to care much about going here lately." She had
finished sewing the last patch into the ring and with the patchwork
smoothed out on her lap and her head tilted back was observing the
effect. "It looks right pretty, don't it?" She got up and took another
roll from the bed. "You know," she said, "I don't believe Rion's ever
got over losing Kate. I mind a day or two before she got married
he come in from work early and went and laid down on the bed in
the loft. I had to go up there for something and there he was, laying
there on the bed and looking out of the window real solemn. I declare,
I felt sorry for the poor fellow. Don't care if he is my brother."

"Rion didn't care nothing about Kate," Jenny said. "Least not
enough to marry her. Rion, he ain't going to be in a hurry to marry
nobody."

"Well, he's old enough," Betsy said.

"He's old enough but I lay he won't be marrying yet a while."

Betsy had laid her work down and was staring at her sister. "I don't know what you're hitting at."

Jenny laughed. "The boys in this neighborhood is a fast-living, dissolute lot. Rion, he ain't no better'n the rest of 'em. He ain't got no girl in trouble yet, far as I know. But it's a wonder he ain't. He runs with Jim Hadley and you heard the preacher a-thundering at him from the pulpit last Sunday."

"I heard him talking about folks being taken in sin," Betsy said. "I knowed he was talking about poor Minty Edgren that had a little baby last Wednesday night."

"And ain't no more married to Jim Hadley than I am," Jenny said.

"Well, they ought to get married," Betsy said. "Now they got this little baby they ought to go on and get married."

Jenny laughed. "Jim ain't going to marry her now. Maybe he'll say it ain't his baby. And maybe it ain't. Maybe Jim warn't the only one."

Cassy raised her head. She looked at Jenny. "It's Jim's baby," she said in a low voice. "She never had anything to do with any man but him."

"Well, that won't keep him from saying it ain't his baby. And she can't contradict him. Won't anybody believe anything she says now."

Betsy had taken her work up again but now she let it fall back on her knee. "I was sleeping in the bed with Minty Edgren," she said in a wondering tone. "A week ago come Tuesday, I was sleeping in the bed with her."

With a quick movement Jenny shoved her chair around so that she faced Betsy. "How come you to be sleeping in the bed with *her?*"

"I was spending the night with Lizzie Mayo and Minty and her ma stopped by for the night. They put Rhoda Edgren in the chamber and me and Minty went up in the loft."

"Didn't she show or nothing?"

"No. I remember once in the night I put my arm around her and I remember thinking 'Minty Edgren is a heap bigger in the waist than I am,' but I didn't think nothing of that."

"*You might a felt it moving!*" Jenny said. She shuddered. "I couldn't a done it. I'd a felt like I was laying up against a snake."

Betsy was silent a second, then she said, "Did you feel like you was a snake when you was laying up inside your ma?"

"I was conceived in holy wedlock. That's different from laying around in cane brakes."

Betsy laughed. "I reckon they were doing the same thing, no matter where they was laying."

"Don't!" Cassy cried sharply, "Don't!"

Jenny had got up and was coming towards Betsy. She was in front of her, bending over until their faces almost touched. Her mouth was working. Her eyes shone. "I'm a-going to tell Ma what you said and I'm going to tell Pa too, how it's all right to lay around in cane brakes. I reckon they won't let you out so much at night, after this, Miss."

Betsy drew back, looking at her sullenly. "I never said nothing of the kind. I never said it was all right to lay around in cane brakes."

"Well, you said it war'n't no harm. Said people was doing the same thing, no matter where they was lying. Said a lot of loose talk. I'm going to tell Ma. . . ."

Betsy suddenly pushed her chair back and sprang to her feet. "No, you ain't," she said. She dug her fingers into Jenny's shoulder until Jenny cried out and backed away. Betsy pursued her. She had hold of both her shoulders now. "You chicken-livered little cripple!" she said between her teeth and shifted her grip from Jenny's shoulders to her throat.

Cassy flung herself between them. She tried to pry Betsy's fingers loose from Jenny's throat but Betsy only laughed at her. Cassy bent her head and bit Betsy in the arm. Betsy shrieked out with the pain and let Jenny go. She backed away, rubbing her arm. "I didn't mean to hurt her," she said, "but she makes me so doggoned mad, always a-picking at me." She turned her head and glared at Jenny. "If I hear any more from you I'll choke you again. Hear that, Miss Aleck?"

Jenny silently left the room. They could hear her on the back porch, splashing water into a pan. When she came back her eyes were red but her face was composed.

Betsy still stood in the middle of the floor, rubbing her arm. She smiled foolishly at Cassy. "I reckon I'll go out and wash my face too. Makes you hot, all this fighting."

Cassy went with her and poured water into the basin for her.

When Betsy had bathed her arm she held it up. "You sure put a ring on me," she said. The two girls watched the red marks fade from the brown arm. "I didn't mean to bite so hard," Cassy said.

Betsy laughed, then caught her breath with a sob. "I might a choked her to death. I don't think about nothing when I get mad like that. And she makes me so mad." She stepped down from the little porch. "I'll take a turn in the yard. If I go in there too soon she might roil me again."

Cassy went back into the room and took up her work. Jenny was sitting in the big chair, sewing away as if nothing had happened. After a few minutes she spoke politely: "I'm about through my strip now."

"I've finished too," Cassy said.

They laid the strips on the bed and then got Betsy's strip from the stool and put it in place. "Another half day's work and it'll be ready for quilting," Jenny said.

Cassy was staring out of the window but she turned her head when Jenny spoke. "Yes," she said, "another day ought to finish it."

Betsy was in the doorway. She held a spray of green in her hand. "I saw this dill in the garden and I thought I'd pluck some for Ma. She was wanting some."

"Let me get you some more," Cassy said quickly, "I got plenty. Let me get you some more."

Betsy shook her head. "No, this is enough." She glanced at her sister and spoke quietly, "Jenny, the sun's most down. We better be starting home."

Jenny was still bending over the bed. "Yes," she said, "soon as I finish rolling up this quilt."

Cassy went forward. Her fingers closed over Jenny's thin wrist, holding the hand back from the work it would accomplish. "Leave it be," she said, "I'll roll it up after you're gone."

"Come on," Betsy said from the doorway. "I just remembered I got to milk tonight."

They were gone down the path, walking side by side, talking, even laughing when the old gobbler came around the corner of the house and made a run at them.

Cassy standing in the doorway, watched them till they had crossed the road, and then she went back into the house. The patchwork quilt lay as they had left it. If you stood a little way off and looked at it through half-closed eyes you could imagine that it was already quilted and finished. She closed her eyes and could see the bright blue and red and yellow disks floating interlaced before her. Double wedding ring!

She leaned over the bed and with a shaking finger pushed one of the strips aside so that the pattern was broken, so that the quilt no longer appeared a finished thing. Then leaning farther over and catching hold of one of the strips she rolled it into a tight ball. She rolled the other strips until there was nothing to see except a half dozen tightly rolled balls of cloth. She packed them into a split basket and pushed the basket under the bed, so far under that one would have to move the bed or crawl under it to get the basket out again.

CHAPTER 13

RION WAITED in the shade of the tulip tree until Frank disappeared around the bend. He crossed the road and walked up the path to the cabin. The door was ajar. He pushed it open. There was no one in the chamber but he could hear stirring in the back of the house. He called: "Cassy! Cassy!"

The sounds stopped but thinking he heard a board rattle on the back porch, he went out into the lean-to. It was empty. He strode out on the back porch. There was no one there, either, but he saw a wisp of smoke rising above a clump of elderberry bushes down by the stream. He walked down the path. On the bank of the stream a fire was going under an iron pot. Cassy stood beside the pot, stirring her wash with a white oak stick. Rion advanced and stood beside her. He picked up a twig from the ground and began whittling on it. "Morning," he said and then glanced at the fire. "Anything I can do for you?"

She shook her head. "I'm much obliged but there's plenty of down wood around here." She laughed, a polite, fine lady laugh. "Not much trouble starting a fire on a day like this."

Rion looked up at the sky. Burning blue though it was not yet eight o'clock and not a cloud in sight. "It's going to be a hot one," he said. He lowered his eyes to her face. She was pale and little beads of perspiration stood out on her forehead. He laughed suddenly. "I'm surprised you're up washing so early," he said, "I'd a thought you'd a laid in bed late this morning."

She advanced to the side of the pot and holding one hand up to shield her face, stirred the clothes up and down in the water. She did not answer till she had gone back to her place, then in a low voice and without looking up at him she said, "I always get up with the sun."

Rion slashed his twig in two with one stroke of the knife and flung it from him. "Even when you're up late?" he asked, "Even when you're up all night with Tom Beard?"

She was looking at him now. There was an expression on her face he'd never seen before. It was like she was trying to make up her mind about something. She opened her lips as if to speak, then closed them. At last she spoke. "Master Beard didn't spend the night here. He just brought me home from church."

Rion laughed harshly. "Master Beard! I'll have to tell Tom. He'll be mighty pleased, having folks call him 'Master,' a whoremaster like him!"

Again she gave him that strange, distant look. "He behaves nice before ladies," she said and kneeling down at the water's edge began rubbing out some clothes.

Rion went and stood over her. "You took up with him mighty sudden. One minute you didn't hardly know him from Adam and the next you cut away and was walking home with him. Without so much as a by-your-leave."

She tilted her head and looked up into his face that was hanging over hers. "A by-your-leave?" she said, "A by *your* leave?" and then she bent her head as if she could not trust herself to speak and began rubbing away at the clothes.

Rion stood gazing down at her. He could still see her eyes as they had been when she looked up at him. There had been pure hate in them. Or was it hate? He had never before had a woman look at him like that. He roused himself. "I didn't ask for the pleasure of your company," he said heavily, "and you know why. I didn't say anything before the rest. I didn't want 'em to catch on."

A sound broke from her, a laugh, or it might have been a cry. She jumped to her feet and ran over to the pot. She took a split basket from the ground and with the white oak stick began hauling clothes out of the boiling water into the basket. A blaze ran up her apron and caught. She did not seem to see it, but went on heaving the steaming clothes up out of the pot.

Rion caught her by the shoulder with one hand then reached down and pinched the flame out between his fingers. "Gre't God," he said, "you don't need to set yourself afire!"

She worked her shoulder out from under his hand and stooped and picked up a shirt that had fallen from the basket into the ashes. It was still steaming. Her lips drew back in a grimace of pain. "It's got ashes on it," she said helplessly, then still holding it in her hand, moved over to the stream.

Rion snatched it from her. "Here," he said, "I'll do it," and wading into the stream he bent over and doused it in the water. When he came back she had fetched the basket of clothes over to the bank and was looking down at them. Before she knew what he was doing he put his hand under her chin. "*Cassy*," he said, "what've I done?"

She did not move, just stood there, her chin tilted up in his hand, her eyes looking straight into his. It was that same strange look, like he was somebody she'd never seen before. Suddenly her lids fell. She jumped back, laughing. "You haven't done anything!" she cried wildly.

"Well, what you carrying on like this for?" Rion said. "What you want me to do?"

She looked away and did not answer.

"Well?" he said.

She looked at him then. "I just want you to go away from here," she said in a dead voice.

Rion had started towards her but he stopped. He stood still on the path, his hands hanging at his sides. "You better think before you say that," he said heavily. "I ain't Tom Beard. You can't whistle me back any time you get ready."

As she stared at him her mouth worked a little, like a child's when it's going to cry, but she didn't cry. She turned away and began taking clothes out of the basket and spreading them on the grass. He watched her spread a big, double sheet out, a towel, then one of Frank's shirts. What had been green grass was all grey and striped with clothes. "You mean that?" he said again but she did not answer, only went on working with the clothes, and after a minute he walked out of the yard.

He kept Bald at a gallop until he was out of sight of the house, then slowed down. He wished now that he hadn't left in such a flurry —it didn't look well. But when he got mad like that he always had to do something, quick. It was her speaking to him that way, like he was somebody she had to be polite to. That roiled him worse than her coldness. But her coldness, her sudden coldness! He had not yet been able to understand it. He didn't suppose he ever would. He suddenly pulled the old horse up short and sat there staring into the woods where a slender young dogwood quivered in a patch of sunlight.

"If you ain't the biggest fool," he murmured.

He thought that he understood it all. Her taking up with first this one and then that one these last few weeks ought to have told him. She was one of these girls couldn't get enough of it. He had pleased her for awhile—there had been times when he doubted that, but he knew now that he had. Then Tom Beard or somebody else had come slipping in that window one night. She liked Tom or whoever it was better than she did him, or she was afraid to try to keep them both hanging on. Or maybe, with another lover, she had just turned against him. There were some men couldn't please women. Maybe he was one of them. Already he had been mistreated by two girls. . . .

He brought the oak stick down on his leg and heard himself grunt with the pain. He whacked the old horse across the rump.

"Get along home," he said.

CHAPTER 14

IN THE FALL and winter of that year Rion saw little of Jocasta. But then he did not go to the parties and infares nowadays. On the first Saturday in April there was a play party at the Beards to which Rion had not intended to go, but the girls and Archy begged him and at the last moment he walked across the fields with them. As they were leaving the house Bill Johnson joined them and he and Betsy walked on ahead of the others, so fast that they were soon out of sight.

Archy laughed. "They're in a mighty hurry."

"They ain't going to be in such a hurry once they get around the bend in the road," Jenny said.

Rion, who had been away from home a great deal, had not realized until now that Bill was waiting on Betsy. "She might go further and fare worse," he said. "Bill Johnson, he's all wool and a yard wide."

"He ain't quite that wide," Jenny said. "I ain't got nothing against him except the way he's always carrying on. Look at that."

Bill and Betsy had come to the river. Betsy had sat down on a log to take her shoes and stockings off when Bill suddenly caught her up, one stocking still dangling from her hand, and carried her across the stream. Rion, not to be outdone, picked Jenny up and splashed through with her. He laughed at Bill as he set her down. "I got the best of the bargain. I'd as soon heave up a sack of salt as yon Betsy."

Bill looked down at Betsy. He put his hand on her shoulder. "Had to carry her across," he said, "she's so sweet I's afraid she'd melt."

Betsy turned red and Archy stuck two fingers in his mouth and whistled. They all went up the bank, laughing. At the turn in the road they met the Robinson girls with the two Davis boys and they all proceeded to the Beards' house together.

Rion walked next to Sarah Robinson who kept talking to him but he did not pay much attention. He was thinking of something Bill had said to him back there at the river. They had been talking about the infare at the Lovelattys' about this time last year. Bill had said to Rion: "You took Cassy home. Remember you all walked through the woods. Wouldn't ride with the rest."

"I walked along the road with her, if that's what you mean," Rion had replied sullenly.

The little hussy, he thought. She had played her cards well. He had been over at the Dawsons' almost every night last summer, but nobody even knew that they were going together. Bill Johnson was probably the first person who had ever coupled their names, unless it was Jenny who had a nose like a fox. He wondered if Cassy would be there tonight. It was at the Beards' house and lately she had been going to all the frolics with Tom. Probably had him sleeping up there in the loft every night. He wondered if Frank suspected. Probably didn't, he was so absent-minded. She could have the loft full of men and he'd never notice. Then, too, he was away from home so much, at meetings two or three times a week. They had too many meetings, and every time a lot of new faces. Men were flocking to join since the Regulators had broken up the court at Hillsborough. Jim Hadley had come to him only the other day, saying he'd heard there'd been a lot of meetings lately and he'd like to come to one. Most everybody was down on Jim Hadley now; said he was the father of Minty Edgren's baby and wasn't man enough to own up to it. He, Rion, didn't know about that, but he never had liked him and he didn't want him in the Regulators. Too many white livers and big talkers among them.

There was talk of the governor sending the militia in. He wondered how many of the boys would stand firm if that happened and then he heard ahead of him a name being called and slowed his steps to listen.

It was Pretitia Lane talking. "I don't know how she can stand to look at him!"

They were talking about Cassy, Cassy and Jim Hadley. She was coming here with him tonight, they said. He had asked her and she had said she would be pleased to have his company.

CHAPTER 15

THE GAMES were already started when Jocasta came in with Jim Hadley. Jim made a break for the circle as soon as they stepped into the room but Jocasta stopped and spoke to Ellen who was not playing, then went into the girls' room to remove her bonnet. Ellen went with her as far as the door, then left her. She walked slowly over to the bed, untied her bonnet strings and laid the bonnet on the bed. There was only one candle burning on the mantel. The shadows were deep in the corner where the bed stood. Cassy sat down on the bed and let her face sink into her cupped hands. From the chamber she could hear the dancers' voices: "*Consolation flowing free. Consolation flowing free. Consolation flowing free. Come, my love, and go with me.*"

The voices sounded far away and yet in a moment she would be in there where the dancing and singing was. There was a rustle beside the bed. She took her hands down from her face. Ellen Beard was standing at the foot of the bed.

"You feel bad, Cassy?"

"My head aches."

"Want to lay down in here a little while?"

Cassy shook her head, then going to the mirror that hung over the chest of drawers began to rearrange her hair. It was so dark that she could not see. She brought the candle from the mantel and set it on the chest. Ellen went out of the room. Cassy re-coiled her hair and stood, staring into eyes that looked back at her from the oval of greenish glass. Eyes as expressionless, as dark as two holes burned in a blanket. The nose and mouth did not seem to belong to them or was it the wavy glass that set the features askew?

She grimaced at her reflection, and as the tired muscles about her lips settled into place she felt her teeth grip the flesh of her cheek and absent-mindedly opened her mouth and ran her tongue over the wall of first one cheek and then the other. The flesh on both sides was sore. It had got that way from being clamped down under her teeth. She could not remember when she begun to set her teeth like that but often nowadays she was aware of the flesh inside her cheeks being sore. She moved away from the mirror and as she did so an hysterical sob broke from her. She stopped and clasped her hands in front of her, nervously kneading the knuckles with the tips of her fingers. She must not do that, out there, in front of the company.

She thought of Minty Edgren. They said that Minty would not even take care of her little baby, just sat in the chimney corner and cried. She, Cassy, used to have crying spells like that when she and Rion first broke off. One night after supper she had started crying and had not been able to stop until Francis, frightened, had slapped her, hard, on the cheek. But that was back in May. It was a long time now since she had cried.

She thought of Minty Edgren again. When she had heard about Minty's baby being born she had said to herself that she would go to see her. She had heard Lizzie Mayo talking about Minty and how now she would not go to parties any more and nobody would visit her except her kin. She had intended to go to see Minty the very day after she heard that but the day had slipped by, and the day after that, and then she had forgotten all about Minty. She could not go now. Minty would not want to see her.

She had forgotten all about Minty when she told Jim Hadley that she would go to the ring games with him. She did not know how it was but she had. He had come by to see Frank. They had talked at the foot of the path. She had sat on the doorstep watching them. Jim was a handsome fellow, the handsomest in the neighborhood, some people said. His brown hair curled all over his head and his skin was as fair as a woman's. He was taller than Frank. At infares he was always the tallest man present. Sometimes just after he had swung his partner he would put his hand up and shake the beam over his head, and once, playing "Skip to my Lou" at the Lovelattys' one of his feet had gone through the floor and he had been pinioned there in the rotten puncheon until two men came and pulled him out. He had made up another verse about that: "Stand there, Big Foot, and don't know what to do. You can't be my darling." Sitting there, watching him leaning down to Frank as he talked, she had remembered how at parties he who always cut the most capers and shouted the loudest would sometimes look around quickly after a loud shout, as if wondering what people thought of him.

She looked away from the two men to where the woods pressed up against the paling fence. A grove of dogwood trees came up there. The leaves were not out yet but the blossoms were as white as paper. Her eyes roved on down the fence. In one place the paling had been pushed aside and a path was worn over the dogwood roots into the forest. As she watched two deer came stepping along the path. She wondered whether they would come up to the fence when she saw that they had fallen to grazing on the dogwood sprouts. She had heard Daniel Boone tell how he crept up on deer, moving while they had their heads down, freezing still as soon as their heads went up. A deer's tail always went up as soon as he raised his head.

She got to her feet and took two steps slowly. There was a flash of white. The deer were bounding off down the path.

Frank and Jim had finished talking and Jim was coming back up the path with Frank. He stopped in front of her. He was laughing, though nobody had said anything. He bent down, his red lips still drawn back from his white teeth.

"There's ring games Saturday night at Beards'. You going?"

She looked at Frank. He was looking away, to the place where the deer had been. The deer are off into the forest. Hairy jacket and the little hoof light on the path. The wind blows a shrivelled puff ball after them.

"May I have the pleasure of your company?"

She had been looking into his eyes, not at their blue, but at the tiny, red veins in the corners. He looked away from her and then back again, quickly. He looks away so that I will think he is here. He is nowhere, for he is nobody. No Man, standing here and asking me to go with him.

"Yes, I'd be pleased with your escort."

He was gone down the path. Frank whittled a stick, frowned. He said: "Jim Hadley. . . . There's been some talk. . . ."

"I don't hold with talk," she said and went into the house.

That was four days ago. Jim had come by for her this evening at six o'clock. Frank did not come. They walked alone through the woods. As soon as they were out of sight of the house Jim put his arm about her shoulders. She let it rest there for a minute, then stepped out from under it, not saying anything, just moving to the other side of the road as if she were walking around a tree. He laughed, then fell to talking about some new people who had moved

into the neighborhood. He talked on all the way to the Beards',
not waiting for her to say anything, not seeming to care whether she
spoke or not. And now from the other room she could hear his voice,
high above all the others.

She must go in there or they would be wondering what was the
matter with her.

She got up and walked into the chamber and would have slipped
in among the crowd but Jim spied her and came towards her. He
took her hand and swung it up and down. He was singing:

"Duck chew tobacco and goose drink wine,
Walk, little chicken, on the pumpkin vine."

CHAPTER 16

THE GAMES had been going on for an hour. Rion stood in the back of the room watching the players. Some of the boys double stamped their feet at the turns until you could feel the timbers of the house sway. The Beard house was built over a deep cellar but any timbers would give under this crowd. Old Ned Raeburn, calling the figures, was worse than the players. He held two shank bones of a cow in his right hand and rattled them at every turn. His old maid sister had put a thimble on her finger and was drumming on a copper wash tub. He, Rion, had not played a single game but he felt like he had been in the ring all evening. That was because of the singing. A tune got started and then went on in your head after they stopped singing it.

> All around the grindstone, the grindstone,
> All around the grindstone, hi yi yea,
> Don't you want a sweetheart, a sweetheart, a sweetheart,
> Don't you want a sweetheart to swing around so gay?

He had never stood back like this at a party before. In some ways you felt like you were at the party more than when you were dancing yourself. When you stood back like this you would take one person and watch him around the room and it was like there wasn't anybody in the room except you and that person. He had been watching Tom Beard and he knew something he hadn't known before. He knew that there wasn't anything between Tom and Cassy. Tom was sweet on her, all right, but there was nothing to it. He could tell that by the way Tom kept looking towards the door while she was in the other room and the way he went up to her as soon as she came in. He had watched them as they stood there together. She spoke to Tom kinder than she'd have spoken if they'd been lovers and she had tried to keep by him. But Jim Hadley came up and claimed her and she went off with him.

Jim went to the shelf where the jugs were as soon as he had come in, before Tom even had a chance to show him the way and he had been back again and again since then to judge from his looks. His eyes were shining like glass and he kept hollering all the time, even when nothing was going on. A minute ago when Dolly Meigs was passing by he had caught her and tried to kiss her but she had ducked under his arm and got away.

The girls over in the corner were talking about him but when the time came up they let him lead them out on the floor as Lizzie Mayo was doing now. They made a handsome couple, even if Jim couldn't stand up straight. Lizzie was almost as tall as he was and as fair. She would be glad when the game was over. You could tell by the set of her mouth. But Jim was enjoying himself, looking around, drunk as he was, to see if folks were noticing what a figure he and Lizzie cut.

Rion studied the handsome face. Jim had a womanish mouth. The lips which had been parted in a smile suddenly drooped at the corners, giving the whole face a worried look. The next moment Jim was smiling again. "Poor fellow," Rion thought, "he knows there ain't anything to him but he has to keep up his foolishness so folks won't catch on."

Tom Beard came up. "Let's get 'em started to playing 'Snap,' " he said.

"Why?" Rion asked. "Who you want to kiss?"

Tom threw his arms out wide. "Every one," he said. "I aim to kiss every girl here tonight before I'm through."

"You better get started then," Rion said.

"I aim to," Tom said but he spoke absently and stayed where he was, looking out over the crowd. A ring broke up. Rion saw the girl they were both looking for.

Cassy was standing by the window. As Rion watched she reached down and picked up a turkey wing that was lying on the sill, as if she were going to fan herself with it, but she held it against her breast. She had on a blue gown and there were blue ribbons in her cap. She was smaller than he had thought she was or was it just that her neck was so slender? She turned her head suddenly. Their eyes met. Rion gazed back though it was like a blow in the face, having her eyes strike on his like that. She felt it too. Her head went back a little but her eyes kept to his face for what seemed a long time. Then she smiled and turned her head.

Rion stared at her after she had turned her head away. He knew what she meant by her smile. She had no hard feelings. It was all over between them. That was what her smile meant. It was all over? She was crazy. She was his girl. He'd have her back again if he wanted her. He took a step forward but Tom Beard was suddenly in front of him. "They're getting ready to play 'Snap,'" Tom said. "There's a couple holding up now."

Rion saw a boy and a girl standing in the middle of the floor with their hands joined. Before they could choose who was to "snap" Jim Hadley ran out on the floor and held up his hand.

The girl nodded her head and he started around the ring. He went around twice, putting his face up close to the girls' faces. Once, before Dolly Meigs, he held his hand up as if he were ready to snap, then took it down before she could move. Finally he stopped before Pretitia Lane and snapped his fingers loudly in front of her face.

The tall, yellow-haired girl did not run as the rules of the game required her to do if she did not want to be kissed. She just stood and looked him in the eye. For a moment Jim didn't seem to know what to do, then he walked off and left her. Rion heard the giggling and shishing all around him. He did not need to crane his neck to know who it was Jim had stopped before this time.

Cassy looked even smaller, running. She had struck back into the crowd and as she ran people made way for her. When she came to Bill Johnson he let her by but stuck his leg out so that Jim tripped and fell on the floor. Jim got up, laughing, but his womanish mouth was set. He ran harder and caught up with Cassy. She saved herself by jumping behind Ellen Beard, then held on to Ellen, pushing her this way and that by the shoulders. When Jim couldn't get past he flung his arms around both of them and tried to kiss Cassy over Ellen's shoulder but she sprang away before he could touch her and left him standing there, his arms about Ellen.

Ellen brought both arms up and broke away from him. "Get away, both of you!" she said and walked off.

Cassy had slipped in among some people over by the window but she heard. She looked at Ellen and turned and looked around the room, from one to another; she put her hands to her face and began running like a crazy person towards the front door. Jim started after her again but somebody called, "Leave the girl alone," and he stopped, grinning like a fool.

Tom Beard was still standing beside Rion. "I'm going after her," he said.

Rion stirred. "No," he said in a quiet tone, "you ain't the one."

He sprang over to the side of the room and had the door open by the time she came to it. She passed through. He followed her, closing the door after him.

She was running down the path. He caught her and put his hand on her arm, jerking her about so that she faced him. "What'd you come with him for?" he asked, then interrupted her before she could answer. "I don't want to know nothing about it. It don't make no difference."

She did not answer, just started on down the path again. He followed her, his hand still on her arm. They came to the big hemlock tree that took up half of the front yard. Rion, looking back over his shoulder at the lighted house, stepped in among the feathery branches, drawing her after him. He set his hands on her shoulders and as he did so he could feel himself trembling all over. *What made you stay away so long?*

CHAPTER 17

RION STOOD on top of the hill and waited for the others to come up the path. The woods were thin, but there was plenty of cover. A big sugar tree that had been blown down last spring lay alongside the road. Three or four men could hide behind it and a little way off was a cedar tree whose branches touched the ground.

He turned around. Bill Alexander stood beside him. He did not cut such a comical figure as he had cut in the kitchen, when he first put the soot on his face, but he looked comical enough. The other fellows were crowding up behind Bill. The soot worked all right. You couldn't see anything of their faces except the whites of the eyes and the teeth. It was like being out with a bunch of negroes. He wanted to laugh. Suppose word got out that a whole gang of negroes was loose and suppose everybody turned out to hunt them. . . .

He motioned with his arm to bring them up closer to him. "Find your cover," he said, "and when I holler jump in on 'em."

"We going to let 'em get right up on us before we do anything?" Josh Hadley asked.

"I don't know," Rion said impatiently, "I can't tell till I see 'em. But don't a man of you move till I say the word."

"I don't like the idea of laying here till they get right up on us," Josh muttered.

Bill Alexander turned on him. "You want to give the word?" He stepped out from the others a little. "Anybody here want to put Josh in the lead?"

"I'll go home if you do," Tom Beard said.

"All right then," Rion said. "Now for God's sake shut up. Them soldiers may be along any minute."

Bill and Tom were ducking in among the branches of the fallen tree. Rion got down beside them. The others were scattering, the four White boys getting behind the cedar tree, Bob Caruthers and Bob Davis and the Cochranes going a little farther off. He crouched down, resting his weight on one knee. He had been mad there a minute ago when Josh Hadley challenged his right to lead but he wasn't mad now, not after the way Tom had stood up for him. A fine fellow, Tom, as staunch as they make 'em. . . . Would it have been better to let him lead tonight?

He turned his head to look at his friend and at that moment Tom turned to him. "Them Hadleys," he growled, "how'd they get in on this?"

"We ain't got time to worry about that now," Rion said. He moved away from the other two to the place where the first big branch of the fallen tree put up. Raising himself on his knees he pressed his body against the branch and leaning a little sidewise, looked out. The road was even narrower than he had remembered it. The woods on the other side were pretty open. Still a man would be hard put to turn a wagon around in them and with three wagons, all pressing on each other! No, the soldiers wouldn't have a chance, if the boys backed him up right. He crawled back to where the other two squatted, their heads just below the level of the tree trunk and he thought as he glanced again at Tom that it wouldn't do to put him in the lead. After all, didn't he, Rion, deserve to lead? It was he who had thought of this plan.

But he couldn't have made the plan, he wouldn't even have known what was going on if he hadn't happened into Franck's ordinary last night just before closing time. Two men from Charlotte were standing at the bar. He heard their talk and turned around and came back after he had started for the door.

"What's that you said?"

The big fellow—his name was Blevins and Rion had seen him often on muster days—said, "I reckon he aims to put the Regulators down." He looked at Rion as if he thought he might be a Regulator. Frank or Rednap would have split themselves trying to make the man believe they weren't, but he was past caring about that. "Who's aiming to put 'em down?" he asked, giving the man back a straight look.

The other fellow spoke up. "The governor. Sent three wagons full of guns into Charlotte yesterday. Don't know what they're for if it ain't for the Regulators. . . . Many of 'em around here?"

"Plenty," Rion said. "You want to join?" and he ran out of the door.

He ran most of the way home. Day was just breaking when he started up the road from the river. He had caught Bald and was just ready to ride out of the lot when he looked up and saw his father standing on the other side of the fence.

"Where you going?" he asked.

"To Rocky river."

Malcolm drew in his breath with a whistle. "You ain't going to ride my horse to Rocky river."

Rion had sat with one leg laid woman-wise across the pommel and looked down at his father. Did the old man know that he was a Regulator? He had been out at a lot of night meetings recently and had made no secret of his comings and goings.

He thrust his foot down into the stirrup. "The governor's sending the militia in. We're going to stop 'em."

Malcolm's long, bony face suddenly seemed to split open in the middle. Rion could see his tongue quivering in the blackish cavern of his mouth. The laughter mounted up from his belly, broke from the cavern, was on the air. His gums snapped shut and opened to release another burst of laughter. He staggered, bent double, then came upright to address an invisible auditor. "He's going to stop 'em!" In his staggering he had brought up at the fence. He leaned against it, still shaking. His arm went up and his face was hidden by his grey shirt sleeve. When he took his arm down he had stopped laughing. His face was in its usual long lines. He looked at Rion, his brown eyes kindly, even friendly.

This look was so compelling that Rion had the impression that he had said something and involuntarily ejaculated, "What?"

"Nothing," Malcolm said. "There ain't nothing I can say to you." He made a sudden motion with his hand. "Go along!"

Rion had shot him a suspicious glance and then had ridden out of the yard. He and Tom and Ben Cochrane—he had stopped long enough to get hold of them—had made straight for the Whites' place on Rocky river. The four Whites and Bob Caruthers and the Hadleys —they'd been in on the thing from the start, anyhow—were there, talking. Joe White had been in Charlotte that afternoon. The wagons were full of guns, all right, a lot of powder too and some flints. They were under a guard of six soldiers. The wagons that had brought the stuff were heading back for South Carolina. The Captain of the guard was trying to find three wagons in Charlotte to haul the loads to Hillsborough. He was having a hard time. Folks had got on to what was in the wagons and nobody had one to spare. One fellow, living there on the edge of town, had stove his wagon up against a tree that very afternoon, only it looked, Joe said, more like it had been done with an axe. They were laughing about that when Bill Alexander came in and said for them not to waste their breath. The Captain had got the wagons, all right. Bill's own cousin, the magistrate, Colonel Moses Alexander, had impressed them. The soldiers had started for Hillsborough.

"We'll stop 'em," Joe White said.

Rion had sat there, wondering how they could do it, and thinking that it was too bad it was such a moonlight night and then the Whites' colored boy came in with fresh logs.

He waited until the negro was out of the room and told them what they must do. Bill Alexander got right up and grabbed a handful of soot out of the chimney. Inside of five minutes they were all blacked up and ready to start. They were all mounted except the two White boys. But they had soon cured that. He grinned, thinking of Old Man White, walking home from the mill, a loaded horse on each side of him.

It was Bill Alexander who had had the idea of taking the horses away from him.

"Pa ain't going to like that," John White said.

"He ain't going to know who you are, blacked up as you be," Bill said. "But you don't have to have nothing to do with it. . . . Here, take my nag off in the bushes."

The White boys and the others dodged off into the woods. Bill and Rion walked down the road. Old Man White came on, whistling: "*Wae's Me For Charlie.*" They waited until they were right up on him, then each one reached up and grabbed a bridle rein. The horse shied, but the mare was worse. She jumped over into the ditch. But she dislodged both sacks in the jump so all Rion had to do was catch her and mount. Bill had to get the sacks off his horse and get rid of the old man who was hanging on to his elbow and yelling for his boys to come help him. One of the sacks knocked him down as it fell but he kept right on yelling, only by that time he was swearing.

When they got up where the others were John White said he felt pretty bad, standing there and hearing his pa call for help and not go to him.

"He might not a been glad to see you after you got there," Bill told him.

"Why?" John wanted to know.

"Old Man White ain't as good a church member as I thought he was," Bill said. "Used some words back there I never even heard before."

Rion laughed to himself now, thinking of Old Man White rolling in the dust and swearing and his boys there in the bushes listening to him.

Bill rose to his knees but as he realized what the sound was, sank back again. "It ought not to take 'em more'n two hours to come from Charlotte," he whispered.

"No," Rion said. "No, they ought to be along any minute now."

His legs were cramped with kneeling. He let himself down on his buttocks with his legs stretched out in front of him. Ahead of him was the bushy cedar tree with the three dark forms crouching behind it. A man shifted his gun and moonlight glinted along the barrel. If it only hadn't been such a moonlight night! He looked past the cedar tree to where a big tulip poplar came up on the very side of the hill. Grass was growing under it and on the new grass the shadow of the blunt poplar leaves lay, so bold they might have been something living. On a night like this things looked bigger than they did by day.

It had been like this last night down in the meadow, lighter if anything. They could have stayed at the house—Frank was over at Braun's but it was better out there in that grassy hollow at the edge of the woods.

They had named it for a meeting place when they parted Monday night. He stood there in the hollow by the same pine tree waiting and she came around the pine and dropped to her knees in the grass. Then, almost before he knew what was happening they were together, his body bearing hers down, his mouth pressed against her soft, cool mouth. "Oh," she said and once more, "Oh," and he raised his head and through his half-closed lids the moon was a long glitter of cold light.

They stayed there together in the grass, she lying close but a little higher up the slope so that she could reach down and curve both arms about his head. She held his head tight in her arms like that, one of her hands slipped down inside his shirt, the other moving sometimes to touch his cheek or his forehead. She shivered all over, then held him tighter, and he thought that he was sorry that he hadn't waited.

They had been parted a long time. There ought to have been something said, some explanations, but when he tried to say something she must have known what it was he was going to say, for she set her lips against his and slid farther down in his arms so that he could feel her bare flesh pressing against his in the place where his shirt was pushed aside and feeling it he took fire again and forgot anything there was to say. . . .

That had been night before last but it was still like it had just happened. All day he had had that feeling, like he was still with her. . . .

He started. Bill Alexander was beside him, whispering. "You hear anything?"

Rion listened. Far off down the road there was a faint rattling sound that might have been anything. . . . No, it was steady now and rising above it came men's voices. "It's the wagons, all right," he said.

He glanced behind him. The White boys were keeping their places behind the cedar tree but one of the other fellows was moving this way. He raised his hand, the palm flattened, and the fellow stepped back into the shadows.

Rion tiptoed out around the branches of the fallen tree. There was a good-sized oak growing near the road. He plastered himself against the trunk. A hundred feet away the hill began its slope. He would keep his post here and he would not give the word until he saw the horses' ears. He turned his head. The boys would all come through that open place there between the cedar and the fallen tree. Was it too small? Would they get in each other's way? No, it was the best place. If they scattered they'd lose time.

He leaned a little to look down the road. There was a rock as high as a man's head jutting out on the edge of the slope. When the horses' ears came past that rock he would yell. He imagined the road that he could not see with the wagons moving slowly along it. That thickety place just before you came to the branch. They ought to be about there. . . . And now they ought to be at the foot of the slope. It could not take them more than three minutes to come up. . . . He let his rifle stock slip through his hands until the butt rested on the ground. He had just realized how quiet it was, no rattling now for several minutes. The wagons had stopped!

He had been staring all this time at the patch of open sky that showed in the cut. It had been deep blue with a frosty sparkle of stars high up and now it showed reddish grey, like crushed raspberries when you pour cream into them.

He left his tree and walked over to the big rock. It was shaley, with fissures all the way up where he could set his foot. He climbed up, crawled a little way along the top, and looked down.

The hollow below him was filled with light. They had built their fire down near the branch. The wagons were halted a little way off, red-coats moving around them. One soldier was taking a team out to lead them to water. Two soldiers were squatting down beside the rear wheel of that wagon. Three or four more were over by the fire, cooking something. His eyes went back to the group beside the wagon. It was a broken axle they were trying to fix!

He crawled to the edge of the rock and dropped to the ground. A shadow sprang up beside him. Bill Alexander had been there, too, watching.

They ran together up the road and dived in behind the fallen tree. The Whites were there and after a second the others came crowding up. Rion tried not to listen to what was being said. If they had only stayed in their places a few minutes he could have thought of what to do. Now he did not know. It was one thing to jump out on men from the bushes and another to rush down hill in the glare of a fire.

". . . and now they're cooking supper," Bill said.

"We'll slip down the side here," John White said. "There's a path straight to the bottom."

"They'll see us," Rion said.

John shook his head. "You can't see it from the road. . . . You know any other way?"

"No," Rion said. "No. You go first, John."

John started off, then turned around. "You'll still give the word?"

"Yes," Rion said.

They went past the great, up-heaved roots of the fallen tree and came to the place between two pines where the path dropped down the hill. It was steep, and sleek with pine needles. You could hear the soft slap every time the man behind you set his open palm against a tree trunk and once there was more noise than that, when somebody stumbled over a root. But if they didn't hold themselves back some way they'd all pile up on each other.

The path was opening up. At the bottom firelight came in

between two broad layers of green like light through a window. A long streak of light running up the side of that big pine. John's head bobbed up into the pool of light, wavered, then was still just this side of the pine. It would be time to shout when they got to the pine. But he must have a look out first.

He slipped up beside John and peered out through the boughs. Two soldiers were working over the axle. The rest were over by the fire. A young, brown-haired officer, his hat cocked back on his head, his hands in his pockets, stood watching their cooking. A soldier came up, dragging a down branch. He waved him back. "No need to blazon the country-side, Grady."

"Aye sir," the man said cheerfully. He put the branch down and kneeling began to rake coals higher about a long-handled skillet. When the officer had walked off through the trees he turned a broad face that shone red in the firelight. "Cor, he'd have had us march to Hillsborough on empty stomachs!"

Rion could feel hard breathing behind him. He turned his head, caught the gleam of eyeballs, then a voice was bawling out and men were jumping past him out of the dark.

He ran as fast as he could across the road, Bill Alexander and John White ahead of him. Two soldiers lunged out from the shadow of the wagon. One had his musket level and was trying to take aim. Bill ran straight at him. Rion saw the gun barrel shoot upward in the man's hand then the two were rolling in the dust.

He veered and ran for the group by the fire. A little way off in the woods the captain stood, his hand that held the pistol coming up slowly, his face calm yet a little frowning as he took aim. "Duck!" Rion yelled and pushed Bob Caruthers so hard he fell to his knees, then ran on.

Over by the fire Joe White and a red-coat were fighting hand to hand. Rion picked his man as he came but before he could get to him the kneeling soldier caught him by the leg. His rifle jolted from his grasp. He went down, the soldier on top of him. They struggled, rolling over and over. The man was stout. On the third roll he got Rion on his back. Rion managed to work his hand down to his belt and slip his hunting knife out of its sheath. He brought it up and pressed the tip against the man's ribs and the fellow jumped off him in a hurry.

Rion got to his feet and picked up his gun. His man was gone through the woods. He caught another one who was coming up behind Jim Davis and he and Jim lashed the two together with a rope that Jim had brought and rolled them over on the ground.

They left them lying by the fire and ran for the wagons. There was some fighting still going on there but it was finished before they came up. Bill Alexander had the captain's pistol and now he was taking the musket away from the last soldier. He had a cut on his face where a knife had nicked him but he was laughing, pointing to the captain. "Says he could have got some of us but he was afraid of shooting his men."

Somebody had brought Rion's fellow back out of the woods. There were nine of them, including the captain, backed up against the wagon bed. The soldiers were quiet enough. The captain, a young fellow about Rion's age, looked as if he were going to cry. He swore at the soldier standing next to him. "I'God, Burke, I ought to have shot you in your tracks." "Yes, sir," the man said quietly and looked straight before him, his hands hanging at his sides.

Bill Alexander laughed. "Get me some more of that rope," he shouted.

Jim came with the rope. They tied the men's wrists together in pairs and Jim marched them at the point of his rifle out into the middle of the road.

Bill Alexander had climbed up on the end pole of one of the wagons and was looking down into the bed. "There's two fifty pound kegs of powder in here," he shouted. John Hadley came running up from the second wagon. "Muskets in this one. What we going to do with 'em?"

"Blow 'em up," Bill said. He let the end piece down and rolled the kegs to the ground. Powder, kegs, muskets, flints, blankets were all heaped on the ground. One of the boys stood there, holding a musket. "How about keeping some of these guns?" Rion knocked the musket out of his hand. "You fool! You want everybody to know we've been here?" He looked at Bill. "Better unhook these horses. 'Tain't no use in blowing *them* up."

Bill looked at the soldiers. "What we going to do with *them?*"

The captain stepped forward, dragging a soldier with him. "You'll hang for this."

Rion scowled at him. "Shut up, you 'tarnal red-coat!" He turned to Bill. "March 'em down the road a piece and turn 'em loose."

"They'll give the alarm."

"Leave their wrists roped. They can't travel very fast then."

"You want to start 'em off?"

Rion shook his head. "No, I want to see these things here burn."
He turned to Ben Cochrane. "Here, Ben, take these critters and turn
'em out to graze."

Jim White had ripped one of the kegs open and up-ending it now
made a train of powder from the pile of arms back across the road.
When it was about three feet long Rion made him stop. "That'll do.
Now stand back, all of you."

They ran off down the road. Rion picked up the captain's pistol
then fired into the train. There was a spark that grew into a blaze.
The blaze whipped like a snake across the road. Rion stood where
he was till it was within a foot of the pile. He ran over and watched
it from the bushes. The open keg of powder had caught. It sizzled
for a moment, then blew up. Scraps of burning blankets rose and
hung in the air. A musket flew off to the side of the road. Rion knew
that he ought to go farther into the woods but it was a fine sight to
leave. He stood there until he heard a sullen boom. The second keg
had burst. He turned to leave and just then there was another explo-
sion. A flying stave struck him, laying one side of his cheek open.
He clapped his hand to his face and ran at full speed. Bill Alexander,
coming back up the road, ran into him so hard that he knocked
him down. "You hurt bad?" Bill asked as Rion struggled to his feet,
blood streaming from his blackened face.

"Not much," Rion gasped, "but a little more and I'd a blown my
fool head off."

CHAPTER 18

MALCOLM OUTLAW came home from Salisbury towards noon with the news of the destruction of the wagons. 'Twas a gang of boys did it. Masqueraded as blacks but there was one of the guards they didn't fool. He says the black warn't nothing but coal soot. Says he recognized one of the boys and can make a good guess at some of the others. The magistrate's sworn he'll hang every one.

Rion looked up from his dinner. His father was staring at the cut on his cheek. Rion looked down. "Which magistrate?" he asked.

"Colonel Alexander. He's offering pardon to anybody that'll turn King's evidence. That'll run 'em out of the bushes."

"It won't if they had the right sort in the gang," Rion said.

He looked his father straight in the eye as he spoke. He had been too tired to come all the way home this morning and had stayed at Cochranes' until just before dawn. Coming into the milking lot he had met his father. Neither of them had spoken but Rion felt certain that the old man would connect his absence with the raid on the wagons. He was not going to confess that he had been in the gang but if the old man guessed, so much the better. "Might keep him from blabbing so much," he thought.

He took a nap under the trees after dinner, then went on down into the south field where he and Archy had been working hilling corn. He worked there all afternoon. Towards dusk he saw Ben Cochrane climb the fence and start down the row. Ben was out of breath when he came up to where Rion was making hills. "The Hadleys have done turned tail," he said.

Rion finished the hill he was making, then stepped over into the next row. "What you mean?" he asked.

"King's evidence," Ben said. "Josh and Jim Hadley. Set out this morning, unknownst to each other and got to Alexander's same time. Colonel Alexander said they'd both be pardoned, according to the proclamation, but they ought to be the first ones hanged." As Ben said "hanged" his lips drew far back, he seemed to hold the word between his teeth, tasting it and finding it bitter.

Rion looked at him curiously. "You didn't think they'd give you a bounty for what you done last night, did you?"

Ben's light blue eyes stared back at him. "I never thought any of the boys'd turn King's evidence."

"No more did I. We ought not to a let those Hadleys in. Never was a Hadley worth picking up in the road." Rion looked away from Ben to where at the end of the row Archy bent over, dropping grains of corn into the hills. "Try not to let the youngster catch on," he said in a lower voice.

"All right," Ben said, "Rion, what you going to do?"

Rion made a hill with swift strokes. "Do?" he said. "Nothing. They ain't nothing to do now."

Ben caught his breath. "I don't know," he said. "I thought I'd go over and talk to Tom Beard. See what he thought. I might get out of the country," he added and as he spoke he turned suddenly and made off between the rows.

Rion made a few more strokes after he had gone, then he flung his hoe down. "Hanged," he said in a wondering tone and then *"God's breeches!"*

The next second he was striding off across the field. Archy saw him going and called after him. "Hey! If you're going to the house bring me a drink of water."

Rion stopped. "Come here, boy," he called.

Archy put his hoe down and came up to where he stood. Rion reached over and touched him lightly on the shoulder. "Son, I'm going away for a few days."

A glint came into Archy's eyes. He nodded, compressing his lips. "I don't know nothing about it," he said.

"That's right," Rion told him. "You didn't see me leave and I never told you where I was going."

Archy nodded again, his eyes fixed on his brother's face. He took a step forward. "Let me go too," he said in a low voice.

Rion shook his head. "Naw, I couldn't take you where I'm going." He looked at Archy and his voice grew sharp. "I'll whale the living daylights out of you if you come after me," he said.

Archy did not answer. He went back down the row, picked up his basket of corn and started dropping seed again and after a second Rion turned and left him.

On his way across the field he passed the hoe that he had flung down. He picked it up and carried it with him until he came to the fence where he leaned it up against a post. He remembered that he still lacked two rows of planting the whole field. He might never finish them now. He stepped over the fence, then looked back over his shoulder. Archy was working at the other end of the field, near a big oak. He could see Archy and could mark behind him the spreading branches of the oak but it was as if he did not see them; as if they and the field too had ceased to exist. He shook his head, frowning. "Best go to Dawsons' first," he muttered and went down the path to the river.

It was dark when he turned in at the Dawson clearing. No lights showed in the cabin but he could make out something white on the doorstep and he knew that Cassy was sitting there. He went up the path and dropped down beside her. She moved over a little to make room for him and gave a soft sigh but did not speak.

"Where's Frank?" he asked after a little.

"In town. He ought to be back by this time."

He reached over and laid his hand on her hand where it lay in her lap. "Cassy, I've got to go away from here."

She turned towards him. In the fading light her eyes searched his face. "Why'n't you tell me you were going out last night?"

"We took an oath," he said.

She did not answer.

"How'd you know? Frank tell you?"

Again she did not answer. He did not repeat the question. It did not make any difference how she had found out. But he wished that he had told her. Well, it was too late for that now. He sat silent, staring at the brown pine needles that covered the door yard. There was a white streak through them where the path went. His eyes followed the white line till it was lost in the shadows and came back to follow it again. He had walked himself out of breath, coming here so fast, but now that he was here there seemed to be no need for hurry. It was as if everything was all right, as if he and Cassy might go on sitting here on the doorstep all evening as they had done so many times. He roused himself.

"I've got to leave here tonight."

Suddenly she was in his arms, her hands locked tight behind his neck, her body shaking as hard as if she had an ague. "You *can't* leave me," she whispered.

He held her to him with one hand while he ran the other caressingly over her hair. "I can't stay, honey."

Her body went slack in his clasp, her arms came from around his neck. She sat down on the door step. She put both hands up to her face and held them there a minute. When she spoke it was in a quiet voice. "Are you going now?"

"I thought I'd better," he said.

She did not speak but it was as if she had spoken, in that dry, strange tone he had heard once before, that time they had quarrelled here by the wood-pile.

He looked down at her face that he could see only dimly in the half dark. A moment ago she had been there beside him, his lover, and now in a flash she was changed. He did not know why and there was not time to find out. He ought to be on the road now and yet he could not leave without having her in his arms again. He put his hand out halfway between them. "*Cassy*," he said.

She got up from the doorstep, moving a little back as if from the touch of his hand. "There's Frank," she said and turned and went into the house. He followed her. They stood together in the dark, hearing the footsteps on the path. Rion laid his hand on her arm. "Cassy," he said again. She moved slightly so that his hand fell away from her arm. "We better have a light," she said. "Would you make a spark?"

He went outside. As he was getting his rifle from where he had leaned it against a tree Frank stepped past him. It was too dark for them to see each other but Frank knew there was somebody on the path. "Cassy," he called sharply, "where are you?"

"It's me out here," Rion said before she could answer. He went in with the gun. She came to him and held a candle over the priming pan. The wick caught from the first spark. As the flame came up Rion looked at her and wondered if she were ill, her face was so drawn. Or was it excitement? Her eyes shone like a jacked deer's.

She seemed to read his thoughts. Her lids fell. She set the candle on the table and moved back towards the hearth. Frank stood in the middle of the floor, breathing hard, staring.

Rion laughed. "Who'd you think I was?"

Frank let his breath out. "Lord knows!" he said and walked over and threw himself down in his big split-bottomed chair.

Rion stood in front of him. "Frank, seems it's out about last night. I've got to get away from here."

Frank looked up abstractedly. "Aye . . . where are you going?"

"How do I know? I'm going to lay out in the woods till things quiet down." He paused and looked at the girl who stood by the mantel shelf, looking not at him but down at her brother. "When I come back Cassy and me aim to get married," he said and as he uttered the words he realized that this was the first time marriage had ever been mentioned between them.

She raised her head. The wildness was gone from her eyes. Her expression was absent and yet questioning, as if he had asked her to walk to a neighbor's with him and she was trying to decide whether or not she would go.

It angered him to have her look at him like that. He took a step towards her, then stopped as Frank's harsh laugh sounded through the room.

"What you laughing at?" Rion demanded.

Frank ran his tongue over his lips to moisten them. "You won't be coming back to this country," he said, "and if you do Cassy won't be here."

Rion stared. "You war'n't there last night," he said, "I can't see how they can mix you up in it."

Frank made an impatient gesture. "Who sent the word around? Who gave Mose Jackson's little Tom a shilling to pry off those covers? And do you think Mose Jackson won't be off to the magistrate now the hue and cry is raised? Nay, man, they'll hang me higher'n they'll hang you."

"I reckon they will," Rion said.

"Aye," Frank said, "I must leave the country." He leaned forward, his head in his hands, then suddenly raised up his head. "I've a message for you. From Jacob Wagner. He wants to go west."

"He can go hellwards for all I care," Rion said.

Frank got up and began walking about the room. "He wants to go west," he repeated. "He's got two horses already loaded for the trip. He and his wife'll be waiting in that grove near the creek, till sun-up he says."

Rion had been staring into the dead ashes of the hearth. "*Jacob?*" he said suddenly. "You mean old Jacob Wagner?"

Frank inclined his head.

"I don't believe he was in it," Rion said, "I never saw him at any of the meetings."

"He was too 'cute to come. But Alexander's got a letter he wrote. Jacob just found that out tonight. He's mad to leave. . . ."

Rion stood with his head bent down, his thumbs hooked in his belt. Finally he raised his head. "The old coot's got plenty of provisions and a belt full of money, I've no doubt. You say he'll be waiting in that pine grove?"

"Aye."

Rion nodded. "We'd best team up with him. Did he say how to get him word?"

"His 'prentice'll be by here any minute. If he takes back word that you'll bring the hides in the morning, Jacob'll· know you're coming."

Rion grinned. "Tell him I'll bring 'em first thing in the morning. And now I'll step over home and get my shot pouch. Meantime," he looked at Cassy, "meantime you can be packing your traps."

CHAPTER 19

WHEN RION came up the road from the river he heard voices and knew that the family must be sitting in the dooryard. He cut around the side of the hill and came up to the house from the back. There was nobody in sight. He opened the back door and tiptoed into the kitchen. It was as black as pitch. He stood his gun up in the corner, felt his way to the mantel, found a candle, and lit it; he took his shot pouch and filled it from the bag that hung from the rafters. His powder horn lay on the mantel, empty. Next to it was an iron gaff that he had beat out on his anvil only a few days ago. He slipped that into his pocket, then filled the horn with powder from the great gourd and was about to leave the room when he heard a rustling and turned around. His mother was in the doorway.

She went to the fireplace, stirred the ashes till they showed red, and lit a candle with a spill. "Why'n't you come to supper?" she asked.

"I was over at Dawsons'."

She came towards him. "We had dewberry cobbler. I saved you some. Want it now?"

"I ain't a caring," he said.

She brought the cobbler from the cupboard, on a plate, with a bowl of milk. He ate and drank, standing. She sat down on a chair that was pushed up to the table and leaning one elbow on the table supported her forehead with her hand. He noticed how swollen the joints of her knuckles were. "Your rheumatism been troubling you?" he asked.

"No," she said with a sigh, "no, I don't have it much in warm weather."

She kept her large blue eyes fixed on his face, so intently that it was hard for him not to look back at her, and he thought how you could look straight into a person's eyes and yet never know what they were thinking—had she known all along that he was a Regulator?— and then he thought how it would be in the morning when she realized he was gone, and he wished things were so he could say goodbye. But it would never do to let on. He would never get away.

"Want another piece?" she asked.

He shook his head. "I'm going down in the bottom after deer. Ben Cochrane he's a-waiting for me now."

"You was out all last night."

He laughed but did not say anything.

She shook her head and slowly rose from the table. He reached over and patted her shoulder. "Don't you worry about me," he said and before she could reply was out the back way.

Outside he paused, then stepped over to the tool shed and selected an axe and hung it in his belt. He started down the path which led through the stable lot and around the side of the hill. As he came down the slope he saw the lighted house above him and heard the murmur of voices. He stopped and called out: "Archy, come here a minute!"

There was silence for a moment. Betsy's voice answered. "He ain't here . . . what you want?"

He considered, then: "I don't want nothing. But Frank Dawson, he says for Archy to come over to his house early in the morning. Says there's something he wants him to do for him. . . ."

"I'll tell him," Betsy called back. Rion stood there in the wet grass until her voice had died away on the quiet air, then he went on around the side of the hill. He walked some distance before he came on the horses, standing together under a tree. He went up to them quietly, put his hand on Bald's neck, and spoke to him by name; then turned and catching the young mare by the foretop put the bridle on her. Bald gave a little whinny as he mounted. Rion slapped him on the neck. "I'd rather had you, old fellow, if you war'n't grey," he said under his breath, then rode off, walking the mare at first, breaking into a trot when he hit the road to the river.

When he came up on the other bank he heard a stir in the woods and stopped to listen. But the sound did not come again and he rode on.

The Dawson cabin looked very different from the way it looked when he left an hour ago. The big table had been pushed back against the wall and was heaped high with household goods: blankets, quilts, down pillow, skillets, plates, knives and cups. As Rion came in Cassy pulled a greatcoat down from its peg on the wall and ran with it over to Frank who was kneeling in the middle of the floor, tying up a bundle.

"Your old matchcoat, Frank. You'll need it, come winter."

Frank shook his head. "I'll wear deerskin." He walked over to the table and picked up a skillet and the small iron pot. "We'll take one skillet and one pot," he said.

She stared at him. "No cups, no plates?"

"I'll make you some green bark troughs," Rion said, "soon as we get out in the woods."

She shook her head and ran out of the room. They heard her outside, rattling the bolt of one of the out-houses, then she was back, carrying a heavy sack of turnip seed. She looked at them defiantly. "I'll take these if I have to drag the sack."

Rion laughed and took the sack from her. "You got any seed corn, Frank?" he asked.

"I'll get some now," Frank said and went out the back door.

Rion looked after him uneasily. "We'd best start," he said. "Somebody might be coming by here any minute."

Frank came in with a dozen ears of corn under his arm. "D'you tell your folks you were leaving?"

Rion shook his head. "And have Ma and the girls start caterwauling and maybe give me away to the sheriff? . . . I left word for Archy to come over here, though. He'll take care of everything."

Frank was fastening the ears of corn on a string. "How'll he know we're gone for good? He might just think we'd gone to town."

"He'll know something's wrong soon as he walks in this room, I reckon. And he'll have sense enough to look after your stock. . . ."

Cassy suddenly clasped her hands in front of her. "I've got a hen coming off tomorrow!"

"Archy'll look after her," Rion said impatiently. He hoisted one of the bundles that Frank had made up, over his shoulder. Frank took the other. They went out, shutting the door behind them. Frank's old horse was standing near the pasture bars. They brought him up, bridled him and fastened the two sacks across his back. Frank was offering his hand to Cassy to mount when she broke away and ran back into the house. They had left the candles lighted. Through the window they could see her standing beside the table. She picked up a plate, then quickly put it down. Her hands went up to her face and fell away. She leaned over and blew out the candle.

They heard the door shut again. She was beside them. She would not mount the horse. "I'll walk a while," she said and Frank did not argue with her. They started off, leading the horses. When they passed the back porch Frank's old stag hound, Killbuck, got up and came after them. Frank stopped and told him to go back. When the dog did not obey Frank picked up a rock and was about to throw it at him when Cassy pulled his arm back. "Don't do it," she said, "I wouldn't want to rock him, last thing we do."

Frank's arm dropped to his side. Rion advanced towards the dog. "Get back, sir," he said threateningly. The dog growled and for a moment seemed about to spring; then, as Rion continued to advance on him he slunk back and they heard his feet rattle on a loose board of the porch and then a light groan as he settled himself for the night. They came to the back gate, passed through and entered the woods. Cassy, walking between the two men, looked back once over her shoulder at the dark house. "Poor Killbuck," she said, "when he wakes up in the morning there won't be nobody there."

CHAPTER 20

WHEN THEY got to town Rion, fearing to be seen on the streets with the loaded horse, made Frank and Cassy turn down a side way, while he himself rode on the other horse past Jacob Wagner's shop. It was dark and so was the room behind the shop. Rion at once turned down the steep road, and crossing the creek got down off his horse, and slipping the bridle through his arm started along the path. In the darkness ahead he could see a shadowy mound looming up, the pine thicket that Orren Sloane had been letting grow up on his land for five years. It was there that Jacob had promised to wait. He came to the edge of the thicket and slipped in among the pines. At first he heard nothing except his horse's hooves sliding on pine needles and then a rustling off to his right; and somebody strangled a cough. The old fool was there, all right!

He went forward quietly until he was almost upon them and called out in a low voice: "D'your 'prentice give you a message for me?"

He could hear Jacob suck in his breath and could hear him say to his wife: "That's him. That's Rion, all right."

He caught the old man by the arm. "Shut up. You want everybody in the country to know we're down here?"

Jacob was silent but Mrs. Wagner was clawing at Rion's shoulder. "I knew you'd come, boy!"

"There's somebody on the path," Jacob whispered.

"It's Frank Dawson and his sister," Rion told them.

He started down the path. Then he heard a noise and stopped. He was quite certain that it was footsteps, not ten feet away.

Old Jacob had come up behind him. "That's Frank, all right, ain't it?"

Rion turned around. He could make out in front of him the outline of the loaded horse. "It's Frank coming along the path," he said, "but that war'n't Frank I heard a minute ago."

"We ought not a left the shop dark," Jacob said, "I told Elsa. And you, you ought to a got here sooner."

"I come on the trot," Rion said. "You go on down there and meet Frank. I'm going to see to these horses. We don't want nobody to get 'em away from us."

He went back to where Mrs. Wagner stood quietly beside the two horses. The horses moved lowered heads, finishing the baits of corn that Jacob had strewn on the ground. Rion walked up and felt over the load that was strapped on each horse's back. One was loaded helter skelter, with a lot of household provisions, blankets, pots and pans, a tightly wrapped bundle that might be a woman's gown. The other horse's load was a neat contrivance of three deer-hide sacks, one hanging down on each side of the horse and one strapped saddle-wise across his back. The sacks were laced with elkskin thongs. Rion slipped his fingers inside the only aperture he could find and touched something that was cold and smooth and pointed. He ran his fingers farther into the sack. The pointed objects lay one on top of each other in rows—hatchets if he was a Christian. He smiled to himself in the dark. Old Jacob was running for his life but he would manage to do a little trading on the way. Rion ran his hand over the other load again and deliberated whether he should not unlash and re-pack it, but it was a mean job to do in the dark. He decided that he would let it go until morning. If any of Mrs. Wagner's stuff fell off she would have her husband to blame. Besides they couldn't strike rough country before daylight.

He untethered his own horse and went to meet the others. Frank, too, had heard somebody moving in the thicket. He mentioned it as soon as he came up. "Well, there ain't anything to do about it," Rion said, "except get away from here as fast as we can. . . . I been thinking. There's a road off here to the north, over the ridge. What say we strike across to that?"

Jacob said that the woods on this side of the creek were "briary to travel in the dark."

"Dark's best time for folks like us," Rion told him. He led his horse up to Mrs. Wagner and bending, offered her his cupped hand. She mounted spryly. Cassy, whom he had hardly seen and had not spoken to since she came, was standing a little way off beside her brother. He picked her up with both hands around her waist and set her beside Mrs. Wagner. She did not speak, even when he seized her so suddenly by the waist, but as he was turning away she laid her hand on his shoulder and leaned down until her face was just over his. He did not kiss her but he caught her ankle and pressed it for a second between his two hands. "You'll have to bend a lot, going through these bushes," he said and gave Gal a slap.

Gal started off. Jacob followed, leading one of his horses. Rion took the bridle of the other horse and Frank brought up the rear with Smiler.

There was a quarter of a mile of thicket to get through before they struck Sloane's woods. The going was not so rough until they came to some broken ground at the north end of the tract. It was up one ravine and down another for the best part of an hour. Jacob got winded and had to rest more than once. After a while Mrs. Wagner made him get up on the horse and she walked. The old fellow didn't want to do it but Frank told him that the women were fresh and wouldn't mind walking for a while.

They got out of the woods and into some flat, briary ground. The horses went better but the women—Cassy was taking turns with Mrs. Wagner, walking—were always catching their feet in the looped vines or stopping to pull briars from their skirts. Rion thought that it would be easier to shoulder one of the horse packs himself and let them both ride but they would have none of it. Mrs. Wagner showed temper. "It's not what you want that makes you fat, young man, it's what you get."

He laughed and said nothing more. They would get along better once it was light. It was this working along in the dark that was hard. The horses didn't like it. You had to lead them every foot of the way. If you tried driving they'd hang their packs up on a limb and then just stand there, waiting till you came up with them and you couldn't afford to let them get two feet away from you, dark as it was. Once Dan got a little ahead and then just melted out of sight. The others stopped and waited while Rion hunted for him. He finally found him hung up against a bushy pine. The fool would have stood there all night without making a sign.

They came out on the big road while it was still dark. Jacob wanted to stop and rest but Rion thought they ought to keep on moving as long as they could. He did not say anything to the others but he was convinced that somebody was following them. While he was hunting for that horse he had heard something moving near him, and when he went towards the sound a dim shape, too tall for game, had broken from cover not ten feet away from him. He started to follow then decided to leave well enough alone. Whoever or whatever it was seemed as anxious to keep away from them as they were to keep away from it. Of course it might be officers planning to surprise them. Still, he couldn't do anything about that except keep going.

When Jacob made such a fuss about stopping to rest, Mrs. Wagner brought some fried pies out and they ate them as they walked. The fried pies were good, each one half the size of an ordinary pie and oozing with sugared apples. After Rion had eaten his he felt as if he could go on for hours and the others, too, showed better spirit, all except Jacob who said that the pie lay heavy on his stomach.

It was getting towards morning, not light yet but the sky a milky grey with a little red showing in the east. Day broke as they went along the sandy ridge road with woods on each side. Jacob suddenly put his hand against his side and sat down on a bank. He moaned "Elsa, you go with the others. I die here, alone."

Rion went over and looked at him. In the grey, uncertain light his mouth was open and he was gasping for breath. A spasm contorted his face. He turned his head to the side and belched, then moaned again.

Mrs. Wagner was kneeling over him, running one hand inside his shirt to feel his heart while with the other she took his pulse. "It's the blood pudding," she said. "He would eat it and it always takes him like this."

"What'd you let him eat it for when he was going on this trip?" Rion asked impatiently.

She turned her face up. Her round eyes fixed his. Suddenly tears spilled down her cheeks. "Dorseys killed last night and Ben brought us the liver and the feet. I was sitting there after supper, thinking about the calf's feet, how we'd make jelly tomorrow, and he come in and he said, 'Elsa, we've got to take to the woods if we don't want to hang for it.'"

"He ought to told you before," Rion said. "He might have known it was coming."

She got to her feet, raised her apron and wiped her eyes. "Get him off in the bushes. I got something that'll cure him."

Jacob, by this time, had turned over on his face, and, still moaning, clawed the ground.

Rion looked around him. The woods came up thick on both sides of the road. One place, he supposed, was as good as another.

Calling to Cassy to hold the horses, he took Jacob's head and Frank took his feet and they started off into the woods with him. Mrs. Wagner wanted to stop at the first brake but Rion said no, they must get out of sight of the road. They stopped finally in a brushy ravine where they laid Jacob on the ground. He sat up, then bent double again. Mrs. Wagner was fumbling in a sack that hung from her waistband. She brought up a package wrapped in old linen, unfolded it and took out some dried leaves. Holding them in her hand she approached Rion. "Can you get me some water?"

He shook his head. "We couldn't light a fire if it's tea you're wanting to make."

She stared at him, then two lines dented her soft, pendulous cheeks. She compressed her lips and going over to Jacob made him open his mouth, then clapped her palm against it and held it there until he had swallowed the leaves.

Jacob lay down again with a groan. His wife sat down beside him, occasionally leaning over to lay her hand on his forehead which was beaded with sweat.

Frank came up to where Rion was standing. He glanced at the sick man. "Maybe we'll have to leave him," he said in a low voice. "Man sick as that can't take to the woods."

Rion shook his head. "I'm going to take him if I have to strap the old coot on the horse's back."

"He'll buck himself off."

Rion laughed. "He'll be better in a little while. Meantime I'm going to see if I can find some water."

He disappeared down the ravine. He had not gone far when he heard something tearing through the bushes. He turned around. Jacob was coming towards him. His face was wild and he beat his chest as he came. Suddenly he stopped and clutching at a sapling for support bent over and vomited with great retchings and groanings. Rion passed him and went back to the others. Frank was standing there watching Jacob. "I hate to see a man doing that," he said, "victuals scarce as they are."

Rion laughed and looked over at Mrs. Wagner. She was sitting on the ground, leaning back against a log. From where she sat Jacob was not visible but she kept her eyes on the bushes which nodding every now and then betrayed that he was having another seizure. As Rion came up she clasped her hands in her lap, sighed, then closed her eyes and seemed almost immediately to be asleep.

Rion looked at Frank. "Reckon we better rest here a while longer?"

"I think we better," Frank said.

Rion looked at Cassy. She had sat down on a rock still holding the reins in her hands. Her eyes were going from Rion's face to Frank's as if she could hardly wait to know what they would say. When Frank spoke she slid from the rock and still holding the reins lay on the ground, face downward, her head pillowed on her arm. Jacob was coming back through the bushes. He grinned sheepishly at Rion and went over and sat down beside his wife. She reached over and took his hand. They lay back against the log and quietly went to sleep.

Rion gently slipped the reins from Cassy's outstretched hand, and led the horses over and sat down on the end of the log. The horses, weary with their night's travel, stood quietly. Rion relaxed, letting all his muscles go slack, even shutting his eyes for a few minutes. Then a bird call in the woods made him open his eyes and look about him. It was good day now. Sunshiny light fell through the leaves and struck on the sleepers' faces. Rion looked at them curiously. Frank was sound asleep, leaning bolt upright against a tree. Cassy looked as if she might be dead, slumped forward like that. She had not moved once since she slid from the rock. Perhaps he had driven them too hard, getting them this far in such a short time: a weakling like Frank, an old man and an old woman and a girl. They couldn't stand what he could stand.

The noise came again. Somebody was coming, not stepping from tree to tree, but moving steadily towards them. He picked up his rifle and got to his feet, then kicked Frank's leg. "Get up. There's somebody coming."

Frank was up in a second. They stepped out from among the others and went towards the head of the ravine. Between two beeches a man's body was visible for a second, then the left hand trunk hid it from sight.

"Damn scoundrel's taken cover," Rion said.

He cocked his gun and stepped behind a tree. "You come out from there or I'll blow the top of your head off."

A head showed from behind the beech trunk, then a man was walking towards them. Not a man, but a boy dressed in deerskins. A coon-skin cap pushed back from a high forehead, brown eyes in a narrow face.

Rion let the butt of his rifle drop to the ground. "Save us and sain us if it ain't Archy Outlaw!"

CHAPTER 21

ARCHY WAS running towards them, so fast that he tripped and his gun fell out of his hand. He was up again and jumping on Rion like a dog that welcomes his master home. "D'you know it was me? D'you know it was me following you?"

"I never dreamt it was you," Rion said. "I thought you had more sense."

Frank spoke up. "Rion, this boy's been laying out in the woods all night. You ought to be glad he thinks enough of you to follow you."

"Well, I ain't," Rion said, "and as for being out in the woods, he's got a good bed at home. Let him lay in it."

Mrs. Wagner was coming towards them. "Lord, Archy, what'll your mother say?"

"I don't care what she says," Archy told her and went over and sat down on a log.

Rion stood over him. "A pretty how-to-do! Here we trying to get away quiet, to save our necks, and this boy's trailed us through the woods. I reckon they's a whole pack following him."

Archy looked up. "They ain't anybody following you. Don't anybody know you're gone but the home folks."

"They know it?"

"You remember when you hollered to Betsy to tell me to go over to Dawsons' in the morning?"

Rion nodded.

"I was laying under the snow-ball bush in the front. I could hear you rounding up Bald and Gal. I reckon Pa did too, for he said, 'That boy's stolen my horses.' Ma wanted to know what you'd be stealing a horse for and he said to make for the woods. She got to crying and carrying on and he said you was born to be hanged anyhow and it was better for you to make off to the woods where they was all ruffians and you wouldn't show up so bad. Then Ben Cochrane come by with a big tale."

"What was it?"

"Well, he said they'd done caught Tom Beard and the talk was all they going to hang him, so Pa said then what did he tell her and she cried some more. They was still carrying on when I left."

"How'd you know where to come?"

Archy laughed and glanced at Cassy. "I knew if you was making for the woods you'd stop by Dawson's first."

Frank laughed too. Mrs. Wagner turned to Rion. "How about making me up a trash fire so I can fry some meat?"

He shook his head. "Ain't you heard how they're rounding 'em up? You want everybody in the country to see our smoke?"

Cassy spoke up. "I've got a parcel of meat and bread but it ain't quite enough for everybody."

"I got something better than that," Mrs. Wagner said. "Rion, there's a five gallon bucket hanging on to one of the horses. You bring it here."

Rion brought it to her. She lifted the lid and took out half a dozen sizable chunks of some dried brown stuff. "Glue broth," she said and looked at Jacob. "You remember that haunch of venison Ed brought in the day after the calf broke her leg and had to be killed? And you had to go to Salem on top of all that? I just boiled that meat down whilst you was gone. Says I, if I can't eat you now I'll eat you later."

Jacob laughed. "You'd think the old lady was a trapper, way she provisions."

Rion rolled the savory brown substance under his tongue until it melted. He put out his hand for the sandwich Cassy was offering him. "That ain't such a bad breakfast," he said. "Jacob, don't you eat none of that pork now. You stick to glue broth."

"I don't care if I never see victuals again," Jacob told him.

Cassy was asking Archy how he had managed to trail them in the dark. He laughed. "You know when you left the house? I was hiding behind the root cellar. I tripped over a board when I got up but you all thought I was Killbuck and didn't pay no attention to me. I was scared to follow you through town, so I just made for the thicket where I heard you say you was going."

"I heard you," Rion said, "and I saw you once, breaking out of an elderberry brake."

He got up and going over to the horse that bore Jacob's household goods, removed the load and threw it on the ground. Mrs. Wagner came and stood beside him, telling him where to stow each piece. He did not answer her but calmly repacked the load and lashed it to the horse. "We been here over an hour now," he said. "We better be moving. Jacob, you ride Smiler and one of the women can take turns behind you. Mrs. Wagner, you give us such a good breakfast you better go first."

Frank took up his rifle and slung his horse's bridle through his arm. Archy, too, picked up his gun and went to the head of the other pack horse. Rion stopped him. "You're going the other way, Son."

Archy said nothing, only hung his head and looked at the ground.

Cassy cried out. "Rion! After he's come all this way?"

Rion did not even look at her. He tapped Archy on the shoulder. "Get started, Son."

Archy raised his head. His brown eyes that Rion had always thought resembled a heifer's fixed his brother's face for a moment; then, as if he read there everything that Rion could have said, he stepped away from the horse. "Goodbye, y'all," he said and raising his hand in a half salute turned away down the road.

Cassy gazed after him. "I don't see how you can treat him like that. And him your baby brother."

"It's time we was getting back on the road," Rion said.

CHAPTER 22

JACOB, pale and silent, was helped on to Smiler, with his wife behind him, and Rion and Cassy and Frank each drove one of the pack horses. The horses were still feeling the bait of corn and were ready to travel. It was hard to hold them down so that the women could keep up with them.

"You wait a while," Rion told them. "You won't be so brash when we strike the thickets."

Frank wondered if they would have much trouble finding forage for the horses.

"Depends on the kind of country we strike," Rion said; "you'll get plenty of cane along the rivers and then again you'll strike country where there ain't any grazing whatsoever. I saw Boone's horse eat a stick big as his hoof once. That was over in that thickety place at the foot of the mountains. We'd a left him there if we hadn't got out pretty quick."

Frank asked how much longer they would travel the road they were on.

"It bends north in about three miles," Rion said. "Then there's a road branches off it but that peters out after you pass the last cabin."

"Daniel and I stopped with those folks on that long hunt we took. There's a tree we took our bearings from, a white oak and it's got D. Boone on it."

They were passing a house. Rion knew the name of the man who lived there, Thomas Allsop. He had driven one of his father's cows over to that man's bull once. A Red Devon. Malcolm Outlaw would have no other. It had seemed a long trip then. Well, he was going on a longer trip than that now.

A tall, thin man was coming around the side of the house. Thomas Allsop himself. Before the others knew what he was doing Rion had driven his horse off to the side of the road. "Good day," he said.

The man's black eyes fixed Rion's face. "I never set eyes on ye before," he said, and then doubtfully "Will ye light?"

Rion shook his head. "I'm Malcolm Outlaw's boy, from Trading Ford."

"Aye," the man said slowly, "it's been five years since you brought the Devon cow over. Ye've had time to grow, but man, ye've made the most of it! And where are ye off to, Rion Outlaw, with four pack horses?"

"Up the road a piece," Rion told him. "My neighbors here are for taking up some of the wild land beyond Peters's. My dad has given 'em the loan of two horses for the trip."

The man came nearer. "I hear the Regulators flogged the clerk at Hillsborough courthouse."

"Aye," Rion said, "but the talk is they've disbanded now. They've a Quaker for leader, you know."

The man laughed harshly. "There's few honest folks about here, only rogues. Will ye light and rest a spell, you and your friends?"

Rion clucked to his horse. "Neighbor Dawson here wants to use the daylight for travelling. But I'll stop with you on my way back."

"So do," the man called and turned back into the yard.

The others were silent until they had got out of earshot. Then Jacob said, "What made you tell him who you were?"

"I was feared he knew me anyhow. But it's no matter. He's an honest man. I can tell by the look of him."

"I've had enough of the honest folk," Jacob muttered.

Rion laughed. "Well, you're getting away from 'em fast as Smiler'll carry you, Old Man." He cut Jacob's horse across the legs with a switch so that he broke into a run.

Mrs. Wagner cried out but the horse was off down the road. When they came up some minutes later, Jacob had halted the horse in the shade of a big mulberry tree beside a spring. They stopped and ate a cold snack, and after that the women took their shoes off and bathed their feet in the little run. Jocasta's shoes had been old when she started and now a hole had come in one sole. Rion cut a piece of leather from his belt and made a patch for it but he knew that it would not hold long. "I'll make you a pair of moccasins soon as I kill a deer," he told her.

At four o'clock they moved on and soon came to the place where the main road bent south. They took the woods road and in a quarter of a mile came to Peters's cabin where Rion and Daniel had once spent the night. There was no smoke in the chimney and the door was shut and latched but Rion thought that the man must still live there, for fowls were scratching on the dung-hill.

The women were almost ready to give out and Jacob, though he had been riding all day, was complaining of weariness. He and Frank both wanted to stop at Peters's for the night but Rion made them start on again as soon as they had drunk from the spring.

The road they had been following stopped at the cabin door. To the north there was not even a path. Rion took his bearings from his pocket compass and struck into the woods, due north just as he and Boone had done three years before.

It was not hard going, for the woods were open, second growth mostly—he remembered that Jeff Peters had told him that it was his grandfather that had cleared the land. Now and then he found a tree that had been blazed. Once he found a beech with one of his own cat faces on it. It was Jocasta who found the place he was looking for. She stumbled on a big, flat rock and fell to her knees. He went to help her but she was up already, scratching leaves away from the rock. "It's a hearthstone," she said, "hearthstone of a house."

The rock was revealed, flat enough and big enough for a hearthstone. Rion looked beyond it and saw the top branches of a white oak tree protruding over the top of a rise. He went to the edge of the rise and looked down: there was a square barked out place on the trunk and letters carved into it.

"It's the place," he said. "We'll rest here the night."

The others came up. The horses were so tired that they stood with lowered heads, not even trying to snatch at the bushes.

"We'll lead 'em down the side of this hill," Rion said. "There's cane growing on this branch."

It was almost dark when they struck the stream. Rion took the packs off the horses, pulled the wisps of grass out of their bells and turned them loose in the cane, telling Jacob to stay there a while and keep an eye on them.

When he came back Frank already had a fire going. Mrs. Wagner had got out her griddle and was frying chunks of salt meat. Cassy was shaping meal dough into cakes.

He went and stood beside her. Her hands were trembling so that she could hardly shape the cakes. "You very tired?" he asked in a low voice. She looked up and it seemed to him that her eyes that were always so clear were bleared like an old person's. "I ain't so tired," she said, "I just got to trembling."

"Let me fix 'em," he said. He greased a flat rock and put the cakes on it and thrust the rock in among the embers.

Mrs. Wagner took the pot Cassy had been using, filled it with water and threw in several handfuls of beans. "You don't expect us to wait till them beans are done before we eat?" he asked her.

She shook her head. "I'm boiling 'em against the morning. I know you ain't going to let me stop long enough to boil beans once we get on the road."

He laughed. "There ain't any road."

Jacob had smelled the meat frying and came up from the branch. "Them horses ain't going to leave that cane," he said, "and I'm hungry. Ain't had nothing inside me now since last night."

Mrs. Wagner took her griddle from the fire. The meat was brown, swimming in rich gravy. Rion dexterously pulled the rock that held the cakes out from the embers. Mrs. Wagner drew a fork from where she. had stuck it in her waist-band, and each person forked up his piece of meat and ate it, then sopped his cake in the rich gravy. There were four cakes apiece and a good-sized chunk of meat for each one. Cassy cut her meat in half and offered it to Rion on her last cake.

He shook his head. "No, I don't want it."

"Take it," Mrs. Wagner told him. "Stands to reason a little creature like her can't eat as much as a man."

The griddle was empty. The last cake had been eaten. Mrs. Wagner took the griddle to the stream and scoured it with sand; then came back to where the others were stretched around the fire. Jacob was leaning against a tree, his hands clasped over his stomach. Mrs. Wagner sat down beside him and took off her shoes. The right foot came out of the shoe hard, and then it looked as if it would never go back again, it was so swollen.

Jacob touched with his finger the red, puffy instep, then held his hand, palm upward, to the firelight. "When she was a *maedchen* I could set both feet here, so," he said.

"I'm going to make 'em both some moccasins soon as I shoot a deer," Rion said.

Mrs. Wagner gave a sigh. "I ain't so tired. It's my head Feels like it'd float off."

"I ain't tired at all now," Rion said. He stood up. "I'm going down and hobble those horses. I don't have no idea they'd stray but we don't want to take no chances."

He stepped to Frank's pack, took out the coil of leather thong, cut off enough for the hobbles and walked down towards the stream. Behind him the fire burned bravely. The light struck glints on the water and illuminated the far bank. The cane came down to the water in a wide sweep, tender shoots of this year's growth. Moving through the green were three dark, rounded objects, and farther on down the bank you could see Smiler's old grey rump. All of them eating their heads off. He could hear the rip-rip as they tore the leaves from the stalk. He stood there a moment listening to the pleasant sound before he waded across and hobbled them.

He started back. Between him and the light figures moved. Frank had dragged up some pine boughs. Mrs. Wagner, her arms wide, was shaking a blanket out over them. Jacob sat quiet on a down log, staring into the fire. As Rion watched, Cassy came forward and taking one end of the blanket from Mrs. Wagner helped her fold it over the boughs.

They were making up their beds for the night. He had not realized that night was actually upon them. They had been traveling so long, at first blundering through the dark, and today walking along that narrow road, head down most of the time. But the night was here. They would rest here, barring accidents, all of this night.

He left the stream and walked into the woods. The fire still dimly lighted his way as he went from tree to tree, cutting off the tips of boughs. When he had his arms full of the green boughs he went back to the fire. The Wagners were already side by side under their blanket. Frank was spreading his blanket as Rion came up. Cassy stood beside him, another blanket in her hands.

Rion went up to her and motioned for her to spread the blanket on the ground. When she had done so he opened his arms and let the pine tips fall upon it, then gathered the blanket up into a sack. He glanced at the Wagners. They were both asleep. But Frank, standing there beside the fire, was eyeing him. There was a peculiar expression on Frank's face, half mirth, half question. Rion looked at him steadily, then laid his hand on Cassy's arm. "Come on," he said and pointed to a level place a little removed from the fire, on the other side of a big elm tree. "Come on, let's get up some more pine boughs and make our bed over there."

PART TWO

"... and as they thought that they might anywhere obtain their necessary daily sustenance, they made little difficulty of removing: and for this cause they were not strong, either in greatness of cities or other resources."

THUCYDIDES

CHAPTER 23

ARCHY had lain down to sleep in a thicket beside a creek. He was waked at dawn by the birds. Through the leaves he could see pale yellow patches of sky. The yellow was deepening and now the light chorus had fallen off as the birds flew away from the thicket.

He jumped up and went to the trap he had set late yesterday evening on the bank of the stream. There was a rabbit in it. He took the rabbit out, put the noose in his pocket, knocked the rabbit in the head and dressed it and cut it in pieces. He made a fire and set the meat broiling on some stones.

While it was cooking he walked a little way up the creek bank. In the grey light the laurel stretched on for miles, to the foot of the mountain. Off to the right rose the dusky shapes of trees. The light grew. The elms were tall against a salmon-colored sky. A thin spiral of smoke mounted and lost itself in the feathery boughs.

He stared until he was certain that it was smoke and went back to his fire. The meat was cooked. He sprinkled it with salt and picking a piece up on the point of his knife, ate, sitting on a rock beside the stream.

It was good light now. That smoke meant that Rion and the others were eating breakfast in that grove of elms there where the creek took a bend. They had followed the creek all day yesterday. They would probably leave it soon and strike out for the mountain. If he could find where they left the creek it would be easy to track them through the laurel. Some time today he would catch up with them.

He watched a trout shoot with one flip of the tail across the stream. This time they could not send him back! He had tracked them for four days through the deep woods, past Pilot Knob and all day yesterday through this thickety plain. Even Rion could not expect him to find his way home after he had gotten this far. And the worst Rion could do was to beat him. He shrugged his shoul-

157

ders. He didn't know that he was going to take a beating from
Rion. He had a right to come west if he wanted to. At least, and
he grinned—there had not been anybody able to stop him.

He ate the last piece of the rabbit, kicked his fire out and started
downstream. The cane pressed in close on each bank but the water
was shallow. He waded most of the way. He came to the bend in
the stream, passed the ashes of their fire and struck out through the
laurel. The horses left a wide track. They must have fed. well last
night. They were making better time than they had yesterday. He
was afraid the laurel would thin out and they would get into another kind of country, where the trail would be harder. He pushed
on, stopping only once during the morning to lap like a dog at a
stream. He was drenched with sweat when he came up on a bluff
and saw between trunks of sycamores a camp fire burning.

He stopped and bringing his arm up wiped his face dry of
sweat; then walked forward boldly. Jacob and Cassy were sitting
side by side on a down tree. She was leaning over, tying the lace of
her moccasin. Mrs. Wagner was standing by the fire, stirring the
pot. She saw him, squealed and clapped her hand to her mouth and
looked over her shoulder.

Rion was coming up from the creek with the carcass of a deer
hoisted up on his shoulders. He stared and without speaking bent
and deposited the carcass on the ground.

None of the others said anything. Archy walked past the fire
and sat down on the log next to Cassy. Her eyes were shining. She
reached over and pinched his arm. "Where'd you sleep last night?"
she whispered.

"In a cane brake right down the creek from you all."

Elsa shook her head. "Poor boy! What you been living on?"

"I didn't give out of meal till yesterday and I've been taking a
rabbit nearly every night."

"Did you come by that place where there was the big landslide?"

He grinned. "I could pick out every one of your tracks plain
as if you was walking in snow." He looked at Rion. "Gal's getting
ready to cast a shoe. That off fore-foot don't make hardly any track
at all."

"Where was you during the storm?" Mrs. Wagner asked.

"Holed up in a draw. But I heard a panther and I was afraid to
fire and anyway my powder war'n't dry. I walked around and got

bewildered. That was the closest I ever came to you all. Saw you by a lightning flash, and almost ran into the four of you, sitting under some rimrock."

Rion was kneeling on the ground, skinning the deer. He looked up. "I wish you had. I'd a sent you straight back. Now it's too late."

Archy's fingers dug down into the rotten wood of the log. He sent Cassy a merry glance sidewise through his dark lashes, then got up and started towards Rion. "Brother Rion, want me to cut that meat out for you?"

Rion pulled a sinew out and hung it carefully on a bush. "Don't lay it on so thick!" he said in a disgusted tone.

They traveled on for another day and a half and came to the foot of the mountain. The laurel was not so tall now but grew more thickety. The horses' sides were bloodied and one of the deer-skin bags that held the provender was ripped in two and what little meal they had left was spilled on the ground. Rion remembered this place from his trip with Daniel. They made camp at noon and he and Archy spent half a day searching for a gap. But they could not find one and Rion said they might as well give up and climb the mountain as he and Boone had done.

It took them a day to get to the top. They camped that night in a pine grove beside a waterfall. The moon was full. It was so light that Archy could not sleep for looking down into the great plain. Rion said that another chain of mountains rose up at the end of it. The land they were seeking lay on the other side of those mountains. In the morning, he said, they would be able to see them in clear light.

They rose at day-break and began the descent. It was not easy, driving the pack horses down the mountain side. At noon they came out on a wide ledge and saw the plain shimmering below and off in the distance the mountains that were called the Blue Ridge piled like clouds on the horizon. They rested a while and cooled themselves in a mountain stream, and went back into the woods. They went down through pine woods most of that day. Towards evening they came off the mountain on to a savannah. They could see woods ahead of them, already blue in the evening light, but the ground they stood on was level and open. Archy was a little ahead of the others. When he saw the plain, free of trees, with the blue grass growing on it waist high he began to run.

He ran, with no boughs touching him, through the wide, cool air until he came to a cany place. He pushed through the cane and was on the bank of a stream. He dropped down, full length, rifle in hand, and drank. He raised his head. The cane on the farther bank was all fallen and trampled. He jumped up and waded across the creek. There, among the broken canes were mounds of such dung as he had never before seen in his life, coarse and dark and of too great size to have been dropped by deer or elk.

"It's buffalo," he said aloud and his thin body trembled.

CHAPTER 24

CASSY LIFTED the top off the pot. "It's ready," she said.

Frank held out his plate. Mrs. Wagner groaned. "I can't eat till Jacob and Rion get back. I'm worrying about *them* now."

"They'll be here any minute," Cassy said.

She filled Frank's plate with stew and sat down on a rock a little way from the fire. Frank ate silently, his head bent over his plate. There was a pinched look about his mouth, and his eyes seemed sunk farther back in his head than usual. Since Archy had been lost the men had taken turns looking for him. Frank had been out all of one night and except for a brief sleep at noon, all of today.

She looked back towards the mountain. Her mind went drearily over the events of the last two days. It had been still light when they came down from the mountain on to the savannah. It had been hard going through those pine woods, and in the twilight this place had seemed pleasant, all level and open. She looked ahead and saw the willows bordering the stream and thought that they would camp here where clover grew thick and the horses could forage all night. She and Rion were on ahead behind the pack horses. Archy had been driving Smiler earlier in the day but Rion had given him leave to hunt a while—they were almost out of meat. Smiler was stopping to graze. They were walking slowly, admiring the white clover that grew waist high when Archy ran past them. She had thought that he was after game but Rion shook his head. "Feeling his oats now he's out of the woods." They watched him run through the clover and disappear in the tall cane. When they came up to the stream half an hour later they could see his track leading down to the creek and up the far bank.

"He's after a deer, I reckon," Rion said.

Dark fell fast. Supper was cooked and eaten and he had not returned. Rion crossed the creek and went up on the other side and called but got no answer.

They had kept the fire high all that night as a signal to him and as soon as it was light Rion crossed the creek again. He found mounds of dung that he said must have been dropped by buffalo and tracked Archy through wild grass to the edge of a wood. He had lost the tracks in the woods but he had kept searching and then in the afternoon rain had begun to fall and he could not find any more signs. He had decided that Archy, following the buffalo, might have dipped into the woods and then doubled back across the creek, and today he and Jacob were hunting on this side of the stream. They had been out since daybreak.

Frank had finished his stew. Cassy got up and set the bucket of wild honey beside him. "Here's some sweetening for you," she said.

He poured some honey out on his plate, ate a spoonful, then gazed at the ground, his spoon in his hand. "Lucretius holds that foods have a pleasant taste according as they are composed of smooth or round atoms," he said. "Contrariwise those foods that taste bitter are held together by atoms that are rough in shape or have jagged edges. Such atoms, he would say, tear their way into our senses."

"Don't you ever quit studying what's in books?" Mrs. Wagner asked.

"Sometimes," he said mildly, "but when I am distraught it is a relief to read a few minutes in a book."

Cassy started. "Here they come!"

Rion and Jacob pushed through the cane and came up to the fire. They were both wet to the waist and the black from the branches was grimed into their cheeks above their tangled beards.

Rion looked at Frank. "How far north did you go?"

Frank gave his report: "I worked over the savannah and back to the mountain. I climbed a tree and sat there an hour, looking. Saw some elk grazing near the branch but nothing else moving."

Old Jacob sat down on the rock and took the plate that Elsa handed him. Cassy gave Rion the venison that she had kept hot in a skillet. He sat down on the ground and put a morsel of meat in his mouth but he held it there without chewing and suddenly spat it out.

"I was back in those woods again today," he said, "and I found ashes. It was an Indian fire, all right. But I couldn't tell how old it was. And the rain had beat out any tracks."

Nobody said anything.

He put the skillet down and got up and stood by the fire. Cassy stood beside him and laid her hand on his arm. "You made him go back once," she said in a low voice.

He laughed. "What good did it do? I ought to have sent him back when he came up with us the other day."

"He'd have trailed us again. He was mad to come."

He raised his hand and brushed it across his face. Under the hovering palm his lips were trembling. He might break down and cry—if she and the others weren't here. For the first time since she had known him she felt that he did not want her with him, that he would rather be alone.

She stepped softly away. Old Jacob watched her go, then looked around at the others. A glint showed in his pale eye. "I reckon we better start home," he said.

Rion looked over his head to where the mountains loomed through the dusk. "No," he said shortly. "We'll go on."

CHAPTER 25

THEY FOUND a gap in the mountains but it was high up; it took them three days to get down into the valley. There was a day's journey through the thickets and they came into another kind of country: rolling land with plenty of streams cutting through it. Jacob wanted to stop in a cove where there was a good limestone spring and both sugar trees and buckeyes growing, but Rion was for pressing on.

"This ain't the kind of country Findley told about."

"One piece of woods is as good as another," Jacob told him. "You ain't going to see nothing but woods if you walk till Doomsday."

"That country he told about there warn't any woods. Just high meadow and level and the land so rich it brings clover waist high."

"And how you going to find this country?"

"He told me, told me how to get there. There's a river with a long island in it. When we get there we strike off northeast. It ain't far then."

"We seen rivers a plenty," Jacob said, "and islands in 'em too."

"We ain't come to this island yet."

Cassy, walking behind the men, listened to their talk, then glanced over at Mrs. Wagner. The woman had half turned her head as they spoke, then as if it were too much effort to listen she fixed her eyes on the ground and plodded on. Her eyes when they looked into Cassy's had seemed darker than usual, with something straining in them. But that was because she was tallow-pale. Cassy could see her jowls shake as she turned her head. There was fat on her still but it hung loose on the bone.

They must all look desperate characters, had there been anybody to look at them. But Cassy herself was clean, she had washed her gown out two days before in a running stream. Mrs. Wagner had two other gowns in her baggage but she had not changed for a long time. There was a greasy spot as big as your hand on the hem of this gown: the bay horse's blood. That was where he had rested his nose when he first came up to them back in that thickety country. Rion had turned the horses loose—they had given up hobbling them —and they were all resting when suddenly the horse broke out of the bushes and rushed up to them, for all the world like a Christian asking for help. His legs went stiff. He fell down in front of Elsa. Blood trickled from his nostrils on to her skirt. The next minute he was up and crashing off through the trees. Rion caught up with him but he could not hold him and he could not come up with him again. He ran, crazily, like that for an hour then fell to the ground in a blackberry brake. When they got to him he was dead. His hair was dark everywhere with sweat and blood and rheum oozed from his nostrils. Rion knelt down beside him and passed his hand over and over him. When he got up he said it was his bladder that had gone bad on him all of a sudden. Nature would not relieve him and the humours accumulated and burst the inner walls of the body. He had seen them like that before. There was nothing they could have done even if they had known about it in time. He stood there a minute, looking down at the dead horse.

"I ain't going to skin him," he said, "Hard time he's had and all. I ain't going to skin him, no matter what you say."

Nobody said anything and they turned away. That night Cassy dreamed that it was Archy, not the horse, that they had left lying in the thicket. She had wanted to stop and bury him but Rion said they must go on, more Indians might come. She had realized then that Archy in the dream had an arrow sticking in his side. He did not seem to mind. He was smiling, lying there with his head turned a little to one side. She had told Rion about the dream, how in it Archy was smiling. He looked at her and did not say anything, but one corner of his mouth flicked up. She knew what he was thinking, that the Indians might have burned Archy or done worse than that to him. They thought of strange things to do. One thing she had heard her father tell about when they first came to this country she had never forgotten. In South Carolina Captain Eliot's body had been cut into pieces and the pieces tied to the bushes. A comrade of his who was hiding in a thicket said that before the Indians did him the kindness of killing him they had heated their gun barrels red hot and thrust them into his bowels.

It was six days since the horse had died; or was it seven? They had been going through this country so long that she had lost count of the days. Jacob said that they had doubled on their trail and were going backwards. He had been saying that ever since the compass slipped from Rion's pocket. Soon after that there had been a rainy spell. The days broke grey and the nights were too dark for stars. It was then that Rion had got bewildered Jacob said. But he was proud and would keep them walking in circles all summer before he would acknowledge that he was lost. A while back they had stopped in a grove of white oaks. Jacob sat down on a log and said that he would stay there until they came back. They had been in that same grove three times already, he said, and pointed out a rock above the spring shaped like an old man's nightcap. When Rion said that rocks were likely to take any shape he said that he recognized twin elms growing beside the spring, one with a gall covering half its trunk.

Rion did not argue. He walked over and kicked him in the behind, so hard that he bounced off the rock. When he did not get up Rion stood over him and told him that he would give him worse than that if he did not start on again.

She lifted her head suddenly. Her nostrils twitched. A tree in front of them was full of white bloom. Rion had stopped under it. He reached up, pulled off a bough and stripped one of the flowers from it. "Here's something for you," he said. She took the flower and raised it to her lips, then loathing the heavy, cloying scent she threw it to the ground. Rion looked surprised but did not say anything. She walked on. After a minute he came up with her.

"You didn't like my blossom?"

"It smelled too sweet," she said.

He laughed. "Didn't know a flower *could* smell too sweet."

They walked on, side by side. They were among pines. The air was cool, with no odor except that of resin. She was glad of that. "Sweet smells or sour," she thought, "they're all one."

For over a week now she had been faint in the mornings, loathing the odors that came from the stew pot. She had thought at first that it was the venison and turkey—they had had them so often, stewed together, and breast of turkey besides for bread, since the meal had given out. She had thought that it was the odor of game that sickened her until—on the day that Archy was lost—Rion had brought her a piece of comb with honey oozing from it, and the same loathing had come over her. She had known then what it was.

Rion was speaking, in a tone so low that Jacob and Elsa could not hear. "Stands to reason a man comes this far he wants to get hold of the good land."

She did not answer. She was thinking of the day when she had first become certain that she was going to have a baby, the day that Archy was lost. She had kept the news to herself, expecting to tell Rion when he came to bed. But Rion had not come to bed until nearly dawn. He had sat beside the fire, keeping it high for a signal to Archy in case he might still be near.

As he was getting into bed he spoke: "We're here because we can't help ourselves. He'd no business to take to the woods."

She had lain straight and still, thinking of what he had said. Archy had no need to take to the woods. All the others, Jacob, Elsa, Frank and now she herself had. Yes, it was well for her that she had come with them. What could she have done if she had remained in the settlements, a lone woman with her fair fame gone? Her heart hardened against Rion and yet at the same time she asked herself what she would do when in a minute he should turn to her. But he did not turn to her. He lay quiet in the same position in which he had fallen on the boughs, like a man stunned or stricken, and after a long time she knew that he was asleep. . . .

Rion stopped suddenly and faced around. She turned too. Mrs. Wagner had sat down on a rock. Jacob was kneeling beside her, unlacing one of her moccasins. As Rion and Cassy came up he let the moccasin fall to the ground. They saw the woman's ankle, fish-belly white except where the thongs had cut two deep red ruts in the flesh.

Jacob gently laid his finger on one of the ruts. Mrs. Wagner's lips quivered. She moaned. Jacob looked up at Rion. "She can't travel no more today," he said. "Hit'll mortify on her if she ain't careful."

"She laces 'em too tight every time," Rion said.

"Here," Rion said, "let me fix 'em." He knelt beside Mrs. Wagner and re-tied the thongs, padding them with a piece of old linen so that they could not slip back into their original position. "Now," he said, "you try 'em that way for a while."

Mrs. Wagner got up without a word and started walking. Rion

and Jacob and Frank went ahead to catch up with the horses. Cassy walked beside Mrs. Wagner. The woman moved erratically, not seeming to look where she was going. Once she fetched up against a tree trunk and stood a moment, her eyes closed, her head sunk on her breast. Cassy went up to her and took her hand. "You feel mighty bad, don't you?" she asked softly.

"It's gone up my leg now," Mrs. Wagner whimpered. "It's shooting pains all over me."

"We'll have to stop then," Cassy said. "We can't go on, you in a fever like this."

Mrs. Wagner lurched towards her. She was smiling, slily, confidentially. "Don't you say anything. Don't you get him roiled. No telling what he might do."

Cassy shook the woman's hand off and walked swiftly on ahead. Rion heard her coming and waited. "We got to stop," she told him. "She's in a fever."

"How you know?"

"She laid her hand on me. It's fit to burn you."

Rion scowled at the ground. The pack horse had stopped and was eating some cottonwood sprouts. Rion suddenly stepped forward and laid his hand on the horse's flank. "They ain't had nothing but sprouts for three days," he said.

"Well, we keep on walking all night and they won't get nothing else."

He looked at her, astonished. "Ain't you noticed?" he asked in a suddenly gentle voice. "Ain't you noticed the country changing?"

She shook her head but the suddenly gentle tone of his voice broke her mood. She looked about her. They had been going through pine country all day and there were still pines about her, but there were other trees, a fine elm not ten feet away and on beyond she could see white branches gleaming. Sycamores! They could not be far from a stream.

She felt her stiff lips crack into a smile. "You reckon we could make it to water before it's dark?"

Mrs. Wagner pushed through the bushes and was standing beside them. He turned to her. "You going to ride the rest of the way, Elsa," he said. He removed the pack from one of the horses and laying it on the ground lifted the huge woman on to the horse. "You walk alongside of her," he told Cassy and settled the pack on his own shoulders.

Frank had come up. He said that they ought to divide the pack —it was too much for one man. Rion paid no attention to him. "I could carry this ten miles," he said, "but it ain't going to be more'n three miles before we strike water."

Jacob laughed out. Cassy turned on him. "Shut up!" she screamed. "Nothing he does suits you. Do something yourself."

Frank and Jacob went on ahead, driving the horses. Rion followed, balancing the heavy pack on his shoulders. Smiler fell in behind him. Mrs. Wagner rode as if she were giddy, swaying about so that Cassy had to hold her on the horse. It was hard to keep beside him. She could have managed well enough in open woods but the way had grown thickety.

They passed Rion. He went almost as blindly as Mrs. Wagner, bowed from the waist, the pack sliding from side to side with each of his stiff-legged steps. Cassy ran up beside him and, stooping, peered into his face. "You'll kill yourself!" she cried. "Kill yourself and then where'll we be?" He put one hand out and pushed her aside, then as if he resented expending that much energy on her, said harshly, "Go on! Get out of my way!"

She left him and went back to the nodding woman and the horse. Smiler had stopped beside a blackberry thicket and was hungrily eating the young leaves and the white bloom. She broke off a switch and beat him till he moved on. From that time forward she had to beat him almost every step of the way, for the thickets grew more plentiful. It was growing dusk but the setting sun was red through the trees. She was wondering how much longer they could see to travel when Frank and Jacob stopped. When she came up with them they were standing on top of a rise beside an enormous beech tree. The ravine below was in shadow but she could hear water flowing and even if she had not heard it, would have known by the ferns that they were on the bed of a stream.

She wondered why the men did not speak; then she saw that they were examining the descent before them. The roots of the trees going down fifty feet, made a staircase. Frank suddenly leaned over and slapped Gal on the rump. The mare started down and the other horses followed. Frank and Jacob went after them. Rion came up. He pushed past the women and went lumbering down with his pack. Cassy turned to Mrs. Wagner. "You better get down," she said, "It'll be all Smiler can do to make it by himself." Mrs. Wagner was about to dismount when Cassy saw that Rion, halfway down, was craning his neck out from under his pack to look up at her. "See the cane!" he cried and gestured with his hand. She looked where he pointed and in the fading light saw far below the fresh green of young cane. All of a sudden her knees felt weak. "I can't make it" she called to him.

He had thrown the pack off his shoulders and was leaping up the path. Standing beside the horse he smiled at her. "It don't make no difference. We'll camp here the night." He had his arm about Mrs. Wagner. His other hand was on Smiler's bridle. He was guiding the horse down the staircase. She waited until they were a few feet ahead, then walked down easily over the matted roots.

The others had stopped on flat ground that was covered with pine needles. "Better camp here," Frank said. "It'll be wet down nearer the river." He was flinging Gal's pack off as he spoke. Mrs. Wagner sat down on the ground. Cassy got two quilts and folded them, then wadded up one of her spare gowns for a pillow. "You just lay here now," she said, "and we'll make you some tea soon as we get a fire."

Rion came over and laid his hand on her forehead. "She ain't got much fever," he said. "Yarrow's what we want. Hit'll bring that swelling down. I'll drive the horses into that cane and hunt for some on the way back."

He had drawn his hunting knife and was off through the woods. Frank had set about making a fire. She went to help him. They dragged up some down boughs. Frank was breaking them with his axe when they saw Rion coming back towards them. "What's the matter?" Frank said. "Couldn't you find any yarrow?"

Rion stood still, staring at them. "There's a field over there," he said, "a cleared field and corn growing in it. And there's a path on yon side of the field with trees girdled."

Frank dropped his axe, swept his hat from his head and sailed it high into the air. "Well, ain't there a cabin?" he said. "Man, ain't there a cabin?"

"I don't know," Rion said, "I saw them trees and I run back to tell you fast as I could."

"Let's go now," Frank had started running, but Rion called him back. "Let's load up now. If there ain't anything we can camp on the other side of the river as well as this one. And if there is anything we won't have to come back."

"Is it a river," Frank asked, "or just a creek?"

"It's a river," Rion said, "Prettiest river you ever seen. Eddies in it big enough to turn a wheel."

"How'll we git across?" Jacob quavered. "I ain't no notion to git wet this time of night."

Nobody paid any attention to him. Rion and Frank went off to round up the horses. They had to beat them to get them out of the cane and Star even lashed out with her hind legs when they started loading her. "I don't blame the poor creature," Jacob said. "First mouthful she's had in days and you flog her out of it."

Rion laughed as he cut the horse over the legs with a willow switch. "Just seeing all that fodder has put spirit into her," he said.

He and Frank lifted Mrs. Wagner on to the other horse and they started off over the sloping ground towards the river. Mrs. Wagner was bewildered. "Thought we's going to rest," she kept saying fretfully. "Thought you's going to let me lay down." Cassy patted her knee. "You going to lie down. You going to lie down in just a minute. There's a house across the river and you going to lie down there." She heard the words leave her lips and was startled by the sound. "Lord forgive me!" she thought. "There ain't no house across that river and here I am getting the poor thing's hopes up."

They walked through bracken that was knee-high and came out on a shelving sandy beach. The river was before them, its waters still glinting a little in the fading light. Rion was running up the bank like a hound on the scent. And now he was coming back. "Here's the place," he cried. "Here's where it's shallowest."

They splashed in, the pack horses going first and Smiler coming after. The bed of the stream was loose rock. The water flowed swiftly but was not deep. Cassy managed to stay beside Smiler until they were halfway across, then without warning she stepped from a slippery rock and plunged into water that seemed to have no bottom. She found a footing—the water was breast high—then lost it and went under. She came up, gasping, flung her head back and saw the cold stars shining through the leaves and in the same instant felt the swift water lap at her throat. "I'll be swept down before they miss me," she thought. She struck out with her arms the way she had seen boys do in the swimming hole and kicked desperately. Pain flashed through her whole body—she had struck her toe on the rock. She turned around and kicked herself towards it, then laid hold of the edge and hauled herself up and got to her feet. She could see Smiler, a little ahead of her. The water ran just under his belly. She floundered towards him, on her hands and knees part of the time. The pack horses were already across and Smiler was stepping out of the water. Rion and Frank were turning back to see how she was making out.

She straightened up, her nose and throat still tingling from the cold water. "It ain't anything," she called, "I just stepped in a hole."

Rion stood by her while she wrung the water out of her gown. He laughed at her. "One hole in the river and you had to find it."

She laughed too, looking around her. There was not much beach on this side. The woods came right down to the water, but it was not woods, it was new ground. You could see the white girdles shining on the trees.

Rion laid his hand on her arm. "Come on. There's a path along here."

They started along the path. Jacob walked beside his wife. Cassy went first with Rion.

The path was snaky, whipping in and out among the trees, making a big loop once to avoid a blackberry thicket. Was it a path or just a trail made by game? She shivered in her wet gown and put her hand out and felt the marks on the nearest tree. "It ain't beaver," she said. "Beaver couldn't cut a tree like that."

"Beaver couldn't reach that high," Rion said. She felt the muscles of his arm tighten under her hand as he halted suddenly. "What's that?" he asked.

"It's a woman," Cassy said calmly. "It's a woman calling her children."

The sound came again, a woman's peremptory voice "Jimmie . . . you come here!"

Rion moved on and Cassy ran to catch up with him. They rounded a blackberry thicket and were in a clearing. Before them a cabin sat under girdled oaks and maples. A child ran out from behind a tree and slipped into the open doorway. A woman who had been standing in the doorway stepped back. The door went to. They could hear the sound of the bolt being drawn.

Rion let the rifle he had been cradling in his arm drop to the ground. He stepped out from the others. "Hello," he called. "Hello the house!"

CHAPTER 26

THEY HEARD steps inside, and a hand came out and pulled the shutter to. They did not hear steps going away from the window and knew that the woman must be looking at them though a crack in the shutter.

"What's your name?" she called in a moment.

"Rion Outlaw, from over the mountains. And this here's my wife and her brother and Jacob Wagner and his wife. She's sick."

There was silence, then the voice said incredulously: "Jacob Wagner that keeps store at Salisbury?"

Jacob rushed forward. "Jacob Wagner," he cried. "The honest merchant! Furs, Hides, Feathers, Notions . . . Mistress, you been in my store? You traded with me?"

The door opened. A small, dark-haired woman was off the doorstep and coming down the path. Jacob ran to her. He shook her by the hand. "You been in Salisbury? You've bought salt from me? Ribbons? Mebbe lace? One spring I had fourteen bolts of Irish lace brought on from Philadelphia . . ."

"It was ribbon," the woman said. "Blue. Half a yard. For my wedding cap." She looked up at Mrs. Wagner swaying above them in the dusk. "That's your wife? D'you say she was sick?"

Jacob had the woman by the arm, propelling her towards his wife. "She's got a bad foot. It's mortifying on her. She's got fever too. Been out of her head these last miles."

The woman turned away from him to Rion. "Get her down off that horse, will you?" She ran ahead of them, scattering a flock of children out of the doorway. "Scat, now! There's a sick woman coming."

The two men half walked, half carried Mrs. Wagner into the house. Cassy followed. The woman stripped a new patchwork quilt from the bed, disclosing one that was more worn. "Lay her there," she commanded and then ran to the fire and stirred up the gathering coals and flung a handful of bark on top of them.

173

The bark flared up, lighting all the room. Mrs. Wagner, propped against the headboard, opened her eyes suddenly and laughed out as if amazed to find herself within walls, then closed her eyes and turned her head to one side. Cassy stepped over to the bed. "It's her leg," she said and lifted the gown to show the swollen ankle. The small, dark-haired woman came and stood beside her. She touched the swollen place gently and laid her hand on the sick woman's forehead. "She's got a bit of fever but it ain't no more'n that swelling would account for."

"We'll poultice that ankle." She straightened up and looked at the two men. They looked back, seeing a small woman in a butter-nut-colored gown with dark, curling hair cut short about her face. Her rather large blue eyes were fixed on them now in wonder. "You from Rowan, from Salisbury town, and I wasn't going to let you in!" She shook her head and laughed nervously. "But you can't blame me. There's all kinds coming over the mountains now."

"Are there many coming?" Rion asked.

She had crossed the room and was standing before a row of shelves placed high on the wall. She took a jar down from the top shelf. "Here, Jim," she called to one of the children. "Get me a bucket of water and I'll put these catnip leaves on to simmer." She turned back to Rion. "Our name's Robertson. James Robertson's my husband. We came here last fall from Wake county . . . Yes, there's a lot of 'em coming through now it's spring. When we moved here there wasn't anybody but Honeycutts and Beans over on Reedy creek." She gestured to a row of three-legged stools against the wall. "Get you a chair. Make yourselves at home."

"We'd better unload the horses," Rion said. "Shall we turn 'em into the cane, or is there danger of 'em getting into the crop?"

"The crop's over on this side of the house. But maybe you'd better drive 'em down the river a piece. Here, Jim, you go with the gentlemen and show them the way."

Frank and Rion left the room. The children straggled after them. Mrs. Robertson pursued them to the door and caught the two-year-old up in her arms and brought him back. "This one's mine," she said. "The others belong to Sally Honeycutt. She's down with her fourth and I brought these ones over to take care of till she's up and about." She had sat down on one of the stools, the child in her arms, and looked at Cassy over her child's yellow head. "The big fellow your husband?"

"Yes," Cassy said. "The other one's my brother."

The woman, still holding the child in her lap, hitched her stool across the floor and lifted the lid of the pot she had set to boil. "It's simmering. We'll just set it aside and poultice her soon as the water cools."

She put the child down and went over and stood by the sick woman a moment, and came back to the hearth. "Lord," she exclaimed, "you're soaking wet. Push up here to the fire. May be May but it's cool down here by the river." And she flung another handful of bark on the coals.

Cassy drew her stool nearer the fire and set about drying her dress. At the other end of the hearth her hostess had started preparations for supper. Venison was cooking in the big pot but another pot swung on the lug pole. The woman pulled it towards her and began stirring meal into it.

Cassy looked over at Jacob who had been sitting quietly on a bench against the wall. He was bending a little forward. Under his grey, bushy brows his eyes were as bright as a squirrel's. She felt the moisture gush up in her own mouth as she watched the white grains fall into the boiling water. She looked away, for fear she might disgrace herself by her eagerness.

"You got meal?" she asked faintly. "You made a crop? You got meal?"

Mrs. Robertson had finished stirring the meal in and laid the iron spoon on a clean ash board at the edge of the hearth. "My husband rode over the mountains last spring and planted him a crop. Then he came back and brought us. We got here in September and the first thing we did was run look at the corn. It was a pretty sight, I tell you. Course the deer had got in some and the chipmunks but they left us nigh two hundred bushels. We've had meal all winter."

She left the room and was back in a few minutes with a bark trough heaped high with greens. "Last mess from the turnip patch," she said. "I was saving them till tomorrow but when company comes you've got to have sauce." She gave Cassy her sudden, brilliant smile and handed her a turnip and a knife. "There's a few sound ones left in the bin. You scrape that while you're waiting. I won't take these greens long to boil now the fire's up."

Cassy cut the turnip in two, gave half to Jacob, and set to scraping her half. It was a little withered on the surface but inside it was sound. She chewed it slowly, holding each morsel in her mouth a long time before swallowing it. The bitter-sweet pulp tasted good and kept her mind off the odor of the mush. She looked deliberately away from the hearth about the room.

It was a good size and nicely chinked with white clay. There was a kind of cupboard standing against the wall with pewter basins and spoons on it and there were half a dozen stools, rounds of white oak with three stout legs pegged in. The bed was a platform of boards with a shuck mattress on top but it was wide enough for three or four people. There was a trundle bed under the big bed and in front of the trundle bed lay an oval-shaped rug made out of sewn rags.

"They must have worked hard to get all this," she thought; "worked hard, every one."

Frank and Rion came in. There was another man with them. James Robertson, the master of the house. He came up to Cassy and taking her by the hand told her with a touch of fine manners that now she had come the house was hers. He was tall, with blue eyes in a long face. A steady looking man. His wife was proud of him. She had looked up when he came in and she kept looking towards him every now and then as she worked.

He had been to the store for salt. There was a store, Carter's and Parker's, in the next valley. He had been gone a day and a night and had been worried about his family all the time. He had not thought to find company when he got back. He was from Wake county and had often been to Salisbury. He knew the Goforths and the Lovelattys. He had heard of Rion's father, Malcolm Outlaw, but never had met up with him, had just never happened to go to Trading Ford. He knew, too, about the Regulators. He was asking about Harmon Husbands.

"There ain't anything to him," Rion said. "I knew that first time I set eyes on him." He hesitated a second, looking hard at Robertson, then said, "I had to leave. Me and my friends here, we had to leave. They was after us."

Robertson did not seem surprised. "We passed through Hillsborough last September," he said. "There was talk then of bringing the clerk to trial."

"They tried him," Rion said, "tried him and fined him, but it didn't do no good. They set the red-coats on us. We had to leave."

Jacob spoke in a musing tone. "My store I left, my goods. Two tons of salt, two thousand pounds of hides . . . I just walked out of the store and left them."

Rion laughed. "And a good thing, too, old man, if you wanted to save your neck." He came over and dropped down on the floor beside Cassy.

"Sh-h," Cassy said and glanced towards the bed. Mrs. Robertson was beside the sick woman now, putting a poultice on the inflamed ankle. Cassy got up to help but she waved her back. "Sit down and rest. Much as you've walked today."

Cassy moved back to the fire. The children came up to her, bringing the baby. The two younger ones hung back but the boy, Jim, stood out in front of her and stared. "I live on Reedy creek," he said in a croaking voice. "We got a spring. It ain't wet weather either."

Mrs. Robertson stepped over and shooed him away. "Been so long since they seen anybody they don't know how to act," she said, laughing.

Cassy held her arms out to the baby. He came to her and she picked him up and held him on her knee while she listened to the men. They were talking about this valley they were in now. The Indians called it the Watauga Old Fields. This country used to be a sacred place to them, Robertson said. These fields had been cleared time out of mind. They still held their peace talks at a place near here, the Long Island of the Holston river.

"Must be the place Findley talked about," Rion said excitedly. "Has it got a fort on it?"

Robertson said that the fort had been built by Colonel Byrd and his men when they came out with help for Fort Loudon and then had to fall back.

Cassy put her hand on Rion's shoulder and called his attention to the baby who was standing up in her lap, his arms clasped about her neck. "Ain't he a sweet little feller, Rion?"

"He sure is," Rion said, but he did not look up. He was listening to Robertson.

" . . . I came out here year before last," Robertson said. "I saw this place here between these two rivers, Watauga and Doe they call 'em. I saw these old fields already pretty well cleared off, you might say, and I says I'll bring my family back and make me a home. I planted a crop and stayed long enough to lay it by, then I started for the Yadkin. I was trying to go back the same way I had come but heavy rains set in and I couldn't strike that trail. There were days and days I didn't see the sun and going through rhododendron and laurel all the time. I turned my horse loose and tried it on foot. I'd find the biggest hill I could and then climb a tree and sight off at the mountains. But there was so much mist I couldn't make out the ranges and some days I'd fall down out of that tree and just lay there, I'd be so weak. I couldn't keep my powder dry so I couldn't kill no game. Didn't have anything but a knife. It was rutting time. Bears used to come and play around me when I'd be laying there at the foot of a tree, trying to get my strength up . . . Finally I met up with two hunters. They let me have their extra horse and I made it back to the settlements . . . I stayed long enough to rest and get my business fixed up and then I started back here with fifteen others. No, I haven't been any farther west than this. I was glad enough when I saw these old fields already cleared by the Indians."

"We aim to go on farther," Rion said. "We aim to go on to Kentuck."

"He can't ever be satisfied," Cassy thought. "He's always got to be going on."

She looked at Robertson. He would stay here, stay here and make a home. A steady man, with a touch of the methodical in everything he said or did. He was telling now about building the cabin. He had set to work on it before he so much as girdled a tree in the fields. It had taken him a solid month and would have taken longer but that his friend, Amos Eaton, had come over and lent a hand. They had kept at it and got in before cold weather. It had been a hard winter but they had made out all right.

Rion was not listening so intently now. His hand, the fingers wide spread, had been lying on Cassy's knee. The fingers curved in, gently pressing her leg. She laid her palm over his with a reproving pressure, then felt her nerves stir at the touch of the loved flesh. She looked down at his cheek, gaunt under the red, curling beard. "We're together, anyhow," she thought; "all the way through the wilderness, and still together!"

CHAPTER 27

It was past midnight when they went to bed. Rion and Cassy were separated. Mrs. Robertson said that the girl was worn out and made her share the bed with the sick woman. She and her husband and the children bedded down on some old quilts, and Rion and Jacob and Frank were each given a buffalo robe and told to make the best of it. Rion lay down on his robe near the door but he could not sleep. The room was still warm—they had had a little fire going all evening—and the breaths of the sleepers made it seem foul to him, he had been accustomed for so long to sleeping in the open air. He took his rifle and robe outdoors and settled himself under a tree.

It was a clear night with stars shining. From where he lay he could hear the sound of water going past. Robertson had said that this place was between two rivers, the Watauga and the Doe. The Watauga was a fork of another river, the Holston. The Holston forked twice. The long island with the fort on it of which Findley had spoken was in its upper fork, or Robertson was as big a liar as ever lived. The country of which Boone told, the great meadow that was a grazing place for game, could not be far from here. They might reach it in three days' journey, maybe less, if he could get these people on their feet. There was the sick woman, and old Jacob was a drawback all the time. Even Cassy seemed to be pining of late and Frank had got so he never spoke, just walked with his eyes down like every step would be his last. A man was a fool to start out with that many people. Robertson, traveling alone, had made it here and back to the Yadkin in one season. He told about how he had nearly starved and lay down at the foot of a tree, thinking he was going to die, but a man might expect to starve if he went to the woods and didn't have wit enough to keep his powder dry and to cap that couldn't even throw a knife, with game roaming all around him. It was a wonder the fellow ever got through. Well, Frank and Jacob and the rest never would have got through if it hadn't been for him, Rion. There had been times when he felt like he was carrying the whole lot on his back as he had carried the pack those last few miles.

He thought of the pack—old Jacob's hatchets had weighed like lead before he put them down—and was suddenly weary again. He shifted his rifle so that it lay between his legs, pillowed his head on his arm and went to sleep.

When he woke the sun was shining through the trees. Cassy was standing over him, holding a piggin in her hand.

He leaped to his feet. "By Godly! This is the first time in my life I ever slept through day-break."

"I'm glad you did. You were dog tired."

He took the piggin from her. "Where you going with this?"

"To the spring. Breakfast's most ready."

He walked down to the river with her. The spring came up between two encircling roots of a sycamore tree. He handed her the gourd and while she was dipping up water he knelt beside the stream and plunged his head under. He came up puffing and shaking himself like a dog until the water was gone from his hair and beard. She was sitting on a rock, staring across the river. There was an expression on her face he had never seen before, a still, withdrawn look. He suddenly felt lonely, there in the bright sun with the water flowing past. He went to her, put his hands on her shoulders, leaned over and kissed her on the mouth. He pointed to an elder thicket a little way down the stream. "Let's go over there," he whispered, "ain't no hurry about getting back."

She shook her head and slid from the rock. "We better get on back. She's needing the water."

"As he picked up the piggin and followed her he thought of the breakfast that was being put on the table. "I bet they have mush again," he said.

Cassy looked at him. Her lips curled. "That mush tasted real good last night but this morning I smelled it cooking and I had to get out of the house quick."

He stared at her. "You don't like mush, and going without meal for two months!"

She shook her head again. "I like it well as anything. It all tastes the same. Except deer meat. I believe in my soul I'd lie down and die before I'd taste deer meat again." She came nearer and laid her hand on his arm and at the same time looked up into the trees over their heads, "I was thinking last night, if I could only get some of those little winter grapes."

"It'll be a long time before they're ripe," he said, thinking that it was like a woman to want something out of season; then some memory arose, talk he had heard, playing around among the women when he was a chap. He stopped and set the piggin down. "What's the matter with you?" he asked roughly.

Cassy picked the piggin up. "You know what's the matter with me," she said, "least you ought to know." And without waiting to see what he had to say to that she walked before him into the house.

He followed in a few minutes. The family was sitting down to breakfast. There was last night's stew warmed over, with journey cakes, and mush and molasses and milk for the young ones. Robertson said that their cow had come fresh the week before.

Rion took his bowl and stood in the doorway looking out as he ate. He had been traveling through this same country for a week but it looked different this morning, fresher, somehow, as if any minute it might turn full summer.

He glanced at the bed. Mrs. Wagner, propped up on a down pillow, was eating as heartily as anybody else. Her ankle still hurt her, she said, but the swelling was going down fast and she had had no fever since early morning.

"You feel like you'd be able to travel today?" Rion asked her.

"Naw," Jacob said querulously before she had time to answer. "She ain't goin' to be able to travel today nor tomorrow neither."

"What you going to do?" Rion asked him. "Stay here and eat these folks out of house and home?"

Jacob looked uneasy. "I'll work for my keep," he said, "I'll lend him a hand with that corn. Needs chopping out. I was down looking at it a while ago. As for you, if you're so full of dash why'n't you take to the woods and shoot us some meat? That'd keep the pot boiling."

"I aim to," Rion said; "I aim to start right after breakfast." He looked at Robertson who had raised a deprecatory hand. "Reckon you can set me on the way to that island?"

"It's all of thirty miles," Robertson said.

"I can make it there and back by tomorrow night," Rion said, "if I don't wander from the way. Frank here can go along with me. In the meantime I'd be obliged if you'd keep these womenfolks till

I get back. You ought not to lose by it." He looked at Jacob. "Master Wagner here he's brought some of his savings along. He can pay for their keep these two, three days."

The women were clearing the table. Rion went outside. Robertson followed him. "Don't concern yourself for the board, Master Outlaw," he said. "There ain't many Rowan folks come through here. We're proud to have you stay a day or two."

"I'm obliged," Rion said, "but you're a poor man, same as me, and liable to run short of meal long before harvest. That old coot's got money sewed in his belt. Let him pay."

Robertson was silent. Presently he picked up a stick and began drawing a map on the dirt. "The Holston forks here," he said. "The island is right in the forks." He prolonged the line he had just drawn, then set a dot beside it. "Here we are," he said, "between the Watauga and the Doe rivers. You go out here back of the cabin and start up the river. When the river forks you bear to the left. You follow that river and it'll take you to the Long Island."

"What about the country in between?" Rion asked. "Any land where a man might settle?"

"You follow any of those creeks up a way and you'll find as pretty a cove as a man'd want. Ridges in between, of course, but there's plenty of good bottom land. If you're thinking of settling here I'll help you locate your land. Or Honeycutt would. He knows all the land around Reedy creek."

"I was thinking of going on to Kentuck," he said.

Robertson nodded. He sat down on the doorstep and began whittling on the stick with which he had drawn his map. "I made a trip up above the head of the island once," he said. "The hills open up in a fine valley. Must be more'n a mile long. I didn't get to the end of it." He lowered his stick and began drawing the map of the Holston and its forks again. "I wouldn't want to go further into that country," he said.

"Why?" Rion asked. "I believe the whole country's going to settle up, and settle up fast."

"I believe it will. But I wouldn't want to take my chances with the Indians up that way."

"They're all pretty much alike, ain't they?" Rion asked.

Robertson shook his head. "I've known a few Wyandots and I've known a few Mingoes. They're as different from the Indians around here as you are from a Frenchman."

"What's the difference?"

"The Cherokee are reasonable, reasonable, that is, for Indians. You make a bargain with them and they'll stick to their side of it if you'll stick to yours."

"I never knew any Indians," Rion said, "except some Saponas I used to go hunting with . . . You had many dealings with the Cherokee?"

"I bought this land from them, that is to say I leased it."

"If you was going to buy it whyn't you buy it outright?"

"Since the King's proclamation a man is not allowed to buy land. I judged it best to stay within the letter of the law and leased it from the Little Carpenter."

"Who's he? The chief?"

"The peace chief. A very reasonable man. In some ways he is not like an Indian. He has been across the water, to London, and has been received by the King."

Rion laughed. "Never heard of such a thing."

Frank had followed them out into the yard. He spoke up. "If I had any means that's what I'd do. I'd buy the land from 'em if I could and if I couldn't buy it I'd lease it. Then you could settle down and know they wouldn't bother you. Ever have any trouble with Indians around here?"

"No. That's on account of the Carpenter. He likes white folks."

Rion frowned, looking from one to the other. "I've come a long way through the woods," he said, "but I never had it in mind to pay anybody for the land after I got here. The Indians ain't using it. They ain't got a right to keep people from settling on it."

"If you'd take my advice you'd pay 'em a little something," Robertson said. "It'd save trouble in the long run."

"I ain't got any money," Rion said. He laughed. "But I got. . . ." he calculated on his figures, "I got thirty hatchets, good ones, too, with a scalping edge on 'em. Least they ought to be mine. I brought 'em across the mountains."

Robertson stood up. "They'd lease you four or five hundred acres of land for them. Nothing they like better'n a hatchet, unless it's a gun."

Rion picked his rifle up from where it was leaning against a tree. "Come on, Frank," he said. "If we going to see this country we better get started."

CHAPTER 28

RION HELD out the stick that had impaled on it a nicely browned piece of deer's liver. "*You* eat it," he said.

Frank shook his head. "I've had one too many of those collops already. Come on. We'd better start." He got up and began stamping out the embers of the fire.

Rion ate the morsel of liver and licked his fingers. "I always said I couldn't get enough deer liver, but this is one time I've had a-plenty. . . . Here, you le'me do that."

He walked over to where the carcass of the deer was hanging, took the axe from Frank and cracked the pelvis bone in two, then split the carcass down the back and took the forequarters off. The ribs he left on the ground but he cut out the saddle and the shoulders and laid them beside the two haunches. "We better take as much of this as we can," he said. "That Robertson don't look like much of a hunter to me."

They loaded up. Frank started off south at once but Rion said that he wanted to have another look at the end of the island. He went back, pushed through the willows, and stood on the river bank. This place where he stood was the head of the island. The point thrust out here, sharp as an arrowhead; the river forked around it, the two streams about equal in size, running swiftly on each side of the island to converge in a master tumbler below.

He raised his eyes and studied the country across the river. It was broken, little hills, covered mostly with pine. Directly opposite, between two sparsely wooded ridges, was a valley. Here at the bank it was hardly large enough to accommodate a pack train but as it bent north it opened out. You could see the ridges withdrawing from it, fold on fold, until it was lost in the blue distance. That would be the valley Robertson talked about, the way to Kentuck.

He had thirty bullets already molded and his horn was full of powder. He could cross the river without even getting his feet wet, there on that down log. In two minutes he could be across the river and on his way through that valley. He put his hand down to feel if his cutty was in its sheath. The hand came up, remained motionless a moment, then reached out to break off a twig of spicewood. He wondered if Frank was out of hearing. It would be all right if he could just call out to Frank that he was off across the river to see what the country was like. But if he got back within talking distance Frank would argue him out of going.

He stood there, chewing the spicewood and the call he dreaded came: "Rion, you coming?"

He threw the twig down and turned back through the willows. He had not gone far before he saw Frank, sitting on the roots of a tree, his pack beside him—he always took his pack off if he stopped to rest so much as a minute. He looked up as Rion approached. "You took so long I thought you'd decided to go on to Kentuck!"

Rion did not answer. Frank got up. They walked on. "I wish we could have come horse-back," Rion said presently. "We might have crossed the river then. If Mrs. Wagner hadn't got sick we could all a been up here by this time."

Frank shook his head. "You're crazy, man. Those horses couldn't have lasted another day. And if they could have made it the women couldn't. Cassy was white around the gills this morning."

"She ain't sick. She's just in the family way," Rion said.

Frank laughed. "I'm not surprised."

Rion stopped short. "What do you mean by that? You think I ain't been treating your sister right?"

Frank gave him back a straight look. "I don't mean a thing by it, Outlaw. You can make something out of it if you want to."

They walked on in silence. In a few minutes Rion increased his pace in order to get ahead of Frank. For over two months now he had been with Frank, day in, day out. He was sick of looking at him, sick of hearing his voice that always sounded, even when he was looking right at you, as if he were 'way off somewhere else. And half the time he was using outlandish words that nobody knew the meaning of. A born schoolmaster. He had no business in the woods. It was a waste of powder to let him draw a bead on game. He couldn't even dress game after somebody else had brought it down. That doe yesterday. He had dragged the carcass off while Rion was trying to get another shot. When Rion got back the camp was running in blood and Frank was greasy up to his elbows. Rion rarely said anything to

Frank but the sight had angered him. "Here," he told him, "there's a right and a wrong way to do everything. You let me dress my own meat after this." Most men would have got their backs up but Frank just laughed and handed him the knife.

He wondered what would become of Frank if you turned him out in the woods by himself. Most likely he would starve to death and somebody some day would find a few buttons or those books he carried in his pack scattered at the foot of a tree and that would be the end of Master Francis Dawson, son of the Church of England minister.

He was pleased by the picture and his anger died. He began to look about him. This was the island Findley talked about, all right. He liked the looks of it. Several times in his wanderings in the woods he had come on places that he liked better than others. He would be going along, not paying much attention to the country except to look for trace of game, and all of a sudden he would ford a stream or push through underbrush and there the place would be and it would be like he had been there before. They were not always the same kind of places. Sometimes it would be a rich bottom with a creek running through it where a man might build a house, or sometimes a wild, piney place on top of a mountain where a man couldn't live unless it was like a bird on a bough, but no matter how different the places were, the feeling was the same, and it would come over him as soon as he saw the place, and would make him turn back as he was leaving and make him see it sometimes months after he was gone—that feeling like he ought to stop, like he was *meant* to stop there.

He had got that feeling a few minutes ago, when he turned back from the head of the island. Standing where he was you could almost see over the whole island. Three hundred acres, at least, and all of it as flat as the palm of your hand. Rich land, too. The trees showed that. Beech and sugar trees and elms and hickories and no undergrowth, just the black trunks rising out of last year's pale beech leaves. It was a place a man could sit down in and get his breath, a place to live, if a man could get possession. But no man could. Robertson said that this land had been cleared time out of mind by the Indians. They never lived here but they came back to have their talks here, and according to Robertson those Cherokee Indians did a lot of talking.

The fort up there on the bluff just across from the island stood, in a way, for an Indian victory. Colonel William Byrd had come through here with a company of militia ten years ago to aid the soldiers besieged at Fort Loudon. But on their way they had got the news that the fort had fallen. Officers and men had all been massacred two days after they marched out of the fort and Colonel Montgomery, coming up from South Carolina to join the Virginians, had turned tail when he heard that. There was no good going to help men who were already dead or scalped; so Byrd and his Virginians had fallen back to this place and had built that fort up there on the bluff. He and Frank had walked around it in the half-dark after they had got up here last night. Two log houses and a double line of palisades making a yard for horses, all stoutly built, though somewhat fallen into disrepair.

The stockade gate was wide open, the door of the houses not even bolted. There was nothing inside but some rubbish the soldiers had left. Last night Frank had wanted to cook their game on the big fireplace and sleep inside, too, but Rion had said no. He had got to the point where he didn't like being inside walls. If any Indians did come roaming around they would think nothing of seeing two hunters cooking their meat over their own fire, but white men inside a fort would be something else again and two men shut in there would have no chance at all if it came to fighting.

He had come to the lower end of the island. The streams united again here, then broke in white falls over a wide stone ledge. An ideal site for a mill. On the right was a small mountain—its headland rose in a black bluff sheer from the water. On the other side of the river was a ridge, shaped like a cat lying down. He had a fancy to see what was beyond it, so without saying anything to Frank he waded the stream and climbed the ridge. It sloped down into a sizable valley. At the end of the valley was another mountain, longer but not as high as the one across the river.

He remembered that Robertson had said that a white man, by the name of Eaton lived on a long ridge not twenty miles from his own house and not far from the Long Island.

"That'd be the ridge," he said to himself. He looked back. Frank was in sight, just about to ford the stream. He called to him. "I'm going down here a ways," and plunged down the slope into the valley.

The land was rolling, as well timbered as the island, though the woods were not quite as open. He looked back, saw that Frank was following him and hurried on. He was in the river bottom now. The trees were opening up: sugar trees, and buckeyes growing alongside of them, and blue ash and gum and hickory. He stooped down and scooping up some of the loamy, dark earth, held it in his hands a moment, then flung it to the ground. "Beats our bottom at home," he thought. "Any land around here'll beat it all hollow."

He thought for the first time in weeks of what he would be doing if he were back on the Yadkin. The middle of June, or was it the last? The corn he had planted before he left would be knee-high by now. He would just about be chopping it out for the last time. If he kept going on as he planned to do he'd have no crop this season. He couldn't get where he was going soon enough to make a crop. The tail of August: he'd be lucky if he got settled then. Another year would roll around before he got a chance to put a seed in the ground. A queer thing to go through a whole season without raising anything. He remembered once he'd asked Daniel Boone about that, how he felt on those long hunts of his when spring came. Didn't he ever want to break up some ground? Boone said no; said when he was off in the woods away from everybody the seasons weren't the same as in the settlements. He could go off and stay a year, ten years, if it warn't for his family, and be content not to put his hand to a plough.

Rion came to where a creek flowed into the river. He struck up through the cane and followed it. Narrow, with a deep bed, a master tumbler. "Falls creek," he said aloud. "Falls creek. That's you," for he found himself giving things names as he went along. "That right over to the left now, that's Eaton's ridge. Bound to be. Robertson, he'd name it the same." The idea warmed him. He and Robertson, when he got back to Doe creek, could talk about the country. He had ranged far enough in two days to learn the lay of the land. When Robertson mentioned a stream or a mountain he would know in reason where it was.

The stream bent farther to the left. He followed it. He was at the base of the ridge. Another stream came down the ridge to join his Falls creek. He debated whether he should follow it up the hill but he turned still farther to the left with the main stream and came out in a grove of beeches. The ridge rose sharply here. One big beech there on the side of the hill would go in the next storm. The earth had fallen away from under it. The roots, clawing like great fingers, went down ten or fifteen feet to solid ground. A spring came up between these roots. He bent and looked into it. The basin was not much bigger than a scalding kettle but the water was deep and clear over a white sand bottom. He turned and looked behind him. The stream ran through a sandy ravine. A little higher up where there was mold the sides of the ravine were plumed with ferns but down here it was all white sand. All about him were big beeches, as fine trees as he'd ever seen. One there on his right had so much room to itself that it had put out branches almost to the ground. Clearing must have been done here some time or other.

He came up over a little rise and was on level ground. The beeches were giving way to sugar trees. A regular grove of them. But there were some fine elms down near the river.

Frank was moving towards him. He held in his hand a plant whose dark green leaves sprang from a thick red stem.

"That ain't nothing but old Jamestown weed," Rion told him.

Frank nodded. "It grows on rich land. There's white clover down in that bottom." He sat down on a fallen tree, took some plants out of his shot pouch, and laid them out on the trunk; then sat with bent head, studying them.

Rion suddenly realized that all the way over the mountains Frank had not plucked a single weed. "Seems more like himself today than he has for a long time," he thought. Aloud he said, "You going to start you another collection when we get settled?"

"The minute we get settled," Frank said. He picked up one of the weeds, a gross looking plant with thick leaves and two spiky flowers growing on it. "You don't often find these growing in twos," he said.

"It's just old Adam and Eve," Rion said, "Break them bulbs and you'll get glue."

Frank laughed. "You'd make a good naturalist, Rion. I don't believe I ever brought you a plant that you couldn't tell me something about it."

"I don't go through the woods blindfold," Rion said, "but I don't holler out every time I come across a weed: 'Oh, la, la, the pretty thing!'" And he mimicked his brother-in-law's voice.

The next minute he felt ashamed of himself and looked at Frank to see how he was taking what he had said. But Frank hardly seemed to have heard him. He was studying his plants. "He don't hardly know I'm here," Rion thought. "He'd sit here all day on this log studying those weeds if I'd let him." He stood up. "I believe I'll have a look over the top of the hill."

Frank's eyes were still bent on the plant. "Oughtn't we to be starting back?" he asked absently.

"The sun's still high," Rion told him, "and it ain't going to take me long to get on top of that ridge. I just want to see what it's like on the other side."

He walked swiftly back towards the spring, then struck up the side of the hill. It was rough going until he emerged on the top of the ridge. It was broader than he had thought it would be, so broad that standing there in what he judged would be the middle he could not see across it. The growth was the same as down in the valley except that there was more pine and fewer beeches. He glanced at the sun and moved northwest. He had not gone far before he heard a rustling in the bushes. The sound continued for a moment and stopped. Some fellow might be watching him from the bushes.

He walked on. He did not think it was Indians. There was nothing to bring them up on this ridge—game wasn't likely to range up here with all that water and grass down in the valley. It might be Eaton. Robertson said that he lived on a ridge not far from Long Island. Coming up the way he had he'd be likely to strike Eaton's place. He turned and walked back in the direction from which the noise came.

"Is that Amos Eaton?" he called out.

There was no answer. Rion stepped quickly behind a tree and primed his gun.

There was silence for several minutes, then he heard the sound again, not one sound but a succession of heavy rustlings. He stepped out from behind the tree and moved off north, walking as softly as he could. In that moment the quiet was shattered by a deep-throated bay.

Rion worked through the brush and came upon an open, grassy spot. Before a big oak tree an old hound bitch stood, hind legs braced, head back, giving tongue.

Rion squatted down and called to her: "Come here, Gal!"

Her tail wagged once. She cocked an ear back but kept her eyes on the tree. The trunk was stout and had a split near the base. The low hanging boughs concealed the hollow. A bough suddenly shook. A sand-colored muzzle showed for a second through the red leaves.

Rion rose and fired. A heavy body tumbled to the ground. The bitch leaped forward and began tearing at it.

Rion went over quickly. The blood pumped from the bear's side. His eyes were glazing. Rion put another bullet in him. He clawed once and was still. The bitch was worrying the carcass. Rion quieted her with a hand laid on the scruff of her neck while he examined an old wound, obviously made by a bear, on her hind leg. He slapped her on the shoulder. "Come on, Gal, let's go home!"

She leaped off across the glade, barking. He followed. Between two laurel bushes the ground was worn smooth. He pushed through and was on a path. The hound had disappeared. He did not have another sight of her until he emerged at the end of the long green tunnel and saw before him a one-room cabin with a small lean-to built on the side. An enormous, flat rock up-tilted itself almost at the doorstep. A tall, bearded man lay sprawled on the rock, chewing a sassafras twig. The bitch was jumping up against the rock, trying to reach the man. Three young hounds who had been sunning themselves behind the man rose, yawning. The man sat up, his legs dangling over the edge of the rock. He looked at Rion and called over his shoulder, "Jane, come here!"

A thin, tall woman who looked not unlike the man appeared in the doorway and stood silently looking at Rion.

The man cursed the bitch and gently pushed her down with his foot. "Hit's a stranger," he said to the woman.

Rion stepped forward. "Howdy," he said. "My name's Outlaw. I been staying down on Doe creek with James Robertson. . . . I reckon you'll be Amos Eaton?"

The man spat out his twig and dropped his bare feet to the ground. "That's my name," he said, "and I don't care who knows it." His eyes went from Rion's face to his blood-spattered leg.

"I got me a bear," Rion said. "There's six hundred pounds of bear meat laying out there in the thicket. You give me a hand and I'll help you get it to the house." He laughed. "It's your meat, I reckon. When I come up that old bitch of yours was getting ready to go in on him by herself."

Eaton looked at the hound, standing with her yellow eyes fixed on him. "That old Chloe," he said. "We can't do nothing with her. Come spring she's out after b'ar. Go by herself if she can't git nobody to go with her."

"Y'ought not to let her out by herself," Rion said. "She'll get killed one of these days."

The man shook his head. "I can't help that. Besides I got three of her pups."

"You better give me one," Rion said boldly. "I been wanting me a good bear dog."

"You can have one," Eaton said. "You can have whiche'er one you'll lead off." He motioned to the doorstep. "Sit down, Stranger." He turned again and called to the woman, "Ain't you got no persimmon wine or nothing? Master Outlaw's done come all the way from Doe creek."

The woman had been standing there all the time in the doorway. As her husband spoke she disappeared into the dark of the cabin and came back with a jug and two horns. She fixed her eyes on Rion again and did not take them off, even looking back over her shoulder at him, as she moved between the two men to set the jug and the horns on the rock.

The man drew a corncob stopper from the jug and tilted it. "Hit's three year old," he said. "Jenny made it first year we come here." He poured the horn full. The woman came and took the horn from him and handed it to Rion, then took a hornful for herself. As she drank her eyes still fixed Rion over the rim of the horn. They were strange eyes, light and clear and as green as the grass that sprang up there at the side of the rock. And she had a strange way of looking at you. It wasn't natural to look at a person as hard as that.

Rion moved over to set his horn down on the rock. She motioned to him to have it filled again. Her lips worked for a moment; then she spoke in a harsh voice: "How's Mistress Robertson?"

"She's well," Rion said, "but she's got her hands full. There's me and my wife and her brother and an old couple in our party. The old lady's down sick. But Mrs. Robertson was curing her up fast. We look to be able to travel in a day or two."

The woman put her hand to her throat as if to ease out the words. "You bring 'em by here," she said and then as if frightened by the sound of her own voice darted past him into the house.

Eaton looked after her. "She ain't e'er had any little ones," he said. "Reminds me of a mare I had once. Barren she was from the start but as fine a traveler as you'd see. That was back in Pennsylvania where there was rods. She was a fine traveler, I say, and easiest horse I ever had to keep in good order, except when she come in. She'd take a spell then and she'd mope and she'd mow, one time kicked right out of the stable. I didn't bother breeding her when I wasn't going to get anything out of her, but I've thought me since I'd have saved myself trouble if I'd taken her to the stallion."

He patted the rock. "You set down here by me. Say you come from Robertson's?" He laughed excitedly, "I mind when they come into the country. I was hunting down on Doe creek and come to a crib full of corn. Thinks I, that's queer; and I pushed through the bushes and there was folks rolling logs for a house. Folks," he repeated, "rolling logs for a house. I stayed with 'em three days, I did, and lent a hand. Robertson, he's a particular man and every joist had to be just right but I'd a helped him if he'd worked me harder than he did. We'd been here two winters by that time and seemed like I was hungry to see some folks. Jane, she had a fit when I come back and told her. Wanted to move down there by 'em. Said she could do for the children. I told her there war'n't but one. I took her down there after they got in the house. Charles Robertson was there with his wife and children. She was after them children all the time, wanted to bring one home with her. Mrs. Charles wouldn't let her do it and the little chap didn't want to come. Looks like she scared him, making so much of him."

"Why don't you move down that way," Rion said, "seeing as she's so set on neighbors?"

Eaton shook his head. "I built that lean-to there and that's all the building I'm going to do for a while. I ain't going to stay here long. This land, it don't suit me. I stopped here in the first place because this house was already built."

"You mean you found a house already built?"

"I come through the woods one day in early fall and there was this house with the land already cleared. We'd aimed to go on further, up above the island. But I says if somebody has done already built me a house and cleared me some land I don't want their work to go to waste, so we moved in and been here ever since."

"Ain't you afraid the man that built the house'll come back and put you out?"

Eaton shook his head. "He ain't coming back."

"Where'd he go?"

Eaton rose. "You come with me. I'll show you where he went."

Rion followed him around the back of the house. The laurel closed
in again here but the dogs had worn paths through the thicket. They
followed a path for a quarter of a mile and came out on the edge of
the mountain. They stood on a ledge of rock that overhung the edge.
Eaton pointed to the valley below. "Thar's whar he went. Down in
the valley and been thar ever since."

The valley was perfectly level, a meadow covered with blue grass.
Rion studied it, chewing his under lip. "I ain't ever seen anything
prettier'n that," he said finally. His voice rose. "A man wouldn't
want better land than that. It'd be a pleasure to put a plough in it.
Ain't it rich? I bet it's rich as cream!"

"It's rich, all right," Eaton said. "Fletcher—that was the feller fell
off this rock—took him up some land down there and built him a
house, right there where you see them cliffs shining. He'd cleared
him an acre or so—you can see the stumps there now—and he was
gitting along fine when a party of surveyors come through here and
told him he'd have to move, that the King had done granted all that
land to the Pendletons. That's the Pendleton grant. Eight hundred
thousand acres of it, them surveyors said, and all belongs to the Pendletons."

"Who are the Pendletons?"

"They stay back in Virginia. But there the land is waiting for
them if they ever take a notion to come. There was two or three
other fellers settled in there but they got off, too, soon as they got
the word."

He had started back up the path. Rion took a last look at the valley
and followed him. "What made Fletcher settle up on this ridge?" he
asked Eaton when he had caught up with him.

"I don't know. Reckon he liked to look down at that valley and
think about how rich it was. He was a fiddling man. Used to bring
a jug out here on this rock and fiddle, cuss the Pendletons, some said.
He was fiddling here on that rock one night, towards sundown when
he went over, give one whoop and over he went. They was an Indian
out hunting that day heard him. Come and found the fiddle on the
rock and knew what happened. Said he'd have gone down after him
but it warn't no use." He laughed. "Jane, when we first come here,
she used to be after me to go down and find what was left and bury
hit and put up a stone. But I told her that warn't no use either. He
was down where he wanted to be, with plenty of tombstones all
around him and the leaves'd put dirt over him fast enough."

They were at the house. The woman was sitting on the doorstep. "What you going to give us for supper?" he asked her. "You got company now. What you going to give him?"

Rion looked over his shoulder at the sun. Its rays were already slanting. "I can't stay the night," he said. "Thank you kindly but I can't stay the night. I left my brother-in-law sitting on a log down at the foot of the ridge."

"Well, you can holler him up, can't you? We'll step over here to the brow and holler him up."

Rion shook his head. "I been away two nights. They might be worrying about me. I'm a married man."

"Well," Eaton said, "you going to settle?"

"I don't know," Rion said. "I've got to get back to the Doe now."

The woman when he said he could not stay the night, had turned her face away from him to stare straight ahead. She looked back at him now. "You got any children?"

"No," he said, "I ain't got any yet."

The man laughed. "You'll have 'em. You settle down near us and I'll give 'em one of Chloe's pups. Ever' child you put up I'll match him with a pup. That's fair now, ain't it?"

Rion laughed. "Fair enough." He picked his pack up from where he had laid it on the rock. "You come along with me now and I'll help you get that bear meat up to the house. It's more'n one man can handle."

Eaton shook his head. "I got a horse. I'll take him over and load up what I want. I don't want to get all of that meat up here to the house. Ain't but two of us to eat. It'd go bad on us and that'd bring the buzzards around. You help yourself now. Don't you stint yourself on that meat."

"I'll cut off steaks," Rion said, "and I'll take the toes. I always did like the toes. Brown 'em right and you got a tasty tid-bit." He shouldered his pack and held up his hand in salute. "Thank you kindly. I'll be starting."

Neither of them spoke. The man had dropped down beside the woman. They sat staring after him and he knew as he turned into the green tunnel of laurel, that they were still staring. He traversed the thicket, found the bear's carcass undisturbed, took what meat he could carry and started down the ridge. It was later than he had thought. Down here in the valley it was almost dark except where a few splinters of gold light struck through the broad sugar tree leaves.

Frank was kneeling under a tree building up a crib of twigs, Indian fashion. As Rion approached he reached for his rifle, primed it and brought the lock down. The spark flashed in the pan. Frank lit a splinter from it, then flung the splinter on to the twigs. They caught one after another. A single pointed flame shot up. Rion strode into the circle of its light.

Frank, still on his knees, looked up. "I got hungry," he said, "so I built a fire. Thought we might as well fry some of those collops."

Rion did not answer. He was staring at the flame. It burned so purely. And now others were springing up around it, lighting this one place under the tree but seeming to deepen the dusk beyond. If he took up this land he might build a house in this grove. His hearthstone might be right where this fire was burning now, between the big sugar tree and the elm. He wished that there were more daylight left so that he could walk about in the grove to see if he could find a better place. He unknotted the thongs that held his pack and let it drop to the ground.

"You did right," he said. "We'll stop here the night."

CHAPTER 29

IT WAS LATE afternoon when Rion and Frank and Robertson got to the island. The Indians were waiting on the bluff just outside the fort. The old chief—he was as yellow as a guinea and his ears hung as low as a hound's under the weight of his silver ear-rings—was sitting on a chopping block beside the gate. A white man lay on the grass at his feet. Another younger Indian stood a little to the side of them.

The Robertson party crossed the sluice and started up the path. Rion as he went kept looking up at the Indians. The old chief and the white man had risen and were coming to meet them. The other Indian stood facing them, with his arms folded, staring straight over their heads. The old chief wore a shirt of stroud cloth but this one had on nothing but his flap and the feather in his scalp lock. He had a broad face for an Indian and he had had smallpox at some time; there were pits in his face deep enough to hide a currant in.

"He's a mean looking devil, ain't he?" Rion whispered to Robertson.

Robertson turned his head, stared out of his pale grey eyes and compressed his lips but did not answer. Rion was sorry he had spoken. All the way up here Robertson had been preaching about being careful not to get the Indians' dander up. The old boy up there on the chopping block was a very important Indian, what they called "the peace chief," which meant that he managed everything except when they went to war. His name was Atta Kulla Kulla and when he was just a chap he had been taken across the water and had dined with the King and a lot of government bigwigs besides, and had never forgotten it. He was vain as the devil and took a lot of handling, Robertson said. Well, he, Rion, would keep his mouth shut after this and leave things to Robertson. He had done his part this morning when he got the hatchets and the rest of the gear away from Jacob. The old coot had got saucy after two or three days of fat living. When Rion first broached the matter to him he refused right off, said that he would ask Robertson if he would stand by and see an old man robbed of his goods. They were out under the trees when he said that. Rion took him by the arm and walked him down to the river. "Now see here," he told him, "you wouldn't never have known Robertson but for me. You'd be laying out there amongst the pines, what the buzzards hadn't carried off, and your hatchets and your stroud cloth'd be alongside of you, doing nobody no good. I brought you across the mountains and I'm going to have my pay. Thirty hatchets for me and ten for Frank and a bolt of cloth for the two of us for helping Robertson make the deal with the Indians. I've thought it all out and that's fair. You don't think about nothing but trading, but a man's sweat is worth something. You going to pay me for mine." He looked him straight in the eye when he said that. "You going to pay me for mine," he repeated, "or you ain't going to ever be in a shape to pay anybody else."

Jacob had flung his hands up over his head. "You'll hang yet!" he said in a whisper and turned and made for the house. Rion followed him. "I don't want you mouthing to the womenfolks about this," he said, "or Robertson either."

Jacob did not answer him, but when they got ready to start for the island he said he would not go, that he was satisfied to have Rion and Frank represent him.

They were at the top of the bluff now. The white man was standing before them, the old chief a little behind him and the big, young Indian was walking slowly over to join the old chief.

The dark, long-nosed man gave a quick, nervous smile and held out his hand. "Good day to you, Master Robertson."

"Good day to you, John Vann," Robertson said. "Here's my friends. Master Outlaw and Master Dawson."

The white man shook hands with Rion and Frank, then slightly turned his head. As if at the signal, the two Indians stepped forward, the old one slightly in advance. He stopped before Robertson, looked at him for a second, then leaning forward slipped his right arm through Robertson's left arm and held Robertson pressed against his side for as long as it would take to kiss a woman, then released him.

His thin, yellow face was on a level with Rion's now. A moment ago his eyes had been dark slits under the heavy lids. They were opening wider. He smiled a little as he pressed Rion to him in the gesture that was strangely like the caress one might give a woman. He stepped aside. The young chief came up. He did not smile and his black gaze flickered over the white man's face so swiftly that Rion had for a second the feeling that something hot and molten had flowed over him.

Rion stepped back, keeping his features impassive by an effort. It was a good thing, he thought, that Robertson had warned him. If he'd followed his feelings he'd have given that last devil a whack that would have sent him winding instead of standing up there and all but kissing him.

He became aware that the linguister was staring at him. The corners of the man's mouth turned up a little as he said, "They take you by the arms instead of shaking hands."

"I've seen Indians before," Rion told him.

"Cherokees?"

"No. Catawbas and Saponas."

Robertson suddenly spoke, saying each word slowly and carefully as if he were speaking to a child: "I would walk a long way through the woods to take the great Atta Kulla Kulla by the arm."

The linguister turned his head and said something. Evidently he was repeating what Robertson had said. The old chief smiled and bowed his head, then motioned towards the fort. They walked over there and he sat down on the chopping block while Rion and the others sat down on nearby logs, all except the young chief. He stood behind his father with his arms folded. As he took his place half a dozen young bucks came up out of the bushes and stood with him.

Robertson paid no attention to them but proceeded to business. Rion had laid the deerskin sack that held the gear at his feet. He pointed to the sack now as he spoke. He and his friends had started up from Doe creek, he said, as soon as they heard that the great Atta Kulla Kulla was coming to the island. They had come because they wanted to have a talk with him. They would come to the Long Island or any other place where he was going to be any time he would send them word.

The linguister had flung himself down on the ground between the whites and the Indians and had not seemed to be listening very carefully but as soon as Robertson stopped he sat up and spoke in their language.

When he stopped speaking Robertson got up. He stood with his hands hanging at his sides, his head a little lifted, and looking off through the trees delivered a speech. It was about a young chief called the White Owl. When this chief was a boy he had shot down a great bear. Then he had killed a lot of men in some battle. Several years later, when he was only nineteen he had been chosen to sail across the water in a great boat with other chiefs to talk with the White Father. And the White Father had taken him by the hand and drawn the briars from his feet.

This same chief, older now but still strong, sat in the councils of his nation. He was a beloved man. Among all the Cherokees there was no chief greater than Atta Kulla Kulla."

Rion had not known till then that the speech was about Atta Kulla Kulla. He looked over at him quickly. The old man's head was thrown back, the eyes almost closed, the lips parted. As Rion watched, the chief's nostrils flickered. His black eyes opened wide. They looked enormous in the yellow face and they glistened as Rion had once seen the petals of a lily glisten under the vigorous strokes of a bumblebee's legs. "Robertson knows how to tickle him, all right," he thought.

Robertson was bending over to unfasten the sack when the young chief suddenly began speaking.

Robertson, still bending over, raised his head. "What does he say?" he asked sharply.

Vann seemed on the point of laughing. "He says they better go look at this land before they hand it over to you," he reported.

Robertson looked over at the Carpenter. The old chief's eyes were again slits under half-fallen lids; the whole face seemed to have shrunk. A moment ago he had cast his shirt aside and had been sitting with his body exposed to the warm sun but now he drew his shirt on and rose.

Vann got up too. "Seeing as the Canoe wants it we better go look at the land," he told Robertson.

Robertson made a gesture towards the bundle on the ground. Rion picked it up. Robertson went on ahead with the old chief. The young chief whom Vann had called 'the Canoe' followed them, and Rion and Frank and the linguister came after. When they got to the foot of the bluff Rion looked back for the other Indians. They had disappeared.

Rion walked on beside the linguister. The young chief was just in front of them. He was over six feet tall and broad for an Indian, but he stepped as light as a woman. No, he moved like a 'coon, that same sidewise gait that Rion had often found himself comparing to the swaying of a branch. It came from putting one foot down in the track that the other foot had just made.

Rion gazed at the naked back, finding a fascination in contemplating flesh so unlike his own. He jerked his thumb towards the Indian. "What did you say his name was?"

"Tsu-gun-sini. Means Dragging Canoe."

"Dragon Canoe?" Rion asked.

The man shook his head. "Like you drag a canoe. Reckon it's because he lives on an island. He's chief of a big island down in the Tellico river. He's the old chief's son."

Frank came up on the linguister's other side. "How long have you lived with these Indians?" he asked.

The man turned his head and gave him a sharp glance. "I don't, so to speak, live with them. I got business in the Nation so I been staying there 'tending to it. I was at Chota all this winter but before that I was at Tellico."

"Are there many other white men at Chota?" Frank asked.

"Well, there's my partner, Dick Pearis and Isaac Fallin and Jarrot Williams. They come in pretty regular. And there's Captain Gist. He's there representing the governor."

"I should like to learn the language," Frank said thoughtfully. "How long did it take you to learn it?"

"I couldn't rightly say. You stay around 'em and listen to 'em talk and all of a sudden it kind of makes sense to you, and the first thing you know you're linguisting. I been linguisting for the Carpenter for a good while now."

"What makes you call him 'the Carpenter'?" Rion said.

"It's because he can join a treaty up so neat, like you notch logs for a house. I forget who it was gave him that name. He likes you to call him by it."

They had come through the river bottom and were walking up through the grove of sugar trees. The Carpenter stopped and sat down on a log near the spring. Robertson sat down beside him. The young bucks whom Rion had last seen at the fort suddenly appeared from the side of the ridge and took up their stand behind the Carpenter's log. As they crossed the open space in front of the log, Rion noticed that they all had the same gait that he had noticed in the Canoe.

"Don't they move like 'coons?" he said to Frank.

Frank did not hear him. He was watching the Canoe. The Canoe had not stopped where the others did. He had gone on straight ahead to the spring. He stopped for a second near a pile of stones, then dived into the bushes. In a few minutes he came out, carrying in his hand a rock the size of a brick bat. He threw it down on the pile and joined the others. The Carpenter had been talking to the linguister but his eyes were on his son. He got up at once, searched until he found a sizable rock, then threw it on the pile. The young bucks also set off on a hunt for rocks until every Indian there had thrown one on the pile.

Vann said something to the Canoe, then translated his reply: "He says that a brave warrior is buried there. He has forgotten his name but he says that he was a brave man. That's the way they do," he added. "Every time they pass where a good fighter is buried they put another rock on his grave. Makes a nice little tombstone in time."

The Carpenter had taken up a stick and was drawing a map on the ground. It had a little the shape of a bat flying with out-stretched wings. The head would be the spring here, the left wing the river bottom and that other wing the land across the river that Rion had promised to take up for Jacob. Rion wondered how much would be included in the whole tract. Six or seven hundred acres, Robertson calculated, if you counted Jacob's land in too. It was a pretty little valley, all right. The more he saw of it the better he liked it. Robertson was talking again. If the Cherokees wanted to give their white brothers this land to sit down on for a while, the white brothers would be glad and would promise to keep peace always. In return they wished to give their brothers, the Cherokees, the presents they had brought across the mountains. The thirty hatchets were of the best quality and the stroud cloth was of the finest dye and new.

The Carpenter was not listening to Robertson. He was staring at his son. The Dragging Canoe had come up and was standing looking down on the map. His arms were folded. His broad, pitted face was sunk on his chest. He raised his head suddenly and spoke.

"What does he say?" Robertson asked eagerly.

"He says it's not the land, it's the trees. This is a holy place, he says."

The Carpenter rose from his log and was speaking. Rion had the feeling that the man would like to be taller than he was. His thin frame was held as taut as a bowstring. His chin was elevated. He spoke rapidly with nervous gestures, looking past his son.

When he stopped Vann said: "Atta Kulla Kulla is now an old man but he has been in the council forty winters and he has been head man for over forty winters. He never heard before that this was a sacred grove."

The Canoe spoke and Vann again translated: "The Canoe says that he came this way many years ago, when he was a boy, with Old Hop—that's their emperor. He says that Old Hop made him throw a rock on that grave there and told him that this was a holy place. Old Hop said he did not know why it was holy but that when *he* was a boy they always visited this grove when they came to the Long Island."

The Carpenter sat down again. He sat for a few minutes, his eyes bent on the ground. When he finally spoke it was in a gentle, almost sweet voice. The look as if he might be laughing at you all the time came over Vann's face as he translated. "He says that he is an old man and has sat in council for over fifty years but he says that times have changed. It used to be that it was the old men who knew which ways were right and which places were sacred, but now the young men tell the old. He says that times have changed."

There was a long silence. Dragging Canoe kept his eyes on the ground and did not answer. Finally Vann said to Robertson, "You better go ahead."

Robertson untied the sack and laid the hatchets out on the red stroud cloth. The Canoe did not pay any attention to the goods but the other young Indians came up and looked at them and the Carpenter picked up several of the hatchets and hefted them in his hand.

The trade seemed to be over. Robertson was getting out the sheet of paper on which Frank had drawn up the lease. He took from his pocket the quill and the flask of ink he had made last night from oak gall. He was motioning to Rion. Rion stepped forward and signed his name. Frank signed his. Then Vann took the quill and after he was through handed it to the Carpenter, who made his mark. When the Carpenter had made his mark, he handed the quill back to Vann who boldly took it up to the Canoe. The Canoe came forward and made his mark like the others. And now Robertson was signing, last of all.

Rion drew his breath in sharply and looked at Frank. It was over.

For a time there it had looked as if there might be a hitch but things had gone off all right after all. The land was his, to sit down on as they said, as long as he pleased.

Robertson was telling Vann that they could not stay the night with their Cherokee brothers. They had promised Amos Eaton to come to his cabin this night. By this time he would be waiting for them up there on the brow.

There was the arm-shaking all over again and they were off up the ridge. Nobody had spoken except for one quick whisper from Frank to Robertson. "I'm glad you got us away before they changed their minds."

They climbed on up the ridge. When they were halfway up Rion looked back. He saw something flash through the leaves and knew it was the glint of a musket barrel. Then he heard a light chatter of voices, very different from the tones he had heard while he was with the Indians. The chatter went on. A wisp of smoke was rising.

"I believe those devils are going to camp there the night," he said. "Camp right there on my land."

CHAPTER 30

RION AND FRANK AND ROBERTSON got back to Doe creek by sundown on Wednesday. The next morning the Outlaw party started up the Watauga. They had to camp on the way one night and reached the creek that Rion had named Falls early the next morning. They stood on the left bank of the river and looked across. The Holston was narrower than the Yadkin and flowed faster. There were deep pools but they always ended in white water. The water in these pools was colored green by the reflection of the leaves. Even the spray of the falls seemed tinged with green.

Rion turned his eyes and looked up the river. "She falls pretty fast after she leaves the island," he said. He turned his eyes to the opposite bank. Willows fringed the river but there were giant sycamores mingled with them. Beyond the sycamores he could see the sleek grey trunks of the beeches that covered all the bottom. A little farther on, he knew, the river took a great bend—this bottom land was enclosed on three sides by water.

"Where's my land?" Jacob was asking.

Rion pointed to the land on the other side of Falls creek. "It lays about the same as this bottom," he said, "except there ain't any big spring on it. But if you build your house up towards the ridge you'll be nigh as close to the spring as we are."

Jacob was looking at the place where the creek flowed into the river. "I may not build up that way. I may build me right here where the creek flows in. That high spot there'd do for a mill site. Plenty flow to turn the wheel."

Rion looked where he was pointing. It was true. The place was ideal for a mill site. He wondered why he had not thought of that himself. "There ain't anything wrong with the other bank," he said quickly. "I may put up a mill myself."

Frank laughed. "You both better get across the river first."

They went up the river for some distance but found no place shallower than the place where they had first stopped. Rion stepped in there and found that except for a few holes it was never more than waist deep. "I reckon it's as good a ford as we'll find," he told them.

He and Frank drove the horses across and then came back and helped the women with their bundles. As they started up through the bottom, Rion looked back over his shoulder at the tumbling water. "Ain't it funny? Here I was living on a ford on the Yadkin and now I come all the way through the wilderness and found me another ford."

They came to the rise, passed it, and went on down to the spring and drank the cold water where it bubbled up between the sycamore roots. They stood looking back into the grove.

"That place there on the rise," Cassy said, "that'd be a good place for the house."

"It's what I thought," Rion said. "It's what I thought first day I come here."

Rion and Cassy went on ahead of the others back up the rise. Down in the ravine where the trees were sparser a little light broke through but up here it was all shade. They threw their heads back and looked up into dense layers of green that were unbroken except where a stray shaft of sunlight would fringe the edge of some leaf.

"It'll take a sight of clearing," Rion said.

Cassy still had her head back, gazing. "When I was little I used to look up into the sugar tree leaves and I'd think it was like the ocean."

"It's because the leaves are so broad," Rion said. "They don't let the light through."

She had left him and was walking towards the ashes of the camp-fires. It was the remains of two fires: the Indians had made their fire on top of the one he and Frank had made. She had dropped her bundle and was stepping lightly around an imaginary rectangle. "The house could go in here. . . . All these sugar trees," she raised her finger and counted, "three, four, six, eight, all these sugar trees they'd have to go, but that big shellbark hickory, you could leave it standing."

"Yes," Rion said, "it'd be handy, having a shellbark right at your door."

"Front door," she said, "The house would face this way."

"South," he said mechanically. "It'll face a little southwest." He looked about him as he spoke. The dense shade suddenly seemed lighter. That was because the trees were gone. They were gone and in their place rose four walls, hewn logs, not white but already weathered, one window, maybe two, and a shingle roof. He might even build a lean-to. . . .

He set his rifle against a tree, turned back to Gal who had come up and was standing patiently behind him, unstrapped the pack and flung it to the ground. "Here," he said to Cassy, "you and Mrs. Wagner finish unloading and drive them horses towards the bottom. Ain't no use to hobble them. When you git there salt 'em a little and let 'em go." He took his heavy axe from the pack, then got Frank's from the other pack and took it over to him. "Come on," he said, "we might as well start on them trees now."

The three men walked down towards the river. Jacob would have stopped at the foot of the slope but Rion went on farther. "Let's get to the bottom land. I want to clear that first."

"The varmints'll eat your crop if you get that far from the house," Jacob told him.

"No, they won't. I'll have me a close fence up time this crop is out of the ground."

" 'Tain't much use to plant corn now," Jacob said. "It ain't going to have time to make."

"We might have a late fall," Rion said, "and if we don't we'll get ro's'n ears and fodder."

They were in the bottom now. He walked about looking at the trees and stopped before a tall, slender white oak. "Let's start on this one," he said and heaved his axe back and set it quivering in the oak's side. After a half hour's chopping it fell with a crash, as perfect a house log as you'd find anywhere in thick woods but with its heart still green.

They stood eyeing the great spread of the branches. "We felled her just right," Frank said. "See, she brought that beech down with her."

Jacob took his axe and stepped in among the boughs. "I'll just cut off these limbs," he said.

Frank and Rion found another oak and set to work on it. When it was ready to fall it balanced on a thin white strip no larger around than a man's leg. Frank stepped back but Rion delivered one more blow from his side. It was one blow too many. The white strip buckled, the trunk twisted sidewise and fell on top of the newly fallen tree. Jacob clapped his hands to his ears and Frank jumped as if he thought he might be standing in the wrong place. Then he laughed. "There go the timbers for your house."

Jacob went up and examined the two trunks at the place where they had collided. "It ain't hurt none. Just a little place dented here where she hit. I'd go on and use her if 't'was me."

Rion shook his head. "No, I ain't going to put her in my house. She may not be strained but I'd be worrying all the time for fear she was. I ain't going to put her in my house."

They cut down five more oaks, then set to work on the beeches. Rion looked about him from time to time calculating how much ground they had covered. A quarter acre at least he thought.

At noon Cassy came down with a bucket full of water and the big skillet full of turkey stew. With her came Amos Eaton. He had heard the trees falling, he said, and knew that the clearing must have started. He brought with him wrapped in a piece of old cloth a handful of pumpkin and melon seeds and he was leading one of Chloe's pups.

Rion thanked him. "We'll put us a truck patch in the middle of the corn," he said.

He watched Amos fasten the young hound to a sapling. "Is that my bear dog?" he asked.

Amos gave Cassy a sly glance. "I told you I'd match ever' child you put up," he said.

"He ain't going to stay," Mrs. Wagner said. "It's too close. He'll be running home."

"I'll give him a bait of venison tonight," Rion said. "And I'll take him out one of these days soon."

Frank looked at the dog thoughtfully. "You'd better call him Sirius."

Rion shook his head. "That don't call so well. . . . Where'd you get that name?"

"Sirius was the name of Orion's hound."

"Sir'us," Rion said. "Well, I better call him that then. Here, Sir'us," and he snapped his fingers at the hound.

Eaton squatted on the ground and watched them for a while. When he left he promised to bring his wife with him next time he came down.

They worked into the late afternoon. Frank put down his axe, stood back, and wiped his forehead on his sleeve. "I'm through for the day," he said.

Jacob got up from the stump where he had been resting. "Rion, it'll be dark pretty soon. You better quit too."

Rion looked up. Between him and the other two lay a great mass of fallen trees. Many trunks had fallen across each other. Here and there an arm thrust up wildly out of a sea of leaves. He gazed into the branches of a great ash and was amazed to find its pointed leaves as fresh, as green as if they still inhabited the upper air. "It's like they don't know they're down," he thought.

He let his eyes rove over the green. He had cut out nearly an acre of trees. Under that great mass of writhen boughs lay his field. He looked into the forest. Here beside his field more trunks went up, oak, ash, beech, hickory and elm. Another field was there waiting for him to uncover it. He could do it with another day's work, if the other two men would stay with him.

Jacob called again. "Come on. It'll be dark here in a minute. You'll cut yourself if you try to chop in the dark."

A moment ago Rion had flung his axe from him when he had finished felling a tree. He stooped and picked it up, and felt the pull of the muscles across the small of his back and realized that this was the hardest day's work he had done in many a day. "You can talk all you want to about driving a pack train," he thought, "but ain't anything like a day's chopping to twist a man's insides. No wonder old Jacob's been perched on a stump half the day."

He walked around the side of the fallen trees and caught up with Frank and Jacob. They walked slowly towards the camp. They could see the fire flickering through the trees and the figures of the two women moving above it. They had unpacked everything and had the camp neatly arranged. Mrs. Wagner's pots and pans were set out on one end of the big down log where the old chief had sat. She had contrived to bring a good many things with her. He noticed a pewter pitcher and there were four pewter plates set out on the end of the log, for all the world like a table. He set his rifle and axe against a tree and walked over and lifted one of the plates.

"I didn't know you had these with you."

The old woman looked up from the stew she was stirring. "I wasn't going to bring 'em out on the trip. If I had you'd a made me throw 'em away."

She took the skillet from the fire and dished out the stew. They took up their plates and began eating. Cassy looked at a blue platter. "I don't know what made me bring that," she said. "There's a lot of other things I'd rather have."

"If I'd only brought some kind of a bowl," Mrs. Wagner said. "I ain't got any bowl big enough to mix bread in."

Rion threw back his head and laughed. "You ain't got any flour, you ain't got any meal and here you are worrying about a bowl to mix 'em in!"

"This land wouldn't bring good wheat," Jacob said. "Too loamy."

"Well, it'll bring corn till the world looks level," Rion said. "Amos Eaton, he got a hundred bushel off that acre of his up there on the ridge."

The stew was all gone. Cassy had taken the big skillet up and was scouring it with sand from the ravine. She stayed her hand and straightened up. "Amos Eaton says he'll have snap beans inside of two weeks." She gazed past them into the fire. "In two weeks," she said.

"He'll divide with us," Rion said. "He's a cross-grained fellow but he's free-handed. He'll divide with us."

She turned around and looked at him, fixedly and yet as if she did not see him. Her eyes were a little dilated and shone. There was fierceness in their shine. You got that look sometimes from a beast when it knew its hour was come but it was strange to see it in the eyes of a woman. He noticed what he had not really noticed until now—how thin her face was. A little cup was sunk in each cheek and the skin over her brow was drawn so tight that it shone. He thought of the child that was making. "It ain't her," he thought, "it's the baby crying out in her. It's afraid it ain't going to get enough to eat."

He cursed the slowness of the seasons. The middle of June and most if not all of the wild greens gone. Amos Eaton was not the man to make much of a garden. He would divide with them what he had but it would be just a few messes of snaps. Corn would not be in silk before August. Till then she'd have to get along without bread or greens. But how could she? She was eating less every day, had got so now she could hardly touch game. . . .

He could not sit still. He took his axe and walking a little way from the fire felled a sizable tree, and then cut down half a dozen saplings. There was a big down log near by. He rolled it up to the fire, cleared out the space in front of it, then set up his cross-pole and slanted the other poles from it to the log. He got the two old buffalo robes and some quilts from the packs and placed them over the slanting poles with rocks laid at the edges to keep them down. "Now," he said to the woman, "you got your house. Least it's all the house you'll have till the land is cleared."

Mrs. Wagner was pleased. "Jacob, go cut me some boughs," she said, "I'll make my bed right up against that log."

The men went out and cut some boughs. The two married couples made their beds inside the tent but Frank said he would sleep outside. Mrs. Wagner and Jacob crawled in and Cassy followed them in a few minutes. Rion still sat with Frank beside the fire. He was tired and at the same time he felt exhilarated, as if his muscles were reluctant to stop working. He got his axe and hunted around till he found a buckeye tree and cut it down. He chopped out a big chunk and brought it to the fire and whittled on it with his knife until he had fashioned it into a bowl. He set it down, looked at it a moment, then spoke to Mrs. Wagner asleep now in the tent: "There! You got you a bread bowl, can you get any dough to put in it."

CHAPTER 31

WHEN RION got up the next morning nobody was stirring. He remembered a long, shallow stretch of water that they had passed just before the creek flowed into the Holston. The bank shelved down to the water gently. He had noticed deer droppings there and the sharp tracks of the little hoofs. It was probably a watering place.

The place was at least a mile from the house. He crossed the creek and was on what they were already calling "Jacob's land." He had not examined this bottom as carefully as he had examined his own land, and as he went down through the dawning light he looked about him. The bottom lay just as well as his own and seemed to have the same kind of growth but it was not quite as big. That was as it should be. Jacob could not expect to ride over here on another man's shoulders and come out as well as he did. It was worth something to the old coot to live near a strong neighbor who would protect him if need be.

He went down to the river, walked along the bank, and came to the pool he remembered. There was more cover here than there was on the other bank. He crouched down, primed his gun, rested it in the crotch of a willow and waited.

It had been quiet enough as he came along but now the birds were starting, all at once, like a crowd of people in church. They were perched in the trees along the bank but every so often one would fly down to bathe in the shallows. Something scarlet flashed past him: a parakeet skimming up from the water to rest on a limb over his head. The woods were full of those little devils. He wished he could capture one for Jocasta. He had known an Indian once had one for a pet. It sat on his shoulder and pecked crumbs from between his lips. A wild thing trusted you a lot to do that.

Light was growing everywhere but here in the woods it was not the sharp light that comes with the sun's rays. It was rather a gradual withdrawing of darkness. There was little wind but the mist on the river was lifting, swirling upward slowly as he had seen clouds lifting once from a mountain top.

There was a rustle in the forest that might have been made by a dry twig falling. Another of those slight rustles and then he saw the delicate forms crowding through the mist: a buck and two does. The buck came first. He stepped out into the middle of the pool and stood still, his head up. The does on either side of him lowered their heads and drank. While they drank the buck turned his head to the left and brought his muzzle slowly down along the edge of the gentle wind. Rion waited until the muzzle had swung almost full circle and was pointed downstream. Then he fired.

The buck dropped in his tracks, falling sidewise against one of the does. She whirled and was up the bank almost as fast as the other one. Their tails blazed white. They were gone.

Rion came out from the willows and stooped over the buck. He was already dead, full grown, with a coat as red as madder and the burr of his antlers just formed. Rion cut his head off and let it float downstream, doused the bleeding neck in the water for several minutes, then dragged the carcass to the bank, heaved it over his shoulders and set off for the camp.

Up at the camp they were stirring. Rion cut the meat out and Mrs. Wagner broiled some collops for breakfast. "Makes a change from turkey," she said and tried to make Cassy eat one. But Cassy refused and said that she would boil herself some milkweed she had found. "I can't eat deer meat this early in the morning," she said.

When the men had finished eating they took their axes and went to the bottom. They worked all morning and most of the afternoon. Then, just as the sun's rays were beginning to slant they prepared to burn the acre off. Jacob had been cutting limbs off the logs they were going to save. Rion and Frank helped him roll these logs to a safe distance, then heaped the limbs and brush into a big pile in the middle of the clearing and raked the ground about the pile free from twigs for ten or fifteen feet on every side.

The women had come down to see the sight. The air was full of the sweet smell of fading leaves. Mrs. Wagner shook her head when she saw the fallen boughs rearing halfway to the tops of the trees left standing. "How in the Name you ever going to get all that green wood to burn?"

Rion came up, dragging some small pine trees that he had cut on the ridge. He put several of them at the side of the mound and dropped shellbark in amongst them. The other pines he laid end to end all the way around the base of the heap, then set fire to the shellbark. It kindled at once. The light wood caught and the small pine trees. The blaze spread from tree to tree until the whole mound was encircled with a thin garland of fire.

Cassy stood beside Rion. She drew her breath in as the odor of burning resin filled the air. "Don't it smell good?"

"Wait till the hickory starts burning," Rion said. "Ain't nothing smells as good as burning hickory."

He left her and walked to the other side of the mound. The pines were nearly all burned now but the fire had started in only a few places. He might have to cut more pines and start it all over again. He rounded the circle and came back to where Cassy was still standing. A shellbark hickory had caught and the fire was going in at last. The tree, as large as any they had cut down, was not sound enough for timber so they had not lopped its branches off. It lay slanting, its trunk protruding from the base of the pile, its branches stretching almost to the top. The flames had started on the loose curls of bark on the trunk and were spreading fast. The whole tree flamed, then the flames died suddenly: the red, glowing skeleton was suspended there in the heart of the heap. There was a rush of wind from the south. The skeleton crumbled into embers which whirled and fell smoldering on the green leaves. Smoke arose in great plumes and drifted upwards among the trees still left standing.

The women moved back, coughing, but Rion stayed where he was watching the flames struggle with the smoke. Other hickories had caught from that shower of sparks. Here and there a flame was creeping along the outside of the mound. But some of the trees were sullen and slow to burn. When the flames reached a buckeye they stopped and had to go around some other way. But they kept mounting. A bed of burning coals was forming in the middle. It grew all the time as the embers dropped down on it. Suddenly a great wall of flame rose from that glowing bed and raced upward. It towered above the pile and licked at the boughs of an oak tree near by as if it would take the trees still left standing. The whole pile crackled. The heat was now so fierce that it burned his face. But Rion did not move. He stood rubbing his hands as if their motion could hasten the burning. If he could only use fire to clear all his land! Set it burning as this great flame was now burning and consume the forest instead of felling each tree laboriously by hand.

They were calling him from the slope. He turned away into the cooler air. As he went he put his hand up to his face. The flesh felt hot even to his calloused fingers. "Little more and I'd a burnt myself," he muttered.

At the camp Cassy was waiting for him, and they went down to the spring. Rion was already stripped to a breech clout. He waded downstream till he found a little falls and sat there at the foot of the ledge, letting the water foam up over his shoulders and throwing it on his face and chest until he was cool all through, then rose and waded upstream to where Cassy was sitting on the cairn of stones. She was looking off up the ridge. He followed the direction of her eyes. A figure was moving off through the pines. He stooped over quickly and picked up his rifle. Cassy laughed. "It ain't anybody but Jane Eaton. She's been around here all day."

"She come to visit?"

She laughed again. "She came to visit but she don't dare. She won't come nearer than this and if we holler at her she runs off."

He gazed after the woman. "She's left something," he said. "Ain't that something setting up there on the rock?"

He ascended the ridge a little way and found, sitting on a flat rock beside the path that was already beginning to be worn, an open piggin full of buttermilk. He carried it back to Cassy. "She's brought you some buttermilk," he said.

She looked down into the white round piggin, then up at him. "Buttermilk," she said in a whisper.

"You take a drink," he said and tilted the vessel before her.

She put her head down and drank, as he had seen thirsty horses drink, in one long, powerful gulp, then she raised her head and stepped back a little. "I better not drink it all up. The others ought to have some."

"They don't crave it like you do," he said, continuing to hold the vessel up to her. She lowered her lips to it and drank again, not quite as much this time, and then for a while she was raising her head and lowering it, taking little sips, holding the milk in her mouth sometimes, as if she wanted to get all the taste she could out of it. Finally she stopped drinking and just stood there, looking down at what was left.

"Did it taste good?" he asked.

She smiled at him and ran her tongue over her lips to remove the little beads of milks. "I haven't ever had anything as good in my whole life."

PART THREE

"Such were the first inhabitants of Kentucky and Tennessee, of whom there are now remaining but very few. It was they who began to clear those fertile countries, and wrested them from the savages who ferociously disputed their right; it was they, in short, who made themselves masters of the possessions, after five or six years bloody war: but the long habit of a wandering and idle life has prevented their enjoying the fruits of their labours. . . ."

FRANÇOIS ANDRÉ MICHAUX

CHAPTER 32

AFTER ARCHY had come up on the other side of the creek and had seen the buffalo sign, he walked about over the trampled ground, searching for a lick. There was no lick, no salt cropping out anywhere but they evidently came here often; there was one place where you could tell they had been wallowing. He left the creek and walked up over the rise. There were a few trees here, mostly ash and hickory. The trunks had great, peeled places where the buffalo had been rubbing themselves. You could see the tracks plain, even up here where the ground was not so moist. The tracks were fresh, the particles of earth still glistening where they had been thrown up by the big cowhoofs. He walked on to the end of the grove. The prairie began. There was an opening in the tall grass before him, wide at first, then narrowing to what looked like a giant rabbit run: the buffalo street. He'd heard the old folks tell about them and now here he was standing on one. He loaded his rifle and set the trigger, then, half crouching, crept down the green alley. When he had gone a little way he stopped and, raising his head level with the grass, strained his eyes to look over the prairie. In these few minutes it had grown darker, and the ground was more broken on this side of the creek, and there was some brush mixed with the grass. Those dark lumps that he saw dotting the prairie might be only clumps of wild plum. He waited, motionless, holding his breath. The dark blot nearest him split, into two moving forms. One headed north, slowly. The other was coming this way.

He stood there cursing the failing light and watching the dark back slide through the grass. He would have to move soon or the beast would graze right over him. And there were others grazing the same way; he would have to move. But that might stampede the herd. He took two steps backward as softly as he could and in that moment the wind changed. The nearest buffalo caught his scent and stopped grazing. His great, woolly head rose, hung there, black against the sky. Archy fired, aiming for the shoulder. There was a bellow. Hoofs struck the earth. Archy dove to the side. The grasses whistled as the beast rushed past him and then there was no sound: the beast had stopped and was watching him. The wind fanned Archy's cheek as he got to his feet and he knew that it was taking his scent straight to the herd. They were making for the woods, the lot of them, with a noise like the pounding of a thousand flails on a threshing floor. The wounded beast heard them, too, and was off, coughing. Archy, listening, thought that the bullet must have lodged in the lungs. In that case the buffalo might choke on the blood and drop soon. There was still a chance, if he could trail him a little way.

He re-loaded and started running. He struck the street and kept to it, thinking he might make better time that way. The herd had disappeared into the woods but he could still hear the hoofs in the distance, and now out here on the prairie he heard a sound that might come from the wounded buffalo. He had stopped to listen, fearing that the beast might already have dropped and he gone past him when the sound came again, a low such as a cow gives when she has cried for her calf a long time.

He stepped forward cautiously. The beast might be down but he could get up again: there was no use taking chances. The grasses in front of him whispered. A form rose out of the tall grass. A man. He thrust the muzzle of his musket into Archy's belly and said something Archy could not understand.

Archy stepped back quickly. The muzzle followed him. With his left hand the man took Archy's gun away from him, then he laughed and spoke again, seeming to ask a question in a kind of talk Archy had never heard before.

The steel ring bit into Archy's stomach. He heard himself speaking: "All right . . . All right!" and then in a voice that sounded high and angry, "You better watch out. My folks'll be along in a minute."

The man lowered his musket and almost in the same motion leaned forward and laid his hand on Archy's shoulder, pressing him into step beside him. They were moving towards the woods. Archy turned his head and looked back. Dusk had settled over the prairie but there in the grove a thin point of fire flickered. The folks had come up and were camped for the night.

He flung his arm up, catching the Indian across the face, then dodged and made off through the grass. The blood roared in his ears. His legs moved faster than they had ever moved before in his life. His arms beat the air and he fancied as each arm shot out that it clutched and thrust behind him part of the prairie. He had been for some minutes in this delicious, headlong flight when he tripped in a noosed vine and went down. He was halfway to his feet when suddenly his whole body was cloven by fire. He went down again, face forward in the grass. The fire licked over him, then it was gone, all but one sharp flame. That burned in his shoulder. He put his hand up and drew it away wet with blood and at the same time felt the blade of the flame protruding cold and sharp from his shoulder.

The flame was dying. His body that had been so taut went limp. He rolled over on his side, feeling, drowsy. But something was touching his bare leg. He opened his eyes. The Indian was bending over him.

He drew the hatchet from the boy's shoulder and pulled him to his feet. He put his arm around him and drew him forward swiftly over the prairie. He said something, then looked behind him to where the fire burned in the grove and said the same thing again, and went forward even faster.

They went through deep woods for a long time. Finally they saw a light shining through the trees. As they drew near it, the Indian began to shout and drew Archy forward on the run.

There were half a dozen Indians squatting around the fire. When Archy's Indian started shouting they stood up. The Indian dragged Archy into the circle of the firelight and the other Indians crowded around the two of them. They looked at Archy as if they had never seen a white man before. One of them felt his thin arms, then passed his hand wonderingly over his hair which he had had Mrs. Wagner clip short for coolness only that morning. Another Indian touched the edge of his wound and made a soft, mournful sound. Finally his captor made the others stand back and led him over and sat him down with his back against a tree, then passed a buckskin thong about his body. His wound—it was in the fleshy part of his shoulder —was still bleeding. He was beginning to feel faint. He closed his eyes, not caring, now that they had tied him up, what happened.

After a while he felt something hard and hot pressing against his lips and opened his eyes. A pannikin fresh from the fire was being held up to him. The liquid in it was not rum or brandy but blood: the buffalo's blood. He sickened at the odor and turned his head aside but the Indian kept the pannikin against his lips and finally he drank. The Indian—it was his captor—then knelt down beside him and bound a poultice of wet leaves on his shoulder. The wound had begun to ache. The cool, wet leaves soothed it a little.

The Indian got up from where he had been squatting and looked down at Archy. He was a young Indian, not much older than Archy himself, though better muscled. He had on nothing but a breech clout. His head was shaved or plucked except for the one long black lock of hair that dangled down to the small of his back.

He looked at Archy and smiled and pointed. Archy looked where he was pointing and saw two more Indians coming into camp. They had rawhide thongs slung over their shoulders and were bending forward, straining like oxen. The burden bumped up over a root and Archy saw that it was the buffalo cut into quarters. A third Indian suddenly ran up behind them, balancing the buffalo head on his shoulders.

He laid it down on the ground beside the quartered carcass. Archy's Indian went over and picked it up. Suddenly he was crouching, coming towards Archy, holding the great, woolly head up beside his own. He kicked out with one leg and gave the same plaintive low that Archy had heard out on the prairie, at the same time looking at Archy and laughing.

Archy made a smile with his stiff lips, and looked away from the dark, bright eyes. The Indian laid the head down and ran and leaped into the air and gave again the cry that he had given when they first came into camp.

Some Indians who were kneeling on the other side of the fire, working at something, turned around and smiled over their shoulders at the leaping Indian. Their smiles turned him grave. He stopped his capering and drawing his knife out of its sheath began to help the others cut up the buffalo meat.

Archy's head felt clearer and his wound did not burn so much. He leaned back against the tree and stretched his legs.

A big Indian got up and came over to the fire. He held a little, cup-like thing in his hand. He bent over and warmed it in the flames then chipped at it with the point of his knife. Archy's eyes went to the gap he had made in the circle and he saw what it was they were working over: a dead man. A young, dead Indian. He lay on a litter of boughs, his feet pointing up straight and his hands folded on his chest. He was naked except for his flap, and his body was sleek with grease up to the peak of his scalp. His face was painted red. A pipe was laid on his breast. A quiver full of arrows was by his side. There was a hole in his left breast just under the tittie. The place around it was dark under the grease as if much blood had run there.

The big Indian went over to the corpse. He flaked a little paint from the stone cup into his palm, then with the tip of a feather he outlined the dead man's eyelids and ran the feather over the groove in the upper lip. He stood a moment, looking down at the dead man, then he gave a cry so low and so mournful that it sent a chill down Archy's spine. He sat down at the foot of the litter, his arms folded, his head sunk on his breast.

The other Indians moved slowly away from the corpse and Archy saw, leaning against a tree not ten feet away from him, a white man bound in the same way that he was.

This white man was looking in Archy's direction but he was not looking at Archy or even at the dead Indian. He was looking off through the trees. A young fellow, not more than eighteen or twenty, with a yellow beard covering most of his face. His eyes were grey, rather pale, and had a dead look to them. They were fixed on something that was about on a level with Archy's head and a little to the left of him and then suddenly they began moving, the man's eyes, swinging from tree to tree as if he were watching something that was going by fast—no, as if he himself were out there in his own look, dodging from tree to tree.

Archy turned his head to see what the man was watching but there was nothing under the trees. He looked back at the man and saw a muscle in the left cheek flicker as if it would leap out of the skin, and then he heard the cry and the mournful Indian was there, leaping at the white man and giving his terrible cry over and over again.

The other Indians ran up and held him back and spoke to him in soothing tones; they led him back to the foot of the bier where he sat down again with his arms folded and his head sunk on his chest.

The white man had not moved except to throw his head a little back and he did not speak now, only let out his breath in a long sigh and sent his eyes to dodging through the trees again.

They came on Archy's face, passed it, then came back again. He winked and stared and was running his tongue over his lips as if he were about to speak, when two Indians came up and lifted the litter that held the corpse. They walked off through the trees with it, the big Indian nearest the litter and the others following single file. As they went they were singing in melancholy voices.

The white man spoke: "Where'd they get you?"

Archy jerked his thumb over his shoulder. "Out there on the prairie. I was chasing a buffalo and run into 'em."

The white man's eyes swung away before Archy had finished. He was watching the Indians. He said: "It was that big fellow's brother I shot."

"Where'd they get hold of you?" Archy asked.

"Three days ago," the man said, "going through that first gap. The others went on. But we was needing meat, so Tom Murphy and I stayed behind to do a day's hunting."

They were both silent, watching the Indians through the trees. They had filled the grave and now they were marching around it. Three times they made the circuit; then they scattered into the woods. The grave was there alone for a long time. At last they came back. Each one had a rock in his hand and he stood a little way off and cast it upon the grave.

They were coming back through the trees. The white man watched them a minute; then he said: "Tom Murphy run like a deer . . . I wouldn't a thought it of him."

Archy was silent, watching the Indians approach. They were talking among themselves, all except the big Indian who went off by himself and sat down against a tree. The others were cutting up the buffalo meat. One had part of the hump and was roasting it on a spit and another broiled the heart on the coals.

When the meat was done they brought some to Archy. He ate it, washing it down with a kind of tea they gave him. They offered meat and drink to the other white man. He took a morsel of meat in his mouth but spat it out, pointing to his throat.

The Indians had finished their meal. They got up. One of them was stamping out the embers. Another was tying up the rest of the hump in an elkskin. They picked up their rifles and seemed ready to start somewhere. Archy's captor came over, smiling, and untied him and took him by the arm. Two other Indians were getting the white man up. He had evidently been tied up longer than Archy had. He stumbled when he got to his feet. One of the Indians had to kneel down and rub his legs before they would hold up under him. The big Indian got up and stood near while this was going on, as if he could not bear to see the white man get so much attention. The white man would not look at him while the others were rubbing his legs. He looked at Archy. "It was Tom running that made me fire so quick," he said, "he run and that got me rattled."

The Indian holding his arm made a sign that they were ready to start. He jerked his eyes away from Archy's face. They set off, with the Indians, through the deep woods.

CHAPTER 33

THEY TRAVELED through the woods for eight days, then one evening they came upon a valley shaped like a bowl and shallow, with a rim of low mountains encircling it on every side. Archy had been feverish from his wound for three days and nights and the Indians stopped to let him rest as soon as they came in sight of this valley. He sat down on a big rock in the pass and stayed there a while, hardly knowing what went on around him until someone touched him on the arm. He looked up. His captor was standing beside him, smiling and pointing down into the valley.

The sun had just gone down. It was already hazy here in the mountains but light still played on the plain below. Archy could see a river winding through the plain, with a smaller river flowing into it. There were stretches of woods all over the valley but there were open spaces, with dark spots in them that looked like houses, and beside these houses were broad patches of bright green. Staring with dull eyes, he knew these for corn fields, and the thought came to him that it was too fair a land to be possessed by savages.

He got up without making any answer to the Indian and they went on down the slope. After a while they came to what looked like a town. The Indians stopped when they came in sight of it. The smiling Indian stepped off into the woods and with his hatchet felled a hickory sapling. Out of the heart of it he split a stout withe and then sat down, cross legged, and began bending it into a hoop. The other Indians fell on Archy and the other white man, Grady, and stripped them of their clothes. Archy's Indian came back with the hickory withe fashioned into a yoke such as is put on breachy stock. He held it high and slid it over Archy's head. Archy felt the cool, wet wood settle on his shoulders and felt the haft strike against his ankle and thought that there was little chance for him to get away from them now. He heard Grady speak:

"Why don't they put one on me?"

"I don't know," he said.

Another Indian came up with two peeled wands. He handed one to Archy and one to Grady and made a sign that they were to wave the wands and sing. Then the Indians drew up in two lines of four each, with Archy and Grady in the middle, and went whooping and yelling into the town.

They ran down a lane, between log houses that were wattled with mud, till they came to a big open square. There was a great elm tree in this square and at the end of the square a cabin larger than any of the others. They ran around this square three times, yelling louder now that people had come out of the cabins to look at them. Finally they stopped. Archy had tripped on his yoke several times and had been struck once when he stopped yelling for a minute. The clamor died. He shut his eyes and stood with his head down, not caring, for the moment, whether they hit him or not, wanting only to get his breath back. When he looked up the square was full of people. Women mostly. No, there was an old, white-headed man and next to him another Indian whose hair was almost as white.

He felt a hand on the back of his head. An Indian had come up behind him and was lifting a lock of his hair. He looked over the heads of the old men, up into the branches of the elm. *An elm threw its branches up bolder than any tree in the world. They'll scalp us now. It's time to scalp us.*

He shut his eyes. In a second the sharp point would cut into the flesh. Hold it back! . . . *Hold it back*! . . . Lessie Robinson. Last August, the way home from church. *She come up and put her hands on me* then turned off into the bushes. White dust makes leaves grey where we are laying. *Sudden and hot* . . . No matter, Promise never again sin, never sin again, never . . .

There was a little tug, the hiss of a blade through hair and the hand was gone. He opened his eyes. The two bent old Indians were still looking at him. There was another man with them, an old, blue-eyed white man, stark naked like them except for his breech clout. He was looking past Archy, past Grady to where some of the Indians were digging around the roots of the big tree.

Archy turned his head and saw them drop the hair they had taken from him and Grady down into the hole. Three or four of them jumped on it and stamped the dirt down and now they were coming back. Archy's captor, the smiling Indian, was beating himself on the breast and giving again the cry he had given so often coming through the woods.

The white man half put out his hand, then drew it back. He said: "My name is Mouncy. Fred Mouncy. I been here in the Nation since the fall of Fort Loudon."

"What nation?" Grady said. "We been in the woods. We don't know where we are."

"You in the Overhill Cherokees. The town of Setticoe." He stood there and looked from one to the other. "Which one of you fellers killed Pumpkin Boy?"

"I shot him," Grady said.

The man had been looking at Grady hard but he took his eyes away quick. The Indians were coming up. He went over and talked to them in their language. They talked back like they were mad. The man said the same thing to them over and over again, but they would not listen. Finally the Indian whose brother had been killed broke away and went running around yelling and waving his toma-hawk.

The man stood a minute, looking around, at the women, at the old men; then he came back to Archy and Grady. He took hold of Archy's arm. "You better come with me," he said.

Archy started off with him, but stopped. "Can't Grady come too?" he asked.

The old white man shook his head. "We'll come back and get him in a few minutes."

Archy did not know whether Grady had heard what the man said. He went up to him. "He says we'll be back in a few min-utes."

Grady was watching an Indian who was squatting on the ground, mixing some black stuff in a stone pot but he turned around and looked at Archy. His eyes were bright and steady. They took in Archy and even took in Mouncy there behind him. "Where you going?" he asked.

Archy did not know what to answer, but Mouncy called out, "Over here, to one of these houses."

Grady turned around again without waiting for the answer. Archy stood there beside him, so close to him that he could feel the heat from his body, could smell his sweat. He put his hand out and touched Grady's arm and would have said something else, but Grady did not seem to know he was there; he was watching where the black stuff was being mixed in the stone pot.

They went off between two rows of houses. They turned a corner and were out of sight of the big tree and the staring Indians. They passed one old woman smoking a pipe in a doorway, then went on down to the end of the street and stopped before a house. It was like all the others, the doorway small and black. Archy had to bend down to go inside.

He straightened up and he felt that somebody had come and taken his head off his shoulders and left nothing there at all. But he could see. A big stone pot stood on a bench there by the door and over in the far corner was a low couch covered with skins.

Mouncy had him by the arm. "You lay down," he said. "You lay down over there in the corner."

He helped Archy over to the couch and laid his hand on his forehead. "You got fever, boy," he said.

He went away. Archy shut his eyes. The couch was higher than it had been when he lay down on it and he himself was lighter. That was because of his head; it felt like a dried cymling. He was afraid he would fall off the couch and he put his hand out and clutched at the coarse bear skin. But the hairs came away in his hand and he was sliding. "Mouncy!" he called. "You said your name was Mouncy?"

The man was back beside him. "You drink this," he said. "Drink this and it might help. Ain't no use in feeding you."

Archy opened his eyes suddenly. "Get me those apples up there on that tree."

"I'll get 'em for you in a minute," the man said. "You ain't got no business eating now. You got fever."

He went away. Archy kept his eyes open but he was lying on his back and could not see anything except the ceiling of the hut. It was dark up there but he could see two little men walking like flies on the arched timbers. Their eyes stuck out of their heads like bug's eyes and were made of phosphorus. They had bows and arrows and the little arrows they shot kept pelting the bearskin. Archy was afraid they would shoot at him and he called to Mouncy to come get them down.

"It's the Thunder Boys," Mouncy said. "They ain't going to do no harm. You shut your eyes and go to sleep."

Archy rolled over on his side and now he could not see the ceiling or anything except over on the other side of the room a grey oval that had something shaped like a man's head sticking up in the middle of it.

Mouncy sat in the doorway and smoked. He spoke aloud in a musing voice: "If there was any of the headmen here they wouldn't do it. If they hadn't all gone to the ball play . . ."

"Where is the ball play?" Archy asked in a quiet, natural tone.

"It's at Chota. And you're here in Setticoe. I wish *I* warn't. I never liked this town. Don't never come here when I can help it. . . . They brought 'em here because it was in this town it all started. But I reckon if Willenawah was here he'd let 'em go ahead. He ain't ever forgot Fort Loudon."

Archy started up. "They going to take us to Fort Loudon?"

"They can't take you there. They ain't no fort now."

"I live at Trading Ford," Archy said. "You can see our house from the river."

"You poor loony! You ain't likely to see it again. Lay down now. Ain't nobody going to hurt *you*."

Archy began to cry. "You said you was my friend!"

"I ain't nobody's friend."

Archy snivelled into the coarse hair of the skin. The man paid no attention to him but went on talking. "Fred Mouncy . . . His Majesty's Tenth Essex. I been here in the Nation ever since the fall of Fort Loudon . . ."

There was a rush of feet outside, a mighty yelling.

"They're taking him to the mound," the man said softly, then went on talking to himself:

"They say I ain't no live man, say something come and got my soul. And they don't like it because I don't take a woman. I couldn't do nothing with no woman. I ain't had my manhood since Fort Loudon. The tenth day after they sieged us I woke up and it was gone."

From some distance off came the beat of a drum. Then one lone voice was singing. Then the drum beat again and then yells, sharp and rhythmical. "They've started round," the man said in the same soft tone.

The odor of burning wood rose and hung on the May air. The old man got up and walked over to the bed. Archy was lying on his back, his eyes closed. The old man listened to his harsh breathing for a moment and went back to his seat in the doorway.

"I come up there behind the parapet. Luke Croft was doing guard. It was the tenth day. The horseflesh was all gone and the cattle. We was down to beans. A quart to divide between three men. The Carpenter, he come in that day and eat with the officers and Captain Demere asked him: 'What news of the towns?' He laughed and said he warn't the man to ask, that the Indians kept everything from him . . . I went up on the parapet where Luke was doing guard. I said, 'Luke, I been starved so long I lost my manhood.' He laughed and said them wasn't the parts to worry about and just then them devils rose from the bushes across the river and laughed and held their hands up and said they was sore from scalping and said they had beaten Montgomery back and taken his drums and a horse load of ammunition . . ."

There was a sudden high scream and then another. The white man shifted his feet and his pipe fell out of his hand, clattering on to a stone.

"We hauled our flag down August ninth," he said, "and paraded the garrison. There was one hundred and eighty men and sixty women and some children. We buried the cannon in the well and some swords and we started out. One hundred and forty miles to Fort Prince George. We marched fifteen miles that day and camped where Cane creek empties into Tellico. Oconostota and Judd's Friend had promised to march with us but they didn't come. Only Judd's Friend come into camp late that evening and stayed awhile and then went off to Tellico.

"Captain Demere knew they ought to a marched with us. We kept watch all that night. It was just after reveille sounded in the morning. Lieutenant Adamson was getting the orders for the day when they fired on him and the captain from ambush. He fired back and wounded one of them and then they was all over the camp. They say now there was seven hundred of them. We couldn't a done nothing if we'd tried. But the officers called to surrender . . ."

The screams kept on all the time now, sharp but running together so that they made a continuous high keening. The man did not seem to hear them. He said:

"They scalped the captain there on the field and made him dance a long time and when he give out they cut off his arms and legs and stuffed dirt in his mouth and they said 'You want land. You got it now.'

"They brought me and the others to this town, Setticoe. In the late evening it was and they took us out to the mound. They made us dance with rattles and then they took Luke Croft and put him on the mound and built the fire around him, low so he wouldn't breathe in the flame. They tied me there and told me it was my turn, after Luke. Luke lasted all night. He wouldn't holler, so they took him out and put water on his face and gave him drink and rested him, then built the fire up again. I was near and I called to him, 'Give up, man! For God's sake, give up!'

"He turned his head and looked at me. I can't ever forget his eyes, red from the fire. 'I'll get out,' he said, 'I'll get out and I'll kill 'em. I'll rip 'em open,' he said and told what he'd do with the guts after he got them out.

"They came up and took him out of the fire. They had gun barrels heated and they stuck 'em up him. He hollered then. I don't know whether he was dead when they cut his arms and legs off . . . They didn't burn me. A runner come from Oconostota, saying there was peace . . ."

The moaning had died long ago. There had been for a while a yelling and singing from the Indians but that had died too and the whole air was still.

Mouncy stopped talking, suddenly, as if he were just then hearing his own voice. He got up and going over to the bed stood for several minutes beside the sleeping boy. He came back and stood in the doorway. "Ain't it quiet?" he said.

CHAPTER 34

THE DARK LANTHORN stood in her small field and looked over her rows of beans. The plants were sturdy, already showing the second tier of broad green leaves. Three times since they had been planted she had stirred the earth in every hill and yesterday she had given the corn the same working. There was nothing to do now for several days. She laid her hoe against the fence post and walked down the rows. When she came to where the small corn was planted she pulled a stalk towards her and stripped the husks back: the grains were the size of an eight-month baby's tooth. She smoothed the husks back over the gleaming ear and let the stalk swing away from her. As she stepped over the two suspended hickory withes that formed her fence she glanced up over her head. Between the drooping plumes of the hemlock a patch of sky was visible, blue except for the milk-pale disc of the new moon. She raised her wrinkled right hand in an old gesture. "I greet thee, Father of my Mother. When it is like this again we will still be seeing each other." She murmured the words under her breath and as she went along the path, still gazing at the moon, she thought that the next time the pale disc hung there her corn would be in the milk, ready for roasting.

She followed the path to the summer house. Inside she stopped before a tall earthen jar and dipped up a gourd full of sour corn gruel. As she did so she laid her palm against the side of the jar, feeling with pleasure the moisture that had gathered there. She had been hoeing in the field for several hours, in the heat of the day, and she was sweating all over. She took another drink of the gruel, relishing its coolness as much as its sharp, agreeable flavor, then turned away to a chest in the far corner. She lifted the lid and took out half a dozen small earthenware pots on a big tray. She crossed the room, going slowly, looking about her as if it had been some other woman's house. A little light came in through the slits in the wall which her husband had made to admit the summer air. It fell in slanting rays on a white-washed floor, on white stools and on walls that had been

233

white-washed as high as the Lanthorn's thin old arms would reach. The pot of marly clay and the twig brush still stood there at the side of the hearth but she would not need them again, until, in the time of the green-eared moon she would make her hearth ready for the new fire.

Balancing her tray of pots she went out through the narrow doorway. Everything inside the summer house was in order—even the reed couches showed white legs under their coverings of skins—and she still had many hours of daylight left. She went swiftly towards the corner of the yard where her carpet hung in its wooden frame.

She had gathered the hemp last summer in the open lands and all during the fall of the leaf she had worked, pulling it, steeping it, beating it and finally in the dark winter house spinning it off the distaff. Others, lying on the couches, would ask why she worked so hard in the cold moon and she had no answer except that she wanted to have her carpet ready for the frame by the time the dogwood was white. The dogwood and the redbud, too, were gone from the woods, but she had worked all the time they bloomed, pulling her thread through with the long cane needle until now her carpet hung in the frame, finished to the last thread, ready for the painting.

She set the tray of pots down on the ground; then for a few minutes she walked back and forth before the frame, measuring with her eye the suspended tawny square, trying to decide with what figures she would paint it.

A noise made her turn her head. A few feet away her foster-son the Bear Killer, slept, leaning against a tree. He was not comfortable. His head would jerk to the side and he would slide from the tree trunk. When this happened he did not wake up but, keeping his eyes shut would rise to the same position again. The Lanthorn smiled. A young man who could not sleep for an hour against a tree trunk would not go far on the warpath.

She took a sharpened stick and, squatting, drew on the hard baked earth the outline of her carpet, then made rough sketches of the figures with which she would adorn it. In one corner a wolf, for her husband's clan. In the opposite corner her own ancestor, the deer. In the lower left-hand corner a cedar tree, in the lower right-hand corner a great dogwood blossom because the carpet had been woven in the time that the dogwood was in bloom. In the middle she would depict some event in the life of her husband, the great peace chief,

Atta Kulla Kulla. As always when she thought of that small, wrinkled old man, her heart grew warm. She wondered how she should show him, whether on the hunt, on the warpath, or in council. When he was a young man he had had great honor: he had crossed the far waters in a boat to talk with the White Father. But even before that he had been distinguished as a warrior, and as a young wife she had heard from the old men and women many tales of his boyhood. When he was twelve years old he had, unaided, shot down a great, raging she-bear and captured her cubs. He had won his boy's name, Bear Killer, from that hunt. It might please him to see the bear, himself, and the cubs here on the last carpet she might ever weave. When a man grows old his thoughts turn to his youth.

Her husband had given his own boy's name, Bear Killer, to this youth sleeping against the tree. She turned to look at him again. He had slid from the tree and was lying on the ground, on his back, breathing hard, his lips that always seemed to her so thick, a little opened. She ought to go over and rouse him. A gnat or some other evil thing might fly between those parted lips. She frowned. It was shameful that she, an old woman, had to spend so much time taking care of a young man old enough to be a warrior. Yesterday he had sat motionless on a log while a cluster of ants as large as a spread hand moved steadily towards him. When she explained that he must not crush these insects or they would settle under his skin, causing him to have malignant ulcers, he stared at her stupidly as if he did not believe what she said. Three moons ago her youngest son, the Little Owl, had had to turn back from a hunt before they were out of sight of the town: the Bear Killer in spite of all he had been told had stopped to make water on the Path. Angry as he was the Owl could not help laughing as he showed them how his foster-brother stood up to make water, like a dog or a two-year-old child. But the Owl was patient, like his father. He had purified himself and then had started again on his hunt, taking the white boy with him. It was on this very hunt that the boy had got his name, but the bear was not very large and a he-bear, weak from his winter's fast.

At first it had made her uneasy to have this boy under her roof. She had been afraid of the evil he might bring in with him. Her husband, however, had explained to her that white people, being ignorant, were incapable of doing evil and therefore not subject to the same punishments as the Real People. Indeed, the physician, Climbing Bear, had confessed to her that he would not undertake to cure a white man of any but the simplest ailment. Their constitutions, he said, were so different from those of the Real People that it was impossible to predict the effect of medicine upon them: a dose of physic that would cure a man might kill a dog. The physician did not believe that the white people were human beings and he cited a tale he had had from his father's father, a great man of the north, how in the old days when a white man took the life of an Ana-gun-wi-yi the lives of ten white men were exacted in payment, for it took ten of the short-tailed eunuchs (as the old people called them) to make up the life of one man of the Real People.

She had said nothing of this to her husband, however, only looked into his eyes and repeated: "They do not cause diseases?" He knew what she was thinking about: the epidemic that had come upon the Real People when he and she were a young married couple. It had been in the summer, not long after the festival of the green corn. Young men and women, some of them the handsomest of the tribe, had waked to find their bodies covered with watery blisters that swelled and reddened and finally burst, leaving ugly holes in the flesh. Some of the young men, finding themselves disfigured, had drowned themselves. Her own uncle, the Kingfisher, deprived by his family of all sharp-pointed instruments, had fallen again and again on an old hoe helve that had been left in the field until finally the blood welled up in his pierced throat, and he died. The physician —it was before Climbing Bear's time—said that the disease came from the lascivious conduct of the young men with the married women, and indeed there were many couples lying out in the fields that summer. But she knew that that was not the cause. Her oldest son, then eleven years old, too young to lie with any woman, had been covered all over with the dreadful sores. He had grown up, not knowing what it was to be unscarred, but she remembered his sleek boy's skin and to this day she never looked upon him without remembering that the disease had come from the white people.

She glanced again at the sleeping boy, recalling the way he had looked when her son brought him, still weak with fever, to their house. A thin, grayish, worm-like creature, his head covered with matted brown hair, his arse tied up like a woman's in strips of filthy cloth. Even after he was well of the fever he would not speak or laugh and would hardly put out his hand to receive his food, only sat in a corner and stared out of dull eyes. Once the Owl, scuffling with him, had tried to rip the strips of cloth off his arse. The boy had squeaked like a bat and had showed fight and the Owl, out of kindness, had let him go. For months after that he had insisted on wearing his filthy, torn bandages until at last the young men had laughed him out of the womanish custom.

Lately he had been anointing himself with bear's grease until his skin had taken on a perceptible glow but under the shine it was still a muddy brown. It would never have any of the reddish lights that so delight the eye when a man is walking past and the sun plays on his naked limbs. Even when he wore the warrior's white crown of swan's feathers he would still be ugly. Why had the Man Above made such a creature?

The boy woke suddenly and sat up. He stared around him as if he hardly knew where he was, then his clouded eye brightened as it fell on her. He got up and coming towards her asked where they all were. She understood that he referred to the Owl and the other young men and told him that they had gone to the river to fish.

"I went to sleep," he said, rubbing his eyes.

She laughed at that. "I heard you sleeping," she said.

He laughed too—he had got so that he now joked and laughed with the family—and taking up his long cane spear set off down the village street.

When he had gone it seemed quieter. The Dark Lanthorn stepped over to a bush and cutting off a twig sharpened it to a fine point, then dipped it into one of her pots. It came up covered with flakes of white paint. She approached the carpet and began tracing in one corner the outline of a deer. She worked swiftly, with a sure hand. Had she not traced the form of this great heraldic deer on five other carpets? Besides it was best to work swiftly once the picture was in the mind. Otherwise it might leave one and go to some other weaver. She showed her still fine teeth in a brief smile. Since her friend, Ganasita, had died there was no other woman in Chota industrious enough to weave carpets, not even the Ghigau whom in the last few years it was the fashion to praise above all other women.

She bent nearer the frame and as she did so she felt a familiar twinge in the muscles of her lower back. The physician said it was rheumatism and for two years now he had made her abstain from the meat of rabbits or any other hunched-up animal and had scratched her all over with a flint arrow-head; but though he was a good physician and cured others he had not been able to take the pain from her back. She, an ignorant woman, did not know what caused it but she well remembered that the pain had first come to her that winter they had had to spend in the forest, when Willenawah and Oconostota, the Great Warrior, had besieged the white men's fort on the river. They had taken the fort and had killed and scalped a hundred white men but more white men had come after that and burned six of the towns and all of the crops and the people had had to spend the winter in the forest without shelter. She did not like to think of that old, unhappy time and was bending closer to her work when a noise on the street made her look up.

A woman was approaching, leaning on a white oak stick, her husband's niece, Nancy Ward, the Ghigau. The Ghigau was younger than the Lanthorn but of late years she had grown heavy and walked always now with a stick. The Lanthorn went to her and offered her her arm. The Ghigau took it as if she and not the Lanthorn were the old woman and the Lanthorn escorted her into the yard. As they went they talked. The Ghigau praised her aunt's industry, saying what was true, that few women nowadays understood the art of carpet weaving. The Lanthorn thanked her for the praise and stood listening with bent head while the Ghigau described a particularly succulent dish she had had that day: last year's beans stewed with the wild sweet potato.

The Lanthorn raised her head and stole a glance at the massive face framed between the silver earrings. The Ghigau's hair was threaded with white. Her eyes were still large and lustrous but they had an absent glare. The Lanthorn looked into them, then looked away quickly. *She does not see me. She does not hear my voice!* She took a step backward: a strange thought had come to her. The Ghigau was one of those persons—like the old white man, Fred Mouncy—who live on after the soul is reft from them. The Lanthorn wondered why she had not known before; one can tell such persons by the look in the eye. A shiver ran up her spine. *Some evil will befall us!* It was from this woman that she and many others of the tribe would receive the first fruits of the new year and the new fire for the hearths. The Ghigau always officiated: she was the most beloved woman in the whole Nation. She had won her title years ago when in the battle against the Creeks she had taken up her dead husband's musket and all the rest of that day had fought like a warrior. She *was* accounted a warrior—in council she spoke and was listened to as if she were a man. The Lanthorn had seen her raise the swan's wing of her office and save from burning a captive already noosed to the stake. But the wife of a headman sees in her lifetime many strange things. The Lanthorn could not forget the night ten years ago when the trader, Brian Ward, left the Nation. Atta Kulla Kulla had discovered that his niece was following the man and had gone with his son, the young Dragging Canoe, to fetch her back. It was late at night when they brought her, bound with rawhide thongs, into the winter house. She had flung herself from the couch where they laid her down, screaming out that she would not live without the man and all that night she had raged, using words that were strange on a modest woman's lips. The young Canoe, helping to hold her on the couch, had wept tears of anger that a woman of his family should be so mad for love of a white man. The Lanthorn, listening now to the Ghigau's decorous talk, went back in her mind to that old time and she wondered how an Indian woman could bring herself to lie with one of the accursed ugly ones. For herself she would as soon take for lover a beast of the forest and yet others of the Real People did not feel as she did. Her husband called the white man, John Stuart, brother—indeed he had once given up everything he owned in order to save the life of that man. And her son, the Dragging Canoe, loved Alexander Cameron, the agent, as he loved no other man.

The Ghigau was making her farewells. The Lanthorn was about to go back to her work when she saw three young girls coming towards her. She recognized the young widow, Monon, and walking next to Monon, her arm about her shoulder, was her own granddaughter, Na-Kwi'-si. Na-Kwi'-si lived ten miles away, on the Great Island, of which her father, the Lanthorn's oldest son, was chief. The Lanthorn had not known that her granddaughter was in the town and she called the girls to her. They came and stood before her, their arms still twined about each other's shoulders. They wore new red cotton skirts and their hair hung loose and was newly oiled. They wore silver earrings. Drops of water shone on their black hair. Their faces had the fresh look of those who have just bathed.

The Lanthorn spoke to them sternly: "You have been bathing in the river?"

Na-Kwi′-si answered, looking down, "Yes, Grandmother."

"But you went to the river from the *osi*, to purify yourselves?"

"Yes, Grandmother."

The old woman fixed her eyes on her granddaughter. "And why do you spend your dark time in the *osi* here instead of in your own woman's lodge on the Island?"

"I was visiting my cousin and my sickness came upon me suddenly."

The Lanthorn gave a dry laugh. "And how came you to be visiting at such a time? A woman who cannot reckon her own moons will come to no good end."

She continued to regard the girls sternly for a moment, then as they only looked down without speaking she dismissed them with a gesture of the hand. "Go now. But do not go to the river. The young men are fishing there and do not want to be disturbed."

They were gone in a flutter of red skirts. They would run past the next house and the next and then, taking care to keep out of her sight, they would circle back to the river and would spend the rest of the afternoon there. If they could, they would lure the men out of the river; if the young men would not come they would stay on the bank, chattering and pretending to admire the fishers' skill.

She remembered what it was to be young. Girls were always wild after their seven days in the dark lodge. It had been twenty years since she had been inside its doors but she could still feel the dark of the place, hot with its womanish smells and always from the corner the wailing of some girl child brought in for the first time by her mother. The old women who guarded the doorway would not talk or look at the unclean ones, even when they placed food before them but always sat looking out into the green world. Once when she was a very young girl she had tried to break past one of those women. The old creature hardly moved, only switched her with a long bough, and she turned and ran back into the lodge. Standing now under the green boughs, clean these many years and free to go where she would she felt a longing to be back in that close, dark place.

"I am an old woman," she thought and then, amazed, "I shall not be here much longer!"

She left her carpet and took two steps forward. They carried her to the edge of the street. The path, in front of her house, was hard trampled, but a little farther down it was white with blossoms fallen from the crab apple tree in her neighbor's yard. She walked down and stood under the tree and looked up into its boughs. There were no blossoms left. All were on the ground and the leaves that last week had been so frail were hardened into the dark green of summer.

Standing under the green boughs she gazed towards the square. She could not see the town house for the overhanging leaves but she could hear a murmur of voices and knew that they came from the old men who gathered there in the late afternoons.

She walked slowly back towards her own house and as she went she glanced up at the ridge-pole. The rag of scalp that fluttered there was so ancient that she could not remember the name of the enemy or how he had been taken. She had lived in this house ever since she was married, all but that one winter in the woods, and she had come back to this house that spring, for the white men out of respect had spared the beloved peace town of Chota when they laid the rest of the country waste. She had been born on the Great Island, ten miles from here. She was fourteen years of age when she first saw the peace town of Chota, with its town house large enough to accommodate a hundred men, its holy square, its ancient elms, but ever since she had first beheld it she had had her home here. For nearly sixty years she had lived within a stone's throw of the square, of the holy relics.

Few women, she thought, had had such honor in the course of a long life. She stepped back into her own yard and took her place before the carpet frame. She could hear her husband's voice now, rising above that of the other men. Hearing his voice, which she had not heard for several hours, a feeling of tenderness came over her. She knew the picture she would paint. She picked up the sharpened stick and began tracing it on the earth: a man with a plume in his hair, standing in a boat. Under the boat she drew three wavy lines. Her husband as the young chief, White Owl, crossing the great water to talk with the White Father. He liked to think of that time. She would make a picture of it for him, here in the middle of her carpet.

CHAPTER 35

Archy had gone to the river with the other young men that morning to fish. Towards noon he got hungry and went back to the house to get some stewed meat. He washed his meat down with a gourdful of gruel, then, feeling a little heavy, sat down against a tree trunk to rest. He had not meant to go to sleep and he felt foolish when he woke and found the old Lanthorn looking at him. Anxious to get out of her sight he rose and, taking his fish spear, went down the street.

He walked fast to the end of the street and turned into the double row of elms that ran through the middle of the town. As he walked along this avenue he slowed his steps, glancing towards the square. At this time of day the town house was deep in the shade of its great elm. Some of the older men were gathered in front of it, some sitting on reed divans, others sprawled on the ground or leaning against trees. He recognized his foster-father, the Carpenter, among them and beside him, towering over most of the men, the war chief, Oconostota.

The shadows of the elm leaves were thick on the road he was traveling. A breeze sprang up. The shadows quivered like running water. From the river the shouts of the fishermen came to him faintly. He shifted his hand down his pole until he found its middle and began to run lightly over the hard ground. He was nearing the avenue when he heard some one calling and stopped.

"Yo-na-di-hi!"

They were calling him, the Bear Killer. He turned around and went towards them. There were half a dozen men taking their ease under the great tree. In the center the Carpenter sat on one of the long reed divans. The divan had been pushed up against the tree and the Carpenter leaned against the trunk as if it were the back of a chair. There was room for two or three men on each side of him but he sat alone. Facing him on another divan were the Old Tassel, head chief of all the Nation and Oconostota, the war chief, and his nephew, the Raven. The others, mostly old men, squatted on their haunches or leaned against trees.

The Carpenter raised his yellow hand as Archy came up. "Sit among us old men for a while, my son."

Archy thanked him and would have squatted on the ground but the old chief patted the vacant place beside him. Archy rose and silently took the place the chief indicated. He was aware as he did so that the eyes of all the men in the circle had swung towards him and he kept his own eyes bent on the ground as he had seen the other young bucks do in the presence of the headman. But he wished that the Carpenter had not made him sit beside him. It was not fitting that a man as young as he, and a white man to boot, should be asked to sit beside the peace chief. But the Carpenter was used to having his way and at times thought little of his own dignity. He leaned over now and laying his arm lightly about Archy's shoulders asked him where his brother, the Owl, was. Archy replied that the Owl and most of the other young men were at the river fishing. "Shall I go to them, Father?"

The chief smiled and shook his head. "It is pleasant here in the shade and the company is the best in the Nation. If the Bear Killer will sit with the old men he will learn wisdom."

Archy looked up and murmured the speech that politeness required, then bent his eyes on the ground again. He had looked down almost immediately after speaking but not before he had caught the flicker of an ironical smile on the lips of the Raven. The war chief's nephew didn't think much of him. He wondered why. The other young men seemed to like him.

The war chief spoke. "Atta Kulla Kulla has two sons to sit beside him now."

The other Indians all looked up. A big, tall man was coming swiftly around the side of the house. Archy had never seen him before but he recognized him by his size and his pock-marked face: Atta Kulla Kulla's oldest son, the Dragging Canoe, chief of the Great Island.

The Dragging Canoe went first to his father and took him by the arm, then to each of the other headmen, then sat down on the divan beside his father. A middle-aged warrior rose and kneeling before him went through the motions of drawing the briars from his feet. The Canoe looked down at the fellow absent-mindedly, then checked him with a gesture when he would have brought water to pour over the dusty feet.

"My feet are not hot," he said.

The Carpenter, his head tilted back, had been staring at a buzzard that sailed high above their heads in the blue. He looked at his son now and asked him the news from the island.

The young chief replied that things were well with all his people, except the warrior, Going Deer, who had left on a hunt three weeks before and had not returned. The Carpenter said that his son should send a party out to search for the lost hunter. Dragging Canoe said that the party had already left.

There was a long silence. The buzzard swooped, so low that they could make out the V of his wings, then he was out of sight behind a clump of trees. Somebody hoisted a water jug up and drank with a gurgle. The Old Tassel folded his hands over his stomach, belched once and was asleep.

Archy, his head still bent, stared from under drooping lids out over the square. The whole town must be asleep. No, there was one woman moving at the north end of the square, a broad figure in a striped gown. She turned her head as she went and the sun struck light from her long silver earrings.

Oconostota spoke in a quiet, meditative voice: "Atta Kulla Kulla, who is the most beautiful girl you ever saw in your life?"

There was a titter from one of the young men. The peace chief had closed his eyes and seemed to be asleep but he opened them readily. "A woman's beauty lies in her spirit. My wife, the Dark Lanthorn, was fourteen years of age when I first met her, here under these elms. The most beautiful woman I have ever seen, then or since."

Oconostota smiled at his friend, his eyes still following the figure moving at the other end of the square. "The Ghigau was older than that when she first came to Chota. I believe she was the most beautiful woman I ever saw. Ten years ago she was still handsome but then—then, I tell you, she moved like a moon beam!"

His nephew, the Raven, laughed. "Our grandmother, the Ghigau moves more like a cow these days."

The pock-marked chief, Dragging Canoe, spoke in a harsh voice. "She drinks the milk of the cow. Perhaps it makes her heavy—or it may be the heaviness comes from lying with white men."

"It has been many years since Nancy Ward had a white lover," his father said mildly.

"It has been ten years since she had a white lover here in the Nation," the Canoe said, "but she is like the moonbeam. She slips through the woods."

Oconostota laughed. "That's so. She has gone many times to visit her old lover. She begs him to come back and live in the Nation. He won't come, she says, but he always receives her honorably."

Dragging Canoe laughed too but said nothing. The Raven had been looking at the Canoe. Now he spoke. "Do you consider the cow an unholy beast?"

"For those who do not wish to move like a cow. . . . I have not touched cow's milk these five years."

The Raven smiled and touched the blanket he was sitting on. "You wear a blanket when it is cold."

The Canoe shook his head. "I do not love the white man's gifts. My wife weaves my blanket out of the hair of the buffalo."

"But there are no buffalo left in the land."

"They may come back."

The Raven, his dark eyes shining, leaned forward and laid his hand on the musket that rested between the Canoe's knees. "This is the white man's best gift."

"I keep it only till they are all run out of the land," Dragging Canoe said. "When they are gone I'll shoot my game with the bow and arrow."

"The white men will never go," Oconostota said sadly. "They are like lice. Each one so small he is nothing. A hundred and you have an itching head."

"I would cut my head off before it should become a breeding place for vermin," Dragging Canoe said.

The Carpenter raised a thin, yellow hand that trembled ever so slightly. "The white men are our brothers," he said. "We are all children of the same Father. I was told that when I crossed the great water . . ."

Some of the men exchanged glances. One yawned. Archy wished that he could get up and leave. The Carpenter, when he started on the story of his voyage, would talk for at least an hour. And no one would dare to interrupt the great peace chief. He glanced at the Canoe. He was not even pretending to listen to his father but sat, his sinewy legs thrust straight out in front of him, staring at the ground.

Archy let his eyes travel up the naked body to the massive head. The Canoe was the biggest Indian he'd ever seen and the handsomest, in spite of his pock-marked face. The Owl said that he was the strongest man in the Nation. Once when the river was in flood he had swum across it three times, rescuing children and women who were too old to swim . . . He hated white men, all except the British agent, Alexander Cameron, whom the Indians called "Scotchie." But then, as the Owl said, Scotchie was his blood brother—he was bound to love him. "The way I love you," the Owl had said.

Archy gazed down at his own thin brown wrist. He could still feel the grip of the Owl's fingers, that day they made him into an Indian. They had just finished pulling out all his hair except the scalp lock and had painted him up and loaded him with wampum and silver bracelets when the Owl suddenly grabbed him by the wrist and yanked him out into the street. Round and round they had gone until it seemed as if their two hands had grown together, the Owl yelling and the whole town streaming after them. It had been a relief when they turned him over to the women to wash in the river. They had done the job well. He had been as limp as a soaked herring when he came out. . . . He could not remember much of what went on after that. They had been in the council house a long time, all the warriors sitting around, the smoke thick enough to choke you. The Carpenter had made the speech:

"My son, you are now flesh of our flesh and bone of our bone. By the ceremony which was performed this day every drop of white blood was washed out of your veins. You are now one of us by an old strong law and custom. My Son, you have nothing to fear . . ."

It was the Carpenter who had said all that. It was the Carpenter who was talking now. ". . . houses on each side of the street as thick as beans in a pod. The Great Father's winter house is as big as this whole town. The warriors that guard it are covered all over with cloth and the cloth shines . . ."

The Dragging Canoe stood up. "I am going back to the Island," he said. His eyes rested for a second on his father. "The searching party came in last night," he said. "They brought the Going Deer on a litter, in four pieces."

The Carpenter's black eyes opened wide and fixed his son's face. His lips formed a soundless question.

The Canoe passed his hand in front of his throat, then with a rapid gesture he indicated the severing of legs from a trunk. His hand came back to his side, then went out again, rested a second on his privates. "Five pieces," he said. "They cut this off too."

The Raven muttered a word. Archy had never heard it before but he knew what it meant, that the white men were all eunuchs. The Indians were always saying that the white men could not enjoy loving.

He realized that the Dragging Canoe, still standing there in the middle of the crowd, was staring at him, absent-mindedly as if he hardly knew who he was. He looked back. All Indians had black eyes but this man's eyes were blacker than any he'd ever seen, except for that spark that cleft the pupil. A shining spark, shaped like a knife. White men had used a cutty knife to dismember the Going Deer's body. A thin knife that shone, cutting through red flesh. . . . *"My son, you are now one of us by an old strong law and custom. My son, you have nothing to fear. . . ."*

He took a step backward and could have burst into tears. He had moved then only because the Canoe was turning away!

The Canoe was walking off slowly between the two divans. He passed from under the shade of the big elm and disappeared around the corner of the town house.

Oconostota had sat down again on his divan. His great, dome-shaped head was bowed a little forward. He studied the ground. The Carpenter was talking with the Raven and two other warriors.

Archy slipped from the Carpenter's side to the edge of the crowd. He turned then and spoke in a low voice. "I am going to the river to fish, Father."

He picked up his spear, crossed the square and turned into the avenue. It was quiet here in the dense shade. Nobody in sight. . . . Yes, ahead of him three girls were walking. They heard steps behind them. One of them turned to look over her shoulder: Amo-gun-yi, the war chief's daughter. One of the other girls Archy had never seen before, but the third figure, taller and thinner than the others, was familiar. He hurried and fell into steps beside them.

"Good evening, beautiful daughters of the Wind and the River," he said, using the kind of talk he had heard the Owl and the other young fellows use.

Amo-gun-yi laughed. "Good evening, Bear Killer, are you still sucking eggs?"

Archy stared at her. At first he did not know what she meant; then he remembered. She had come by the other day when the Lanthorn was boiling him some eggs. The Indians boiled theirs till they were as hard and blue as bullets but he always made the Lanthorn take his out while they were still soft.

He laughed too. "Yes, I have sucked up all the hen eggs and now I am going to the river to look for turtle eggs."

Amo-gun-yi leaned forward, making a barking sound and imitating a dog robbing a hen's nest. One of the girls laughed. The other girl looked straight ahead.

Archy looked at her across the bent bodies of the other two. He was not even certain that it was Monon but he asked the question anyhow. "Where have you been? I haven't seen you in a long time?"

The other two were straightening up. Their heads came between him and her and so he did not see her face as she answered, only heard her voice.

"I have been mourning my husband."

Amo-gun-yi was the kind of girl who couldn't stop anything once it got started. She was making the offensive sound again. This time she was a snake, climbing a tree to get birds' eggs.

He gave her a hard look. "The daughter of the great chief ought not to travel with a suck-egg dog," he said and fell behind them.

They were walking on. Amo-gun-yi had wanted to stop and rally him some more but the others pulled her forward. She was looking back at him over her shoulder now, her face working, ready to start giggling all over again. He stuck his tongue out at her, at the same time bringing his right hand up in an obscene gesture. That settled her. Her face changed. She turned around and went about her business.

They turned off into one of the side streets. Just as they rounded the corner Monon looked back at him over the other girl's shoulder. He could have laughed. She was like him, wondering if this was the man or whether it could have been some other fellow!

He walked on, balancing the light spear in his hand. *I have been mourning my husband.* That was why he had not seen her anywhere.

It seemed a long time since the festival but it was just a year ago this month—the festival of the green-eared moon when the first young corn was ripe. It had been his first big Indian shindig. They painted the town house white and the headmen went around with wreaths of white swan's feathers on their heads and white wands in their hands. There had been a lot of singing and dancing. He had kept himself as scarce as he could. They fasted for eight days before they had the big dinner. That was when you had to walk mighty straight. It was a sin for a man to so much as touch the skin of a girl-child during those eight days, the Owl said. After it was all over they had the big dinner and some more singing and dancing. It was when they were all dancing in the square that the Owl had come to him, bouncing along like a bird, laughing all over. "Time now," he said, and took Archy down into the grove on the side of the square.

As they went he explained. Most of the young men were waiting on the other side of the square. The women always made a break when the dancing was over. The Raven and his crowd figured they would head that way and, being in the first line, would get the pick. They forgot that it was the women's night. Some sour old bitch was likely to get hold of you and not let go. It was better to do the choosing yourself. This morning at the spring he had been talking with a very attractive young married woman, the wife of—oh, he would never tell the name of her brave husband! He had asked her about the festival, particularly about the hour after the dancing when the women were free to take what man they chose. She said that that was very nice for women who did not have a fine husband like hers or women who were such fools that they did not know a fine husband when they had one. As for her, she took no part in such frolics and always went straight to her house as soon as the dancing was over. He asked her which side of the square she traveled on her way home and she said that on her way home she always looked towards the sun. Somebody had come up just then and they had not had a chance to finish their talk but as she was leaving he called after her to know how many women went with her into the open lands to pick sallet the other day. She called back that she had had only one friend with her so he would take only one man with him. The Bear Killer was his brother and he would share everything with him, even the pleasures of the blanket and he came close and laughed and squeezed Archy's arm the way he was always doing.

It was a cedar grove there on the east side of the square. The trees

stood up straight and tall, like people, no, like giants—the biggest
cedars he had ever seen in his life. They had had to go quite a way
into the grove to get out of the light from the torches. They stood
behind a big cedar whose boughs came down to the ground and
waited. The Owl kept talking about the girl he'd had last year.
Archy didn't talk. He was hoping the Owl wouldn't find out how
green he was—if you didn't count Lessie Robinson. He was having
a round with her in the bushes on the way home from church but
he hadn't more than got her down when Rion came up on them and
yanked him off by the scruff of the neck and said that the Robinsons
were trash and that he'd give him the beating of his life if he ever
caught him with her again.

The Indian girls had come weaving their way through the big
cedars, talking and laughing but keeping their voice low so that a
person a few feet off couldn't have recognized them. The Owl knew
his girl and went up to her. They turned off into the dark.

He couldn't even see his girl's face. He didn't know what name
to call her by. He had stood there like a fool—until she leaned over
and put her hands on him. He was startled but he took the hands and
pulled her up against him. They went down together there in the
grass. She didn't wait for him to make the first move, took it away
from him as they said. He'd often wondered what it would be like.
Now he knew. But he wondered still. Would it be very different
with a white girl? You had to make over them, warm them up, he'd
always heard. But this Cherokee girl was hotter than he was. When
he got weak she could hardly wait for him to get strong again. . . .
He had gone to sleep with her lying across him, her arms tight around
his neck. When he woke the moon was gone. It was almost day.
The Owl was standing over him.

The Owl wouldn't wait long enough for him to say goodbye
even. And he wouldn't tell him the girl's name but he had let slip
the name of her husband. That was when Archy said that he would
like to see her again. The Owl laughed until he had to lean against
a tree. "Round O will shoot you if you come to his cabin," he said.

But Round O had been killed, a month later, falling off a big
rock somewhere over in the mountains. Archy had attended the
burial service, had seen the widow from afar off, standing with other
members of her family but she had disappeared after the burial.
He had never talked to her again, until today. . . .

He had come to the end of the avenue. From here a broad plain sloped down to the river. They had cleared out most of the trees but a few were left standing. Three or four houses stood in the shade of these trees. One of them was the house of the white trader, Captain Gist who, three years ago, had married Wurteh, sister to the Old Tassel, and ever since then had resided in the Nation.

Captain Gist was sitting in his yard. Archy raised his hand in salute and walked past, then on an impulse turned back into the yard. Gist, naked, Indian fashion, except for his flap, was sitting on a stool under a china-berry tree. A gun lay across his knee. He was changing the flint. As Archy approached he held the gun up in front of him.

"What do you think of this for the best smooth-bore that has come into the Nation, Master Outlaw?"

Archy took the gun and examined it. It was of British make.

"It's worth all of five guineas," he said, "and if I had 'em I'd give it ye."

Gist smiled and taking up a tuft of rabbit's hair dipped it into a cup of grease and began to oil the gun. "I'll sell it to the Dragging Canoe," he said. "I hear he's in the town today."

"He was over at the town house," Archy said, "but he left. Said he was going back to the island."

"The Raven then. Or maybe the Old Tassel himself'll fancy it. It's a gun for a headman now surely."

"The Dragging Canoe says he'll use a gun only till the white men are run out of the land," Archy said.

Gist glanced up sharply but said nothing. Archy watched him as he leaned over to drop the tuft of rabbit's hair back into the cup. The twisting movement sucked his belly in and made his ribs stand out until you could almost count them. He was as hollow-ribbed as an Indian and his flesh was as red. The red came from bear's grease but aside from that he could have passed for an Indian, with his black eyes and his coarse black hair.

Archy wondered if the Indians liked him because he was so much like themselves. No man in the Nation had ever risen as quickly as he had. He had come to Chota five years ago, to trade, and now he was married to the sister of the head chief and spoke in council. It was not only his wife's relatives that favored him. The Indians all liked him, so much that they had given him a whole island—an island far to the north, longer than the one Dragging Canoe was chief of. But Gist had never gone to take up his island. He preferred to stay on here in the Nation, living the life of a warrior and trading a little on the side.

There was a sound from the bushes behind them, a bleat such as a lamb might make. Archy turned around and saw a young child hanging in his board from the limb of a tree. Gist got up and took the board down, then unfastened the thongs and tumbled the child out on the ground. A boy, fat for an Indian baby, not yet old enough to stand. He started crawling. Gist watched him a minute, picked him up and, extending his arms to their full length, shot him up over his head. The child shut his eyes tight but made no sound except to gulp when he took in his breath. Gist set him on the ground. He gulped again and without looking up started crawling. Gist laughed. "They don't get to stretch their legs much in those boards. I take him down every now and then to give him a chance."

They sat watching the baby crawl off over the ground. Finally Archy spoke:

"One of Dragging Canoe's men got killed the other day."

"Who killed him?"

"White men."

They sat there. Gist's eyes were still on the crawling child. Archy studied the half-averted cheek.

Gist suddenly turned around. His black eyes were on Archy's face. "The Canoe have any idea who did it?"

"He said it was white men. . . . Reckon there'll be a war?"

Gist shook his head. When he did not say anything else Archy got to his feet and went and stood in front of him and stared down into his face. "I'm a white man," he said. His voice rose and cracked. "I don't want to be here 'mongst these Indians if there's going to be a war."

Black eyes can get a film over them. The man twisted his head to one side, as if, stark naked as he was, he was wearing a collar that galled him. When he spoke his voice was quiet. "The Carpenter is a reasonable man. So is the Tassel."

Archy could feel the sweat break out on his forehead. "But what if there *was* a war?"

Gist suddenly got up. His voice changed, became sharp, as if Archy were a dog or a horse that he was commanding to stand still. "Shut up, Outlaw!"

Archy stared at him, his mouth open. But Gist was not looking at him. He was looking towards the house. Wurteh was just coming through the doorway. Her long braids swung to one side as she stooped to get through the opening. She straightened up and smiled at her husband. Gist stepped over, picked up the child and started towards her.

Archy took a step after them and stopped. He and Gist had been talking English. He called out now to Wurteh in Cherokee: "Goodbye. I have had a talk with your husband and now I am going to the river. Goodbye."

He left them and walked off fast, down the first path he came to. After a while he stopped. This was not the way to the river. He must have taken the wrong turn, back there where the path forked. This path led to the town. He faced about. He could still hear the shouts of the fishermen but faintly. Spearing fish from the canoes; probably working up the river. If he struck through the woods and walked up the path along the river he would come up with them. He had his spear. The Owl would be tired by this time and would let him have his canoe.

He chose the path that would take him to the river, followed it a few steps, and sat down with his back against a tree. His lips moved. In his mind he was still talking to Gist. "You're a white man. You ain't an Indian. You can't go on all your life pretending you're an Indian. You're a white man. Same as me."

He drew a long, sobbing breath, then was silent, looking about him. This was a place he'd never seen before, but he'd know it for Cherokee country if he came to it in his sleep.

The giant sycamore in front of him had ferns growing on its lower branches. The trunk was split up to where the first branch put out. He got up and walked over to it. The split had come a long time ago. The inner wall was hollowed out and covered with a smooth substance that was as hard as bark, only not white. He slipped through the opening and, stretching his hands out on each side of him, touched only air. A yoke of oxen could stable here and not tramp each other. He looked down at the mold in which his feet were sunk. Black, fine as gunpowder and so rich nothing would grow in it. How many years had it been piling up here inside the hollow trunk? He glanced up over his head where ferny moss and leaves mingled. These trees were taller even than the ones on the square. When you asked the Indians about these big trees they smiled in a secret way or laughed out. Was this country older than other countries? Had these trees always been here, since the beginning of time?

He stepped out from the hollow trunk and threw himself down on the ground, burying his face in the dead leaves. At first he kept on seeing white trunks in black air and then ferns and leaves. But they went away. There was left only the black. He pressed his face deeper into the rustling leaves and thrust his fingers into his ears. Keep out the white trunks, keep out the sound of this river, and he could hear the Yadkin flowing over its bright marble rocks, could see his father's house set in its grove on the green hill. He shut his eyes tighter, but he could not see the house or hear the Yadkin water. He was moving slowly, through bright air, over ground so hot that it burned his feet. The hickory handle was warm and sweaty in his grasp. He sank the hoe into a hill. It struck on a clod. There was a place there in the south field where the dirt was always cross-grained and caked. Once, years ago, it had been plowed when it was wet. It would always be like that, Rion said, ruined forever. . . . On a hot day Rion would hoe faster than usual, then get through before you did and wait for you at the end of the row. If you hoed up and tried to catch him he would laugh. . . . Rion was the strongest man anywhere around Trading Ford. He didn't suppose there was any man in all of Rowan stronger than Rion, unless it would be that blacksmith at Hillsborough. . . .

Somebody was coming. He sat up suddenly, rubbing his eyes. The young widow, Monon, stepped over the roots of a big beech and came and squatted on the ground in front of him.

She did not speak or touch him, just squatted there looking at him. After a little she said something but he did not know what she was saying and he did not answer. She looked away, studying a clump of ferns that came up there between them. He studied her face. It was thinner than he remembered it and the upper lip was shorter than in most of the Cherokee women. She turned her head to the side. Light slid through the leaves and fell on her cheek. There was a lily that grew in the fields at home, tiny, perfect flowers on a brave stalk. Her skin was the light, pure red of those petals.

She was standing up, saying again the words he did not understand. "I don't know," he said vaguely, not realizing that he spoke English.

She came up to him and laid her hand on his arm. She smiled and, making the same little gentle sound, looked away, to one of the paths that went through the brake. He set his left hand against the small of her back and drew her to him. With his other hand he ripped off the fathom of stroud cloth that was tied about her loins. When he would have torn away the wad of moss bound against her, she broke away from him. She was at the edge of the brake, gathering up the strip of cloth, turning to look over her shoulder. He caught up with her and they ran together into the brake.

CHAPTER 36

THERE WERE two hours of sun left when Rion finished planting his last hill of corn. He went to the river to get a drink and came back and sat on a stump to rest and looked over the field. He was glad now he hadn't gone to the Watauga with Frank and Jacob. It would have taken a day each way for the trip and another day for the frolic —he would have been into next week planting his corn. As it was he'd got it in before the rain that was blowing up. A week could make a mighty difference.

He got up and walked down the field towards the creek, a zig-zag course, for he had to walk around a stump every few minutes. He would like to know how much land—how much solid dirt—he had cleared but it was hard to figure when the stumps took up as much room as the dirt itself. He thought of that first year. The fire had licked over this land for three days running. They had got the logs burned off or burned down to where they could handle them, but most of the stumps were only charred on the outside. They would be here for many a year yet. Still, counting stumps and girdled trees, he must have two whole acres cleared. And the land was rich. He'd make two hundred bushels of corn this year.

He was about to turn up the path to his house when he remembered that Elsa had asked him to step over some time soon and put seats on some stools. She had the hides ready and Jacob had drilled the holes for the thongs, but she thought Rion had a better sleight than Jacob at putting the thongs through.

He crossed the creek and walked up to the Wagners' house. Elsa was sitting on the doorstep scouring her plates. He dropped down beside her. "How you making out, with your old man gone?"

She did not look up, just went on scouring her plate. "Cat got your tongue?" he asked.

She looked up then. "I wish I had a cat or something to make a fuss. There ain't been a sound in this house all day. I got so I was feared to hear myself move around."

"Yet you couldn't wait this spring till you got you a house built over here."

"A body wants her own house, but she don't want to be alone in it."

"I can't see as Jacob is much company," Rion said. "He don't have much to say."

"Hunh! You'll do well if you're as good company, time you're his age. It ain't so much what he says as having him around. That man, he's like a baby about me. If I run off here into the bushes a minute he's a-calling, 'Ma, what you doing?' I told him the other day, 'There's times folks don't want to tell what they're doing, even if they ain't anybody to hear 'em.'" And she laughed and a little color came up in her cheeks.

Rion laughed too, thinking how different this old woman was from Cassy, who would never mention running off into the bushes to anybody, let alone joke about it.

She had put her plate to one side and sat, her hands limp in her lap, gazing before her. Jacob had cut out a mighty small dooryard. The trees pressed right up to the house, so thick you couldn't even see the creek for them. She took a quick breath and turned to him. "Hit's still, ain't it?"

"Hit's still," he agreed, "if you don't listen to the water."

She let her breath out in a long sigh. "If Jacob or me dies out here, we'd be buried by this creek."

"What's the difference? If you was to die at home you'd be buried by the Yadkin. Close to it probably. Ain't the Free Baptist burying ground down by the river?"

"Hit's down there," she said absently and went on talking, more to herself than to him. "It ain't being so far from home. It's being out here where the woods is so thick, where nobody don't hardly know where you are. If we was buried by this creek chances are wouldn't nobody ever pass by our grave, and if they did they wouldn't know who we was. If you folks moved off, that is."

Rion stood up. "What about them stools?"

She went with him into the house and brought the stools and hides and set them before him. He squatted on the floor and laced the thongs through, making her hold the hides down while he fastened them as tight as he could.

"There," he said, "I reckon that'll hold up anybody comes to this house."

"You about the heaviest man comes here," she said. "Frank nor Amos Eaton don't weigh much more'n a scarecrow, either of them."

She stepped to the shelf and took down a platter half full of walnut meats. In the old days when he and Jacob finished trading she would always bring him a tart or a "wonder," but now that she didn't have flour or sugar to do with, it was walnuts. But she took just as much care now as she did then, getting the boy's breeches out whole every time.

He took a handful and set the platter back on the shelf. As he ate he looked around the room. Ten by eight, two feet shorter than his own house each way, but a neat, tight house all the same. After all, there were only two of them in it. He stepped to the fire, pulled the lug pole out and let it swing back. "It's cracked," he said. "You ought to get Jacob to fix it."

"He keeps promising, but now he's started his sluice he ain't got no time for anything else."

"His sluice?" Rion said. "You mean he's building him a sluice?"

She nodded. Rion pushed past her and went outside. He walked a little away from the house towards the creek, Elsa following him. They had not gone far before they found the place. She was right. The old coot was starting a sluice. Ten uprights in already and more lying on the ground ready to set up.

"If he ain't a fool!" Rion said. "How's he going to get him a wheel after he gets the sluice built?"

"Amos Eaton says they's a wright over in Carter's Valley got tools to work with. Amos, he took the man's word and he sent back word he'd come when Jacob was ready for him."

Rion laughed. "Say he gets a wheel set up. Who's going to bring him corn?"

"He says they'll be plenty to come time he gets the wheel turning. Says he met some folks on the south end of Eaton's ridge the other day was looking for land to settle."

"Lots of folks say they're going to settle and don't, and if they do, how's he know they got enough git-up to make a crop?"

She was not listening, looking back over her shoulder. "They's somebody at the house," she said, and made off through the bushes.

Rion followed her. Jacob and Frank were standing in front of the house, looking dog-tired. He went up to them. "Well, I see you're starting a mill," he said to Jacob.

Jacob looked at him as if he hardly knew who he was. "They must a been two hundred men there," he said.

"White folks or Indians?"

"White folks. I ain't counting the Indians. They was men from the Doe and men from the Watauga and some from up as far as Carter's Valley. They was some from as far off as the Clinch, and they must a been a dozen from Wolf Hills. They piled the goods up in a heap and the Indians walked round and round 'em. They was eight dozen matchcoats and wristbands and a lot of duffields, besides the guns and powder. Some of it was mighty sorry stuff, but they made it out two thousand dollars' worth. . . . But it was good enough for them Indians. They was some of them there looked like they'd never seen a bolt of cloth before. Take it and wrap around themselves and laugh like children. . . ."

"What did the white folks do?" Rion said. "After they come all that way what did they do?"

"They set up a government," Frank told him. He looked at his brother-in-law and laughed. "You better walk straight now. We got magistrates and a clerk and a sheriff too."

Rion squatted against a tree. "The country's ruined," he said.

Elsa came to the door and asked Jacob and Frank if they wanted their supper now. They said they did and she turned back into the house to prepare it. Jacob and Frank sat down side by side on the doorstep.

Rion squatted in front of them, chewing on a grass blade. "I can't see what they done that for. We come out here, the most of us, to get shut of the law."

Frank said: "They set up a government to make the lease lawful."

Rion started. "You mean to say that after all that talk, all we done was lease the land again?"

Frank shook his head impatiently. "You don't see, Rion, many times as I've told you. They've got us in a cleft stick. Ever since the Virginians ran that new line. You ain't in Virginia and you ain't in Carolina, then where are you?"

"I be dog if I know," Rion said.

"You're on Indian land. And you can't buy land from any Indians. The King made a law about that."

"There's too much law," Rion said. "I come out here to get shut of it."

"You'd have to go a far piece to get shut of the law," Frank said, "and even then it'd follow you."

Elsa called the men in to their supper. Rion stood up. "I'll be going up to the house. Frank, you come when you get ready."

"Whyn't he stay here the night?" Elsa asked. "Dog-tired as he is he don't want to be walking no farther."

Frank looked up, his mouth full of turkey. "I'll be up first thing in the morning," he said.

Rion crossed the creek and started up the path he had cut out between the houses last spring. He walked slowly, thinking over what had been said. If he'd only pushed farther up the Holston when he first came out! He'd be in Virginia then and could claim his land as a first settler. But no, he had to stop rig.. '..e where the trouble was. He'd been on this land two years and there'd been trouble from the start. The new line had been run the very year he came. All the south Holston settlements—the Watauga, the Doe, the Nolichucky— had come out on the Indian side. How was a man to know just by looking at land whether it belonged to whites or Indians? He'd done his part, paid the Indians a little something for the land instead of taking it the way most folks did. But that hadn't helped. The British agent said they must all move off. Jacob Brown, over on the Nolichucky, had picked up and moved overnight. Maybe he ought to go too. Go to Kentuck where he'd planned to go in the first place. . . .

He emerged from the path and suddenly was in the clearing. Coming up from the river like this you'd never know there was a clearing and a house in here unless you happened to strike this path. That was what Elsa didn't like, being where folks might pass by and never know that you were there, but he didn't know that he'd want his house out on the road for all the world to see. Every night when he came up through the woods it was a surprise to come on the clearing like this. You'd think that it was dark, but when you got in here it'd still be light. And it was getting lighter all the time, the way he kept falling trees. Sometimes when he was resting after dinner he'd get up right quick and fall one and sometimes he'd stop and fall one on the way to the field. If a man kept his axe handy he could fall a lot of trees in a lifetime. And as he told them every one down was one out of the way. His dooryard would be bare now if it wasn't for Cassy. She made him leave some just because she liked to look at them. That big fir there in the south corner. She said he was never to fall it on any account. And she'd made him leave the big shellbark hickories, one at each corner of the house.

He looked at the house where it sat under the interlacing boughs. A good-sized crib, twelve by twelve, each way. Now that the roof and chimney were on it looked larger. They'd wanted him to cat and clay the chimney, said he'd never get it done before frost any other way, but he'd held out to use the rocks over in that pile by the spring. They were the right size and flat, most of them, so that they worked up nicely. It'd taken him all of two weeks to build the chimney, but when he was done it drew. Suck a corn shuck up like a March wind.

It was a hard thing to have to put puncheon on for a roof, but he had no way in God's world to rive out shingles. Puncheon it had to be. But it was tight. Not a leak in two years. A good house, every log matched at the corners. And yet it didn't look right to him. That was because of the room that wasn't built yet. He'd had it in his mind now for a whole year. It had got so the house looked lop-sided to him without it.

Cassy wanted him to make a lean-to at the north. Said that way the room'd get some heat from the chimney. But he was a mind to make another crib facing south. That was the way the old house was at home. No sense building unless you did it right, even if it did take you longer. They could put a lean-to on later if they needed it. . . . If he moved, like Brown and the rest, he wouldn't be building either crib or lean-to. . . .

He walked through the dooryard and was about to step up into the house when he saw Malcolm coming around the corner. He had on nothing but his hippens and he was dragging a brush broom. It was hard pulling for him. Each time he flung out a leg it wobbled and seemed about to double on him, but he kept his balance and made it as far as the hickory tree, then sat down on a root with a plop.

Rion waited until he had sat down, then went and squatted in front of him. "What you doing, boy?"

Malcolm had been so busy holding on to his broom that he had not realized that his father was there until Rion was right in front of him. He started and his face settled into the solemn expression it always had when he knew anybody was looking at him. Rion, looking into his eyes, observed that in the last few weeks the pupils had grown darker. When he had been born they were blue, like all young things, but they'd been turning ever since. They'd be a blackish grey like Cassy's before he was through.

He picked the child up, and getting to his feet danced around with him until he himself was dizzy and had to lean against a tree. "How you like that?" he asked.

Malcolm had crowed out when they first started going around, but now he was squirming in Rion's arms. Rion set him down. Malcolm reached for his broom, and as soon as he had hold of it sat down again on the root of the tree.

Rion glanced over his shoulder, but no one was in sight. He bent over the baby. "Say Daddy!" he whispered.

Malcolm raised his head and gave his father the same solemn stare; then his gaze wandered. Suddenly a light came into his eye. His mouth opened wide and he held out his arms. "Mammy!" he cried. "Mammy!"

Rion turned around. Jocasta was coming up the path from the garden. He went to meet her. He slipped his arm about her and he could feel the swelling under her waist-band. She was six months gone, though you wouldn't think it, seeing her step along so light. "What you been doing?" he asked.

She leaned up against him for a second, then suddenly sprang away, catching at his hand. "Come here. I got something to show you."

He followed her around the house to the garden patch. "You want inside?" he asked, and when she nodded he lifted the slab gate back and followed her down the rows. As he went he looked about. The pumpkin seed hadn't been in the ground a week, but they were already pushing through and the beans he had planted six weeks ago were in full blossom.

Cassy was bending over the beans now. "Look," she said, and pulled a stalk towards him.

He looked at the lavender and white blossoms and saw where two or three were withered and the tiny, perfect little beans already formed.

"You got sharp eyes," he said. "I looked here yesterday and didn't see a bean."

She was bending farther down the row, running her hand in

among the leaves. "Here," she said and pulled another stalk out. There, swinging under the broad leaves, were half-a-dozen beans as long as his index finger.

Still stooping she looked up at him. "Aren't they forward?"

He bent and fingered one of the slim, green beans. "We'll have snaps inside a week," he said.

He held his hands out and drew her to her feet. They walked back up the row. At the gate he stopped and looked over the garden again. "I'll try to git in here for an hour or two tomorrow."

"I'll hoe the pumpkins," she told him, "and I'll give the snaps another little working while I'm at it."

"You better not be hoeing now," he said. "You might strain yourself."

They had come to the corner of the house where they could see into the front dooryard. Malcolm was holding the brush broom in both hands and pushing it back and forth over the bare ground.

"Look at him," Cassy said. "Sweeping. Now, ain't that sweet?"

The child looked up. He did not drop the broom immediately, but he made only a few more strokes after she had spoken, and in a few seconds he laid it down.

Rion frowned. "What makes him do that way?"

"He don't ever like for you to look at him when he's playing," she said.

She moved past him to the bench that sat beside the back door. Both water buckets were empty. He took them to the spring and filled them. When he came back Cassy called out that the back log was about gone, so he stood a chunk of buckeye on end and split it in two with his axe. When he had finished splitting the chunk he picked up one of the back logs. As he walked across the yard he looked up at the house. It was almost dark outside, but the little fire that was on the hearth showed a glow through the doorway. Cassy was in the corner, rocking the cradle. He could see her hand come out each time to meet it and push it away.

He stepped up into the house, tip-toed across the floor, and put the log on as quietly as he could, and tip-toed to the front door. The cradle was bumping slower each time now. Malcolm ought to drop off any second. He sat down on the doorstep, resting his hands on his spread knees. His thoughts went back to his talk with Frank. Suppose he did move off like the others. Would he better himself?

Jump from the frying pan into the fire, most likely. If the King said you couldn't buy land from the Indians, what was the sense of moving? The same thing would come up again sooner or later. Robertson was probably right when he said stay here and work things out. He'd been talking with the chiefs all spring. Some of them wanted the settlers to stay—if they wouldn't take up more land. Well, the result of all Robertson's work was the meeting today. They had the land for another eight years. When the time was up there'd be some new hanky-panky. The British agent would be telling them to move on again. Yet a lot could happen in eight years. In eight years there might be enough of them to dare the British agent. The government they'd set up today: he'd been against it, back there talking to Frank and Jacob, but he didn't know but that he was wrong. As Frank said, you had to go a far piece to get shut of the law. . . . But the law had to start some time. Somebody had to make it to start with. No sense in men across the water making law for folks on this side. Folks on this side knew the country, knew what they had to deal with. They ought to stand up on their own hind legs and make their own law.

He brought his clenched fist down on his knee. "I'm with 'em," he said aloud.

Cassy was at his back, dropping down fast as a shadow, to clap her hand over his mouth. "Shh!" and in the same whisper, "what you talking about?"

"I don't know," he said, confused. "It's a way I got into, being out in the woods by myself so much."

"Your supper's ready."

"What you got?"

"There was some of the poke sallet left and I can warm you a slice of the deer meat."

"I'll have it in a minute," he said. "I ain't downright hungry yet."

She sat down beside him. He reached over, took her hand, and laid it flat against his thigh with his own hand over it. They watched the great yellow moon rise up behind the trees. Suddenly a harsh scream came from the river.

Cassy jumped. "What's that?"

"It's a swan. Must a gone to roost already and something came prowling around."

"What you reckon it was?"

"Pole cat, most likely . . . I found the place where those swans roost the other day. Little island. Ground just white with down and the droppings a foot thick."

She did not answer. He pressed his hand closer over hers and put his other arm about her shoulders. "Reminds me of the old place on the Yadkin, hearing those swans cry. You could always hear the river there, from any place in the house. Ain't it funny now, I come all this way through the woods and found me another place on a river?"

A little sound came from the room behind them: Malcolm sighing in his sleep. She was on her feet. He followed her into the house. She bent over the cradle a minute, then came back to where he was standing beside the hearth.

The fire had been banked with coals since late afternoon. Only a few embers showed through the ashes. He took the poker and stirred them till they glowed, and brought fresh logs and laid them across the stone andirons. He fanned the embers with a turkey wing and a blaze sprang up; then, still on his knees, he looked over his shoulder into the room now filled with the bright light. His eyes rested on Frank's empty bed, then went to Cassy who had sat down on the stool at the other end of the hearth. He looked into her eyes and smiled. "This is the first night we been here by ourselves," he said, "the very first night."

She got up from the stool and came to him and put her arms about his neck. They were standing together there in the middle of the floor when she suddenly drew away. "There's somebody coming on horseback," she whispered.

Rion glanced at his rifle hung on its pegs over the door. He was moving towards it when a voice spoke from outside:

"Outlaw!"

"It's James Robertson," he said to Cassy. He went to the door. "What's the matter, Robertson?"

Robertson was pulling a limb of the big hickory down, getting ready to hitch his horse. He came up into the room on the trot, breathing hard, his grey eyes looking almost black in the firelight.

"I want you to go with me to Chota," he said.

"Chota?" Rion said. "What you going to Chota for? You had all the Indians in the country over at the Watauga today."

"They went home. All of 'em. In a huff."

"What's the matter?" Rion said. "Frank told me the trade went off all right."

Robertson looked at Cassy as if he were only just now seeing her. "Your pardon, mistress." He turned back to Rion. "The trade went off all right. The trouble started at the ball play. There was some bullies there from Wolf Hills. They killed that Cherokee they call Billie, before anybody knew what was happening. The chiefs and all the others just picked up then and left."

"Hunh," Rion said. He pushed a stool towards Robertson with his foot. Robertson shook his head. "I'm going to Chota," he said. "If I can just get to the Carpenter . . ."

Rion nodded. "They'd listen to you if they'd listen to anybody."

Robertson picked up his hat from where he had flung it on the table. "Well, you ready to go?"

"Now?"

"Now. They can't start anything for three or four days. Takes 'em that long to purify themselves. It ain't two hundred miles, they say. We got just time enough if we push right along."

Rion got his shot pouch and took his rifle down from the pegs. "I'll stop by Jacob's and tell Frank to step up here," he told Cassy; then he turned to Robertson.

"I'm ready."

CHAPTER 37

ROBERTSON HAD FED his horse before he left home and had a sack of corn tied to his saddle rings. They gave Gal ten good ears, then Rion saddled her and they started off. They went up to the head of the Island then took the trail that led along the east bank of the river.

The moon was up over the trees; the path before them was as light as day. It was the one they called the Great War Path, the one all the Indians took coming from their towns over in the hills.

Rion looked at Robertson. "Reckon we're likely to meet any of 'em coming along here?"

"Who?" Robertson said.

Rion had turned away but he looked back at the man. Robertson's old wool hat was clapped on the back of his head so that the brim rode up brash as a rooster's tail. Under it was a long, calm face that he might have been carrying to meeting. You couldn't imagine the expression of Robertson's face changing, no matter what happened. Well, the Lord only knew what was likely to happen on a trip like this. Rion rode a little closer to him.

"Indians," he said. "This is the way they come, ain't it?"

Robertson glanced to the left where the woods pressed up black. "We couldn't make much time traveling in there. And we got to make it in four days."

Rion laughed out. He raised himself stiff-legged in the stirrups the way he used to do long ago and Gal broke into a gallop. Rion let her gallop quite a way before he pulled her up.

"I'm glad we ain't taking anybody else," he said when Robertson caught up with him. "Get three men and you got three minds. . . . What you going to say to 'em after you get there?"

"I'm going to try first off to get to the Carpenter," Robertson said. "I believe I can make him listen."

"How'd it happen?" Rion asked. "How'd they happen to kill that Indian?"

"It was soon after the ball play started. The Crabtree boys was drunk and bragging. That Indian, Lying Fawn they call him, happened to run into one of 'em."

"D'you see it?"

"I was over on the other side of the field. First thing I knew the crowd was all gathering in one place. I pushed in. The Fawn was on the ground, doubled up. All of a sudden he straightened out. I saw where the bullet had gone and I knew it was ten to one it had found the heart. I went hunting for the chiefs."

"What became of the Crabtrees?"

"It was the oldest boy done it. He and the others was to horse and off before folks knew what had happened. . . . I pushed on around the crowd and there was Oconostota and the Carpenter with a lot of their men standing around. I couldn't find the linguister or anybody could talk, but I addressed myself to the Carpenter, best I could, making signs; going on about how sorry I was. He wouldn't even look at me after the first. Just watched the Fawn. The minute he was dead they said something to the young bucks and they picked him up and started up the trail with him. The Carpenter, he looked at me then, and sort of flung out his hand, and then he and Oconostota went after them."

"If you could have got hold of the linguister you might have done something with 'em."

"I don't know. They don't like to be hurried. When one of 'em's killed they're going to take time to mourn, no matter what. It don't do to fool with 'em then."

"I reckon you're right," Rion said, noticing how bright the moonlight was on the path.

They slept in deep woods that first night but the next day they came out on a savannah. There were mountains in the distance but the path led through a broad valley. Towards evening the mountains closed in, the trace got narrower. A river came dashing down the mountain and flowed beside the path.

Robertson called it the Nonachunheh and said the Indians named it that because it laughed so hard.

On the evening of the second day they came to another river, broad and swift, flowing over boulders that it had washed down from the mountainsides. They had no trouble in fording it. The path turned on itself at right angles, went back a way, and there, plain to see, was the ford. They crossed the river and were about to camp in a cane brake on the other side when Rion said, "Let's go up the river a piece."

Robertson reminded him that they had only one more feed of corn. "We ain't likely to find better forage than this. Better let the horses get it while they can." He waited a second, then he said, "They know we're coming along here anyway."

They hobbled the horses and turned them loose in the cane. While Rion was handling the horses Robertson had found a place sheltered by a fallen tree. They made a fire and roasted a turkey that Rion had shot that morning. They ate all they could. Robertson put what was left in his sack. "We can eat on this tomorrow," he said. "Better not fire any more shots than we have to."

Rion thought of what Robertson had said before supper. "What makes you think they know we're coming?" he asked.

"They may not know who it is but they'll know there are white men on the path. Oconostota'll have left some men behind to watch."

Rion thought of a party of Indians they had met the first day out. The silent, watchful eyes that never changed their expression all the time Robertson and the trader were talking. He and Robertson had fancied they saw a glow in the sky last night. It might have been that very party of Indians kindling a fire up on some bluff. They had a regular way of sending news by fires.

He rose and stamped out the embers of the fire. He had been tired when they stopped but he did not feel sleepy now. He looked at Robertson, wrapping his old cloak around him, ready to lie down for the night.

"I'll walk out here a way and see what the country's like," he told him and took his rifle and walked back towards the river. The land was higher than he had thought. They were camped on a bluff. He pushed through the pines and came out on a big boulder that overhung the river. On his left a stream flowed past the boulder to cascade a hundred feet into the river. He walked to the edge of the rock and stood there and watched the play of the little waterfall. It was only a jet of white at one end of a smooth stretch of water. The river was like a lake here, a long, still pool, almost enclosed by reeds. In the moonlight the water looked black. On the beach at the foot of this bluff he was standing on was a long white something.

"Swans," he thought.

He thought of his wife. Two nights ago he had been sitting beside her, telling about a place he'd found on the Holston where swans roosted. If he and Robertson got shot on this trip, would the news of how they died get back to the folks at home or would they just lie here and nobody even find their bodies?

There was a noise behind him. He whirled, ready to fire, and knocked against Robertson.

Robertson laughed and said he wasn't as sleepy as he'd thought he was. They walked along the bluff together. It curved in a little. You could see the swans plain now, a huddle of white a hundred feet below.

"Don't the Indians put swansdown on 'em when they come in peace?" he asked Robertson.

"They make a kind of crown out of the feathers," Robertson said.

"Couldn't we do something like that? To show 'em we're peaceful when we come up to the town?"

"That's for warriors. But we might make some kind of a sign."

Rion walked to the edge of the bluff and took aim. His shot blasted a swan from its roosting place out into the water. It floated, its body tip-tilted at first, then righting itself as the long neck that had been noosed like a vine slowly straightened out. Rion climbed down the side of the bluff and wading into the black water caught the warm, white thing just as it was drifting around the bend.

Back at the camp he took his knife and ripped from the body long pieces of skin that were thick with down. He wrapped the pieces of skin around two peeled sticks. When he had finished he took these wands to the branch, washed them free of blood, and held them up for Robertson to see.

"There's your swansdown. Now it's up to them to recognize their own sign."

All the next day they traveled at the base of a mountain higher than any they'd seen before. After that they came to a wide valley with another river to cross and then the path began to climb through broken hills. They went up hill and down for a whole day, and late in the evening came to a pass between two wooded ranges. The horses were winded by the last climb. They stopped to rest them and realized as they looked down into the valley that they were at the end of their journey.

There was a wide plain with a river running through it and on the banks of the river a collection of houses. The woods were thick next to the river but on this side of the houses were open lands.

"It looks like a town, with real folks living in it!" Rion said in surprise.

They followed the path down into the valley. The woods stopped at the foot of the hills. They rode for a while through open lands that were covered with wild grass, and came suddenly on a field planted in corn. The blades were ankle deep, a good stand, but the hills planted so close that they choked each other. There was a young pumpkin vine putting out its leaves at the base of each stalk, and in the vacant space between the rows something else was growing. Rion was leaning out of the saddle, trying to see whether it was beans or more pumpkins when Robertson behind him said, "Hist!"

Rion straightened up. Over in the middle of the field was a scaffold built of hickory poles. Sitting on top of it, holding long leafy switches in their hands, were two old women. Their bodies, bare above the waist, were the thinnest Rion had ever seen. They held their wizened faces perfectly still, but their black eyes flickered over Robertson, over Rion, and away from them to the village. The next instant they had slid from the scaffold and were off through the corn rows.

Rion laughed. "They look like old grapes," he said, "old dried-up fox grapes. Reckon that's why they put them out here, to dry in the sun?"

"They're out here to scare the deer off," Robertson said, "but I wish they hadn't a been. They're in the town by this time, telling them we're coming."

He had his white wand out and was holding it up before him, stiff as a poker. Rion did the same. They rode slowly through the field and up to the first house.

There were two of them, set almost opposite each other, square cribs but with the logs standing on end instead of supporting each other. Between them a lane opened up. On each side of it were more houses with garden patches beside them.

An Indian was coming out of the first house, a tall, strong-looking fellow with nothing on but a breech clout. He was stooping to get through the low doorway and his eyes were on the ground.

When he straightened up Rion and Robertson were halting their horses in front of him.

He glanced at them and then he looked away to the hills they had just come out of, as if those hills could tell him who they were.

Robertson held his wand up and shook it towards the Indian and said some word he'd learned from them, coupling it with the chief's name. "Atta Kulla Kulla," he said and shook his wand again.

The chief's name seemed to bring the Indian to. He ran his tongue over his lips and stepped towards them and began to talk, so fast that Rion thought they couldn't have understood him even if they'd known the language.

"He's asking something," Robertson said.

"Look out!" Rion said and pointed up the street. A rabble was heading towards them, a few men in front and behind them a lot of women and children.

Robertson leaned towards the Indian. "Take us to Atta Kulla Kulla," he said, loud and sharp.

The Indian gave him a quick look, then grasped his bridle rein and began to lead the horse up the street. Robertson turned and gave Rion a look over his shoulder. Rion smiled. Robertson was rattled, afraid this Indian would take him off by himself.

Rion whipped up his own horse and pressed close behind them. They were heading straight for the mob. Two men who were in the forefront suddenly sprang to one side and came up to the Indian who was leading the horse. He stopped and said something, then started on again. The two men fell in with him and the mob closed in behind.

Rion looked down and saw at his stirrup a boy's thin face and staring eyes. He drew his foot back as if he might dig the child in the ribs. The child laughed but his laughter was cut short by a hand that fell on his shoulder and dragged him back into the crowd.

"Don't tease 'em," Robertson said in a low voice.

They turned down a lane where the houses were even thicker. In some of the yards women were cooking over open fires. They stared at the procession. A few joined it but most of them stayed where they were, staring.

They took another turn. The Indian stopped and pointed to where a glow came from behind a clump of linden trees. Robertson was getting down off his horse, falling over two or three Indian children as he did so. The mob fell back. Rion followed Robertson up a little rise.

There was a house behind the clump of trees. The glow came from a fire outside. Women were cooking around it. There was a bearskin spread on the ground. The old, yellow chief was lounging on it. A naked child, four or five years old, was sitting beside him. As Rion and Robertson came up the rise the chief reached over and with his left hand tumbled and touselled the child as if he had been a puppy or a kitten.

The child's cries were still in the air as the two white men went towards him.

Robertson walked to within a few feet of where the chief was lying and stopped and said his name.

The chief got to his feet and came towards them. The child ran after him and, wanting to play some more, tugged at his hand. He took his hand away and, laying it for a minute on the child's head, stepped away from him.

He looked at Robertson and spoke his name and then his face tightened up and he did not say anything more.

Robertson went towards him, saying the word for friend and brother and holding out his hand. The chief did not take Robertson's hand and draw him to him, the way they usually did. Instead he began talking in a high voice, waving his hands to and fro.

Robertson put on a sad look and brought his hands, one of them still holding the white wand, up in front of him, and then let them fall away quick to his sides to show how bad he felt not to understand. Then he called the name of the man who had linguisted for them at the Island.

The chief shook his head and took his two hands and threw them before him in a sort of galloping motion.

"He means he's ridden off somewhere," Rion whispered.

The chief looked at him hard; then he looked down at the ground as if he were trying to make up his mind. Finally he called one of the women over and said something to her. She started off down the street.

Robertson came over and stood beside Rion. There was sweat on his forehead and his voice was hoarse as if he had been talking a long time. "If he's this hard to handle I don't know what we'll do with Oconostota," he whispered.

Rion felt that the old chief could read their minds even if he didn't understand what they were saying. "Don't try to talk to him any more," he said. "He's sent for a linguister. Wait till he gets here."

"There he comes now," Robertson said. "White man, ain't it?"

Rion did not answer. He was staring at the man who was stepping up into the yard. As naked as an Indian and as red, with his head shaved back to the scalp lock and silver rings hanging heavy from his ears. He came on up to them. The light from the fire was on his face.

"It's Archy," Rion said, "Archy Outlaw."

CHAPTER 38

As THEY MADE their way through the crowd Rion put his hand up and pulled at the collar of his shirt. The leather seemed to have stiffened and no wonder, being out in the wet so much—or was it that his neck was bigger than usual? The last few hours he had felt as if a band was around his throat, not tight enough to choke him but there at the base of his throat ready to be drawn tight. The feeling had come over him when Archy stepped up into that yard and it had stayed with him all through supper. The Indian woman had given them some sort of boiled bread, made out of beans and potatoes. Robertson kept saying it was the best thing he ever tasted. He, Rion, had taken a piece in his hand and was about to bite into it when that feeling came over him, and he had to lay it down. Robertson noticed, and whispered to him that he'd better eat or they might take offense. He'd taken some of the meat then but it was all he could do to get it down, first time in his life he'd ever felt that way at table—if you could call a bearhide spread on the ground a table.

Their guards—they had one apiece—were stooping in the midst of a cleared circle, before a reed couch spread with skins. Robertson was sitting down. Rion did the same. The guards stepped away. Robertson turned his head long enough to whisper:

"You notice they didn't give us anything to drink?"

Rion nodded. Both white men faced towards the town house. It was built on a little rise so that the chiefs who sat on the seats placed against its long east wall were up above the rest of the people. The old Carpenter sat on the white seat, being peace chief. A few feet away from him was the war chief, Oconostota, on a chair as red as madder. There was another chief, head over all of them: the Old Tassel they called him. He was away on a hunt and that big, pockmarked young chief who had been at the Island that day was with him.

The Indians standing behind Rion and Robertson pressed up, so close that one of them pushed against Rion's shoulder. You could

275

hear them shuffling back, laughing and whispering. It gave a man a strange feeling to have that many of them there at his back even if they weren't doing anything more than mocking him. He had caught one of them at that on the way over here. A long, tall devil, supple as a piece of whang leather. He had suddenly whipped off that piece of cloth he had tied about him and tied it on again, making a pair of breeches the way children might do. After he got them fixed he went straddling along stiff-legged as a goat with his head up in the air. The others howled like wolves. Even Robertson laughed.

"They don't believe in a man tying up his arse," he said.

Rion stared straight ahead. The old Carpenter looked as small as a child up there on his high white seat, the eagle feathers that he held in his lap covering all his feet and legs. The other chief, Oconostota, had a fan of the same feathers in his lap. He was the fiercer looking of the two, being over six feet tall, with the longest head Rion had ever seen on any man. But he did not have the power over the people that the Carpenter had—unless, Robertson said, somebody struck the war pole. Everything would be given over into his hands then. The thing was to keep it from coming to that. That was what Robertson had been working for all the time he had been talking to Archy.

Rion felt suddenly as if he couldn't sit still. He got to his feet. Robertson turned his head quickly and gave him a look. "What you doing?"

"I just thought I'd stand up a while."

"Sit down," Robertson said. "There's some of 'em looking at you now."

Rion sat down. A ring of Indians was crowding up at the corner of the town house. He let his eyes travel over them and then on to the fire that blazed up at the right of where the chiefs sat. It was moonlight but they had kindled a fire just the same. It made the whole square as light as day. He looked back into the crowd. They were not all Indians. A white face every now and then. Traders. They looked away the minute they knew you were looking at them. There was one white man taller than any of the others. A black-haired fellow, leaning against a tree and wearing a blue, frogged coat with an officer's scarlet hat cocked on his head. He kept his arms folded and looked off over the crowd as if he was not much interested in what was going on.

An Indian came out from the town house, carrying a bearskin. He laid it down on the ground in front of the chiefs, then stood, his hands stiff at his sides, looking down at the skin. Another Indian was coming up. He was carrying a gun and a round whitish stone. He laid the things down on the bearskin and stepped around to where the other Indian stood.

They went off together. Big, strong-looking bucks, picked probably because they looked alike, walking off side by side, their arms, even the feathers in their scalp locks, swinging at the same slant. Rion watched the firelight lick up the naked thigh that was nearest him and thought that no matter how big they were or how strong, there was always something womanish looking about them.

"What did they lay that white rock down there for?" he asked Robertson.

"It's a chungke stone, what they play ball with." Robertson half raised himself from the couch, then fell back. "Those are the things belonged to Lying Fawn, I reckon." He gave a sigh. "Well, they got to go through the thing their own way."

Rion was watching the young buck who was coming up to stand in front of the chiefs. Greased all over and his head shaved. Silver rings in his ears, a shell gorget on his breast, and nothing else on but a breech clout. He turned his head a little to one side. There was a feather stuck through his scalp lock. That meant that he was one of their fighting men.

Archy stood with his face turned half to the chiefs and half to the people. There was the same look on his face that he had had this evening when he stepped up into that yard and the light fell on him and Rion knew that he had found his brother here among these Indians.

He had jumped over a baby that was crawling between his legs. "*Archy!*" he cried and his arm was out and over the boy's back. "Archy!" he cried and remembered now the feeling of his hand on the naked back as he drew the boy to him.

But Archy was pulling away even before he'd finished hugging him. Robertson saw that something was up before Rion did. He said, "*Listen to him, Outlaw!*" and Rion listened and felt Archy's eyes on him hard as flint, though he was smiling. "*Don't tell 'em I'm your brother. Make out you know me, all right, but don't tell 'em I'm your brother.*"

Rion had looked away without saying anything. The old chief came up. Archy spoke to him. The old chief made a sound like a clucking hen or like women being polite at meeting. Then Archy turned back and began talking again, asking questions about the folks, pleasant, laughing, and all the time holding him off with his eyes. At the last he had said, sticking it in with some linguisting, "Don't you try to see me. I'll fix it so we can get together."

"Things were mixed up enough without this," Robertson said when he was gone.

"You want he should stay with these Indians the rest of his life?"

Robertson shook his head. "I'll go as far as the next man to help him get out, but one thing at a time I always say. We got enough on our hands."

"I ain't going out of this town without him," Rion said.

"All right," Robertson said, "but don't do anything brash. You heard what he said?"

"I heard what he said," Rion told him, "and I saw him too. All fixed up like a raree show. Turned my stomach."

"Well, a man lands in one of these towns he's got to do the best he can," Robertson said.

That had been three or four hours ago. Rion and Robertson had not been alone together since then. Under guard every minute, even when they were sitting at supper with the old chief. The old chief had thawed a little while they were eating supper. It looked like he was willing to forget about the Lying Fawn, but of course it would all depend on what was said at the council. . . .

A big Indian was coming up to where the bearskin lay. He picked the gun up in one hand and the chungke stone in the other, and walked out in front of the chiefs.

"That's the Raven of Chota," Robertson whispered. "He's nephew to the war chief."

The Raven called the Lying Fawn's name, and leaned over and with the barrel of his gun slowly made marks on the ground; he rose, looking at Archy.

Archy faced around towards the crowd. "Ten winters," he said. "He was ten winters drilling his stone and polishing it but he will not be at the ball play again. His chungke stone goes to his son. . . ."

A boy came leaping out of the crowd, moaning. The Raven handed the stone to him; then turning to the crowd, he talked wildly, shaking the gun at them, all of a sudden stopping short, panting as if he had been running a mile.

Archy's voice might have come out of the man's own mouth. "This gun is burning in my hand and I know that your guns are burning too."

A yell rose, as strange a sound as Rion had ever heard in his life. It came from the Fawn's son. Rion could see the boy's mouth, still open, but the sound seemed to come from far off, from somebody walking by himself in the forest. It died. Other mouths opened. It rose again but now it did not seem far off but as if the man was coming towards you.

"Gr't God!" Robertson said under his breath.

Rion kept his eyes on Archy. "Don't he *know* he's working 'em up?"

"He has to tell 'em what's said. There's traders here know English." Robertson drew a long breath. "I' God *he's* going to talk now!"

The old Carpenter was standing up. He laid his eagle feathers down on the chair and walked out towards the crowd. He stood a minute, looking at them and then he smiled, a kind of pitying smile.

"You say that your guns are burning in your hands. That is always the way with brave young men. But the gun can speak only one word. It cannot even tell you which way it wants to send the bullet. Are you sure that these guns burn to send bullets against the white men? Remember that it was our white brothers gave us these guns. Will these guns turn against their fathers? It may be that they burn to send bullets against the Creeks."

He was still smiling and his black eyes were wide open and glistening the way they had been that day at the island. All the time Archy was linguisting he kept those black, shining eyes on the crowd. When Archy stopped speaking he turned them suddenly on Robertson.

Robertson was on his feet, speaking in a voice that sounded windy and broken. "The white men that killed the Lying Fawn were no friends of ours. Rascals. If we had known what was toward we'd have barred them from the play."

There was a long silence. The Raven stood there, his hands hanging at his sides, his eyes on the ground.

Robertson looked around him. None of the Indians looked back at him. They all kept their eyes on the ground. That seemed to rattle Robertson. He took a step towards the Carpenter. "We're done now," Rion thought, "He's lost his head." But the Carpenter was shifting his stance. His left foot, going back, put a pace between him and Robertson. That seemed to bring Robertson to. His face changed. His right hand swept back to point to the path over the hills. "We have come from a far river to talk to our brothers about this mistake that has been made. Would we have come all this way if our hearts had not been right?"

The Carpenter did not answer. It was the Raven. His voice was stony, his look sad. "The Lying Fawn was a brave warrior but he did not fall in the fight. He fell, visiting friends, before he even had time to be weighed on the Path."

Robertson was going to answer but the chief spoke: "Our white brother does not speak with a snake's tongue. It is true that the Lying Fawn is gone and gone before he had time to be weighed on the Path, but many a brave man has gone the same way. Last winter Round O, one of our bravest young men, fell from a big rock and his body was broken in pieces. It was not Round O's heart failed him. It was his foot slipped. So with our white brothers. Their hearts are right towards us. It was the foot that slipped . . ."

The Raven looked at the peace chief and then he looked up at his uncle. The war chief had moved while the others were talking but now he sat with his arms folded, staring off over the crowd as if what was going on was no concern of his. The Raven looked back at the Carpenter and then cast his eyes sullenly on the ground. The Carpenter waited a second and spoke again:

"Blood has been spilled on the path but it has been covered up. These two white men, our brothers, came along the path and found the blood there and kneeled down and covered it up with their hands. It is all covered up now. . . . We shall not even look where it lies."

He was walking back to his seat, turning his back on them as if there was nothing more to say.

Robertson was sitting down beside Rion. Rion laid his hand on his knee. "I believe that fixed 'em," he whispered.

"I don't know," Robertson said. He leaned forward to peer around the corner of the town house. When he looked back at Rion his long face was split in two by a smile. "It's all right. They're fixing to drink with us!"

They sat there and waited while two Indians came stepping up and waved fans of eagle feather over their heads. After that they were led up to where the chiefs were sitting. A seat covered with some white stuff was brought out of the town house and set between the two chiefs. They sat there and drank the black drink out of big conch shells, and after that they ate some more and there was dancing.

Late at night they were taken to the cabin where they were to sleep. Half a dozen young bucks went with them, carrying guns, and fastened the door of the cabin after them.

They had been in there only a few minutes when the door was unfastened and a man stepped into the room. It was the man Rion had noticed wearing an officer's hat and leaning against a tree. His name was Captain Nat Gist, he said. He had come to take Rion to his brother.

CHAPTER 39

RION WANTED to take Robertson with him but Gist said it was better not. He'd only asked for one of the white men. "I told 'em we wanted to talk over old times. Old friends, I told 'em, raised in the same town."

"Go on," Robertson said. "Don't pay any attention to me. Go on."

Rion looked at the man and decided to trust him. They went outside. The Indians lying on the ground before the cabin rose up as they passed, then sank down again without saying anything.

"I told 'em I'd be responsible for getting you back inside an hour," Gist said.

Rion did not say anything.

They walked on down the street and came to a house that sat off a little from the others. Rion noticed a wild plum thicket growing up at the back of it.

Gist stood back. Rion went inside. Archy was there. Rion went to him and catching him by the elbows half lifted him from the floor.

"Archy, hinny!" he said.

Archy laughed out as he broke away from him. "I didn't know what to do when I came up in the yard and saw you standing there," he said, "and then I remembered they couldn't understand, no matter what we said."

He sat down on a bench that was placed against the wall. Rion sat down beside him, looking around as he did so. There was furniture in the room. A chest over against the far wall and in that same corner a couch with skins piled on it. There was another smaller piece of furniture that he couldn't make out beside the couch. This must be a summer house for there was no chimney to be seen anywhere. He realized suddenly that there was no window either but there was not much need for one. No chinking between any of the logs. The moonlight lay in broad stripes all over the floor.

He looked at Archy. "You got your own house?" he asked.

Archy was sitting full in a shaft of light that came in between the logs. He had his head tilted to one side, studying Rion's face. "Yes," he said; and then, "you ain't changed much, Rion."

Rion laughed. "It ain't been so long as all that."

"No," Archy said, "it ain't been so long."

Rion tried to think back to the day Archy had been lost. He could remember searching all that night and the next day and then the long days after that when they were gradually giving up hope, but he could not remember the moment when they first knew the boy was gone.

"How'd they get hold of you?" he asked.

"It was when we came down on to that savannah. Remember? I was ahead of the rest. I came up to that creek and found buffalo trace and started up the other side."

"And they was waiting there to get you?"

"I ran into 'em."

"And you been here ever since? . . . They good to you?"

Archy raised his head and looked Rion full in the eyes. "Like I was one of *them*," he said.

There was a sudden sharp, querulous sound from the corner of the room. Rion did not know what it was at first. He saw that what had seemed a heap of skins there on the couch was raising itself. A girl, half naked, with long black hair hanging loose around her shoulders.

She sat up on the couch, leaned over, and with her foot rocked the log cradle that was setting in front of her.

"That your woman?" Rion asked.

Archy said "Yes," then called out something to her in Cherokee. She answered and kept on rocking the cradle with her foot. But the baby that was in the cradle would not be quiet. The woman finally took him up and held him in her arms, patting him on the back.

"Maybe he's got colic," Rion said, thinking of the way Cassy used to hold Malcolm up to her shoulder and pat the wind out of him after each meal.

Archy did not answer. After a minute he said, "You ever heard anything from the folks?"

Rion shook his head. "Nobody's coming through from that way. But the country's settling up fast, I tell you."

"Where did you settle?" Archy asked.

"On the lower Holston. Not far from the Long Island. I got me two acres cleared already and a house built. I'll make two hundred bushel of corn this year if the varmints don't get it. Pretty good garden patch too."

"How's Cassy?" Archy asked.

"Tolerable. We've got a boy. Born last January."

"What'd you name him?"

"Malcolm, after the old man," Rion said. He did not say that Cassy had wanted to name him Archy. They had almost quarreled over that. "I ain't going to have it," Rion had said at the last. "You reckon I want to hear him called a dozen times a day: '*Archy! Archy! Archy!*'" and he had got up and left the house and flung off into the woods.

He looked over at the woman and the baby on the couch. "How old's that one?"

"Near a year old."

"What you call him?"

"The Fox. But he'll have three or four names before he's done," Archy said wearily.

"All of their names mean something?"

"Most of 'em."

The woman suddenly laughed; she called out something and set the baby on the floor.

"What's she say?" Rion asked curiously.

"Says it's too light in here for him to sleep."

The baby was crawling towards them. When he was halfway there Archy picked him up and sat down again. The baby dug his toes into Archy's thighs and stiffening his whole body reached up and caught at the feather that was stuck through his hair.

Rion looked away from them. "You been here nearly three years," he said. "Didn't you ever try to run off?"

"Once. They'd taken my gun but I started out with a knife I stole. I was out in the woods four days. Nothing to eat but a rabbit I brought down with the knife."

"So you come on back?"

"I run into a hunting party. I come on home with them."

The baby was squirming in Archy's hold. Archy leaned over and put him on the floor. As he was crawling off he set his hand on Rion's moccasin, then as if realizing that the foot was strange to him he tilted his little head and looked up. Rion held himself still and looked down at him. The little round face was topped by coarse dark hair. In this light his eyes looked black too, but you couldn't tell. By daylight they might be as light a brown as Archy's.

The hand was lifted. The baby was crawling off. Rion eased his breath out and turned to Archy.

"This Captain Gist that brought me over here, can you depend on him?"

Archy did not answer for a minute; then he said: "I ain't ever had much to do with him but they say he's a stout man and knows the woods as well as any white man in the Nation."

"He looks like he could fight if it came to that," Rion said. "The question is, would he stand by you?"

"How you mean?"

"Would he help you get away from here?" Rion said sharply. "You been here three years now. You want to stay here the rest of your life?"

Archy did not answer.

"Well," Rion said, "what you think?"

Still Archy did not answer.

Rion turned away from him and began walking up and down the room. The girl on the couch was staring at him but he did not pay any attention to her. Finally he stopped in front of Archy.

"All right then, if you don't want to take Gist in on it. I don't trust" (he did not realize until afterwards what he had said), "I don't trust a squaw man anyhow. We can manage by ourselves. Just us two'll be best. There's a thicket grows right up to the back of your house here. A man could hide in that." He went over and ran his whole arm and shoulder into an aperture between the logs; then he was back before Archy. "Well, what say?"

Archy got to his feet. He put his hand on Rion's arm. "We couldn't get out of here tonight. There's a man watching every brake."

He was whispering. It suddenly occurred to Rion that the woman on the couch might have learned some English from him. "Well?" he said in a low tone. "How you want to go about it?"

Archy walked over to a bench just inside the door. There was a jug sitting on the bench with a long-necked gourd lying beside it. Archy dipped down into the jug and brought the gourd up full. "Want a drink?"

Rion shook his head.

Archy drank his dipper off, then put it back in its place. "You go on back with Gist," he said. "And in the morning you and Robertson start off, just like you hadn't seen me. I'll catch up with you."

"How'll you get away?"

Archy shook his head and smiled. There was an expression on his face Rion had seen often, when Archy was a boy and would slip off to the swimming hole to get out of work, and then when he came back to the field try to act as if he never had been gone, or when their father would try to find out who it was had left the hoes in the field or the pasture bars down. A sly one Archy had always been and slyer than ever since living with these Indians. But probably his way was the best, to slip out of town by himself and join them on the trail after they were out of sight of the town. . . .

There was a knocking at the door, not loud but prolonged.

"All right," Rion called.

He struck Archy lightly on the shoulder. "Goodnight, boy. You be careful."

"Goodnight," Archy said and followed him through the door. He was still there, a long, black shadow beside the door when Rion looked back just before rounding the bend in the path.

CHAPTER 40

RION TRIED to talk to the white man, Gist, on his way back to their prison. But Gist would not talk, except about the settlements on the Watauga and the Holston. He was curious to know about them, how many head of people there were, where they came from and whether they were likely to stay on the western waters.

"They'll stay if the Indians don't run 'em off," Rion told him.

"The head men here are willing for 'em to stay," Gist said. "They signed to that, didn't they?"

"They made their mark on it," Rion said, "but that ain't saying they'll keep their word."

Gist was ahead of him on the path. He turned around. "The Cherokees think a lot of their word," he said, "specially the head men. I never knew 'em to break it." He was silent a minute, and then he said, "Of course the agent may not think the way they do about the settlers staying. After all, the law says for 'em to remove."

"We got a law of our own now on the Holston," Rion told him. "We may choose to go by our law instead of the British agent's."

"It ain't the agent's law. It's His Majesty's government."

"His Majesty ain't ever been on this side of the water. He don't even know how much land there is. Looks to me like he ain't got no right to say who shall settle where, when there's land enough to go around."

Gist turned around again and looked at him. "You're talking treason, ain't you?"

"Maybe so. You come to the Watauga or the Holston and you'll hear a lot of the same talk."

They were at the cabin. Rion told the captain that he was much obliged to him, and stepped inside without offering to shake hands. A minute later he heard the bolt shut and knew they were shut in for the night.

Robertson was kneeling by the chimney that went up in the middle of the room, holding his gun in his hand. "I thought I better

not go to sleep," he said. "There's been somebody around here. I
could hear 'em on the roof."

Rion stooped and thrust his head up the chimney. It was ill
made and very small. The scrap of starlight that he could see was
no larger than a man's hand. "I don't believe a man could get down
it," he said. "Maybe they was just up there spying on us."

"Maybe," Robertson said, "but we better not go to sleep at the
same time. You go over and lay down. I'll watch awhile."

"I don't feel like sleeping," Rion said. "You lay down first."

Robertson went over to the couch and lay down. Rion squatted
down near the chimney. He wondered what time it was and con-
cluded that it must be after midnight. For a while there had been
yelling and singing off towards the square but that had quieted
down. There was no sound to be heard at all now except night
noises, the cry of some animal now and then or the creaking of a
branch in the wind. Of course that owl he'd just heard hooting
might be one Indian signalling to another. They could imitate any
sound in the woods he'd heard. He looked around him watchfully.
The moon was waning, but there was still light enough to see everything in the room. The bed Robertson was sleeping on was made
out of stout pieces of cane; buffalo tugs threaded through the hollows held the pieces of cane together. A nice piece of work. He
had thought that these Indians lived like beasts of the wood, but they
had houses like everybody else, only everything was different from
the way a white man would have it, this chimney here in the middle
of the floor instead of going up outside the wall the way a Christian
would have it. There was a neat little out-house at the back of
Archy's cabin. A hen-house; he had heard the chickens cra-aking as
they came up the path. Archy had accumulated as much gear as
he had in these three years, only it was Indian gear, not white
man's.

He ought not to have said that about not trusting a squaw man,
but that was what Archy was. It was too bad he'd been here long
enough to get him a woman and father a child, but it was to be
expected. The traders all had Indian wives. The boy had gone on
and done like the rest without thinking much about it. He'd always
been one to go with the crowd, not taking any thought of who he
was or what his folks stood for. . . . That time on the way home
from church, rolling around in the leaves with Lessie Robinson. The

boy might have got mixed up with that trash for life if he, Rion, hadn't come along.

He thought of Cassy and became excited imagining how it would be when they got home: he and Robertson coming up the path and Cassy standing in the door and seeing the man with them and maybe not being able to make out who it was. Let her live a long life. She'd never get a bigger surprise than she would have then. They must put a shirt on him, cover up that paint and those pictures, a deer it looked like, pricked into him with gun-powder.

Something fell on the roof with a plop. He was on his feet and then he realized what it was: an acorn dropping. That was what Robertson had heard when he thought somebody was scampering on the roof. He, Rion, had been sitting here all night ready to fire against the acorns dropping off the trees!

The noise had waked Robertson. He was coming over. "Here, you lay down awhile. I've had a good sleep."

"All right," Rion said and went over and lay down on the couch. He closed his eyes and for awhile could think of nothing but the moment when he got home, and the folks would look out and see that he had Archy with him. The vision grew less bright each time he summoned it and finally faded before the strange Indian faces that seemed to come crowding around his bed. He told himself that he would not let them keep him awake and shut his eyes and, grasping his rifle firmly in his right hand, turned on his side and went to sleep.

Robertson woke him at daylight to tell him that a lot of Indians were heading for the cabin. They were the guards of the night before, come to take them to the Carpenter's house. A fire was going in the same place there under the linden trees and women were cooking around it.

Archy was not there. The white man, John Vann, who had been with the Carpenter when Rion first saw him at the Long Island, acted as linguister. He came and stood beside them as they ate, and asked about the settlements on the Watauga and the Holston. Robertson told him that he did not get around much and could not say how many settlers there were or where they came from.

The man laughed. "This is a long trip for you then."

"I hope I never have to take it again," Robertson told him.

The old Carpenter was getting on his horse, said he would ride with them a way. Rion wondered whether Archy knew that they would have an escort out of town and decided that he probably did. That might be the reason that he did not appear at breakfast. He might have gone on ahead, might even now be at the place where they would meet.

They rode out of town the same way they had come in. The Carpenter had a dozen young bucks with him. They wanted to go on farther but he would not let them. When he was ready to go back he got down off his horse and came over to Rion and Robertson and "took them by the arm," as the Indians put it, and said that they were his friends and brothers and his heart would always be straight towards them. When they looked back, after entering the open lands, they could still see him, sitting there on his horse, looking after them.

"He'll sit there till we're clean out of sight," Robertson said.

"It don't make much difference," Rion said. "I've an idea Archy's on ahead."

"He won't have a horse."

"He might. If he don't we can ride and tie."

As they rode on they looked around, wondering where Archy could be hid. There was not much cover. A big oak here and there or a wild plum thicket, but for the most part the land was covered with wild grass. It was waist high in some places. A man could lie hid in it but he could not hide his horse. Rion looked off to the right and saw, where the road took a bend, an out-cropping of rock, one big boulder, with half a dozen smaller ones scattered around it.

"He could hide there," he said.

They rode on. When they were almost level with the rocks a man stepped out into the road in front of them. A tall man, heavier built than Archy, wearing an officer's hat.

"I've a message for you, Master Outlaw, from your brother. He says for you to go on ahead."

"Go on ahead? What's he mean? Ain't he coming too?"

"He can't get away."

Rion rode over closer to the man. "Has something gone wrong?"

"Not that I know of."

"Well, why'n't he come then?"

"He said for you to go on ahead."

Rion turned around and glared at Robertson. "I ain't going without him," he said. "You can go on by yourself if you want. I'm going back."

Captain Gist had sat down on a rock and was studying the toe of his moccasin. He looked up. "I wouldn't go back if I was you."

"Why not? There's a linguister there can talk for me. Archy can, for that matter."

"It won't do you any good."

"That old yellow chief. I'll put a bullet in him."

"And git yourself and me killed too," Robertson murmured.

"Shut up!" Rion said. "It ain't your brother."

Captain Gist stood up. "It won't do any good to talk to the Carpenter. He can't make your brother come."

Rion slowly lowered his eyes to the ground. In the silence he could hear Robertson's horse tearing away at the grass; then Robertson gave a sigh.

Gist took a step towards Rion. "Any message you want to send?"

Rion raised his head. The two men watching him were startled to see how in those few seconds the blood had risen in his cheeks until the whole face was swollen up to the eye-lids. He fixed his shining, red-brown eyes on Gist. "No," he said.

A curious expression came on Gist's face. He was about to turn away but he stopped. "Don't you take it too hard," he said softly. "There's many a man comes here to the Nation and stays awhile and don't want to leave."

Rion looked at the man as if he were surprised to find him still there. "Hanh?" he said, and when he found Gist's black eyes still fixed on him he made a weary gesture with his hand. "No," he said again, "there ain't any message."

CHAPTER 41

CASSY'S SECOND CHILD was born that summer, a girl whom they named Sarah for Rion's mother. Rion worked harder than usual that fall, clearing another quarter of an acre and building a crib to hold his corn. He also built Jocasta a hen-house, for she had got a setting of eggs from Charles Robertson's wife early in the spring and now had a small flock of chickens.

Charles Robertson often came by the Outlaws on his way to the store in Carter's valley. He was more of a talker than his brother, James, and always stopped long enough to pass the time of day and tell the news over his way.

There were neighbors to visit now if a man wanted to spend his time gadding. Two families had settled across the river from Rion's place. One family had a parcel of children. The other family consisted of a middle-aged man and his sister. He was a fiddler. Some said he had kept school and would like to keep one again if he could find scholars. Cassy didn't like his looks and said that she didn't know that she'd want Malcolm or Sarah to be under him. Rion laughed at that. Sarah hadn't begun to notice yet and Malcolm wouldn't be learning his AB-Abs for many a day yet and when he did wouldn't need to go from home with a schoolmaster right in the house.

Cassy said that if there was a school Frank ought to keep it. He was the most learned man on the waters anywhere around. Charles Robertson said there was no doubt of that but added that there'd probably be enough scholars soon to keep two masters busy, the way the country was settling up.

That was in January. It was the hour of the noon-day rest, an unseasonably warm day. They were all out in the dooryard, Cassy on the steps, the men sitting on up-ended chunks of wood when Charles Robertson came up the path and sat down among them. He sat down, facing the river. "I declare," he said, "I can see the water shining through them leaves."

"We been noticing that ever since the last clearing," Cassy told him.

Charles turned to her. His broad Irish face was solemn; then he grinned, the way a man does when he has news he is anxious to tell. "You clear out a few more trees and you can see the road," he said.

"I'd be feared to," Rion told him. "It might hurt my eyes, watching all them carriages go past."

A robin that had stayed the winter suddenly flew to the top of the hickory tree and piped a few sharp notes. They looked up and saw the bare bough the bird perched on with the other black boughs crowding against it and thought of all the wintry skeletons that lay between them and their old homes, and they laughed. Charles Robertson laughed loudest of all, and nervously, then suddenly leaned forward, looking at Rion. "You'll live to see wagons, and plenty of 'em, going through this valley," he said.

Rion said: "I come of long-lived folks but ain't none of 'em lived to be old as Methuselah yet." But his eyes rested on Charles' face speculatively.

Charles jumped up and came towards him. "There's a road going to be cut at the head of the Long Island. I talked to the men who're going to cut it."

"And who be they?"

"They's twenty or thirty of 'em, from North Carolina. They stopped by James' place yesterday, to bring him a letter from Judge Henderson."

"Henderson . . ." Rion said. "I used to know a Judge Henderson in Carolina. Dick Henderson he was."

"Richard Henderson and Company," Charles said. "There's nine in the company, but this Judge Henderson he's top bear dog. He's a going to buy up the whole country, done already traded with the Indians for it, and now he's sent some men on ahead to cut a road."

"What country is it he's got hold of?" Rion asked. He suddenly sat up straighter. "It better not be any of the land around here, after all the trouble James and me had fixing things up with the Cherokee."

"It's far above the Island," Charles said, "what they call the Kentuck. All the country between the Louisa and the Shawano. *He's done already traded with the Indians for it.*"

"He might trade with 'em and not be able to take it up," Rion said slowly.

"He ain't going to try to take it up himself. He's going to sell it off in parcels, to settlers. Three, four hundred acres in a tract. James has had two letters from him setting it all forth." He laughed, calmer now that he had got his news told. "Charlotte says James had better hurry up and get him some learning now he's hearing from all these big men."

"How's he getting along with his learning?" Cassy asked.

"He's clean through the primer and reading some in the Bible now. Every night he writes up two whole sheets of foolscap. A fair letter he wrote the other night, Charlotte said. Next time he gets a letter she's going to let him answer it himself."

"I tried to learn once," Rion said absently. "Went to Frank here a whole winter but it never done me no good. . . . How come all these big men writing to James?"

"Why, on account of what he done, him and you. News of it had got down to Charleston, through the Indians, I reckon. Judge Henderson he'd heard all about it, and said in his letter that the Watauga men ought to be proud to have James living amongst them. He didn't say anything about you. Don't reckon he knew you were along."

"I didn't do any of the talking," Rion said. He was silent a moment; then: "You say you seen these men are going to cut the road for Henderson's company?"

"There's twenty or thirty of 'em, mostly from Rutherford. Man named Boone at the head of 'em. He's been through here before. You know him?"

"Aye," Rion said. "I knew him too. In Carolina." He rose and picked up his axe. "I better be getting back to work," he said, but after he had spoken he stood a minute looking off into the woods. "Daniel Boone, still going to Kentuck!"

"I never thought he'd come through here," Cassy said.

"It's on the way," Rion said. "That fine grazing country he used to talk of lies up here above the Island, from all folks tell me." He glanced at Cassy. She'd been as excited as the rest while Robertson was telling his news but now she looked sad as if, lonesome as she was, she was sorry to hear about the country opening up. He walked over and laid his hand on her hair. "What you so down in the mouth for?"

She turned her face up to his and she smiled. "I was thinking about the folks that'll be coming, on the road, only there ain't no road, camping every night and moving on the next day. It's a hard way to live."

"Well, they can go on past," he said. "We don't have to move, not if we're satisfied."

She kept her face turned up while her eyes searched his. "No," she said, "not if we're satisfied."

CHAPTER 42

DURING the next few months the people living on the waters of the lower Holston heard a great deal about Richard Henderson and Company's Purchase. The deeds were not signed yet, but Judge Henderson had interviewed all the influential chiefs and had their word. The Little Carpenter had even made a trip to Cross creek with Henderson to see the goods that were to be traded for the lands. Two houses full. The Carpenter's wife had gone with him to inspect the goods on behalf of the women. Both the chief and his wife had seemed to be satisfied with what was offered. The Carpenter, the Old Tassel, Oconostota and other important chiefs were to come to the Watauga in the spring to sign the treaty.

Henderson was offering liberal terms to men who were willing to go out and settle the new country. Every man who would stay there until September of the next year could take up five hundred acres of land for himself and two hundred and fifty acres for each tithable person whom he should take with him, on the payment of twenty shillings sterling per hundred and an annual quit rent of two shillings per hundred.

The Outlaws, sitting before the fire at night, talking, sometimes saw themselves in imagination settled in the new country.

"Five hundred acres of land," Rion said. "If we sold out everything we got here we could get up enough to pay the tax."

"We could take up seven hundred and fifty acres, you and me together," Frank reminded him.

"Nigh on to a thousand acres of rich land. Maybe we ought to go."

"There may be some catch," Jocasta said. "This Judge Henderson, he may not do all he promises."

"Dick Henderson's an honest man," Rion said, "though a lawyer."

"How'd he git around the law? I thought the King said couldn't nobody buy any more land from Indians."

"He's got a decision of the Lord Chancellor's," Frank said. "The

Lord Chancellor held that when countries are acquired from Indian princes the property rights are vested in the grantee by the nature of the grant itself. . . . I saw it copied out in the last letter Robertson had."

Cassy laughed. Rion shook his head. "You'd a been a big man, Frank, if you'd stayed in the old country. Would you mind saying that again?"

Frank repeated what he had said. Rion looked into the fire. "I reckon what it means is that you and me can't patent three hundred acres from these Indians, but a man can make a deal with 'em for twenty million."

"I don't believe the decision'll hold," Frank said. "It goes against the proclamation of '63."

"I wish I could get hold of Daniel Boone," Rion said. "He'd have the inside track. He'd know."

"Well, James Robertson looks to be Henderson's right-hand man in these parts," Frank said. "I reckon we can find out from him. . . . When you reckon Charles'll be up this way again?"

They did not see either Charles or James Robertson for several months. But Amos Eaton made a trip to the Watauga and came back with word that the treaty was to be held the middle of March, within a mile of Charles Robertson's station, right on the river, at the place they called the Sycamore Shoals.

Daniel Boone was not there now but had been in and out several times. The Indians were already gathering. Two or three hundred fighting men and a sprinkling of women and children. The company had undertaken to feed them all. A score of hunters were in the woods, but they were not bringing in much game. Henderson would have to have beef and corn, too, if he fed all those Indians. The word had gone around and people were already driving cattle in. He, Amos, was thinking of driving his two steers down.

James Robertson had sent Rion a message by Amos. This was the chance for the South Holston men. Buy their land outright from the Indians at the same time that Henderson was making his great purchase. If the Indians would sign one deed they'd sign the other. Judge Henderson, who was as clever a man as you'd find, though a lawyer, was drawing up the deed. Charles Robertson was to be trustee and already had two thousand pounds worth of goods contracted for. Rion could come in with the others on payment of twenty shillings.

"I ain't got twenty shillings," Rion said.

"There's the bull calf," Cassy reminded him.

"They ain't no question but that you can sell him," Amos said. "Henderson's going to be put to it to feed 'em. There's Indians coming in every day. They look for a thousand before they're through."

"I reckon I better go down with you," Rion said.

They started Wednesday, two days before the treaty was to begin, but had bad luck on the way with the cattle straying and did not reach the Shoals until Friday. They got to Charles Robertson's place early in the afternoon. The door was latched. Nobody at home except the dung-hill fowls and the pig in its pen.

"They're all over at the Shoals," Amos said.

The cattle were tired and were standing quietly. They drove them to water in the branch that ran just below Robertson's house, then started along the path to the river. They had not gone far before they heard a noise like the humming of many bees.

Amos slapped his thigh. "There's more of 'em come in since I was here. . . . Now say, d'you ever see anything like that?"

They had come up over a little rise. The Sycamore Flats were before them. Far off, water glinting in the sun but between them and it sycamores growing everywhere, and moving through the pale trunks dark figures: white men, Indians, women and children, even a few blacks. Rion stood looking and thought that he had never in his life seen so many people in one place before.

He shook his head. "What'll we do with these cattle?"

"They've got a pen over here," Amos said.

They drove the cattle on through the trees. The pen was down near the branch. A three rail fence, room inside for fifty head of cattle. The bars were down and cattle were being driven through. There were a lot of drovers standing around. One big fellow sat on the top rail shouting at the men who were driving the cattle.

As Rion and Amos came up an Indian left the crowd. A tall young buck with silver rings dangling from his ears. He had on a matchcoat. Under it his naked legs shone with grease. Rion stood still while those shining, reddish legs swung past him. That night at Chota Archy had had rings in his ears and he had been greased all over, just like one of them. He looked off past the pen to the far end of the grounds. That must be the main Indian encampment. One good-sized cabin up already and Indians milling all around it. Three or four hundred at least. . . . Would Archy dare to show his face here among white men?

The other cattle were through. The drovers were coming out of the pen. Amos was starting his two steers in when the big fellow on the fence suddenly bawled out to the man who was handling the bars not to let any more through.

The fellow stood back as if he was surprised. "Why not?"

The big one turned around, almost losing his balance, and looked over the pen. "They's too many of 'em in there already."

Amos gave a long whistle.

"I ain't going to start nothing now," Rion said to himself. "I ain't going to start nothing." He walked up to the fence. There looked to be fifty head at least but they were all steers and standing quietly. There was room for a dozen more without crowding.

"You want to tie 'em up outside?" he asked Amos in a low voice.

Amos was eyeing the fellow on the fence. "I wouldn't mind if it was anybody but John Choate." He looked at the little man. "He was a-riding Tilman when I was down here last week."

Tilman heard him. He dropped the bar he was holding and kicked the other two out of the way. "He ain't going to ride me no more," he said.

Choate was down off the fence. His jug hit the ground before he did. The cob flew out and the liquor was spilling on the ground. A man behind him picked the jug up and was calling: "Here, John, you better have another drink."

Choate did not hear him. He was coming towards Tilman. Tight as a tick, but he kept his feet all right; only when he came to Boss he put his hand out and rested it on the steer's broad back.

Rion looked at Tilman. The man was little but knotty. "I was laying any money it'd be on this cock," Rion said to himself. He continued to an imaginary person who sometimes seemed to be standing at his elbow and arguing with him. "Naw, I *ain't* going to stand back. Don't care what you say. . . . Suppose Tilman couldn't handle him!"

Choate had lifted his hand from Boss' back and was walking around the steer towards Tilman.

Rion took a step forward. Tilman flicked him a glance out of the corner of his eye. "Stand back, Stranger," he said and there was that in his voice that would have made Rion stand back if it hadn't been too late, if his blood hadn't already been up. He stepped to Boss' head. The steer stood, placidly slobbering. Rion dropped his left hand on the steer's shoulder and looked at Choate, separated from him now only by the steer's body. "You wouldn't want to stampede my cattle now, Friend?"

Somebody back in the crowd laughed. Choate jerked his head in the direction of the voice then looked at Rion.

"What's that you said?"

"Said I was going to drive my cattle through," Rion answered in a soft voice.

Choate came on, throwing out his arms at first, but that was to get his balance, then stopping so short that he rocked on his heels. He was a man who showed his liquor in his eyes. They glistened like a treed coon's. "I wish he warn't so drunk," Rion thought and shot his fist out and buffeted the man on the chest.

Choate recoiled from the blow. He ducked his head and charged at Rion, who sidestepped and putting out his foot tripped the man. He stooped and turned him face up. He placed his foot on Choate's nose and stood on it, rocking back and forth. Then he lifted him to his feet and tossed him over his head. Choate lay on the ground, moaning. Rion turned away.

He was walking around the edge of the crowd towards the other side of the pen when he saw that Choate had got up. "He's trying to git to his horse," a voice cried. "Throw him his horse so he can be riding!"

There was a laugh from the crowd. Rion laughed too and looked up to see James Robertson and another man watching him. He went towards them, still laughing and making a show of dusting his hands off.

"Some fine folks you got down this way!"

"They'll soon take poplar and push off," Robertson said off-handedly.

The young man who was standing with him frowned, looking after Choate as if the very sight of the man disgusted him. "Many of them like that on the Watauga?" he asked.

Rion glanced at the blue-eyed six-footer. He was not filled out

yet but he was stout enough to take care of himself. He grinned.
"You thinking of settling?"

"Master Sevier rode out from Virginia last November," Robertson said, "and now he's thinking of settling."

"Here on the Watauga?"

"He fancies some land higher up. On the Nollichucky."

"That stream we crossed on our trip?"

"That's right," Robertson said. His right hand fell on Rion's
elbow, closed on it with an affectionate pressure. "This is the boy
who was with me on that trip to Chota, Master Sevier."

Rion grinned again and looked closer at the young Virginian.
He was dressed in deerskin as he himself was, but he had a feeling
that he ought to be dressed finer, for he had a finical manner for
a settler. Probably some big fellow at home, or if he was too young
for that, from some big family. Robertson was in with all the high
muckety-mucks now. Well, there was none of them too good for
him. No finer fellow on the western waters than old Jim. . . .

"You seen Daniel Boone?" he asked.

"I left him over there in the marquee an hour ago."

Rion turned around. "Amos, I'm going over here a piece. You
coming?"

There was a barrel of Monongahela in the fence corner. Amos
had got to it. He waved a full horn at Rion and a little of the whiskey
fell in bright drops to the ground. "God in the mountain!" Amos
said and put his foot over the spots as if to keep them from getting
away. "I'll be 'long in a minute, Rion."

Rion laughed and walked away between the other two men.

Robertson put his hands together, making a tent of his long
fingers. "There'll be many a skull split before this day is over."

"You got to expect that," Rion said. "Well, Jim, is the pot
a-boiling?"

"They started out by saying they didn't want to sell. Then they
wanted to sell that land on the Virginia line that Donelson surveyed.
Henderson told them there wasn't but one piece of land he wanted
to buy, and made out he wasn't very anxious to buy that. Some of
'em came over last night and looked at the goods again and they had
a conference this morning. They ought to sign today, if they're
going to sign at all."

"Reckon they going to sign at all?"

"You can't tell with Indians. Our goods come in today, Rion. The goods that'll pay for our land. You got your money ready?"

"I got a bull calf over in that pen that ought to bring it."

Robertson nodded. "They'll buy him. Got all they can do to feed these Indians."

They walked on towards the white men's encampment. There was a path but it was full of water, the ground on both sides like a hog wallow from the trampling. Rion looked up. Above the wintry branches the sky was a deep, pure blue. There had been a little wind in the morning but that had died and the air was as balmy as May. Ground thawed fast in weather like this. A few more windy days and he could be plowing.

They came to a fire tended by some negroes. Stew was cooking in a big iron pot and a little way off from the fire on trestles lay the carcasses of half a dozen bears. Two white men stood before the trestles, one skinning and one cutting out the meat. The young Virginian stopped and examined one of the unskinned carcasses. A young he, thin from the winter fast, his bowels still plugged with laurel. He wouldn't dress a hundred pounds. "I'd a left that one lying in the woods," he said with a laugh.

A knife came up to point off through the trees. "We got all them Indians to feed," the man said and, pushing the bear over, ripped the skin of his belly down with one drive of the knife.

"They going to ruin them hides," Rion said as they walked on. "But I reckon they have to work fast. . . . Don't the Indians do nothing towards feeding themselves?"

"Lord, no," Robertson said, "they're visiting."

They were in the middle of the grounds. On their left the two log cabins that the white men had built and off in the distance the Indians' tents. Between the two encampments there was an open space where few trees grew, and moving in this open space around the ashes of a dead fire were white men and Indians.

Rion ran his eye over them as if they had been cattle. "Must be five hundred of 'em," he murmured.

"And more coming all the time," Robertson said.

They passed the marquee where grunting negroes were up-ending chunks of wood to make seats, and came to where the two cabins stood side by side. A dignified looking man in broadcloth standing in front of one of them raised his hand in salute to Robertson, then

GREEN CENTURIES 303

walked off down the path. "That's John Reid," Robertson said. "He's here representing the Virginians." He led the way to the second cabin.

There was no window. The place was dark. In the middle of the dirt floor, where it caught the light from the doorway, was a table heaped with papers. A man sat behind it writing. Over on the hearth a good fire was burning. A sandy-haired man with a big nose sat close to it, a blanket over his shoulders, his naked feet plunged into a tub of water. On the other side of the hearth a man with a wool hat pushed back on his head squatted on his heels, oiling a gun.

The man at the table was reading to himself in a droning voice: "This indenture made fifteenth day March year of our Lord one thousand seven hundred and seventy five . . . Oconostota Chief Warrior First Representative Cherokee Nation tribe Indians and Atta Kulla Kulla and Savanooke otherwise Coronoh Chiefs appointed by warriors and other headmen convey for whole Nation Being Aborigines and sole owners by occupancy beginning time lands on the Ohio river from mouth of Tennessee river up said Ohio to mouth or emptying of the Great Canaway or New river and so across a southward line to the Virginia line by an intersection that shall strike or hit the Holston river six English miles above or eastward of the Long Island therein and other lands or territory thereunto adjoining . . ."

He looked up. "I put in eastward of the Long Island after what they said yesterday . . . Well, Jim, d'you talk to any of 'em?"

Judge Henderson. Rion felt like laughing as he thought of the last time they had met. But the judge did not recognize him. He was looking at Robertson.

"I couldn't find the Carpenter," Robertson said, "but I talked to Oconostota. He says the talk yesterday didn't mean much. Says he'll sign and he's pretty sure some of the others will."

Henderson pushed himself back from the table. He snapped his fingers. "I wouldn't give that for a deed unless it was signed in open treaty."

"You're right."

Rion slipped past them, went to the man on the stool and laid his hand on his shoulder. Boone looked up and was on his feet. "By Godly, I been looking for you!"

"I heard you'd been in and out. I just got down here myself today."

"Where you living?"

"On the south Holston. Just below the Long Island . . . Where you going from here?"

"Up above the Island. I got some men up there now cutting the road. I could stop the night at your place when we leave here . . . Rion, you've filled out some. You married and got a family?"

"Parson Dawson's daughter from the Ford," Rion said. "I got a boy and a girl. Where's your folks?"

"On the Clinch. But I aim to go up in the new country. You better come along."

Rion grinned. "I ain't hardly got settled here yet."

The sandy-haired man waved away a negro who wanted to put more hot water in his tub. "Young man, what's your name?"

"Outlaw."

The other shook his head. "That ain't your name. You look like a red Highlander to me. More likely MacGregor or MacIntosh. Maybe even Gordon. Your folks got in some trouble in the old country and had to leave. Took the first name that came into their heads and stuck to it from pure contrariness. Just like you'd do today. You look ornery to me."

"What might your name be?" Rion asked, grinning.

"Me? I'm a damned Hogg. When I's young I thought of taking my mother's name. Alves. Good folks, too, though Spanish. I gave it up for fear of hurting my father's feelings. But a man don't like to be called Hogg all his life. I tell my boys they can change any day they want to. The girls'll have to marry or stay damned Hoggs."

"It is a kind of ridic'lous name," Rion said. "Still, I've known worse. When I was a chap we had a neighbor named Swiveltit."

"I couldn't a stood that," Hogg said. "Hogg I can stand up to. Been doing it all my life. But Swiveltit. . . ."

Robertson, sitting on one of the bunks, was re-lacing his moccasin. "There's some of them Indians don't want to sell, and that's a fact." He spoke in a muffled voice, his head bent down, his fingers fumbling with the moccasin thongs. "I was talking to one today. Kept telling me the game was the Indians' cattle and hogs . . ." He tied the lace with a snap and stood up.

Henderson was pacing the floor in front of him. "If they don't sign today they won't sign at all," he said.

His voice had a dead note in it. He did not look at Robertson as he passed him. Rion, squatting against the wall, eyed him curiously. There was a deep line on each side of his mouth that had not been there three years ago. His eyes were not as bright as they had been. His linen was dirty. Still he looked the big man every inch. Older, but that was natural with all he had on his mind. He realized that it was Henderson who had sent them all west, Henderson who had kept Boone on the move, furnishing him, paying his debts, sending him out again until now they had found what they had been looking for all these years. Twenty million acres. If Henderson made the trade he would be one of the biggest men in the whole country, if not the biggest. "I'll be telling folks about when I knew him," he thought, and then, struck by something about the face, some tenseness of the muscle or expression of the eye, he wondered what the outcome would be. "He don't *look* like a winner," he thought. "Maybe he knows he ain't going to win and it's got him down. He's put everything he's got into this and he's going through with it but he don't feel right about it . . ."

Boone was walking towards the door. He followed him outside. They stood in front of the cabin, watching the crowd.

"How long since you been back on the Yadkin?" Rion asked.

"I got back a few weeks after you left. We must a passed on the way."

"Them boys that shot up the wagons, you hear much talk about them?"

"Some of them left the country," Boone grinned, "like you did. But the year after that there was a battle."

"A battle?"

"At the Alamance river."

"Soldiers put 'em down?"

"The boys didn't have enough ammunition. Come out with enough powder for a day's hunting and when that was gone they had to quit . . . Tryon hanged two from your neighborhood."

"*Hanged?*" Rion said.

"Buried 'em in that grove by the courthouse. Tom Beard and Jesse Andrews."

A woman was coming towards them, holding two children by the hand. The little boy kept looking back over his shoulder at an Indian who stood against a tree, his arms folded on his chest. Rion could see that cellar of Braun's with the muster roll spread out in the light of the one candle:

THOMAS BEARD
ORION OUTLAW

He gave a sigh. "Sometimes I wish I hadn't left the way I did . . . Where was Husbands when this was going on?"

"He left the country before the fighting started. He was against it all along . . ." Boone raised himself up on tiptoe. "I believe those Indians are starting over. Least there's some kind of a stir."

The white men were coming out of the cabin, Hogg last, booted and calling to his nigger: "Boy, fetch me a blanket, I got to go, if I catch my death of cold."

They were taking their seats under the marquee: Henderson in the middle, Thomas Hart on one side of him, Hogg on the other, then James Robertson, John Williams and half a dozen men Rion had never seen before.

Rion and Boone stood behind the marquee, close enough to hear what was being said. Rion looked over at the Indians. The whole crowd was drawing up in two long lines. Suddenly a young warrior came running down the lines. Midway between the two old chiefs he stopped in his tracks long enough to fire his musket into the air, then whirling ran back to the.end of the line. Another one came after him and now the firing was so rapid that it sounded like one continuous shot.

"Pretty, ain't it?" Rion said.

"That's what they call a *feu-de-joie*," Boone told him

Young Sevier had come up and was standing with them. "It's a waste of powder. If it'd a been me I'd taken their guns away from them soon as they came on the grounds."

James Robertson in front of him gave a dry laugh and half turned his head. "You wouldn't a got very far with that."

The last warrior had fired and had run back towards the end of the lines. The chiefs walked slowly over to the seats that had been prepared for them, up-ended chunks of wood, like the white men's, but most of them were covered with furs or cloth.

The linguister was coming forward, the same, dark, long-faced man that had been at the Island that day. He took his place halfway between the red men and the white. After a little the old peace chief, Atta Kulla Kulla, came and stood beside him and began speaking. Although it was warm he wore a matchcoat, cut just like a Christian's but trimmed with red and blue beadings. His ears, weighted with the heavy silver, hung down below his cheekbones. His voice was deep to come from so small a man. He spoke slowly, with pauses in between. The linguister, John Vann, spoke up briskly, his eyes all the time dwelling curiously on the white men: Atta Kulla Kulla was an old man but had for a long time been friend to both white and red. He was glad to see them gathered together here at the Broken Waters where the Cherokees always came in the spring of the year. . . .

Rion yawned and looked around the circle for faces he knew. There was the war chief, Oconostota, on a seat covered with red stroud; next to him the one they had pointed out as the Old Tassel. He had on the most silver of any of them. His eyes went on down the line. There was the Raven who had made the big speech that night at Chota and, sitting beside him, taller by half a head, the big, pock-marked fellow he'd seen on the Long Island that day he leased his land. The others all had silver in their ears and trinkets on their necks and arms, but he wore nothing but his flap and a necklace of the longest bear's claws Rion had ever seen.

"He's like a Quaker," Rion thought, "believes in dressing plain." He laughed at his own conceit.

Boone turned around. "What you laughing at?"

"I don't know. Sometimes they act just like real folks, don't they?"

Boone did not answer. His eyes were on Henderson who was just then standing up to address them in a voice loud enough to carry over the whole crowd.

"I am glad that the headmen and warriors of the Cherokee Nation have come here to talk with their white brothers . . . The white man has not enough land but he has guns, knives, hatchets, blankets . . . The great chief, Atta Kulla Kulla, has seen the goods gathered together there in the cabin . . ."

Rion kept looking at Oconostota. While Atta Kulla Kulla had been talking he had kept his long head sunk on his chest, but now he raised his head and sent a quick, bright look around the circle. "He don't really want to sign," Rion thought, "but he wants those guns for his men . . . He's old but there's mischief in him yet."

"There's the deed," Boone said in a low voice. Henderson was getting a thick roll out of his cow-skin satchel. He spread it out on the block in front of him. Atta Kulla Kulla and Oconostota got up and went forward. Stepping behind them was the Raven and behind him the linguister. They approached the block and stood looking down at the paper, then Oconostota said something and put his hand out and touched the paper.

Henderson looked at the linguister. "It's the same deed," he said impatiently. "Nine copies, one for each partner, all exactly the same, a precaution in case of fire or theft . . ."

The linguister turned and spoke to the Indians in a voice so low you could not hear him. Finally Oconostota nodded his head and advanced his hand towards the quill that Henderson was holding.

The man from Virginia was getting to his feet. "Would it not be proper to read the boundaries of the land before letting the chiefs affix their marks?" he asked in a clear, sharp voice.

Henderson started. "I *pray* you, Master Reid, my partners and I have been at great expense . . ."

The Virginian pursed his lips. An obstinate look came on his face. "It is not generous to get a people to sign a deed if they do not know what it says."

Henderson whirled around toward him. He made an impatient, fiddling gesture with his fingers. "They understand it. It's all been gone over a dozen times. I pray you do not interfere at this juncture!"

The Indians were not paying any attention to Henderson or the Virginian either. They were looking back towards the circle of seated chiefs. One of them had risen and was walking slowly out into the middle of the circle: Dragging Canoe, the big, pock-marked chief of the Great Island.

CHAPTER 43

THE DARK LANTHORN stood on the south bank of the river and watched the water flow smoothly down between the widening banks to break on the great boulders that in this place covered the whole bed of the stream. It was early afternoon. The sun had left the north bank and hung directly over the river. Its rays struck sparkles from the eddies that curled about the rocks. She half closed her eyes and yellow light played over the whole surface of fretted water.

"I have seen the Broken Waters," she thought. "I have come to them an old woman but at least I have seen them now before I die."

She stepped out of her moccasins and sitting down on the bank thrust her feet into the water. It was pleasant to feel it lapping against her bare flesh. She hitched herself along the bank and thrust her feet in deeper. It was as if she were touching water for the first time today and yet she had gone to bathe at dawn with the other women. But the bathing had not brought its usual refreshment. She had seen more than one woman looking over her shoulder as she flung the water to the Four Winds and she herself had felt as if one of the ugly white men might step out from behind the willows at any moment, although, she reflected, the river was the last place they would come. Four days she had been on the Broken Waters and in all that time she had not once seen a white man going down to the water.

She had asked her husband about that and he had replied that it was not the custom of the whites to go to water, particularly, after the cold weather had set in.

"Perhaps that is what gives the odor," she suggested, and he agreed that when a great crowd of white men was gathered in one place the odor was indeed overpowering.

She leaned her head back against a tree trunk and closed her eyes. Pictures from her long journey rose before her: the long trail to Cross creek, the streets crowded with people, and finally the great house in which the goods were stored. But they had stopped at a larger house than that on the way back, two storeys, made all of brick. The men who lived in it wore long black coats. They had taken her into one room that was as large as the town house at Chota. In the far corner there was a contrivance of reeds and from those reeds, as plainly as she now heard the sighing of the wind in the brush, came the voice of a woman singing. Clearly a piece of magic. There had been other sights and sounds almost as strange. There had been so many things to marvel at she had been afraid she might forget some of them; so every day she came away from the crowd and sat by herself for a while, calling the pictures up and impressing them on her memory.

There was something moving on the bank behind her. She turned around. Her granddaughter, Na-Kwí-si, stood there eyeing her. "Grandmother, my father is speaking in council."

"You mean your grandfather. He has already spoken three times since the council started and doubtless will speak again."

The girl was silent a moment, then she said: "I mean my *father*, the chief of the Great Island."

The Lanthorn watched a weed round up against a rock and slide over it. "He is old enough to speak in council," she said in a dry voice, "but he is a warrior, not an orator. He had better have left it to the older men."

The girl was gone through the trees. The Lanthorn sat still for a few minutes; then she too rose. She was not vainer than other women but if her son, the Dragging Canoe, was speaking in council she would hear him.

She walked swiftly up the path and worked her way in among the crowd until she could see the headmen, seated in a circle as they had been yesterday, all except her son, the Dragging Canoe. He stood in the center of the circle, the linguister, John Vann beside him.

He stood there taller than an ordinary man, wearing no ornament except a necklace of bear's claws. The March sun struck full on his upturned face, on the broad cheekbones, on the nose that thrust out bold as a hatchet. But for those pits that the white men's disease had left, he would have been the handsomest man on the grounds.

"Last night I dreamed that I was with my grandfather . . ."

He resembled his grandfather, Chief Yellow Bird, more than he did his own father. It was not only his stature and the bones of his

face, but the look out of the eye. Ever since he was a little boy he
had had that straight, searching look.

"But my grandfather was sad. He kept his hand to his forehead.
His body leaned to one side . . ."

The voice was sonorous and full. The speech began well. Her
father always began his speeches with a reference to the past. "To
dwell on the glorious deeds of one's ancestors elevates the mind," he
used to say. Chief Yellow Bird, although a warrior, was a man of
thought. In the spring he went with the physicians to the woods to
gather their herbs, and back at the lodge he would sit for hours
discussing the nature of the world: "The Great Spirit has caused
everything in nature to be round except stone, which is the imple-
ment of destruction. Everything that grows from the ground is
round, like the stem of a plant. Everything that breathes is round,
like the body of a man. Since the Great Spirit has caused everything
to be round mankind should look on the circle as sacred . . ."

"*It is the blood. I cannot eat or sleep for the smell of my people's
blood!*"

But we came in peace! She stared at her son, then pressed forward
until she could see her husband's face. His mouth remained set in
the expression of grave politeness, but his eyes, wide open, were fixed
upon the speaker.

Judge Henderson, the one they called Carolina Dick, half rose,
but somebody pushed him back. The white men wanted to know
what had been said. One was calling out now to the linguister.

John Vann spoke to them. The Canoe did not wait for him to
finish. He put out his hand and the man fell back. The Canoe turned
to the chiefs.

"I do not speak to you with my own voice but with that of many
ancient peoples. Our fathers came here long ago, from a great water.
The Muskohge held this land then. They were warlike but they
could not stand against the Real People. We drove them from the
land and we built our towns on the graves of their fathers. In those
days there were other warlike people who lived across the mountains: the Pamunkeys, the Chickahominies. Where are they now?
Gone. Whole nations. Melted away before the white man like snow-
balls before the sun. We have said in council: 'But they will not cross
the mountains. They will not make war on the Real People.' That
hope has vanished. They have crossed the mountains and have settled

upon our land. Our father, Stuart, told them to leave. But they did not go. And now they ask that we give them the land to sit down on forever."

He walked over and stood before his father. "Give them the deed they ask and they will not be content. They will ask for more and yet more land . . ."

Atta Kulla Kulla looked at his son but did not speak.

The Canoe walked away from him and stood before Oconostota. "They will stand finally in your beloved town, in Chota. They will lay it waste as they did Toquo and Tellico. Where will the great war chief be then?" She saw Oconostota's shoulders rising and now the whole column of his body towering opposite her son. It was true what they said of him, that in anger his eyes shone red.

The Dragging Canoe looked into the red eyes and smiled. "The great war chief will have fled, with his people, across the mountains. The white men will follow and cut him down. At the great river or where the mountains start again. What does the place matter?"

He turned his back on the war chief. He took his tomahawk out of his belt and threw it towards a log that lay halfway between the Real People and the Whites. The blade sank deep into the wood. He waited until the handle had stopped quivering.

"I am for war," he said. "My very breath is bloody!"

He raised his head. The war chief stood with his eyes on the ground. The Canoe looked around the circle but no one gave him back his glance, and he turned and left the council.

CHAPTER 44

RION WANTED Cassy to stay at Jacob's while he and Frank were away but she had just started making some soap from fat she had been saving and didn't want to leave her work. "Get Jane to stay with me," she told him. "That'll be company enough."

"All right," Rion said, "if you'll sleep at Jacob's you can both stay around here in the day time, I reckon."

Jane came down the next morning, leading her Devon cow and the three-weeks-old calf. Cassy had not seen the heifer since she came in. She stood in the doorway, watching, while Jane tied the heifer to a tree. Looking at the bag, still distended to the size of a hominy mortar, with the blue veins standing out from the sleek, cream-coloured skin, Cassy thought how long it had been since she had had a cow's teat in her hand. She ran out and squatting down beside the beast poked her head into the warm flank, and grasping one of the teats sent a stream of milk on to the ground. She turned around to Jane, laughing.

"Le'me milk tonight!"

"I'll let you milk every night and morning too," Jane said. She gave the heifer a slap on the flank as she turned away. "You going to be more trouble than you're worth."

"No, she isn't," Cassy said. "I'll feed her."

"You do it then," Jane said, "and I'll take care of the baby."

During the next three days she nursed Malcolm while Cassy did the outdoor work. Malcolm would not have much to do with Jane but as she said she could watch him, he couldn't bar her from that.

Cassy was glad to get away from the house for a change. The fodder had been gone for two weeks. The cattle—the Outlaws' dry cow and the heifer—had to browse for their living. Every morning Cassy drove them into the woods. She had not realized until she got out of the clearing how far spring was advanced. There were a few patches of snow left, on the north sides of slopes and in hollow trees, but the air was balmy and the trees were already showing buds. The

slippery elms had the biggest buds. Cassy carried Rion's light axe
along and felled as many little elm trees as she could find, and when
they gave out she would reach up as high as she could and cut from
the larger trees all the boughs that had swollen tips. Then she would
leave the two cows in the woods, grazing on the boughs, until late
afternoon when she would drive them up to milk.

On Wednesday afternoon while she was driving them home she
found a good sized patch of wild mustard growing in a sheltered
place along the creek. She stopped and gathered her dress-tail full.
"We'll have 'em for supper," she told Jane.

Jane was on the floor, making a twig pen for Malcolm. "I don't
see no use cooking when you haven't got men folks," she said.

"We'll have men folks," Cassy told her. "Rion said they'd be
home tonight."

"Then you ain't fixin to sleep at Jacob's tonight?"

"There won't be no need. Rion said they'd be in tonight."

Cassy put the greens on to boil with a piece of deer meat. She
went out and milked the cow and fed the calf. When she came in
with the half gallon of milk, which was all that was left after the calf
was fed, Jane had the hearth brushed and the fire made up bright.
Cassy took her old cloak off and hung it on its peg, and went over
and stood in front of the fire.

"I declare, I wish we had something to cook tonight," she said.

"There's two deer hams hanging in the loft," Jane told her.

Cassy shook her head. She looked down at Malcolm, who had
run up to clasp her about the knees. "When this one was on the way
I took a scunner against deer meat and it hasn't ever left me. I crave
something besides game."

"You got them two cockerels left," Jane said. "You got to kill
'em some time. Why'n't you have 'em tonight, seeing as you're so
set on eating?"

"I believe I'll do it," Cassy said.

"You'll have to cut their heads off. Them necks is too tough to
wring."

Cassy got the axe down and started for the door. When she got
there she paused. "I always did hate to kill a chicken after I raised it."

Jane laughed and came over and took the axe from her. "Here, I'll
do it. Them roosters ain't nothing to me."

She went out with the axe and in a few minutes came back with the headless bodies of the cockerels. Cassy had hot water ready. The two women scalded the chickens and knelt on the hearth and picked them, stowing the feathers in a deerskin bag that Cassy brought out.

A few minutes later Cassy had put them to stew in the iron pot.

"What you goin' to cook your mush in?" Sarah asked. "You got chickens in one pot and greens in the other."

"We'll have ash cake," Cassy told her.

She drew a stool up to the fire and took Malcolm on her knee. "It'd be nice if we could have dumplings with those chickens."

Jane laughed. "You couldn't make dumplings out of corn meal. Wouldn't be no way to bind it together."

The two women sat silent for a while looking into the fire. Jane said:

"Back in Otey township I went to an infare once. It was a cousin of mine, getting married. She was getting along, all of twenty-two years old, and I reckon the old folks was glad to git her off their hands. Anyway they give her a big blow-out. I warn't more'n eight year old at the time but I always remember that supper."

"What did they have?"

"Everything you could think of. They was one thing. A little pie. Chess pie they called it. I stood there and I ate twelve of 'em before Ma come along and stopped me."

"Twelve pies!" Cassy said.

"They warn't big pies. Doll size, but, Man, they was rich!"

"What was they made out of?"

"It was a kind of custard baked in a crust. Made out of eggs and sugar and milk, I reckon."

Cassy looked down and saw that Malcolm had fallen asleep. She got up and laid him in his crib, and came back to the fire. "When I was a chap we used to have suet pudding."

"D'your mother make it good?"

"My mother died when I was born and my father put me out to board. This woman I stayed with, Mistress Slaughter her name was, used to make suet pudding every Thursday. Sometimes when the big bag was full she'd steam a little bag for us children."

"Was she good to you?" Jane asked.

"Good as she knew how to be. There warn't much to her."

"Ain't it strange now," Jane said absently. "They's folks don't think much of children and have the raisin' of 'em and there's others thinks the world and all of 'em and don't have none around."

"The Lord's ways are hard to understand," Cassy said. She turned her head and glanced up at the shelf. "Jane, I got three eggs."

"You mean for a pudding? You ain't got no sugar and you ain't got no currants. You ain't even got no suet. We used all the fat in the house in that soap."

"There's a little ball of suet up on that shelf but I don't mean for a pudding. I mean for a pie like you were talking about. I could sweeten it with some of that pumpkin molasses."

"And make the crust out of meal? You might try. You bolt meal two or three times and it's most as fine as flour."

Cassy stood up. "I'm going to start it now before the men come."

Jane opened the door and looked out. "If they don't come pretty soon we'll have to start for Jacob's. They ain't more'n an hour of sun left."

Cassy was already bolting meal through a piece of muslin into the buckeye bread bowl. "I'll go ahead and make the pie," she said, "and if they don't come we can take it down to Jacob's with us. Jacob and Sarah won't mind having pie for supper." And she laughed excitedly.

She mixed the crust, using the little deer fat she had left for shortening, then stirred up her custard in the small brass kettle and set the kettle on a bed of coals. While the custard was thickening she prepared the pie crust, patting it with her hands instead of rolling it, as she had no rolling pin. "What in the Nation am I going to bake it in?" she asked when she had finished.

Jane was ranging before the shelf where Cassy kept her cooking vessels. She took down the long-handled iron skillet. "It's the only thing anywhere near the right shape," she said, "and the handle'll be handy when you get ready to brown it."

Cassy fitted the crust into the skillet and poured the custard in on top of it and was about to set the skillet on the bed of coals when she suddenly raised it up. "I ain't goin' to cook it till they come. That way we'll have it hot."

"There they come now," Jane said.

They opened the door and looked out. Some men were riding up into the clearing, Rion first, then Frank and Amos, and behind them a stranger dressed in deerskin.

Cassy looked at him and said: "It's Daniel Boone, from the Yadkin!"

She pushed past Jane and ran to meet them. Rion had just halted his horse under the hickory tree. He leaned down and kissed her hard on the lips, and with one hand still on her shoulder spun her around to face the visitor. "Here she is, Daniel."

Daniel Boone had just thrown his leg back to dismount. He got off his horse and coming up to her took her hand and held it while he looked earnestly into her eyes. "Parson Dawson's daughter," he said, "from Trading Ford."

Cassy made him a curtsey, something she had not done in a long time. "You are not like to remember me, Master Boone. I was a chap last time I saw you."

"And when was that?" Boone asked, his grey eyes still holding hers.

"You were after deer in the woods back of our house and stopped for a drink of water."

"I remember," Boone said. " 'Twas in buck running time. I came out of the woods and found a house where none had been a month before. A gentleman came to the door and told me I'd better take brandy, so I put a drink of his brandy on top of the water from the spring."

Frank laughed. " 'Twas my father. He held that brandy was a sovereign cure for all ills."

Cassy released her hand from Boone's grasp and stepped back. "Here's my neighbor, Mistress Eaton, come to keep me company while the men were away."

Rion had left them and was unsaddling the horses. "Git me some salt, Cassy," he called. "I'll salt Daniel's horse here under the tree and then they won't be no fear of his straying."

Cassy ran into the house for the salt but suddenly remembering her manners ran back and held the door open. "Come in all and rest you. Supper's on the coals."

Jane Eaton affected delicacy. "We'd best be going, Mistress Outlaw. You've a house full as 'tis."

Cassy was on her way out with the salt but she stopped long enough to catch Jane by the shoulder and shake her. "Ye'll not leave this house without your supper, so say no more."

She handed Rion the panikin that held the salt and ran back into the house. Frank was standing in front of the fire, stretching himself and yawning. Daniel Boone was over in the corner on one knee, unfastening his pack. Frank saw him lift a book out and lay it on the floor while he rummaged for something else. He went over to him quickly.

"You've a book?"

Boone handed him the book and rose. "I always take a book along for my pleasure when I go to the woods."

They were coming towards the fire. Frank went to his stool in the corner and began turning the pages of the book. He looked up at Boone. "*Gulliver's Travels*," he said.

"We were reading that book around the fire one night," Boone said, "when a band of Indians came and surprised us. I lost the book in the fracas but I went back next morning and retrieved it. We had to swim a creek to get to the place, trying to come up to it another way, you see. Alex Neely, he was with me, said we should name the creek out of the book so we called it Lulbegrud. Because we were reading about the Lulbegruds when the Indians came . . ."

Frank looked up, the vague look in his eye that Cassy knew so well. "Aye," he said. "Aye." He gestured towards the shelf on the east wall. "I've Lucretius there and Pliny and Hesiod too. Do you read the Greek or maybe a bit of Latin?"

"Thank ye," Boone said. "I'm no scholar."

There was a cry from the far corner of the room. The baby was awake and Malcolm was sitting up and peering over the bark wall of her crib. Cassy was going to her but Jane Eaton was before her. She had the baby in her arms—the first time she had ever allowed her to hold her—and was bringing her over to show to Boone.

"Eighteen months old," she said, "and walks as good as anybody. Got twelve teeth. Open your mouth, Sarah. Show Master Boone."

Sarah looked down at the floor and pursed her lips up tight.

Boone laughed. "Cat's got her tongue and I don't believe she's got no teeth either." He leaned towards the child and sang in a deep voice:

> "Oh you little dear,
> Who made your breeches?
> Daddy cut 'em out
> And Mammy sewed the stitches."

Jane laughed her high, excited laugh and sat down, holding the child in her lap.

Cassy soothed the baby, then went back to the hearth and lifting the lid of the pot stuck a fork in one of the chickens. It was almost done. She replaced the lid on the pot and stood a moment, considering what had best be done next. Rion would be calling for his supper in a minute and there were the ash cakes still to be made and the pie to brown and the table to set. She glanced at Jane who was clasping Sarah to her with a silly smile while she listened to Boone's foolishness.

"You'd think it was her own child," Cassy thought with a flash of the malice that beset her sometimes when things did not go to suit her, and then she told herself that it was easier to have the three of them there at the side of the hearth where they were out of the way.

Rion and Amos had come in. Rion watched Cassy holding the long-handled skillet close to the flame in order to brown the pie. "What in the Nation you got there?" he asked.

"Larroes to catch meddlars," she said tartly. "I'd be obliged if you'd fix me a bed of coals for the cake."

"I'll do it as soon as I bring in a back log," he told her.

"Why can't you do it now?" she flared.

He stopped and looked at her, surprised. "I can't fix the ashes right till I get the back log in," he said and went out the door.

In a few minutes he came back with a back log and a forestick. He arranged them with his usual deliberate care and then took the shovel and raked glowing coals into a bed and covered them with ashes. When he had done this he brought the ash board over to the table to Cassy, and held it for her while she put the cakes on it. He had to wait while she patted the last one into shape. "You warn't in such a big hurry after all, was you?" he asked. And when she looked away from him and did not answer, he said: "Having company don't seem to agree with you."

Cassy felt as if she were going to cry. She set the last cake on the board in a hurry, then walked over to the far corner of the room. The wash basin and jug were there on a bench. She washed her hands and took a long time drying them.

She started back towards the fire. Sarah saw her and began crying for her. Jane handed her over. "I'll set the table whilst you give her and Malcolm their supper," she said and went and got the cup of milk and bowl of cold mush that had been set up for them.

The baby ate greedily and dropped off to sleep as soon as she was through. When Cassy came back to the fire after putting her into her crib, Jane was pulling the pie back from the fire. "It's browned nice," she said, "and you better take these chickens up too. I stuck 'em a minute ago and they was done."

Rion came quickly to Cassy's side, holding the big iron fork. "Here," he said, "let me do that." He had the chickens out of the pot and on to the platter. Turning back to the fire he drew the ash board out and slid half a dozen cakes into a bowl.

"Hit's on the table now," he said. "Sit down."

Cassy cast a glance around the table as she took up the greens. Jane had not wasted these last few minutes. She had known without being told that the little pat of butter they'd been saving for two days was to be used tonight. And she had thought to put the jug of milk on too.

Rion was putting a drum stick and slices of both dark and light meat in Boone's bowl. "Hit's a change from venison," he said, then, "here, you'll want some of the gravy." He got up and going over to the pot dipped up the little pewter jug full of gravy and divided it between the Eatons and Boone. He was back with another jugful. "Here," and he would have poured some in Cassy's bowl but she shook her head.

"I ain't hungry right now."

He bent closer to her. "What's the matter?"

She smiled up into his face. "Nothing."

"I'll send you a piece of the breast," he said and went back to his place.

Cassy ate her piece of breast and sopped an ash cake in a little gravy which she finally poured from the pitcher, then sat back a little from the table, watching the others eat. It took them a long time to eat all of the chickens and greens but now they were through.

"I never had a chicken taste better to me," Amos said as he pushed his stool back.

"Set down," Jane told him. "You ain't through yet."

Cassy brought the pie. Rion handed her his cutty knife and she cut it into five big pieces. The crust had stuck to the pan a little but she was able to get it out by running the knife around under it, and the custard stayed firm.

"It's a pie!" Daniel Boone said. He looked at Cassy and smiled. "You mind me of my Rebecca. I tell her she can make more out of nothing than any woman I know."

He took a bite. "Hit's good," he said. "How did you sweeten it?"

"Pumpkin molasses," she told him. "You want another piece?"

"You keep one for yourself."

She shook her head. "I'd rather you all ate it."

"There won't be no trouble about that," Amos said.

The pie was eaten. They were rising from the table. Cassy began clearing away the dishes. Jane helped her carry them to the bench in the corner and took the dish clout and dried the pewter for her. When they had ranged all the dishes on the shelf and had tidied up the hearth, they took the dishpan outside and emptied it at the edge of the clearing. As they were going back Jane said, "Wait a minute," and stepped off into the bushes.

Cassy stood there holding the dishpan and looked up at the sky. It had been so warm earlier in the day that they had thought a rain was blowing up from the south, but towards sun-down it had turned off cold and now all the stars were out. It would be cold and fair tomorrow. She remembered a night at her old home on the Yadkin when she and Rion had stood out in the yard looking up at the stars. A night in spring and the stars had been bright with sparkles of gold fire to them like they had tonight. The same stars shining on both sides of the mountains. It made you feel like you weren't so far from home. And tonight, around the table, with everybody eating and talking about how good things were, it had been like old times back on the Yadkin . . .

Jane had come up at the side of the house and was standing on the doorstep, waiting.

"All right," Cassy said and followed her into the house.

Malcolm was asleep. Frank was still reading in Boone's book. The other three men were drawn up close to the fire, talking. Rion and Boone were cleaning their guns. Amos, who never did today what he could put off till tomorrow, sat there, watching them.

Rion looked over at Cassy. "We got another deed to our land," he said.

"How come?"

"They got to talking and James said as long as Lawyer Henderson was there we'd better get him to make a deed for our land along with the rest of the Purchase so they drew up a deed quick and the Cherokees signed it." He looked at Boone. "That makes the third time I've treated with 'em for this land. . . . You know for a while there I thought warn't any of the deeds going to get signed, when that big chief they call 'the Canoe' walked out. That was quite a speech he made, warn't it?"

"I didn't like the looks of things," Boone said.

"Well, they went on and signed."

"That was the Carpenter, and I don't know yet how he turned the trick. The young bucks'd have followed the Canoe at the drop of a hat. I saw two of them standing there after the goods had been given out. One of 'em had on a shirt that was his share of the purchase. He felt it and I heard him say they'd given the land away, that he could have killed enough deer on it in one day to buy that shirt."

Rion laughed. "So he could. The ignorant savage!"

"How much do we have to pay?" Cassy asked.

"Two thousand pounds in leather goods. Charles Robertson's trustee. He isn't sure how many men are coming in on it yet."

"That ain't high for the land," Boone said, "but you don't want to fool with this land around here. Wait till you see Kentucky."

"Is it much richer than this?" Rion asked curiously.

"Richer and lies level. And the game! I seen a sight there I'll never forget. John Findley and I come out on top of a big hill and there below was a meadow, big as all Carolina and full of white clover, and grazing on that clover must have been three or four hundred buffalo. We went down the side of the hill and up to the place. It was a sight to see 'em making off, some running, some loping and the young calves playing alongside their mothers."

"It's like Findley said it was, ain't it?" Rion said. "Remember he told us about them big licks and the game so thick? . . . Whatever became of that fellow, Daniel?"

"Well, we located that place on the Louisa where he traded with the Indians soon after we got out there. Soon as he found it, seemed like he sort of lost interest in the country. Then we had a brush with the Indians. Holden and Mooney and Cooley were for going back after that. Findley said he'd guide them as far as the gap."

"Where was he heading from there?"

"Back to Pennsylvania. Least that's what he said one night, sitting around the fire. In early June that was. Next morning after breakfast I went to the spring for a drink. When I got back Findley was riding off through the trees. He turned around and he saw me standing there by a big tamarack, looking after him. He saw me but he didn't make no sign and I didn't either, just stood there and watched him go." He glanced from one face to the other with a puzzled expression. "A strange way to part, warn't it?"

"Had you had any difference?" Rion asked.

Boone shook his head. "No, it was just his way . . . When I got back to the camp Holden and the rest was loading their horses fast as they could to make after him. Said he didn't give them any warning either. Just stood up and said he was for the gap and anybody wanted to could go along."

"Well, that was like him," Rion said. "That fellow, he didn't care for nobody nor nothing but traipsing around the country . . . Daniel, it's been six years, ain't it, since you first started to Kentuck?"

"I tried to settle there two years ago," Boone said, "in the fall of '73. Sold out in North Carolina and started with Rebecca and the children. The Bryans come too, and some other families. They was forty of us in all."

"D'you come through here?"

"We come through here," Boone said, "and we got as far as Powell's Valley. We had to turn back there. The others went on to the Yadkin but we stayed the winter on the Clinch, at David Gass' station."

"The Clinch!" Rion cried. "Us here on the Holston and you no farther away than the Clinch!"

Boone was looking into the fire and did not seem to hear him. "It was in September," he said. "We got as far as Powell's Valley and then I thought we needed some more flour so I sent Jamie back to Captain Russell's . . ."

Cassy made a little murmur. "Jamie's the oldest, ain't he?"

"Seventeen," Boone said heavily, "he'd a been seventeen this year."

Rion looked at Boone, then laid his hand on Cassy's knee and gave it a light pressure. "Go on, Daniel," he said gently.

"He got the flour and started after us, with Captain Russell's boy

and a negro boy and two men was working for Russell. They must
have lost their way or maybe the cattle lagged—that nigger, Petty
they called him, couldn't get the straight of anything—but they
camped about three miles behind us that night. That nigger said they
heard wolves howling but they didn't think anything of it." He raised
his head. He glared at the company. "Nobody expected any trouble,"
he said, "it was just a month before the McAfees had come through,
and no trouble, no trouble at all."

"The Indians come?"

"Just before day. They fired into the boys while they was sleeping. Jamie and young Russell was both shot through the hips. One
fellow got away—never was heard of again. That nigger hid in a
pile of drift."

"You say the nigger got away?"

"He stayed hid in that pile of drift all night. There was one of
the Indians we all knew. A Shawnee. Big Jim they called him. Petty
heard Jamie talking to him when they first came up and then he
could hear him begging and begging. That was after they started."

"What did they use?" Rion asked in a low voice.

"Knives. The boys kept trying to turn 'em back with their hands.
That was how come the bodies was slashed so bad."

Cassy turned her head and looked at him. "They killed those
young boys?"

"Yes, ma'am. One boy was mine and one was William Russell's."

"Did you turn back and find 'em?" Rion asked.

Boone shook his head. "There was a fellow had deserted from
our party, came up just after the Indians had left. He was standing
there, not knowing what to do, and William Russell came up on his
way to join us. They sent a man ahead to warn us and Russell and
that fellow, Choate, dug the graves. Jamie was buried by the time
I got there and the other boy too." He was silent a while; then he
added: "Rebecca felt bad. She'd sent a sheet back, wanted I should
wrap Jamie in it."

"They ought to a waited to bury him till you came," Cassy said,
weeping.

Boone reached across Rion to touch her knee. "Don't cry now
. . . William Russell thought best not to wait. Folks have to do the
best they can in the woods." They were all silent. He looked into the
fire for a few minutes, and he said: "I went back to Powell's Valley

in May of last year, to Jamie's grave. They'd put logs on it but the wolves had pawed them off and dug part way in. I opened up the grave—they buried them together—and made sure that nothing hadn't got to them, and then I covered 'em up again, so deep that nothing couldn't ever get in."

"I don't know whether I could have done it," Rion said. "D'you go by yourself?"

"There wasn't anybody convenient to go with me," Boone said, "and Rebecca was worrying, feared they hadn't put the logs on the grave. I was glad I went. After I got home I was glad I went but that night I had one of my spells, the worst one I ever had in my life . . ."

"What kind of spell?" Rion asked.

"Melancholy," Boone said. "Profound melancholy. I've had those spells three or four times in my life. While they last I'm not a natural man."

Frank looked up suddenly from his book. "How did you feel, Master Boone?"

"Like I couldn't live," Boone said, "like there warn't no sense in living on."

Frank closed his book and stood over him. "Your spirit had been weakened by the shock," he said. "It is a phenomenon recognized by the Ancients. Lucretius has written of it." He stepped to the shelf and took down his copy of *"De Rerum Natura."* I will read you what he says, or rather I will translate, for you tell me you have no Latin."

"I'd be obliged," Boone said.

Frank read: ". . . the spirit weakened by some cause or other often appears to wish to depart and to be released from the whole body, and even the countenance appears to grow languid as at the last hour, and all the limbs of the bloodless trunk to relax and fall . . ."

"I was weak as a cat," Boone said. "I remember I was laying there looking up at the sky and I heard Indians creeping up and I knew I'd have to ride for it. I got up and I got on my horse but it wasn't like I was doing it myself, it was like somebody else was telling me what to do."

"Lucretius argues that the spirit is mortal," Frank said. "He cites the putrefaction of the body when the spirit has left it, and holds that the spirit suffers a similar putrefaction when torn from the body."

Boone shook his head. A wise look came on his face. "You mean the spirit rots same as the body? When I was a boy and used to go to meeting I heard 'em talk about man's soul being immortal . . ."

Rion looked into the fire, thinking of Jamie. It was hard to realize that he was grown, old enough to send off through the woods like that. He always thought of him as he had been when they took him with them on that trip over the mountains. Long ago that was. He couldn't have been more than ten but he had toughened up quick once he got in the woods. They had the most trouble with him at night. It had turned off cold and they'd been afraid he'd freeze if they left him to sleep by himself, so they took turns holding him up against them. He kicked a good deal and he ground his teeth all night long. Too much buffalo tongue, but Daniel never could see it and would let him eat his fill of it every time . . .

He looked over at Boone. It had been a long time since they two had been in the woods together. Some of the feeling of those old days came over him. He remembered the first time that Daniel Boone had ever spoken to him, had ever taken any notice of him. There had been a muster in Salisbury, and after it was over a lot of men went down near the river and drove a nail in a big sycamore and started shooting. Daniel was one of them. He, Rion, hadn't been more than thirteen at the time. He stood back, of course, whilst the older men were at it, but he was itching to shoot and every time a fellow stepped out he'd raise old Betsy and sight down her like he was shooting too. They got down to the two best shots finally. Daniel beat the other fellow. He must have noticed how bad Rion wanted to shoot, for when the crowd was breaking up he called Rion over and drove in a new nail and told him to have a shot at it, then stood by until he had finally put a bullet through it—it took him three shots. The crowd was all gone by that time and they walked up from the river bank together. Daniel said—it was before he went to live on the upper Yadkin—that he was going over in the Dunn's Mountain country the next day and asked Rion to go along with him . . . That was the first time they ever went hunting together.

Boone turned his head and smiled, not at Rion but at something Frank was saying, then his features settled into their usual, calm resolute expression. Rion studied his face. When he, Rion, was a

chap and Daniel first started taking notice of him, he had thought
that Daniel was the finest looking fellow he had ever seen. It had
hurt his feelings the way his family talked about Daniel. A vagrant,
he heard his mother call him once. Daniel hadn't changed much in
these six years, but looking into his face tonight he saw something
that he had never seen before—had they seen it all along? That look
he had, almost too bold for a human. When a beast was set on going
its way you couldn't stop it, short of killing it. Daniel talked about
Kentuck and likely it was all he said it was, but if it wasn't he
wouldn't care. He'd be off over the next range to see if the land there
wasn't better. Or if Kentuck turned out to be the richest land ever
was anywhere, something would take him away from it. He didn't
have any choice. He was one of those men had to keep moving
on . . .

He looked at Cassy. She sat hunched forward on her stool, gazing
into the fire, not seeming to listen to what Frank was saying. Her
long hair had come uncoiled and the tail of it had slipped down her
back. He had the impulse to lean over and take her hair in his hand
and pull it but something in the expression of her face stayed him.
She was a queer woman. Most of the time she stuck right with him,
closer than a cockle burr; then all of a sudden her head would go up
and that blank look would come into her eyes and if he said anything to her then, he'd get an answer that might have come from a
stranger. It was a thing he never got used to, a thing he dreaded,
that look and the cold, far-off sound her voice would have then.

She turned her head. Their eyes met. He smiled at her and felt
pleasure flood over him as her gaze softened under his. He knew
now what she had been thinking as she gazed into the fire, that he
would be off with Boone to Kentuck, that it was all to do over again,
the building of the house, the settling, the getting together of
gear . . .

He was glad when Boone spoke to him. "Well, Rion, you better
come on to Kentuck."

He shook his head. "No, I been here four years. After a man's
worked land that long it don't look right to turn around and leave it."

CHAPTER 45

ARCHY STOPPED on the trail and looked back. The Owl was several yards behind him. When he saw Archy looking at him, he walked faster. Archy stood there until he had caught up with him then he bent down and examined his friend's foot. New skin had formed over the wound but the flesh under it looked tender and you could still see the dark, purplish spot where the cane had stabbed.

Archy rose and walked a little way off the trail and sat down on a log. "I'll rest here," he said.

The Owl stood where he was, looking down the trail. "They will come soon," he said. "It will be a spectacle! My brother, the Dragging Canoe, at the head of eighty warriors—to say nothing of our white brother's escort. How many warriors do you think he will have?"

Archy shook his head. "Not many."

"Our father, Stuart, would give them to him if he asked?"

"He wouldn't want them."

"But think of the glory!"

Archy grinned. "White men don't think it's much glory to follow a pack train five hundred miles through the woods."

The Owl nodded in the way he had learned from Archy. "You are right. I have heard my brother, the Dragging Canoe, say that to a white man glory is no more than a worm crawling on the ground. He will not put out his foot to crush it but it can crawl away if it wishes . . ." The merry look suddenly went from his face. He came over and gently touched Archy's arm. "I hold you fast," he said. "I hold you fast with both hands."

"I hold you fast," Archy repeated mechanically.

He looked past the Owl to where the trail took a turn down hill. The Canoe and his men ought to be coming along any time. The runner who had come into town at noon had said that they were not three hours behind him. They had been away since early March, four months in all. He glanced at the Owl's brown, lively face. But for the Owl he, Archy, would have been one of that band that had gone south with Dragging Canoe to meet the king's agent. The Canoe had come by Chota the morning they started. He had seen Archy standing there in the square and had asked Atta Kulla Kulla if his white brother might not come with them. Atta Kulla Kulla had been agreeable. Archy was about to go to his house for his bandoleer when he stopped, feeling the Owl's eyes on him. There was no question of the Owl's going. It was the very day he had got the cane stab. In fact the women had just finished dressing his wound. He sat there against a tree and watched the others, and the look on his face was more than Archy could stand. He had told the Canoe that the honor was too great, that he was as yet unproved as a warrior and besides did not care to go among white men.

The Canoe did not say anything but he had a curious expression on his face as he turned away. Archy wondered now what the Canoe had made of his saying that he did not care to go among white men. Had he thought that he might possibly be tempted to stay with them and never return to Chota?

There was a tiny nick in his left nostril where a trailing briar had got him yesterday. A gnat was buzzing at it. He put up his hand and absent-mindedly slapped at the gnat. Three months ago these thoughts would never have entered his head, but lately everything seemed changed. All that fall and winter there had been talk that the white men were going to war amongst themselves. The people at Chota and the Great Island did not know what to make of it. "Scotchie"—that was Alexander Cameron, the deputy super-intendent—said that it was all talk, but when the ammunition that the Cherokees were in the habit of receiving from Charleston did not arrive, he did not know what to say. At last a letter came from the superintendent, John Stuart: Men from South Carolina, enemies of the King, had seized the Cherokees' ammunition three days out from Charleston. Their father—as they all called Stuart—could do nothing. He was abed with the old trouble in his foot. But he was sending his brother to them with thirty more horse loads of powder.

Atta Kulla Kulla and Oconostota were glad to hear that the powder was on the way and thought that the trouble might die down. But the Canoe said that his brother, Henry Stuart, might meet more enemies of the King along the way. He and a band of his warriors would go to meet him. They started south in March and no news had been heard of them until this day in mid-summer when the runner had come, saying they were not far behind him.

A locust tree that was being bent for a bow grew near the path. The Owl limped over to it now and swinging himself up stretched his length along the trunk and looked down at Archy through the bright coin-shaped leaves.

"Bear-Killer, is your marriage a make haste or will it last?"

"It's going to last," Archy said.

The Owl smiled. "She was crazy to get you and now you find that she is a good girl to have under your blanket, eh?"

"I wouldn't trade her for any of them," Archy said.

The Owl nodded his head. "They are very passionate, those girls of the Hollow Leaf, and it lasts with them into old age, I have heard my father say. . . . She comes of important people. Cousin to the Ghigau. . . ."

"I don't love that old woman," Archy said.

"My mother does not love her either. My mother, if she had not been a woman, would have been a physician. She knows all the plants and understands the signs. I heard her tell my father once that it was her belief that the Ghigau was one of those who live on without the soul."

"What do you mean?"

"It happens sometimes. The old white man, Mouncy, lost his at Fort Loudon."

"He don't have much life about him," Archy said.

"He would be dead if he were one of the Real People. With a white man it does not seem to matter . . . I did not say so to my mother but it seems to me that there are others in the Nation who live on without the soul. . . ."

Archy wondered if he were going to name his father, but the Owl continued dreamily: "Our great man, Oconostota. All my life I have heard what a great man he is, but he does not seem to have acted like a warrior, when my brother, the Dragging Canoe, threw the hatchet into the ground at the Broken Waters. . . ."

"He didn't seem to want to fight, from what I hear," Archy said. "But then he's getting old."

"I have heard my father tell of one of our chiefs who made war when he was so old his age could not be counted and so blind that two young men went always behind him to hold his eyelids up. . . . No, I think our great man is great no longer. His soul was reft from him at Fort Loudon, along with the old white man's. . . ."

He turned over on his back and lay with his hands crossed on his breast. Archy sat silent, staring off through the trees. He was thinking of Charleston where the Canoe and his men had gone. Once when he was about ten years old his father had had to go there on business and had promised to take him, and then at the last minute had left him at home. Lying awake in bed at night, before he knew that he was not to be allowed to go, he had thought about Charleston until its streets had grown up in his mind. It was probably not the way he imagined it, and yet when it was mentioned he always felt that he had been there. . . .

Rion's face came before him, not the way it had been the last time he saw it, grave, a little suspicious but kindly, but Rion the way he used to look in the early mornings in that loft room they shared together. The call would come from downstairs—their father always rose long before it was light and sat for a long time over the kindling fire. There would be an instant's silence, then Rion would turn over in bed and as he turned would gather his faculties for the day. If he had been alone in that attic room he would have lain a little longer, might even have drowsed off again, but the thought of doing to somebody else what his father had just done to him would get him out of bed and on his feet. He would pull on his breeches so fast it would make your head swim, then come and stand over Archy. "Git up, lummox! You going to lay there all day?" A 'cute one, Rion. You had to get up early in the morning to get ahead of him.

Well, he, Archy had got ahead of him, when Nat Gist carried him that word. He hadn't asked Gist how his brother took it, didn't even talk to him when he got back, but sometimes since then he would wake in the night and try to see how Rion looked when he found he wasn't going with him. Would he get mad all at once or would he be so surprised at first that he couldn't say anything, and then all of a sudden, maybe hours later, rage would well up in him, like a kettle that stays at the boil a long time and then suddenly spatters all the hearth?

Rion would boil, all right. It would be one of the few times he had ever been fooled in his life and by a boy that he had raised from a pup! It was a wonder he hadn't come back into town to get him.

No, his feelings, though he would never admit it, would be too hurt for that. . . . He wished there had been some other way but he had known when he first saw Rion in Atta Kulla Kulla's yard that he would have to fool him. He had never for one moment considered going with him and, indeed, he hardly ever nowadays thought about his old life, only sometimes just before day, or in the day, waiting at a deer stand, he would be overcome with wonder to know how Rion looked in that instant when he got the news. . . .

The Owl spoke: "Bear Killer, of all war medicines there is one that I would most like."

"Which one?"

"It is to put your life up in a tree during the fight. There was one of our great men had that medicine once. In all his battles he was never wounded."

"How did he die then?"

"A Creek captain found out about his medicine and told his men to keep firing into the tree tops until, standing there under the trees, this great man fell dead."

"Then the medicine didn't work."

"It worked for many years." He laughed. "Would you want to live forever?"

"Not that long," Archy said.

The Owl raised himself up a moment, then sank down again. "When will my brother come? . . . Bear Killer, I am going to learn that medicine and use it all my life, and when I am killed I shall tell them to tie my body with vines high up in the trees where I can watch the enemy and send word to our men what they are doing."

"How'll you send word?"

"I will choose some man who understands such things to be my after-death friend."

"It would be fine if you could work it," Archy said and laughed.

The Owl turned over on the tree trunk so that he lay facing Archy. "I can learn it," he said. "Bear Killer, I am not an ordinary individual."

"You're one of the best shots I ever saw," Archy said.

"That is true. But there are many good shots. Bear Killer, I am going to be a warrior such as has never been seen in the Nation."

Archy looked at him curiously. "How do you know?"

The Owl glanced behind him as if some one might be listening.

"It is not good to talk of such things, in summer, when snakes are above ground, but I will tell you. . . . You know that when the time comes boys go to the lodge to fast and dream?"

Archy nodded.

The Owl continued: "It is bad if you do not have a dream. Some do not dream and are ashamed to say so. I was one of those who had a dream."

"What was it?"

"I was in a long ravine, so long that it extended to the ends of the world on both sides. I tried to climb the sides but my strength gave out and I fell back. Suddenly I heard some one talking behind me, saying 'My Son, it is not good to die in the village.' "

"Who was it?"

"It was a great white deer, taller than you are, with the signs of the Four Winds painted on his breast. He danced before me on two feet and then he tore his stomach open with his hoofs and then he made himself holy and healed it again. . . ."

"How old were you when you had this dream?"

"I began fasting when I was seven or eight—in those days we were more religious than we are now—but I was eleven when the great deer came to me. My father made me stop fasting after that. He said that the blessing was too great, that if I accepted it I would always be wanting to go on the war path."

"So you didn't accept the blessing?" Archy said.

The Owl sat up on the tree trunk, laughing. "My mother is of the Deer People. She said that no matter how great the blessing I must accept it. She took me back to the lodge and I poured tobacco and prayed and the deer came again. . . ."

"What did he say this time?"

The Owl shook his head, smiling. "I had better not tell you. It is, after all, a holy thing. . . . But I shall be great in war." He swung himself down from the tree trunk, taking care to land lightly on his lame foot. "It will be dark before my brother comes."

"There he comes now," Archy said.

A procession was coming along the trail. The Canoe rode at the head beside a white man. Winding away behind them were the pack horses and behind them nearly a hundred warriors on horse-back.

The Canoe saw the two young men standing beside the path.

He smiled at them and turning shouted an order that stopped the whole train. He dismounted and going off to the side of the road sat down on a log and holding up the little mirror that hung about his neck looked into it and readjusted the eagle feather in his scalp lock.

The white man on the horse stared, but as he saw other warriors looking into their mirrors and adjusting their ornaments, he halted his own horse and sat with his right leg draped woman-fashion over the pommel of his saddle.

He was a thin, middle-aged man and wore a dust-stained, frogged coat and cockaded hat. Graying brown hair escaped from its club at the nape of his neck. His face was streaked with dust and there was a scratch on one cheek where a briar had got him. He did not seem conscious of his appearance, only sat slumped in his saddle, watching the Indians.

"Our brother, Stuart," the Owl said softly.

Archy would have liked to go to them, to greet the white man and ask the Indians about their journey, but he knew that it would not do. The Owl was already loping off down the trail as fast as his lame foot would let him. If he, Archy, was kind enough to let him outrun him he would be first in the village and would tell his tale to one of the headmen: the Dragging Canoe and all his band had been killed, the pack train scattered, the powder stolen. . . . The headmen would pretend to believe him. They would all begin mourning. The Canoe and his men would wait until the mourning had reached the right pitch before they walked in on them.

The Owl had started whooping. The sound struck the trees and rattled back. Somebody in the village answered. Archy ran faster. The white face he had just seen was still before him. How tired the man looked, and around him all the fresh, smiling Indian faces! A soft-bred Charleston pup, but white men always looked like that when coming off a march. He opened his mouth and let out a yell while his feet pounded the dirt faster. There would be big doings tonight. Maybe a keg of rum. They would dance all night, he and the Owl and the other young men.

CHAPTER 46

THE TALL HIGHLANDER, Alexander Cameron, entered the cabin first. He flung Stuart's saddle bags on the floor and walked over to a skin-covered couch. He thrust his moccasined foot under it and dexterously rolled out a cask of brandy.

Henry Stuart sat down on the couch and bending over felt of the muscles of his back. "It must be five hundred miles," he said.

Cameron drew a tin cup full of brandy and handed it to him. "Nearer seven hundred," he said.

Stuart frowned, still feeling his back. "John assured me that I would find the first hundred miles a torture. The rest of the journey would be pleasurable." He gave a dry laugh. "His predictions were reversed. I found the first hundred miles endurable. The rest," he waved the cup at Cameron, "ah, Master Cameron, the spirit was willing but the flesh was exceeding weak!"

He looked about the room. Cameron was said to keep up some state in his home near Keowee but he lived in a clutter here. A pile of skins as high as a man's head over in one corner was evidently used as a dresser. A hair brush lay there and beside it something that looked like a pomade jar. A pair of boots in the middle of the floor and over in the far corner a heap of garments that looked as if they hadn't been stirred for many a day. The Indians kept their dwelling places neat. His Majesty's Deputy Superintendent did not follow their example.

He eyed Cameron over the rim of his cup. It had been fifteen years since they had met. In his own rooms at Beaufort. John had come by early in the morning with his young deputy who was that day to be dispatched to the Cherokees. Standing at the window Henry had watched them come up the walk, his tall, dark, spry brother—that was before John succumbed to the gout—and the lank Highlander. Cameron had been pale from his voyage and so thin that his black stockings wrinkled on his legs. Now he was stouter, almost as dark as an Indian and wore no stockings, or

335

breeches, either, nothing, in fact, but his flap and a necklace of the longest bear's claws Henry had ever seen.

His brother, John, had told him that young Cameron—he always spoke of him as young though the fellow must have turned forty—would be of great help in the delicate negotiations he was to attempt, but now that they were face to face he found himself embarrassed in the presence of a man who bore himself so much like a savage. "Still he never wore breeks in the Highlands," he thought. Aloud he said politely: "Do you reside at Chota all the time now, Master Cameron?"

The dark face smiled at him. "The Indians call me 'Scotchie.' . . . I've judged it best to stay here, since this trouble started." He turned towards the door and stopped. "The Carpenter and Oconostota want to wait on you tonight."

"Here?"

"Right now. If it is convenient."

"Hadn't I better go to them?"

Cameron shook his head. "You'll meet the other headmen at the dance—they're giving the eagle tail dance to honor you—but this'll be private."

Stuart followed him to the door and when he had gone, stood a few minutes looking out. A fair night with every star showing. Off towards the square a bonfire was blazing. As he watched a figure leaped into the air and for a second was spreadeagled against the blaze. The Cherokees often danced a whole night through, his brother said. He put his hand to his back. It was something to be off the trail and under a roof. There had been one morning towards the last when he had thought he was not going to be able to mount his horse. But it would never have done to ask help from the Indians, least of all the tall chief who had ridden beside him most of the way.

John had been very emphatic about that. Lying there, his gouty foot propped higher than his head, he had groaned when his brother came into the room. "The trip'll kill you, Henry!"

Henry had not then been able to imagine the rigors of four months' travel through the woods. "It's not a question of my comfort, John," he had answered steadily. "It's whether I can take your place."

John had groaned again and buried his face in his pillow. The action brought on a spasm with his foot. It was ten minutes before he could talk. "Od's Leather, Boy! There ain't a man in Carolina could take my place with those Cherokee. But it's better to send somebody of my blood. They'll make allowance. Just do the best you can, Boy. Stand up to it, if it kills you . . . and Henry, try to cut as much of a dash as you can. They think a lot of appearance, you know."

Henry belched, feeling the bear meat he had had for supper lying heavy on his stomach. Three dark figures were approaching, the chiefs probably, with Cameron. He turned back into the house, wondering whether he could remember enough of the language to talk with them.

The Carpenter entered first. He came to Stuart and held his wrist in both his hands for a moment, then shifted his grasp to the elbow and finally to the arm-pit. When he had done this he gently forced Stuart back to the couch, then knelt down before him and drawing off his boots and then his stockings ran his hands over his feet.

Stuart, looking down at the naked back—it was a warm night and the chief wore no covering—noticed that the skin was wrinkled as though the flesh were falling away under it. Well, it was a long time since Fort Loudon fell. . . . Paul Demere had been scalped alive before they cut his arms and legs off. But the Carpenter had taken John Stuart off on pretense of hunting for meat and had guided him three hundred miles through the woods to the Virginia settlements. John Stuart, when he was in his cups, liked to tell how the Carpenter had bought his life from the others, stripping off his coat, his bracelets, his bandoleer and finally giving up his gun and standing there naked down to his flap.

The hands that were brushing over Henry's feet felt hot and dry, like the hands of an old woman. Their touch was tender, too, like a woman's. "It's more than the ceremony with him," Henry thought. "It's John's feet he's drawing the briars from." And he remembered how, when he was leaving, his brother had raised up on his pillow one last time: "Egad, Henry, tell the Carpenter I hold him fast. . . ."

He murmured the message now, finding to his relief that the Cherokee syllables came easily to his tongue. The Carpenter, recalled to himself, stood back. Oconostota came forward and went through the same ceremony, as did Cameron, though he and Stuart had parted only a few minutes before; then all three sat down on the floor in front of Stuart.

Henry had sat down again on the couch. He wished that he hadn't but thought it would be undignified to change his position now. He cleared his throat:

"Your father, John Stuart, asked me to tell you. His old trouble with his foot has laid him on a bad bear skin. While he lay there, unable to move, enemies came and attacked him. But they did not take his life. He is now on a boat on the great water. These same enemies are the ones who stole your powder. Your father could not come through the woods himself but he sent me to you, with more powder. . . ."

He stopped for breath. In the pause the Carpenter spoke: "Who are these enemies? Mounseers?"

Henry looked away, to the papers he had spread out beside him on the couch. He could hear his brother's voice: "You will have a devil of a time with them, Henry. They won't understand how the British can fight among themselves. . . ."

"They are British," Henry said, "but they are bad people who go against their king. There are many now in South Carolina and among the Long Knives, too, I hear."

"That does not surprise me," Oconostota said. "Red men make war on each other. Why not white men?"

"I am for the King," the Carpenter said boldly. He laid his hand on his breast. "It is now many winters since I heard the talk of my father, King George. But it will stay with me, as long as I live."

Henry looked at him sharply. "It is well known, Atta Kulla Kulla, that you are staunch to the King, but tell me this: why did you sell the land on the Kentuck river to the North Carolina people? It is that has made much trouble."

"I am growing old," the Carpenter said, "I could not travel through the woods to my father's house."

"You travelled all the way to Cross creek to look at the goods."

Atta Kulla Kulla glanced at Oconostota and one corner of his mouth crinkled in a smile. "Henry," he said, "hear the truth. I gave them the land because they asked for it. It is no use denying the white men anything. They are like their own flies. A swarm comes. The people beat them out of the town, turn around and another swarm is upon them. Does a man spend his life fighting flies? I wanted them to have land of their own to sit down on. Maybe then they would leave us in peace."

"And you, Oconostota," Stuart said, "why did you put your hand to the treaty?"

The war chief stood up. He took several steps about the room. Suddenly he stopped. He looked down at his own right hand, then flung it out before him. "I value my life no more than that of a dog," he said, "but I can never make war again."

Cameron's black eyes swung to the war chief's face and stayed there. The Carpenter spoke softly: "I have known that for a long time."

"It has not been a long time," Oconostota said. "It has been for two winters. The winter that Round O was killed I stayed in my hot house all the dark months and I thought much. The thoughts I thought in those dark months stay with me. . . ."

"That you cannot ever again make war?" the Carpenter said.

Oconostota shook his head. "You are a wise man, Atta Kulla Kulla, but you do not know my heart. You think that in those months I examined myself and came to the conclusion that I was not a fit leader. Or you think that I am now too old to lead a war party. Either way you talk like a fool. At this moment I would not delegate my power to any man in the Nation, except perhaps to your son, the Dragging Canoe, who is as much of a man as I was in my prime." He looked at Stuart suddenly and smiled. "I have seen you, a child, in Charleston," he said. "Do you remember seeing me when I was a young man?"

Stuart shook his head.

Oconostota bent his eyes on the floor. "It is a pity. There were no looking glasses then such as the young men now carry about their necks, but I have seen my shadow in the water or reflected on copper and I say there was none like me in the entire Nation, and has been none since, unless we name the Dragging Canoe who as I say is a fine looking fellow. . . ."

"Do not name him," the Carpenter said. "My son already has too great an opinion of himself."

Oconostota laughed. "Perhaps you think that I, too, have too great an opinion of myself? There was a time when I would have agreed with you. I will tell you when it was, when I stood with you on that hill in the woods and watched our towns burn. Fifteen towns they burned and the cornfields around them. You and I both suffered great hardships that winter, going about naked and starving. But with me there was the wolf inside. Constantly I examined myself to see how I had failed. . . ."

"You laid siege to the fort and the fort fell," Atta Kulla Kulla said impatiently. "It was another swarm came then and burned our towns. I tell you they are like flies. . . ."

"They are like flies," Oconostota said, "but it is not that only. It is the war medicine. It no longer has power."

Atta Kulla Kulla looked at him. "That thought has come to you too?" he said quietly. "I have never believed, since I crossed the great water."

Oconostota inclined his head. "You are a strange man, Atta Kulla Kulla, and I think have never been truly religious. I, on the contrary, have been a religious man all my life. It was that made me such a great war leader."

"What has changed your heart?"

"The passage of time," Oconostota said. "I have sat in my hot house and in my mind have lived through the siege, from the very moment I struck the war pole. On the Path the war bundle never touched the ground but was always borne high. The place of ambush was chosen well. We rose up and killed and scalped till our hands were sore with holding the knives . . . and yet when we should have been dancing over our scalps we stood in the far woods and watched our towns burn. . . . All that winter and for many winters afterwards I examined myself, thinking that there must have been some impurity, some want of skill. But time has changed that. I look back on my youth. The man I see is not myself. I can judge his actions as I would judge those of any other young man brought before me and now that I am no longer Oconostota I know that in him the Nation had such a war leader as is seldom found. . . . It was not the leader. It was the war medicine that failed. It no longer has power. . . ."

"I have never believed that it has power against the white man," Atta Kulla Kulla said, "since I crossed the great water."

There was a long silence. Alexander Cameron got up and stepped softly to the east wall where he stood looking out. Finally Atta Kulla Kulla spoke:

"It is not now with us the way it has been. Some of the young men no longer look to the war leader. They say that they will make war themselves and get their lands back."

"Led by your son, the Dragging Canoe?" Stuart said.

"He wants to make war, yes. But first he says we must give back all the white man's gifts. The guns, the blankets, the cloth, the powder that has been coming into the Nation since before he was born, he says we must give them all back. . . ."

"The Real People will never do that," Stuart said harshly.

"I do not know," Atta Kulla Kulla said. "It is not with us the way it has been."

The Scotchman suddenly turned from the wall. "There's a band of men just come in to town," he said.

"It is the ambassadors," Oconostota said. "The great chief, Cornstalk, is arriving in Chota tonight, with delegates from the northern nations."

CHAPTER 47

HENRY STUART took the conch shell and held it up to his mouth with both hands. The drink was hot and bitter. He recognized it as the sacred black drink, made out of holly berries, and remembered just in time to spit some out on the ground.

Light raced in a long streak up the trunk of the big elm and lost itself in the dusk of the branches. An Indian moved farther back from the fire without taking his eyes off the man who stood in the cleared circle speaking. There must be five or six hundred of them here in this square. When he had been last in London he had met at one of the coffee houses the editor of the *Gentleman's Magazine.* If he could find words to describe the scene before him. . . .

The massive old woman who had given him the drink went stooping on along the line. Nancy Ward. She was called the Ghigau and he understood that her power in the Nation was enormous. It was she who had waved the swan's wing in the exercises that had preceded the Eagle Tail dance, and now it was her duty to serve the sacred black drink to the headmen and important visitors.

The hot drink was making the sweat start out all over him. He took his handkerchief from his sleeve and wiped his face; then, fearing the Indians might consider the action undignified, he thrust it hastily away. *Egad, Henry, try to cut as much of a dash as you can!*

He sat up straighter. . . . But no matter how straight he sat or how impassive he kept his face during the ceremonies—the Eagle Tail Dance had lasted two full hours—he was not one to cut a dash with Indians—or with women. Those girls there on the gravelled path in front of St. Mary's church. Young Priscilla Lane sweeping him a negligent curtsey while she delivered her aunt's message. He could see beyond her all the time the other girl laughing over her shoulder. "My compliments to your aunt but I shall be unable to dine at the Retreat on Sunday." And then something had made him add "By that time I shall be among the savages." He could hear the two of them tittering as he moved away and could have told what they were saying, that he did not look the man to be entrusted with such a mission.

The Mohawk ambassador was rising and walking out to stand beside the linguister, a thin, wizened old man with white tufts of eyebrows. His belt was of white wampum with black strings attached. He spoke in a high, reedy voice and the young linguister imitated his every gesture and even the tones of his voice.

"I suppose there is not a man present who cannot read my talk. These white beads"—when he said that he ran the wampum over his hand so that the beads caught the light and sparkled "—these white beads are our people who were at peace. The black beads are the Long Knives"—his voice rose even shriller—"the Long Knives who came into our towns without provocation and killed our people and the son of our greatly beloved man, Sir William Johnson. . . ."

So Sir William Johnson's son had been killed! He had not known that before. Sir William Johnson's influence and prestige were enormous. There would almost certainly be the devil to pay among the northern Indians. . . . He looked away from the speaker. The black drink was having its effect on him. He did not feel the heat so much now and there was a kind of singing in his blood. Even his eyesight was improved. The people, the trees, all seemed fixed in a cool, luminous light and yet when he bent his attention on any object he was capable of observing the most minute detail. The boy immediately in front of him had a nick no wider than a hair in one nostril. It gave him a spirited air as of a hound sniffing the wind.

The Raven of Chota was accepting the belt from the Mohawk ambassador. A straight, tall fellow with something of his uncle's look about him. He was mentioned always as Oconostota's successor. Did Oconostota really have any regard for him? He had not mentioned him once last night, when they had had that strange, confidential conversation. . . .

Atta Kulla Kulla beside him gave a sudden grunt and leaned forward. He too leaned out a little. The great Shawnee chief, Cornstalk, was rising. He had heard his brother say that he considered this chief the most dangerous man among all the tribes. At the battle of Point Pleasant two years ago he had commanded the allied armies, fighting them in lines like white men. He was speaking in a grave melancholy voice:

"The Shawnees once possessed land reaching almost to the sea-

shore. Now they have hardly ground to stand upon. . . ." His
hand that had been hanging at his side came up, trailing something.
A belt of wampum, twice as long as the Mohawk belt, twice as wide
and of a deep purple colour. Atta Kulla Kulla was sitting back as if
he had seen what he expected to see and there was no need to look
further. "It is a war belt," Stuart thought. "The others were ordinary messages. But this is a war belt."

The boy with the nicked nostril moved his head slightly. His
dark eyes were so full of light they looked as if they might spill out
of his head. Stuart looked over his shoulder into the crowd. Everywhere the same steady stare fixed on Cornstalk. One or two were
spitting on the ground, a sure sign of excitement with Indians.

". . . The French have long seemed dead but they have risen.
They have supplied us with guns, with powder, with lead for bullets.
It is not too late—if we fight like men. You Cherokees have a hatchet
that was brought to you six years ago. It is time to take it up. . . ."

The purple belt slid through Cornstalk's hand and lay, a great,
swollen snake at his feet. He was detaching a little panikin from
his belt. It flashed in the firelight as he turned it upside down. What
poured out was crimson, a steady stream settling on the snake's body
in one great wound.

The boy in front of Stuart was spitting in a frenzy; then suddenly
he leaped to one side. A big man was making his way forward, Atta
Kulla Kulla's son, the chief of the Great Island.

He held something in his hand, four hairy objects strung like a
child's toy on a string. Two were yellow, the third brown; the one
at the end of the string was grey. They whirled in the wind of his
approach. One of them turning over disclosed the circling hoop, the
fresh painted red skin.

Stuart turned to Atta Kulla Kulla. "Did they take those scalps
on the way to Charleston?"

"On the Kentuck," Atta Kulla Kulla said softly. "They are
young men and did not love to return empty-handed."

The Dragging Canoe handed the string of scalps to Cornstalk and
stooped and picked up the long belt. "I am for war," he said in a
loud, grave voice.

There was a yell. A warrior rushed out from the crowd and
hurled his tomahawk at the flag pole. It struck near the base. He ran
nearer and began running round and round the quivering pole, his

head thrown far back, his wide-stretched mouth releasing shriek after shriek.

One of the northern delegates suddenly pushed forward. He fixed beady eyes on Stuart and uttered harsh, unfamiliar syllables. "What is he saying, Atta Kulla Kulla?" Stuart asked irritably. "I cannot understand what he is saying."

The chief turned and gave his ironic smile. "He is saying that you have forgotten that I saved your brother's life; he is saying that it is true that you have brought the Cherokees ammunition but you want to keep it till it falls into the hands of the Virginians."

Stuart looked up. Dragging Canoe was looking at him. He spoke in a voice that carried above the shrieking:'

"Our brother has brought us no belt but he has words for us from our Father. Listen!"

"Stand up!" Atta Kulla Kulla hissed.

Stuart got to his feet.

"The red men do not understand the written talks of the white men. Even so the white men do not understand the red men's belts. But I know this . . ." To his dismay he felt his voice crack and grow shrill. "Ambassadors have come to you from the north, urging you to make war. If your Father, Captain Stuart, were here he would tell you not to listen to these men. . . . What has he always advised you? To consider well before you act and get talks from those who have your welfare at heart. The troops will be coming up from Florida before another moon. They will march through the Creek country. The Creeks and the Chickasaws have each promised to furnish five hundred men. We will have an army large enough to invade the whole frontier. And while the Rebels are fighting you here on the land, they will also have to fight men who will be in boats on the sea. They will have no chance to escape. You can destroy them all. . . ."

Cornstalk had been standing with his head a little bent. He raised his head now and through lowered lids eyed Henry. Henry looked back at him. The black eyes were hostile and incredulous. His own eyes went to Dragging Canoe's face. He took a step forward.

"The northern nations have proper white men to direct them but you Cherokees have not. If you go over the border now you will fall on the King's friends as well as his enemies and then . . ." He was about to say "And then the King's troops will come against you" but he realized that he must not bring up that possibility. Searching for a word he stared out over the crowd. The boy with the nicked nostril had moved out from under the elm tree. His eyes met Stuart's, then sheered away. Not black but a clear, glancing brown. But he had an Indian look for all that, rapt, unseeing.

Stuart took a fresh breath. "I ask you only to wait. The troops are on the way . . ." He heard his voice roll on, making sentences easily, and all the time thought of a sorrel mare he had had as a boy, how when sometimes he would lean his cheek against the satiny cheek and cup her nostril in his hand, the nostril would flutter wildly and the brown eye he looked into would stare past him while the head jerked from side to side.

"I am not the man to talk to them," he thought. "I cannot make them listen," and felt a hand touch his arm.

Atta Kulla Kulla was standing beside him, with Oconostota. "Has my brother said all that is in his heart?" Atta Kulla Kulla asked.

"Yes," he said, "oh, yes," and followed the two old chiefs through the crowd out of the square.

CHAPTER 48

OFF TOWARDS THE EAST the forest was as light as day—they had built up another fire in the middle of the square and were dancing around it; but here in the cabin it was dark. Henry Stuart sat on the reed couch, leaning forward, his elbows on his knees. His eyes fixed the dirt floor, his lips, moving, shaped broken sentences. Ever since the two old chiefs had left he had sat here like this while phrases of the speech he ought to have made formed themselves in his mind.

He knew as well as any man the conventions of Indian oratory. A reference to their glorious past, then a graceful allusion to the tie that bound his brother to them—the northern delegates had accused him of forgetting Cane creek!—then a tribute to Atta Kulla Kulla or Oconostota, perhaps to both. He would have had them in the mood to listen then. Instead he had plunged into the heart of the matter, telling them what they should do, all but threatening them. Yes, he had been as near as anything to threatening them. He had pulled himself up just in time and after that had become incoherent. No wonder Atta Kulla Kulla had stopped him.

"I am not the man to handle them," he muttered, "not the man for the mission," then sat upright on the reed couch while the hair prickled over his scalp.

The yelling that accompanied the dancing had for a long time been steady and ominous. But in that moment a new sound had risen and hung above the other yells the way sheet lightning might crackle over a forest. He sat there on the couch and felt the hair of his head sink down slowly like the ruff on a dog's back.

He got up and walked about the room. The hoarse, sullen yelling had started afresh. That other sound might not come again for a few minutes, might not come again tonight. He kicked one of Cameron's boots aside. Cameron was out there with them now. He had caught sight of him only once in the crowd and then his face had seemed drunken, with the eyes gleaming. An Indian in all but color. He would get no help from him.

He walked to the west wall and looked out between the logs. It was not so light here where the house tossed its wavering oblong of shadow over the green thicket. Elderberry bushes mostly, some of them as high as a man's head. The Indian children or some smaller animals had made runways through all the brake. A man might slip out of town through one of these brakes.

He looked up over the trees and found the north star. The Watauga country must lie northeast from here, over beyond that great elm. Nearly ten thousand people in those settlements. A great many "Rogues" amongst them, Atta Kulla Kulla said, but there must still be many who were loyal to the King.

The sound came again, more prolonged this time and with a quaver at the end that it had not had before. The first time he had felt it in the hair of his head, but now in the pit of his stomach. They were dancing over those scalps that the Canoe had brought, probably re-enacting the taking of them. When an Indian got ready to scalp an enemy he put his foot on his neck and catching hold of the hair gave the neck a twist that usually broke it before he ran his knife around the scalp. A good warrior could give that twist of the neck at the same time that he raised the scalp holler. . . . If they fell on the border they would take hair where they found it, women and children as well as men. . . .

He stood quietly regarding a spray of elderberries that thrust up beside the wall until the cry had died away. A sound behind him made him turn then. A woman had come in and was standing near the doorway. A big woman with grey-streaked hair, the one they called the Ghigau.

He made a motion for her to be seated. She dropped down on the floor. He walked over and sat on his couch. They sat there looking at each other. Her eyes were very bright under her dark hair. There was something about the wide mouth that reminded him of Atta Kulla Kulla. Well, she was his niece.

She was speaking. "You have left the council?"

"The red men do not understand the white men's written talks. Even so the white men do not understand the red men's belts. . . ."

She was smiling. She knew that was not the reason he had left the council. A remarkable family, that of the Paint Clan. John had said once that all the brains of the Nation were concentrated in that one tribe.

The excitement of the drink had died out of him. He was tired.

He had been talking to them in this cabin for a long time and what good did it do? If she were not the Ghigau he would take her by her fat shoulders and walk her out of here.

"You are for the King?" she asked suddenly.

He stood up. "I am His Majesty's Deputy Superintendent." He gestured towards the papers that were still flung down there on the couch. "I am preparing my speech for tomorrow's council. I have no time for talk with women."

The dark eyes lighted into amusement. She got to her feet. "You will not make any more talks in council. I heard Atta Kulla Kulla and Oconostota talking, planning how to get you out of the town."

"This is the peace town," he said, "and Atta Kulla Kulla is chief here, not a crazy woman."

She did not say anything for a long time, only looked at him. Her eyes were large and full of light. You could distinguish the pupils from the surrounding black, a rare thing with Indians. She smiled and suddenly it was as if she knew all that was in his mind, as if they had been talking together for a long time. He went towards her. "I do not care for that," he said. "I am not afraid. . . . But my brother . . . I was to hold them *back* from war . . ."

She was leaning towards him and now her lips were set against his cheek. Moist and firm. Against them his own flesh must feel withered. It had been a long time since a woman had kissed him.

She had drawn back, still smiling. "I know the white men. I have loved them for a long time. . . . Listen, Henry, the Dragging Canoe is leader now and he has struck the war pole. The young men are leaving the square to start their fasts. . . ."

He nodded abstractedly. "It will take them three days. . . ."

She came so close to him that he could smell the rancid bear's grease on her hair. "Give me a talking paper," she whispered. "There is a white man outside will take it to the Watauga."

"Who is he?"

"One of the traders."

He had turned from her and was unstrapping his saddle bags. He had mixed ink only that morning and there was a fresh made quill. He found the roll of paper and sat down on the couch and using his saddle bag for a desk, began writing:

"To His Majesty's Loyal Subjects in the Settlements on the Watauga and on the South Holston and on the Nolluchucky, Warning. . . ."

CHAPTER 49

RION LAID his crop by on the tenth of July that year. The next day he and Frank started girdling trees for another acre of new ground. They were working in the bottom in the late afternoon when they saw dust pinging up through the bushes on the other side of the river and knew that somebody must be riding along the trail. It had been several weeks since they had had any news from their friends on the Watauga. This rider might be coming from there. They put their axes down and walked over to the ford.

The rider came on at a trot. When he got to the ford he pulled his horse up and let him drink. Rion had sat down on a stump and he called out now across the water: "Light and set awhile!"

The stranger raised his head. A young fellow, and he had been on the trail a long time; his face was streaked with dust and his yellow hair was matted with dust and sweat. He fixed bloodshot eyes on Rion.

"Your name Outlaw?"

"That's right."

"You know a fellow lives around here named Wagner?"

"His house is right over there. You could see if it warn't for the trees."

"Well, I got something for him and you too." He rode over to where Rion sat and handed him a paper. Rion was unfolding it slowly when Frank stepped up and took it from him and read:

Fort Lee, July 11, 1776.

"Dear Gentlemen:

Isaac Thomas, William Fawling, Jarot Williams and one other have this moment come in by making their escape from the Indians, and say six hundred Indians and whites were to start for this fort, and intend to drive up the country to New River before they return.

JOHN SEVIER."

"John Sevier?" Rion said. "That the young fellow come out here from Virginia last year?"

"It's Captain Sevier," the messenger said, "and I don't know when he come or where he's going. But him and James Robertson and Charles and a lot of others have done forted up on the Watauga. You better go to Amos Eatons'. They're building a stockade there. . . ." He paused and looked at them sharply. "They was another letter come to Charles Robertson's about two weeks ago," he said.

"Who's it from?" Rion asked.

"Stranger come up to the children where they was swinging on some grape vines and said, 'Git that to your pappy.' It was signed by the Indian agent."

"Well, what'd he say?"

"Said the government was going to land troops in Florida and march them up through the Creeks and Chickasaws. Said they was five hundred warriors promised from each, besides the Cherokee. And said all that was loyal to the King must put their hands to a paper Charles was to send back to him. . . ."

Rion looked into the boy's green eyes. He laughed. "Has Charles got many marks on the paper?"

The green eyes lighted. "He ain't got around to drawing it up yet. . . . What's the name of your neighbors up the river here?"

"Mulroon," Rion said. "There's a man and his sister. How much further you going?"

"Up above the head of the island—if this horse holds out. . . . You tell Wagner for me?"

"I'll tell him," Rion said.

They watched him splash through the ford and up into the woods, then they looked at each other. "I reckon we might a known this was coming," Rion said. "Well, we better get up to Eatons'. Will you step over to Jacob's? Don't let Sarah bring everything she's got. It likely won't be but a night or two."

He went up to the house. Cassy had just come in from the garden with a split basket full of snaps and had sat down under the big trees to string them. The children were playing a little way off under another tree. As he came towards her she smiled and tilting the basket a little showed him a handful of new potatoes lying among the green beans. "I just grabbled one hill," she said, "and look what I got."

"You oughtn't to a done it," he said mechanically.

She turned her face up to his. It was as brown as his own, except for a white triangle on her forehead—she had an old cap that she wore when she worked outdoors. Perspiration had pasted the fine, young hairs flat against this white skin. All at once she became conscious of them and put her hand up and brushed at them with impatience, then as if fearing that he might think the impatience was for him she looked deep into his eyes and smiled.

"What you been doing all evening?" she asked.

He looked over her head towards the house. The door was open. He could see all the way inside. The bed, jutting out from the east corner, took up most of the space framed in the doorway. Above it, running almost the length of the wall was the shelf that held their few dishes. Cassy always kept this shelf neat but it struck him today that there was something different about it, and he realized that it was not the shelf but the bed. It was spread with the new coverlet, the one Cassy had finished weaving only day before yesterday. He was about to tell her that it was handsome but other words came instead. "Honey, we got to go up to Eatons'," he said and let his hand fall on her shoulder.

He felt a muscle jerk up in her shoulder and then the whole shoulder grew rigid. She answered his tone rather than his words. *"What's the matter, Rion?"*

"They was a fellow come by a minute ago said there was some chance of Indians coming."

She was on her feet and turned about so that she faced him. *"Indians?"* Her eyes went quickly to the woods as if she thought the Indians might already be there, then she was looking at him again. "What do we have to go to Eatons' for?" she asked quietly.

"They're building a stockade there. Everybody's coming in."

She started towards the house, pausing once to look towards the children, then running on. He followed her into the house.

She was going swiftly about the room, taking clothing down from the pegs. "I got time to run in the garden and pick some more snaps?" she called as he entered.

He shook his head. "Better just take what you got in the house. . . . Cassy, I'm going to turn the cow and calf together. There won't be room for cattle up there and if there was we couldn't feed 'em."

She turned around. The look he dreaded showed for a second in her eyes. "How long you reckon we'll stay?" she asked.

"Won't be more'n a few days. Maybe just one night."

He went outside and turned the calf out of its pen and unlatched the door of the little smoke house, and took down two sides of meat and slipped them inside deerskin sacks. There was some room left in the sacks after he had put the meat in, so he took them into the garden and filled the space with heads of young cabbage. The mare was grazing on the edge of the woods. He tolled her to him with a wisp of grass, bridled her, and tying the two sacks together, flung them across her back.

Cassy was coming out of the house, some garments thrown over her arm, dragging a sack of meal. He took it from her and loaded it on the horse. While he was doing this she ran to fetch the split basket from under the tree. "I'll take it on my arm," she said. "These snaps'll come in handy for supper."

Malcolm and his little, black-haired sister had come up and were staring at the horse and his load. "Where you going, Daddy?" Malcolm asked solemnly.

Rion laughed and held out his arms to Sarah. "Want a ride?"

She laughed and he swung her up on top of the load. As soon as he saw Sarah up there Malcolm wanted to ride too; so Rion settled him beside her on the sack of meal.

"It's kind of hard on old Gal," Cassy objected.

He laughed. "Don't either one of 'em weigh more'n a fly."

He led the horse around the corner of the house. The old hen that Cassy had put out this morning was scratching for her new brood right in the middle of the path. She went flying out of the horse's way, the chickens scuttling behind her. Cassy looked after them sadly. "Poor things! I was aiming to go out and feed them. Rion, you reckon I got time?"

"*Naw*," he said and then disturbed by the sound of his own voice he added soothingly: "They'll git along. Chickens can always pick up a living."

"What you going to do with the mare?"

"Turn her out soon as we get there. She'll come home."

There was the sound of voices from the front of the house.

"It's Jacob and Sarah," she said.

"Gre't God," he said, "I forgot all about 'em."

She looked up at him suddenly. "No, you didn't. You sent Frank to tell 'em. It was you sent Frank, warn't it?"

"He walked over there on his own two legs," he said drily.

The Wagners came, leading a loaded horse. Sarah and Frank were arguing about something that he had made her leave behind. Jacob paid no attention to them but walked by himself. He held his gnarled hands in front of him but they moved continually as if he were just picking something up or putting it down. Rion felt his spirits suddenly lighter. He walked close to Jacob and poked him in the ribs. "Well, it looks like we no sooner get settled than we have to move, don't it, Old Man?"

Jacob dodged aside without looking up. "They ought to a let them Indians alone," he muttered.

"Where'd you be if we hadn't taken the land? You couldn't stay in Carolina."

Jacob did not answer. Rion did not look at Cassy but he could feel her eyes on him. "Well, they're building a stockade up at Amos'," he said cheerfully. "Indians can't get over that."

They pushed on up the hill. Rion kept thinking of Sevier's letter. *Isaac Thomas. . . . He remembered that fellow from the Shoals . . . escaped from the Indians.* Things must be tight if they wouldn't let traders go in and out. . . . *Six hundred Indians and whites . . . to drive up to New River. . . .*

That other letter, signed by His Majesty's Agent. Suppose he had put his name to it, put his name to it and just stayed there in his cabin and when the Indians came poked a paper at them saying he was loyal? He spat on the ground. "I'll take my chance with the rest," he thought, "only they hadn't no business setting the Indians on us. No, they hadn't no business doing that."

They were at the top of the ridge. The pines gave way here and the laurel began. They approached Amos' house. The laurel bushes around it were slashed and bent and the muddy ground—there had been a heavy rain the night before—had been trampled deep by the feet of men and horses.

They emerged from the thicket and stood in front of the house. A close slab fence ten or twelve feet high started from its wall and was built out ten or fifteen feet towards the spring. Men were working there now. Two or three were riving logs while others set the king post the fence would turn on. From off in the woods came the sound of axes and then all of a sudden the crash of a falling tree.

Malcolm, who had stopped still in his tracks, started. "Daddy, what's the matter with Uncle Amos' house?"

"He's building him a fence," Rion said. "It's a good one. Chickens or nothing else can't get over it."

They stepped over a pile of logs and made their way in behind the stockade. A stockhouse was going up, and men were setting posts for the fence that would join it to the other cabin.

Rion saw the white insides of the oak slabs first and then he saw the people. A mort of them, spilling out of Amos' house and milling around in his yard as thick as ants. Under the persimmon tree a woman had a fire going and was cooking something. Near-by a crowd of children were playing "I Spy." There was hardly a spot in the whole enclosure where somebody was not standing.

He and Frank led the horses over near the fence and unloaded. Rion drove both horses outside the enclosure and gave them a slap to start them home. When he came back he found Jacob and Sarah sitting wearily on their bundles and Cassy standing with the children clinging to her skirts.

"This ain't the place," Malcolm said suddenly and Sarah echoed him, "Dis ain't de place."

Cassy bent and kissed her. "Yes it is. There's Aunt Jane coming now."

Jane and Amos were coming towards them. Jane took Sarah in her arms and stood there holding her. Amos was dripping with sweat and looked as if for once in his life he had been doing some work. He gestured with an axe he held in his hand. "I been riving out boards for 'em. But Abel Lyles he's spelling me whilst I get my breath."

Rion grinned. "Looks like you wouldn't have to do no work with all the force you got around here."

Amos pushed his hat farther back on his head. "Man, they been coming in here since yesterday before daylight."

"How'd they git here? I don't see no cattle."

"First ones come with a yoke of oxen. Drove their wagon right up under the window. Was figuring on stabling the oxen inside, I reckon. I made 'em hide the wagon out in the woods and we built a pen down there on the the run for the cattle. There's some of the boys watching down there now. What'd you do with your stock?"

"Left 'em to range."

"The Indians'll get 'em sure."

"They may. But I didn't see no sense in bringing them up here. Couldn't get enough feed for all these cattle to save us and if things get tight we'll need the room."

"If things get tight enough we'd need the cattle," Amos said.

Rion laughed. "Shoh, we'll never stay in here that long. Indians ain't enough patience to siege a place."

Amos was looking at two men who were picking their way across the muddy ground. "Hi, Captain," he called. "Here's a man done just come in."

Both men turned and started towards them.

"Which one's the captain?" Rion asked.

"Both of 'em?"

"I mean which one's in the lead," Rion asked impatiently.

Amos leaned down and pulled a blade of grass. "Well, I reckon Jim Thompson's seen more Indian fighting than any man here, but that Captain Cocke, he's an up-and-coming fellow, I tell you."

The two men skirted a sheet that a woman had just spread on the ground, and stopped in front of them. Thompson was a tall middle-aged fellow with blue eyes set close together above hairy cheeks. Cocke was younger, with a fair complexion and inclined to be a little plump. He greeted Rion heartily. "I'm glad to see you, friend. Where's your station?"

"Down here at the foot of the ridge," Rion said.

Cocke pursed his full lips. Rion had for a second the impression that he was trying to look older than he actually was. "That makes a hundred and sixty-nine fighting men, Eaton," he said, "a hundred and seventy, counting that stout boy of Bledsoe's."

"He's as much of a man as any of them," Eaton said.

"Ever done any fighting?" Cocke asked Rion.

Rion grinned. "Not with Indians. I was in a kind of battle once, over in North Carolina. It didn't last long."

"I was in North Carolina last year," Cocke said, "recruiting militia."

"Have any luck?"

"I may say I had. Two companies I brought back. Some of those lads are in here with us now." He seemed suddenly to realize that Thompson had not spoken, except for a brief "howdy" and he addressed his next words to him. "It's a good thing some of us realized last year what was coming, Captain. If we hadn't begun organizing militia then where would we be now?"

"I never thought the Cherokee would rise," Thompson said. "I've known that old Carpenter for three years now. Oconostota too. I never thought they'd rise."

"Where'd you see your service, Captain?" Rion asked boldly.

Cocke cleared his throat. "Colonel Preston issued my commission in August two years ago. Before that I was in command of a body of irregular militia."

Thompson had half turned away from them and was watching the work on the stockade fence. "There's that boy of Bledsoe's now," he said as a slight figure suddenly emerged from the willows by the spring.

"We'd better see if he has any news," Cocke said. They walked away.

Amos stood chewing his blade of grass and looking after them. When he turned to Rion one side of his face was drawn up in a grin. "Now ain't that something?" he said.

Rion shook his head. "Sometimes a fellow like that ain't so bad after he gets a little age on him," he said musingly.

Amos laughed and threw his grass blade from him. "I got my breath back now," he said. "We better go down and take a hand on the stockade."

CHAPTER 50

ON THAT DAY, the twentieth of July, Rion went on guard around three o'clock. He had patrolled the rifle range a half hour before, and looking up at the block house had seen a musket poking through the loop-hole he was to man. When he got up in the loft he found that the musket was held suspended in its place by a chunk of wood wedged against the butt. The guard, Bill Durroon, lay flat on his back on the floor, snoring.

Rion trod on the man's hand as he took his place at the lookout. The fellow sat up, rubbing his eyes. "Anything coming?" he asked when he had finished yawning.

"If there had been you'd never known it," Rion said.

Durroon got to his feet. He stood for a second looking over Rion's shoulder at the bit of woods and sky framed in the long slit of the loop-hole. "Ain't no sign of rain," he said and yawned again. "If I was home you know what I'd be doing?"

"Sitting on your butt if you warn't laying down," Rion said.

Durroon laughed. "I'd be eating watermelon. They was three in my patch big enough to eat but they didn't thump just right. Wish now I'd picked them. Varmints probably got 'em by this time."

He went down the ladder. The man at the other loop-hole laughed. "I started to wake that feller," he said, "but I didn't see much use. They don't really need but one man up here."

"Maybe not," Rion said, "but he ought to be a good one."

The man turned away from his loop-hole and leaned back against the wall, his rifle swinging in both hands. "You think them Indians are coming?" he asked.

"I wouldn't be in here if I didn't," Rion said.

The fellow shifted his quid of tobacco and spat on the floor. "I believe if they was coming they'd a been here before this. We been in here over a week now. It ain't the week I'd a chosen to be cooped up either. My corn was late this year—had to plant three times before I got a stand. I was fixing to give it the last working the day the word come."

"It ain't a good time of year to be away from home," Rion said.

The fellow—his name was Bulloch and he came from Reedy Creek—frowned. "If them Indians do come they're likely not to come to this fort. Spread through the settlements and tear up the crops and steal the cattle—that'd be more like 'em."

"You got to take a chance on that," Rion said.

"I don't know about that," Bulloch said. "I ain't said much, but if it wouldn't cause trouble amongst the others I'd take my old woman and walk out of here this day. . . ."

"And you and your old woman maybe not have a hair on your head time night come," Rion said shortly.

"Maybe not," Bulloch said, "but I'd do it, I vow I would—if it wouldn't cause trouble."

Rion did not answer and the other man turned back to his loop-hole.

Rion stared through the narrow slit in the logs off to the east. He had this loop-hole every time he did guard duty. The scene he looked out on had come to be as familiar to him as his own dooryard. Down below the ridge on the left, veiled now by a light haze, was Pendleton's rich valley. On the right was the smaller, shallow valley in which his own home lay, and rising up beyond that Bays' Mountain that always looked to him like a loaf of bread just taken out of some monster oven.

Standing on guard he often turned his eyes to one or the other valley but for the most part he looked straight ahead along the backbone of the ridge. Just beyond the rifle range a laurel thicket began. A bridle path ran through it, due east. The eye could follow the path for a long way when it suddenly vanished in scrub pine. There was quite a lot of scrub pine before the ridge sloped down into the heavy growth that marked the horizon.

That bridle path ran on to join the Warriors' Trail. It was along that trail that the Indians would travel from their towns. He had picked out a certain spot, marked by an unusually tall cluster of pines, where he imagined the two trails joined. Always when he came on guard his eyes went first to that spot but not once in these eight days had he seen so much as a wisp of smoke, and yet he felt that the Indians were on their way.

But they might not come for days. In that case there would be hell to pay. He did not believe you could keep these people cooped up in this fort many more days. Supplies were not running short. There was plenty of meal and side meat still and, thank God, they had had enough sense to fence in the spring. There was water in abundance and even milk for the babies—Amos' three cows came up to the gate every evening to be milked. It was not the lack of anything they needed, or even sickness—a lot of the babies had been sick but you had to expect that—no, it was none of these things but just that a restlessness had come over the people, men and women too. It had come all of a sudden, two days ago. At least that was the first time a man had turned to him and remarked on what he would be doing if he were at home. It was that same day that he noticed two men dropping their work to stand staring off into the woods. He knew what they were thinking, that there was nobody to stop them if they wanted to walk out of here. That was the way this fellow, Bulloch, felt. He didn't know but that he'd feel the same way—if he didn't know that the Indians were coming.

He started, then leaning his rifle against the wall thrust his head out of the loop-hole. A woman was coming up from the brush there on the right, walking along calmly with no effort at concealment. He leaned farther out of the loop-hole. It was Cassy. She had a split basket full of greens in her hand. She had been down in Amos' sallet patch cutting collards.

He was about to call her when a hand fell on his shoulder. He turned around. Amos had come to relieve him. He did not stay to talk to Amos but went on down the ladder. The room below was full of women. He made his way through them hurriedly, on tiptoe, not glancing towards the corner where John Dunham's young wife lay on a pallet, moaning. She had been delivered of a child three days before and had been clean out of her head ever since. He wondered whether the fever had been brought on by fright and confusion or whether she would have been taken that way anyhow. . . . Cassy's third child was due in four months. But they would be out of the fort and back home by that time.

He stepped down into the yard. A little shape fluttered up from the shadow of the wall and glided beside him. A girl about ten years old. She wore a single garment, a man's deerskin hunting shirt, belted at the waist by a leather thong and so old that in places the hide had broken and showed her dirty flesh.

He looked down at her and smiled. "Where you think you going?"

The expression of her face—a wide, curious stare—did not change but the sound of his voice seemed to startle her. She dropped back and hid behind a pile of logs.

The enclosure was full of women, gathered in knots under the few trees or huddled in the scant shadow cast by the stockade fence. The ground which had been muddy when they came in was as dry as a bone and every blade of grass, every shrub had long since been trampled down into the dust. As he walked along he cast a glance up at the sky. Not a skim of cloud in all that burning blue.

Jane was sitting on the ground under the persimmon tree. She had her knees spread wide and Sarah lay across them, sleeping. He had hardly thought about the children in the last few days, but now it occurred to him that Sarah might be sick. He looked at her anxiously as he came up. She was pale and there were purplish shadows under her closed eyes.

"Ain't anything wrong with her, is there?" he asked.

"She ain't been *right* for two days," Jane said.

"She ain't got fever?"

"It's her bowels," Jane said. She was looking past him as she spoke. Cassy was coming towards them with the basket of greens. He went to meet her. "What was you doing out on the range?" he asked.

She looked at him calmly. "I had to get some greens, the baby's bowels are bound up." She stepped past him and laid a stick on some ashes that were smouldering under a pot. "I'm going to cook these greens now." She glanced at Sarah slyly. "Do it this time of day and won't so many children be coming around."

Jane shifted the baby on her knee. "I saved a piece of corn bread to crumble in them," she said.

Rion felt awkward and inexperienced, hearing them talk so authoritatively. "Reckon that'll cure her?" he asked.

"Ain't anything better, short of physic," Jane said.

Rion heard a slight noise and looked up. The strange little girl had crept out from behind the logs and was standing about ten feet away, staring at them. She was very thin. The hair that was pushed back from her forehead was matted like the fur of some mangy animal and might have been almost any color. Her blue eyes were set wide apart in the dirtiest face he had ever seen. But her face was no dirtier than the rest of her. The skin of her neck, her bare arms and feet and legs, all were crusted thick with dirt.

He made a motion towards her with his hand. "Why don't some of you all take and wash that little critter?"

Cassy looked up, smiling faintly. "She belongs to that wild fellow. Comes and stands here like that for an hour at a time." She crooked her finger and whistled as if to a dog. "You want to come and set with us, honey?"

The child whirled and was back behind her pile of logs.

Rion laughed. "I ain't got time to go over and flush her."

He looked towards the spring where some men were gathered in the shade of the willows. They had been sitting there idly, some of them playing cards, but now they were all on their feet, moving around. "They's somebody come in," he said abruptly and hurried off down the slope.

On the way he passed a wild-haired, ragged looking man sitting alone on a log. His face was crusted with dirt. His hunting shirt was slick with grease. Rion remembered seeing this man the day they forted up. He had asked several people who he was but nobody seemed to know—he had just drifted in the day the blockhouse went up. This must be the "wild feller" Cassy had spoken of. He felt sorry for the child if this man was all the dependence she had. He looked to be as near a beast of the forest as a man could get and stand on two legs.

The men were gathering in a circle around the spring. He pushed in among them. The Bowyer boy was stretched out full length, his head bent over the water. As Rion came up he raised his head to answer a man's question. "Must be three or four hundred," he said, and then his head went down again and you could hear him greedily lapping.

"Where'd he come on 'em?" Rion asked the man next to him.

"Up on Cockrill's Run," the man said.

The boy hurriedly plunged his whole head into the pool, then stood up. Beads of water sparkled on his eyebrows and lashes and on the young hairs of his beard. He drew his hand across his mouth, sighing luxuriously as if he could hardly forget his thirst for a moment, then stood straighter. His grey eyes shone through their wet lashes.

"I wouldn't a found 'em," he said, "if I hadn't climbed up on that bluff. I was scouting around there all day yesterday and I lay down and slept in a hollow not three hundred yards from that run. I got up long before it was light and was getting ready to go over on the other side of the ridge, thinking they might have cut through that way, when I come on this big bluff. I decided I'd go up there and have a look around before I left. I had to set up there a while before it was light and then all of a sudden I leaned over and there they was, thick as hops."

"What was they doing?" Jim Thompson asked.

"Sleeping, but they had some guards out. Least I saw one coming up from the run. I took out then."

There was silence. It was broken by William Cocke's voice. "Gentlemen, I think we had better go out to meet them."

Jim Thompson looked up over the stockade into the woods. "That gives 'em a mighty good chance to slip up on us," he said. "What did we build a blockhouse for if we ain't going to stay in it?"

Rion glanced around the circle. Nobody was looking at Thompson. The men were all staring at Cocke. "They know they ain't a thing to him," Rion thought, "and they're wondering why he's so brash." He suddenly felt like laughing. The fellow was scared! His full lips were trembling and his voice when he spoke had been louder than there was any need for. "He's scared to *stay*," Rion thought. "He still wants to do something big but he knows it'll have to be quick." And then he forgot his speculations. Cocke was walking in among the men, speaking in a lower, more persuasive voice:

"They won't attack us here. They won't attack any of the blockhouses. They'll break up into parties and spread through the settlements. There's a lot of folks didn't come in. It'll be hard on them, to say nothing of the destruction of the crops. . . ."

A tall man threw away the stick he had been whittling on. "I don't want those bastards to get my young corn."

"My idea is to fight 'em and get it over with," another man said. "I reckon if we have to go outside to find 'em we'd better do it."

Thompson looked at John Campbell. "What is your feeling, Captain Campbell?"

"You and Captain Cocke have seen more Indian fighting than I have," Campbell said courteously. "I'm willing to abide by your decision."

Thompson looked around the circle at the men and then at the women who had come out of the blockhouse and with the children were pressing up through the young willows. He made a motion with his hand as if to drive them back but he let it fall abruptly at his side.

"Go get your powder," he said.

Men were swarming up the rise to the blockhouse. It was full of women. Rion dove through them and got to the high shelf in the east corner. He had five pounds of good French powder stored there in a big gourd. Cassy had thought it was a bad idea to keep it there where anybody might get at it but.he had said no, it was best to leave it in full sight; then if anybody took it they'd know who they had to reckon with. He lifted the gourd down and tilting it began to pour the fine black powder into his horn when he felt somebody come up behind him and a hand was laid lightly on the arm that held the gourd. He kept on pouring until the horn was filled to within an inch of the rim, then he looked around into Cassy's face. He smiled. She dropped her hand and moved back a little.

"You all going out now?"

"Right this minute," he said and slapping her lightly on the back ran out of the house and down the hill.

The scouts had gone on ahead. The captains were drawing off their companies. Rion had been elected a lieutenant in John Campbell's company. He had men under him. He walked over and called out in a loud voice: "Dress on the right!"

They were forming in two long files. Thompson at the head of one, Cocke at the other. The order came suddenly: "March!"

Grinning boys held the gates back. They passed through and were on the rifle range. Their feet crunched on the crisp, burned soil. They were over the range and into the laurel. The path had been widened by wagons and sleds. Plenty of room for two files of men.

"But maybe we ought not to be in files," Rion thought. "Maybe we ought to each pick us a tree."

The laurel ended. They were in the pines. They could be in here. Yes, there was plenty of cover for them in here. But would they have had time to get this far? Cockrill's Run where the Bowyer boy had seen them sleeping, was all of six miles. He was a fast runner, that boy, and he had come on them before it was good light. If they had slept another half hour or if they had been slow getting started they would not have had time to get this far. Suppose they had got wind of how many men there were in the fort and had turned tail? It was funny, ever since that boy had brought the word, he had not been able to see them, to see them coming through the woods the way he had been seeing them for eight days. But that didn't mean anything, except that now he was busy his mind didn't have time to run on foolishness.

He glanced overhead. Not more than an hour of sun left. If they didn't come on them before dark the men would be turning back to the fort. He stared over the butternut-colored shoulder in front of him and almost prayed. If a dark head would show there on the other side of that hickory or to the right behind those rocks.

The man in front of him suddenly broke step. "What's that?"

"Firing," Rion said. He leaned out to look up the line. "Here come Bob Davis and Bill Biggs."

The scouts came flying up the path. "We run into 'em," Davis gasped.

Thompson was beside them. "How far, boys?"

" 'Tain't no distance—if they haven't fallen back."

Thompson was back at the head of his file, yelling: "Ready. . . . March!"

They were off on the double quick. Out of the scrub pine now and down into the flats. Master oaks, beeches and hickories. Room between the trunks for a man's garden patch. No cover here. Where could the savages have gone to?

Somebody ahead sang out. "Right about face!"

The man in front of Rion turned and stared. "What for?"

"I don't know no more'n you do," Rion said and left his men and ran up the line. Up there the men had already broken ranks. Cocke and Thompson stood off to one side, talking.

Rion went up to them. "You ain't turning back?"

Thompson looked up. "Captain Cocke thinks we'd best turn back. And I don't like the looks of this place much myself." He jerked his hand towards a great oak. "No telling how many of them hiding behind them trees."

Rion heard the pad of a moccasin behind him. Robert Edmiston spoke. "I thought we came out to fight?"

Cocke looked at him. His face was flushed and his eyes had

narrowed but he spoke calmly. "It is a question of where we'll fight. While we're waiting here they may have slipped around us and started for the fort." His voice rose, grew sharp. "Do you want 'em to come on the women and children?"

Thompson looked worried. "I reckon that's so. Besides it'll be dark here in a few minutes."

He walked over towards the men. "Dress on the right," he shouted.

Rion went slowly back towards the ranks. Robert Edmiston walked beside him. When they were out of earshot Edmiston spoke. "He was all for coming out to meet them. Now he wants to turn tail."

"He's a white-livered son of a bitch," Rion said. "Ain't got no business to command."

Edmiston looked at Rion. A grin came on his lean, rather solemn face. He turned around and called out in a loud voice: "Let Captain Cocke go back to the fort and look after the women. The rest of us'll stay here."

Cocke heard him and stopped in his tracks. His rosy face went pale. He threw his head. "Sir, do you impugn my honor?"

Edmiston shook his head. "I just said you ought to go on back to the fort."

Bulloch, the man from Reedy Creek, stepped up beside Edmiston. He looked from one man to the other, then he said: "There's some of us think we ought to stay and fight as long as we've come out."

"That's right," came from somewhere in the crowd. "Let him go back," somebody else shouted.

Cocke paid no attention to any of them. He stared at Edmiston and said in a low, furious voice, "I served against the Shawnees, sir, which is more, I think, than you have to your credit."

Edmiston spat on to the leaves and looked up with a sly smile. "Maybe you've had enough Indian fighting."

There was dead silence. Cocke was walking with little, quick steps across the rustling leaves. He stopped when his pale, furious face was within a few inches of Edmiston's. "Sir, my judgment is one thing, my military reputation another. You are at liberty to question the one but not the other. . . ."

Rion had slipped around through the crowd and was standing beside Thompson. "Hadn't you better pull your cock off?" he asked.

"I know Bob Edmiston. He ain't going to back down for hell or high water."

Thompson shook his head. "That's a good boy, that Cocke, but he gets his back up too easy." He raised his head suddenly to look off through the trees. "Here they come," he said.

There had looked not to be any cover in all that wide, flat place but there was: a draw, far off to the left. The Indians were rising up out of it, spreading through the trees as they came.

Thompson was shouting: "Dress on the right. Dress on the right!"

Men were drawing up in front of a big beech. Rion was running towards them when Bob Davis came at him, yelling. "Too far out. They're going to outflank us."

Rion looked up. The Indians were pushing to the left, skirting some big trees.

Davis was already back of the line, on a little hill, still yelling, beckoning with his left hand. Rion ran straight at the line. "Come on! Form on the hill."

They were coming after him and now they were forming on the hill. He drew a long breath and looked at his priming.

The Indians had seen them and had stopped, striped clowns huddled in the shade. A big chief sprang out from among them and made for the white men's centre. The others crowded after him.

Rion looked down the line. The men were steady. Then suddenly Bill Edmiston and Bob Davis broke from the line. Edmiston looked back over his shoulder. "Come on! Don't wait for 'em!"

Rion ran up beside them. The Indians were coming on fast; the big chief still in the lead. You could see his face now. Black stripes quivering over the stretched, red mouth; a big nose. The one that had been at the Island, the one that had made all the trouble.

He brought his rifle up and aimed, high, for the belly button. He heard the report and in the same instant wind whipped his cheek. He retched and leaning over picked the tomahawk out of the loam.

Frank, beside him, turned white eyes. "You got him!"

Rion shifted the tomahawk to his right hand and ran forward. The chief was on the ground. The blood spilled from his thigh, not his belly. He set his lips together, thrust his fist into the place, was on his knees.

Rion was leaning over to tomahawk him when he felt a hand on his wrist. He looked into black eyes while a knife came up towards his throat. He held the fellow off with his knee while he swung the tomahawk out and then up. It sliced in like butter. The Indian fell backwards on the leaves.

Rion stepped around the body and saw the chief being carried off by two men. He kept twisting in their grasp to look back. His mouth was still stretched wide with his shouting. His eyes were fierce through their glaze.

"He's done," Rion said, and turned quickly, hearing a cry. "They got you, Frank?"

Frank grinned and slumped to the ground. He was crawling off towards a log. Rion looked back at him once and moved on. Off towards the right Thompson's men were closing in on a bunch of Indians. Rion ran towards them. When he got there the Indians had been beaten back through the trees. "Follow 'em," Rion screamed, "don't let 'em get away!"

The Bowyer boy jumped over a dead Indian and was beside him. He pointed to the streaked leaves. "This way. They went this way."

They ran forward. An Indian was crawling between two trees. Rion cracked his skull with his tomahawk and they went on. Jumping over bodies, dodging between tree trunks. The way was sticky with blood—they passed two more who had to be finished off—but nothing walked upright through the trees.

The Bowyer boy spoke, thickly, from a swollen mouth. "Might's well go back."

"I reckon so," Rion said.

Thompson was coming towards them. He laughed and wiped his brow with a bloody hand. "Boys, they've done turned tail!"

Rion looked at the body that lay nearest him, a young Indian with a hole plowed through his chest. There was another one ten feet away. He ran over to it. An older man, wounded in the lungs: the leaves all around him were flicked with red froth. He raised his head and looked over the grove. Prone bodies everywhere and everywhere the trails of blood. He started running and suddenly it was like some day in summer, when going into the field, he would find a melon that had not been there the day before and then another and then another, and would run from row to row, counting the long, dark shapes. So now he ran over the field and the bodies he came on were to him like the fruit he had been used to number on that summer day.

Six he found in one patch and then, on top of a hillock, two more; and fallen behind a log, three in a cluster. No more in sight. He ran, panting up to Thompson. "Twenty-one," he cried.

"There's one right there," Thompson said. An expression of disgust came on his face. "Look out, Man, what you stepping in!"

Rion looked down. The Indian had been killed with a knife. He lay half turned over, blood still oozing from his torn entrails. It was seeping into Rion's moccasin. He laughed and standing on one foot took the moccasin off and shook the dark drops down on to the leaves. "We let it out of 'em, didn't we?" he cried. "We let it out of 'em!"

CHAPTER 51

THE BAND led by the Raven left Chota on Tuesday. Five days later they were in the valley that was called Carter's from the man of that name who kept a store there. In the late evening they dropped down into a hollow that was grown up in young beech and drifted thick with fallen leaves. A spring, welling out from under a rock, sent a bright runnel through the brown drift. The Raven was at the head of the line. He came into the grove at the same swift trot that he had kept up since early afternoon. Archy thought he would pass through the water without stopping, but on the brink of the stream he reached up and touched a low-hanging crooked limb, then gave the grunt that meant that he had found a landmark.

In the same instant a man rose up from where he had been sitting at the foot of a tree and came and took him by the arm. As he made the gesture his face showed for a second over the Raven's shoulder: a black mask striped with red.

In this dim light it was hard to tell who he was, but Archy saw the scar that lifted the upper lid of his right eye a little and he knew that it was Noonday.

He felt angry. "He has not yet killed a man," he thought, "and he is not as good a hunter as the Owl or as myself for that matter. Why was he picked for a scout instead of us?"

And then he forgot himself, listening to what was being said.

". . . five . . . in a cabin . . . a mile from here."

"Why are they not in the fort?"

The black mask cracked wide in two. "They came out to get water."

The Raven turned and threw his hand up with fingers spread wide. The men broke their rank. Archy stood back until the older warriors had drunk. Then he stepped up the slope and knelt and drank the water where it bubbled out between two flat green rocks.

When he had finished he dropped down in the leaves beside the

Owl. He could still feel his gullet string where the clear, cold water had washed it. They had already drunk three times today but that water had come from the hollow reeds that each man carried slung about his neck. A man could drink a gallon of that warm, sweetish stuff and not get the refreshment he could get from one drink of water cold from the spring.

He sat quietly, touching shoulders with the Owl as they leaned against the same young beech. Dusk was already in the hollow. In that soft light the warriors' painted faces were greyish blurs except for the glint of an eye-ball every now and then or the thrust of some feather when a man turned his head.

The Raven and the scout still stood together, talking, but the other warriors all leaned as he and the Owl were leaning against some tree or lay back against the slope, legs and arms sprawling. All except the *Etissu*. He sat on a fallen tree, upright, his hands on his knees, looking straight before him, his war bundle that on no account must ever touch the ground, sticking out from the middle of his back like the handle on a pot.

". . . a hundred," the Raven said, "a strong fort. . . ."

The Owl's shoulder pressed a little harder against Archy's. He turned his head. His eyes gleamed; his lips drawn back in a smile showed his strong, white teeth. He had had that same expression on his face all day. Others had noticed it. Archy had seen one grey-haired warrior look at him curiously and then with an arch glance direct another man's eyes to the mirthful face.

"Atta Kulla Kulla's son is happy now that we go to war," he said softly.

The Raven and Noonday had come over and were sitting down beside the old warrior, Humming Bird. Captain Gist got up from where he had been sitting and joined them. They discussed the situation in the fort. Day before yesterday Noonday had climbed a tall tree and looking down into the fort had seen men handling sacks of corn and had counted ten or twelve head of cattle. "But there is little water," he said.

"How do you know?" Gist asked.

"The cattle low . . . and those men would not have come out if they had not needed it."

"How long have they been in the cabin?" the Raven asked.

"Two days. They have a butt full of water on runners just outside the door but they cannot get the sled across the field. One of us watches and shoots every time they step out."

"Why have you not captured those men?" the Raven asked sharply. "Three of you and they only five."

Noonday was silent a moment; then he said: "We are two now. The Northward is dead. I have hidden his body under some leaves but I am puzzled how to dispose of it. Shall I bury it now or shall we build a scaffold and expose it so that the birds may pick the bones clean?"

"That is an old custom," the Humming Bird said in his deep voice, "and a burial acceptable to a warrior."

The Raven did not seem to want to put his mind on the question. "How did the Northward meet his death?" he asked.

"At the cabin," Noonday said sullenly. "We went there this morning just before day, whooping as loud as we could. But they were ready and shot the Northward through the chest as we broke from the woods. Doublehead and I turned back then—to help him."

"To help him?" the Raven said. He seemed to repeat the words mechanically and yet with a tinge of sarcasm.

There was no answer from Noonday. Archy could hear old Humming Bird's heavy breathing but the old man did not speak and neither did Noonday, who after a few seconds got up and walked away.

He was taking his place quietly in another group of men. He would not mention to them what had passed between him and the Raven, and as long as the Raven was leader he would obey him, but once off the Path he would call him to account. One of them would probably die for what had been said tonight. And yet had anything been said? Had the Raven meant to asperse Noonday's courage or had the emphasis on "help" been accidental?

Archy wished that it were lighter so that he could study the man's face. Was he nervous or merely preoccupied, trying to plan the attack as skilfully as possible? He had a reputation to live up to. A man did not get the name Raven unless he had showed not only courage but wisdom in battle.

He thought of the Owl as he had seen him a few days ago, throwing himself on the ground, howling and digging his fists into his eyes. That was when he discovered that he and Archy would not join the party from the Great Island but must go with the band from

Chota. And yet last night, when they had stopped to eat and drink, the Owl, sitting beside him for a few minutes, had whispered that now they were on the Path he had no regrets but was as happy to follow the Raven as he would be to follow his brother, the Dragging Canoe.

"They have confidence in him," Archy thought, and words he had heard in the town house came to him: "On the warpath do not make new plans. Think only how best to obey the leader."

The Raven broke the silence. "Humming Bird, what do you think? Shall we pass this cabin by and go straight to the fort?"

"I think we had better stop and take it," the old warrior said.

"But the noise of the shooting will alarm the fort."

"They are on guard anyhow," Gist said.

Archy looked up. On the march he had not been near Gist at any time. He had almost forgotten that this white man was with them until now when his voice came out of the half-dark.

The Owl leaned forward suddenly. "And the men from the cabin might come up on us from behind, O Raven."

"That is true," the Raven said thoughtfully. A lighter note came into his voice. "And how shall we take the fort, O Owl?"

"Burn it," the Owl said eagerly. "If you allow, I will be the one to hold the torch."

"We will decide that when the time comes," the Raven said. He stood up and called out the word that meant that the men had rested enough and must now take to the Path again.

It had been dark for several hours when they stopped on the edge of the clearing. It was not a large clearing and the cabin stood square in the middle of it.

There was no light showing anywhere but men's voices were heard.

"Bill, how long we been in here?"

There was a creaking sound as if the man addressed were turning over on the floor. "Two days, I figure. . . . It was just about this time of night we made the break, warn't it?"

The other man laughed. "And I didn't want to bring that sack of meal along! Old Lady Ashcraft came pretty near crying . . . till we said we'd take it."

"That's the way with women. They look ahead. It's their nature."

"And look always for the worst. Well, Old Lady Ashcraft warn't disappointed. . . . She sure is one thin old pee-turkey. That Miller girl is the prettiest of all them young ones, ain't she now?"

"I ain't hardly noticed her, Arthur."

"You take a look at her when we get back," Arthur said and began to sing:

> In Scarlett town where I was born
> There was a fair maid dwelling
> Made all the lads cry "Wellaway!"
> Her name was Barbara Allen.

The warriors were taking cover on the edge of the woods. Archy, lying behind a stump, another man close beside him, heard the song and remembered how Rion used to sing it, coming home from church at night, letting his voice ring out how it would, not caring whether or not he disturbed the neighbors.

> O don't you remember in Scarlett town,
> In Scarlett town a-drinking,
> You gave a health to the girls all around
> And slighted Barbara Allen?

The fellow was getting the verses mixed, having Barbara scorn the dying man before she got to his bedside. He moved his head restlessly and felt the coarse hair of his comrade's dangling scalp lock brush his cheek. He drew a little away from him and stared off across the clearing. Something round and dark came up there against the cabin wall: the water butt hoisted up on a sled. They must have another butt full inside or they would not have held out this long.

For a second it was as if he were in there with them. Four bearded men sprawled on the floor. Another, the one who had been singing, leaned against the west wall. He had a flaxen beard. His head, cocked a little to one side, was thrown far back. He was still singing though there was no noise to be heard anywhere, except off in the woods a mockingbird's fluting.

He got to his hands and knees and looked up at the sky. There were not as many stars out as there had been a while back and the air was softer. It might rain and even if it didn't, it was going to be a black night. Too black to know what you were doing. Perhaps they should have waited till dawn. But that would mean putting off the attack on the fort still another night. The Owl was right. They could not leave those fellows here and go on to the fort. Five men, probably the best marksmen in the lot. They would be on them like catamounts.

Four men came out of the woods, a long dark object swinging between them. . . . All along the wood's edge men were rising. He picked up his rifle and stepped out over the hard ground. Almost as dark here as in the woods. Would the door be in the middle of the wall or would they have to feel for it?

His free hand, swinging out, touched a bare back. The man ahead had stopped. He froze in his tracks and breathing softly stared at the black wall. There was a patter of feet. Four men ran past. The black, blunt log they carried soared up to crash against the wall.

There was a shout inside and then no sound. Four heads bobbed back past him, then the log was rising again. Wood splintered under the stroke, and there was the whish of leather ripping from its hold. Dark heads clustered thick as the warriors put their shoulders to the door.

He shifted his rifle to his other hand and drew his tomahawk from its thong. He could hear the white men against the door, cursing, grunting. Suddenly there was the sound of fire. In the flash the Humming Bird's face showed, a writhen mask, and then the old man reeled off, groaning.

The white men still had the musket barrel thrust through the doorway but three warriors had hold of it. There were more splintering sounds. The door went down with a bump.

He leaped forward and as he leaped heard his own voice raised in the war cry.

The doorway was clear of men. He stepped around the half fallen door and was into the room. He put his hand out and felt nothing but dark. But off to the right men were struggling. He went towards the sound. His hand grazed a naked shoulder. He stepped back and in that instant a man's arms came up and took him around the chest. He sprang and broke the fellow's hold, faced about and swung his tomahawk up, then down, as hard as he could. It struck on flesh and hung. A glancing blow, in the shoulder, he thought. He pulled the blade out and would have struck again when a musket went off. The glare showed him the white man on the floor, a Cherokee bending over him. Sobbing he stumbled off, hack-ing, striking nothing. And then tow flared up on the hearth and all the room was light.

He stood still, brushing his arm across his face to clear his eyes of sweat. The room was full of Cherokees. From the corner groans came but no white man was standing. In front of him the Owl bent, straddling a man. He was rising, holding something in his hand. Archy's eyes went past him to the prostrate body. There was a tomahawk wound in the chest but yes, the shoulder, too, was soaked with blood. He looked away. "He was mine," he thought, "mine if I hadn't stepped off!" and then he saw bright drops of blood falling on the toe of his own moccasin and realized that some one had come to stand beside him. He stared for a moment at the floor where the blood was spattering thick, then let his eyes travel up past the dangling scalp to the Owl's face. Words came to him.

"You have done well, Brother."

The Owl turned to him. He was breathing hard but his face in the dying glow of the fire showed calm and bright.

"I am a warrior now," he said.

The Raven was coming towards them, holding a scalp in his hand. He slipped on a smear of blood, righted himself with a bound then turned and gave a quick look about the room. "They are all dead," he said.

Somebody flung on another handful of tow. The knot of warriors over in the corner parted. A bearded, middle-aged man was propped slackly against the wall, another man's bloody body fallen across his knees. A little way off a young, German-looking fellow lay on his back staring at the roof. His arms, widespread, made him look as if he had just lost his balance and toppled down. It was his yellow hair that the Raven was fastening to his belt.

The glow was dying. The Raven finished tying the thong that affixed the scalp, threw his musket to his shoulder and trotted out of the room.

He went west, the warriors filing after him. On the edge of the clearing they found the Humming Bird lying dead behind a stump, a hole deep enough to hide a man's fist in, blown in the side of his head. They carried the body a little farther into the woods and left it, covered with leaves, under some rim-rock.

Half an hour later they stopped in the deep woods beside a spring. The Creek Killer was there, waiting for them. He had been lying up in a clump of dogwood within earshot of the fort. There had been much talk when the shooting started at the cabin. For a few minutes it had looked as if a band would go out to help the men in the cabin but the ones inside had evidently thought better of that. At any rate the gate had not opened. He could swear to that, for his post had been on that side of the fort.

Noonday had something at his belt, larger and whiter than any scalp could be. He was holding it up. "This will help the fire," he said.

A man came suddenly from behind Archy and snatched the bundle of tow from his hand. "Let me set the torch," the Owl said. "O Raven, let me set the torch!"

An older warrior spoke. "The Owl is Man-Killer now. Let him touch off the fire."

The Raven turned to the Owl and gave him his directions. He and the Creek Killer were to lie hid in the woods on the other side of the clearing. When they heard firing they were to start for the fort. The shooting would draw the settlers to that side and give the Owl and his companion time to get the fire to burning.

The Creek Killer grunted his approval. "It is better than flaming arrows. That is too slow."

Archy felt a hand on his arm. "Come with me," the Owl whispered, then said aloud calmly, "My elder brother, the Bear Killer, goes with us. . . . *Na-hwun-yu-ga-í, O Raven.*"

"*Hwi-la-hí,*" the Raven said.

The Creek Killer was already on the path. They followed him. They came out in a grove of elms. The ground was covered with young limbs that had been lopped off for browse last winter. On the edge of the clearing the brush had been raked into a long pile. Archy stooped and felt the frail boughs; they were as dry as tinder. The Creek Killer was dropping down behind the brush. He stretched himself out full length beside him. They looked over at the fort.

A watch fire leaped in the southwest corner. The fort stood up big in its glare. A high stockade fence with a blockhouse at every corner. Room for fifty head of cattle in there besides the people. They were fixed for a siege, all right, if it weren't for the water.

Something showed up suddenly on one of the roofs, moving along like a man's bent form. "They keep a guard along there too?" he whispered.

"They are putting out blankets," the Creek Killer said. "In the morning they wring the dew out of them."

The Owl had been off in the woods cutting a pole for his torch. He came up now and dropped down beside them. "In the morning!" he said and laughed, and then broke into excited whispering about the fight that was just over. "I got in there and I struck about but I could not find anybody. I thought, 'There are not enough to go around. They will all be killed before I get a chance.'"

"That was just the way with me," Archy said, thinking of the arms that had come around him in the dark and then of the blow that he had struck.

"I found mine with my foot," the Owl said. "I heard the fall and thought somebody else had brought him down and then he caught at my ankle and I was on him. Aieh! I was on him. I grow excited now, telling you about it, but I was calm at the time. I struck one blow only but it was a good one and then my foot went to his chest and I grasped the hair and pulled, and I heard his neck snap and knew that I had made the *coup*." His voice sank. "But it is hard to take a scalp in the dark. I am afraid this one will come out small when it is dried."

"They'll all know you took it in a night fight," Archy said. His voice sounded harsh in his own ears. The contrast between his own warm tones and Archy's grating voice must have struck the Owl. He reached out suddenly and laid his hand on Archy's wrist. "I hold you fast," he said.

"I hold you fast," Archy said and lay quiet, staring at the fort. When they had first come up it had seemed that there were no sounds from there but now you could hear sounds a-plenty. The measured footfalls of men on guard, and occasionally a rumble or a little flurry of hoofs from the cattle penned up in there, and once a child's fretful wail rose and was promptly hushed. Off in the woods the mockingbird was still going it, imitating a catbird now. How many times had he and the Owl, pretending that they were mockingbirds, run through all the calls they could give! This was the night they had been waiting for so long. Well, things had gone well for the Owl, so far. . . . A few minutes back he had been jealous of the Owl, wishing he would stop his talk. But now he did not care so much. It was the Owl's touching him like that and reminding him that they were brothers, or maybe it was just that he had had time to think it over. Anyhow it seemed right that the Owl should be the first to get a scalp. He was the chief's son, and he was one of the Real People. He, Archy was just a *Hoobuk Waske*, though they never reminded him of it, but always treated him as if he were one of them. And he himself didn't remember except once in a while. If he got something to take back he might never think of it again!

Something soft and wet flicked his nose. Rain? Or a bird flying past? He looked overhead. The sky had changed in the last half hour, dark grey now, with no stars showing. Still, no other drops were falling. It might hold off a long time or not come at all. He was turning to ask the others if they had felt anything when a gun went off in the woods on the other side of the fort. There was another report and then another before a gun answered from the fort. It did not sound like a rifle but like some sort of blunderbuss.

There was the crackle of broken twigs. The Owl and the Creek Killer were off with their loads of brush. Archy took up as much as he could carry and went after them. They spread out from each other and, holding their loads high, moved slowly towards the fort.

The fire in the enclosure burned bright, pushing the shadows back, throwing a ring of light far out over the bare, burned ground. Across this band of golden light wavered the blunt shadow of the nearest blockhouse. If they could get into that shadow. . . .

The firing came faster. There were shouts from the fort, and rising and echoing back from the woods, the Cherokee war cry. The Owl was in the light and running.

Archy tripped on a clump of sage, was down, then up. The light struck full on his face, washed over him, then the shadows closed in again. He was running, with the Owl, beside the long stockade fence.

Rosy glints of light struck through the cracks. In the cabins backed up against the fence children were crying but as yet there was no firing from this side. With trembling hands they heaped their brush high against the boards. The Owl was on his knees, his musket a long shadow beside him. There was a snap, a flash and a tiny snake of fire curled bright through the tow.

The blaze spread and now all the twigs were crackling. Archy stared at the boards, on the other side of which cattle were lowing. Slabs of green oak and butternut. Would they burn?

The Owl drew his torch from the fire and running off a few

yards sprang like a cat up the side of the fence and on to the roof.

The Creek Killer raised a startled face. "They will shoot him!"

There were lumbering steps in the blockhouse and then a gun went off. There was no cry from above, only the sound of something falling and then the torch, still flaming, shot out over the edge of the roof, and after it the Owl's body.

He fell heavily, lay still for a second, then was turning over. Blood oozed from his thigh. He groaned.

Archy ran to him, knelt and putting his arm around his back, tried to raise him up. The Owl groaned louder and, pushing him away, crawled towards the burning torch. He had it in his hand and was crawling back towards the wall.

A bullet buried itself in the ground beside them. From above came a steady yelling. Archy could hear another sound, like continuous firing, only it seemed far off.

The Owl was at the wall, raising himself up to hold the torch against the green wood. His head went forward. Archy saw the lips puffed out, straining, and then the head went slack on the neck; the body slumped to one side.

He felt a hand touch his arm. "We are alone," the Creek Killer said. "They are not coming up."

Archy caught the Owl under the armpits. The Creek Killer took the feet. They ran, swinging the body between them. A sharp pain ran through the calf of Archy's leg. He looked over his shoulder and did not know whether it was his own blood or the Owl's that left a trail on the ground. They were on the edge of the clearing when the Creek Killer suddenly let go of the feet and staggered off. Archy dragged the Owl on into the woods.

He was bending over him, trying to feel the wound when he heard the Creek Killer come up behind him. "It was not I that let go of him," the Creek Killer said. "It was my hand. It is broken," and he held it up so that Archy could see the blood that flowed down on his arm.

Archy told him that he had better try to stop the bleeding with some leaves. He bent closer over the Owl. He was not groaning now. He lay, as Archy had put him down, one arm doubled under him. Archy straightened the arm out and felt of the wrist. There was no pulse. He let the wrist go and felt the wounded thigh. It was pulpy with blood, and blood was a thick jelly on the leaves.

The Creek Killer spoke. "He is dead. A man cannot lose that much blood and live."

He sat down at the foot of a tree and after a moment Archy sat down beside him. He realized that rain was falling. They sat in the rain, listening to the shots that still came every now and then from the fort.

"The Raven drew off when the rain began to fall," the Creek Killer said. He sighed. "We have three dead now. I wonder if the warriors will want to bury them or put the bodies up in trees. The Humming Bird himself said that it was a burial acceptable to a warrior."

Archy heard another voice: "*And when I am killed tie my body with vines high up in the trees where I can watch the enemy and send word. . . .*"

He looked up into the high, ghostly boughs of an elm. "In the trees," he said.

CHAPTER 52

Archy woke and at first he thought he was at home in Chota, and then he saw the buffalo hide going up beside him and knew that he was in the tent on the mountain. He felt an agreeable warmth along his left side. The Fox was curled up in a ball like a dog against his hip. But there was nobody on his other side. When he had come in from his watch, Monon and the boy were asleep there together. He had flung some wood on the fire so that they might not wake cold, and had crawled in under the same robe.

That had been several hours ago. He had been cold and very tired—for two weeks he had been on watch every night in that same pine grove—and he had gone to sleep almost immediately. But he had not slept the night through; stars still showed through the slit in the tent. Yet Monon had a fire going outside and was bending over a kettle as if she were cooking something. What had got her up so long before day?

He sat up gently, so as not to disturb the sleeping child and slipped out from under the robe. His rifle and shot pouch were where he had put them down beside the pallet. He slung the shot pouch over his shoulder and taking the rifle up went outside.

Frost was white on all the rocks and a cold wind blew up from the valley. He turned the collar of his leather shirt up and, shivering, stepped to leeward of the fire. Monon came to him quickly and leaning against him clasped her arms about his neck. "You have rested?" she whispered.

He yawned, stretching back against the encircling arms. Then as the fire warmed his body his faculties awoke. He stretched a last time, put one hand on her shoulder and with the other bent her body in against his. "What made you leave me?" he asked.

Her lips touched his and she drew back, looking over her shoulder. He glanced in the same direction and saw the Dark Lanthorn sitting on the other side of the fire. He let Monon go and went towards her. "I did not see you there, Mother," he said.

She laughed and pointed to the kettle that was boiling on the fire. "We are cooking rocks, Bear Killer."

"For what purpose?"

"It is for the chief," Monon said. "He has the shaking and in all the kettles we are heating rocks to lay against him and keep him warm."

"You'll burn him," he said.

The Dark Lanthorn laughed and Monon gave him a push. "They are wrapped in hides, Foolish One."

The Dark Lanthorn got up and coming over to the fire bent and touched one of the rocks. "It is almost hot enough," she said. She straightened up and looked at Archy. Light glowed in her deep-set eyes and the muscles about her strong mouth quivered a little but when she spoke it was only to say: "You will bring them to me when they are hot enough, my son." She went swiftly along the path that led to the chief's camp.

He stood looking after her. The expression that had been in her eyes when they rested on his had been one of almost disturbing kindliness. Lately she often looked at him like that. And she made a point of asking him and no other young man to do for the sick chief the things that required a man's strength. And yet a few months ago she had not liked him, had only tolerated his presence. "It's the blood," he thought and remembered with a little flicker of the nerves along his spine the ceremony that he and the Owl had gone through. "She believes we changed blood. I'm all that's left of the Owl."

He turned to Monon. "How is he tonight?"

She shook her head. "They should leave him alone. He is dying, that is all, dying. But they will not believe that the great Atta Kulla Kulla can die like another man. Tonight they have scratched him all over with dawískulà and have given him to drink of the juice of boiled ferns. It has purged him, but what of that? They cannot take his years away from him."

"These last few weeks have been too much for him," he said abstractedly.

Her beautiful upper lip quivered suddenly like a child's, then set in a hard line. She looked away from him at the tent made of skins, at the few cooking vessels that were all they had been able to bring with them when they abandoned the towns. "We live like the beasts in the woods," she said scornfully.

He let his hand rest on her shoulder a moment, then stepped past her to the rock that was his lookout. He took his seat there and stared out over the valley.

At first his eyes, tuned to the firelight, could not make out anything except the wreaths of mist floating up from the trees; then towards the north he found what he was looking for, what had been there when he went to bed. A yellowish grey cloud that had in its centre something bright and leaping. The fires were still burning. Down there in the pine grove, talking to Noonday, he had thought that the burning town must be Chilhowie but from up here it looked more as though it were Settico—if Settico was not already burned. Night before last that yellowish smoke had extended in a long roll across the horizon with flames leaping up in two places.

Three towns at any rate were gone now: Tellico, Chilhowie and Settico. Chota was still standing—the white men had spared it out of respect for Nancy Ward—but there was not a man, woman or child left in it, only the dogs. He thought of the night the Cherokees had left their towns with children crying in fright and women crying for the things they had had to leave behind. And then he thought of the Beloved Woman who had betrayed their plans to the white men and sitting there on the rock he cursed her, slowly, filthily in white man's talk.

Monon looked at him with bright eyes but did not stir from her place by the fire. After a little he got up and went to her. She looked up at him timidly. "Captain Gist is waiting for you on the path."

"What does he want?"

She shook her head. "He is going to make a journey."

He rolled the rocks out of the kettle on to a hide, twisted the hide into a bag and picking it up started along the path. His way led over the brow and a little down the mountainside. Everywhere through the trees low fires burned. Men, women and children, rolled in skins, lay about them, sleeping. This was the encampment of the Middle and Valley people. They had begun coming in here two months ago. By this time all that were not dead or in captivity must be here.

His own people, the Overhills, had had warning when they fled their towns and had brought horses laden with skins and other household equipment, but these people had been surprised in the night and their towns burned over their heads. They had nothing but the skins of the game they had shot since they came—with powder furnished them by the Overhills.

He skirted a fire that was built near the path. Three or four people were sleeping beside it, huddled under one bearskin like peas in a pod. One man sat erect beside the fire with no blanket about him. The chief who had led the fight at Tomassee. The town had been attacked in the night and retreat cut off. The fight had not lasted long. When it was over sixteen dead warriors were found heaped on top of one another in a ravine. Those bodies were all scalped— South Carolina was offering seventy-five pounds for each scalp— and the women and children rounded up to be sold for slaves. Chief Walalue had escaped on the march but had not been able to bring off his wife and children.

As Archy passed now he looked up out of red-rimmed eyes. His lips moved. He seemed about to speak and then his head dropped and he was staring into the fire again.

Archy walked on, faster now, for he saw Captain Gist sitting on a down log waiting for him. He had a pack on his back. His rifle lay across his knees. He did not speak until Archy had come up to him; then he said:

"Harlan's just come in."

The trader, Ellis Harlan, had been sent to the white men's camp three weeks ago with a flag of truce. Many people had thought that he would not return. Colonel Christian, who commanded the white men's army, was said to be a man of unusual ferocity. The Old Tassel had said in council that he would not be surprised if Christian refused to honor the flag and put Harlan to death. But Atta Kulla Kulla had insisted that a message must go and Harlan, who was a brave man, had undertaken to deliver it.

Archy dropped his bag of rocks and stood facing Gist. "How many of them are there?" he asked. "Or could Harlan find out?"

"They took him through their camp so he could see. He says there must be over two thousand."

Archy looked back over his shoulder at the fires dotting the hillside. "We have the Valley warriors to help us now," he said.

Gist gave a short laugh. "They had better leave *them* behind if they go on the warpath," he said.

Archy thought of the eyes he had just looked into. "You are right," he said. "But there are many warriors from the newly burned towns who have not got into camp yet."

Gist said: "The Raven is for peace . . . I am leaving for Christian's camp now, with a flag."

Archy said bitterly: "The *Raven*," giving the name its ritual meaning: a chief on probation. "He commands, now the Great Warrior is in his dotage . . . What message do you carry?"

"To ask for peace and say they will meet Christian at the time he has set, at the Long Island."

"To give them more land?"

Gist stood up. He spoke suddenly in English. "Outlaw, they cannot stop the white man now."

Archy started. It had been a long time since he had been called by his English name.

"You are for peace?" he said stupidly.

Gist stepped out from the shadows of the trees on to the path. The firelight fell on his face. It was thinner than it had been in the summer, and two deep lines, lines that you never saw in an Indian's face, Archy thought suddenly, were drawn from the nostrils to the lips. He brought his dark, haggard face, the eyes brim full of light, closer to Archy's. "I can take you with me," he said.

Archy stood there, stared at him. Once, a long time ago, he had stared into these same black eyes and Gist had called him "Outlaw" and would not give him back his glance.

He took a step backward. Gist spoke again. "*Make up your mind, man!*"

Archy's clenched fist fell at his side. He could feel the hot vapor ascending from the hide-wrapped stones. He ought to be taking them to the sick chief now.

He stepped forward and spoke steadily over his shoulder in Cherokee. "One messenger is enough, Captain Gist. If the great chief, Atta Kulla Kulla, had wanted to send me among the white men he would have called me to him and said so."

There was no answer and no sound except the rustle of a moccasin in the leaves. He walked on past the flickering fires to Atta Kulla Kulla's camp. A good fire was burning near the tent. The sick chief lay inside but with the flaps fastened back so that he could see those who were gathered around him. He lay in a half sitting position, propped against a roll of skins, the naked soles of his feet stretched out to the fire from under his robes. Since his illness, which had lasted for three weeks, he had not plucked his beard and the white hairs frosting his cheeks and chin made his deeply sunken eyes look larger and blacker than usual. Oconostota and the Raven sat on a log near the fire. They were looking at the trader, Ellis Harlan, who sat on a log opposite them. He had a paper in his hand.

The Dark Lanthorn saw Archy and came to him and taking the rocks slipped them in under the bearskin against the chief's side; she tucked the bearskin in until he was swaddled tight. When she had finished she stood a moment looking down at him. "Are they too hot?" she asked.

He settled his body farther down under the coverings with a sick man's fretful "Aaah!" then waved her aside. He turned his enormous black eyes towards Archy, who had sat down on the log beside Harlan.

"Let the Bear Killer read Christian's paper."

Harlan turned to Archy. "He asked me where Scotchie was and I said Pensacola, and then he said where was the Canoe, and I said I didn't know. He give me that paper to bring back and sent word he'd burn the rest of the towns if we didn't send in Scotchie's scalp and the Canoe's too."

"Read the paper," Atta Kulla Kulla said.

Archy unfolded it: "To the Old Tassel and Headmen of the Cherokee Nation: How can you expect peace before you have delivered up to me Alexander Cameron, that enemy of the white men and the red? I shall cross the river and come to your towns. I will distinguish between those towns which have behaved well towards us and those which have not . . ."

His eyes slid from the paper to the fire. It was hard to keep his mind on what the white man said. His thoughts were back there on the path. Gist would be entering the pine grove now. By daylight he would be at the creek . . . That dark, haggard face . . . Where had he seen it before? . . . At the fight in the cabin when the tow had flared a second time. Gist, rising up, a knife in his hand, his lips a little drawn back but not smiling, his eyes staring down at the spongy thing that had been a man's head. "It's the scalping," Archy thought. "Some men can't abide it. Mouncy said that." And he thought for the first time in months of the old, foolish white man who had been his nurse when he first came to live with the Cherokees . . .

The Raven was speaking: "Where was Colonel Christian encamped when he gave you this word?"

The trader raised his head, glancing stealthily between his long, fair lashes. "At the Great Island."

A voice spoke from outside the ring of the firelight. "What price do they set on my scalp?"

"A hundred pounds."

"And on Scotchie's?"

"A hundred pounds."

Archy made himself sit still and kept on gazing into the fire. He had not known that the Dragging Canoe was in the camp. He had not known that he was alive—until this voice had spoken from out of the dark! The Dragging Canoe had not been seen in Chota since last summer, when he had brought in the thirteen scalps taken on the Kentuck Path. That was just after his attack on the white men's fort had failed. He had brought the scalps in, crawling like a wounded dog, and then had disappeared into the mountains. It was rumored that he was dying. A warrior who had been in the fight with him said that the hole in his thigh was big enough to hide a chungke stone in. They had stuffed it with leaves there on the field to keep the blood in. But *tsgáya* had got in with the leaves and started festering. They had had to be burned out with powder, causing great sores. The Canoe, this man said, lay in a cave in the high mountains, rotting . . .

But he was on this mountain now, coming up to the fire, limping but moving strongly! He stopped and held his hands out to the blaze. "It is not enough," he said.

Archy looked up at his face first and then at his left leg where it showed under his open matchcoat. There was a great hole where the flesh had been torn away.

The Canoe shifted his body so that his weight was on his right leg. He was looking at the Raven. "It is not enough," he repeated. "I am worth any ten men in the Nation, and so is Scotchie. Eh, Raven?"

The Raven tilted his head back. His long eyes rested on the

Canoe's face a second and slid down his body to the scarred leg. "I do not know," he said. "I was not at the battle of Island Flats."

The Canoe's laugh was surprised, like that of a man who stumbles suddenly and finds himself on the ground. "No?" he said. "You were prowling like a suck-egg dog in Carter's Valley. But you did not get into the henhouse." He put his hand out and touched the Raven on the shoulder. "I am not going to kill you," he said, "you are needed here to look after these people . . . I will even talk with you further. Listen. Judd's Friend and Willenawah come in here tonight, each with a hundred men, of good heart. We can still stop the white men, at the Hiwassee."

The Raven had sat quiet while the hand was on his shoulder. Now that it was gone he shifted himself a little way down the log. "How will you fight this time?" he asked.

The Canoe looked at him thoughtfully. "I made a mistake in that battle, fighting my men in lines, the way the white men do. I will not make that mistake again. In the woods this time. They will never beat us in the woods."

The old chief, Oconostota, sitting on the log beside the Raven, woke from a doze. He shivered and standing up let his blanket fall straight around him, then gathered it against his chest with his folded arms. "It is cold to be in the woods this time of year," he said.

The Raven let his hand fall down on the log. "I am for peace," he said.

Dragging Canoe looked away from him to Oconostota. "And you?"

Oconostota leaned forward and fixed bleared eyes on his face. "I am an old man . . . It is what the Raven says."

A log broke in two. The Lanthorn rose from her place and dragged up a down branch. As she passed back to her seat Archy had a glimpse of her face, a thin old woman's face but with eyes as wild, as darkly gleaming as a young girl's. She was back on her rock, cross-legged, looking into the fire.

A sound came from the tent. The Dragging Canoe raised his head as if for the first time aware of his father's presence. He walked over and stood before him. "What has resentment against you?" he asked.

Atta Kulla Kulla's black eyes burned into his. "I am as good as dead," he said.

The Canoe inclined his head. "I do not think you will rise from this bearskin."

Atta Kulla Kulla jerked his head to one side. "I had a daughter once," he said in a thin, mournful voice, "but she died in infancy."

"I am glad she did not live to have sons," the Canoe said.* He leaned over and looked steadily into his father's face. He straightened up. When he spoke it was reflectively. "But you fall late. You have been rotten at the heart for a long time."

He was leaving the chief, coming back to the fire. He saw Archy. He spoke. "Bear Killer, make a talking paper for me."

They went over to the rock where the Lanthorn was sitting. She moved a little aside to make room for them. The Canoe took a roll of paper and a quill from his bandoleer. Into the little panikin that was slung at his belt he poured powder from his horn, then spit into the powder and stirred the mixture with a stick.

He dipped the quill into the panikin, brought it up with the tip edged black and handed it to Archy, then began speaking:

"Alexander Cameron, dear Friend and Brother: They have burned our towns, all except Chota which they spared because the Ghigau lives there who betrayed us to the white men. I am glad you are where you are, for our great man Oconostota and his nephew, the Raven, wanted to take your life as well as mine.

"They offer one hundred pounds for you and one hundred for me, to have us killed. Let them bid up and offer what they will, it never disturbs me. My ears will always be open to your talks and our Father's. I will mind no other, let them come from where they will. My thoughts and my heart are for war as long as King George has one enemy in this country. Our hearts are straight towards him and all his people . . ."

He paused. Archy finished writing his last word and would have folded the paper, thinking he was through, but he put his hand out to stay him, and continued:

"Our hearts, I say, for I have some of our people with me now. I have had talks with Willenawah and Judd's Friend and Lying Buck and Hanging Maw and Kitegiska and the Young Tassel. These chiefs and some of the young warriors will go with me to build the new

* The Cherokees had a maternal organization and succession was through the female line. Dragging Canoe succeeded his maternal grandfather as chief of the Great Island, as Atta Kulla Kulla might have been succeeded by his daughter's son had his daughter lived.

towns. The Old Tassel's heart is straight towards us but he cannot leave his people. My father is dying. He will not hear any talk but peace nor will the Great Warrior or his nephew, the Raven . . ."

The woman on the rock beside them drew in her breath with a long sigh. "The new towns?" she said.

He had been staring abstractedly at the ground as he talked but now he looked up at her and smiled and his face was not stern but ardent and dreamy. "On the other side of the great river," he said, "where the rock comes to an end. There is a cave there where I shall live until I have time to build a house. A creek runs out of the cave past a wide meadow. We will build a town house in that meadow. We will call the new towns by the old names and after a while they will be like the old towns to us and we will love that country as we have loved this country here . . ."

"Yes," the Dark Lanthorn said. "Oh, yes."

He stood up. He looked down at Archy. "It is Creek land," he said, "but the messenger who takes this letter to Scotchie will stop in the Creek country and ask the great Creek chief, McGillivray, for permission to settle on this land."

Archy reached up and laid a hand on his arm. "Let me take the message, Dragging Canoe," he said. "Oh, Dragging Canoe, do not let any other than me take the message!"

CHAPTER 53

WHEN THEY got to Eatons' and saw all the people Malcolm was glad. He had never seen that many people before in his life. At first he thought they would surely be leaving soon and he walked around looking at them while he could. But night came and they did not go. And in the morning more people came. There were a lot of children but he never got to play with them much and after a while he didn't think about them being there, and just played by himself or with Sarah the way he always did.

Then after a long time the men all went out of the fort and the women didn't talk and the strange children quit playing. His mother wouldn't answer when he spoke to her and Aunt Jane held Sarah on her lap all the time. He was glad when his father and the other men came back to the fort, for there was laughing then and talking, and nobody put him to bed at all, he just fell asleep under a tree.

There was another long time after that and then his father said they were going home. He was glad to get home. All that first morning he and Sarah played under the trees, fixing a play-house for the shuck dolls. All this summer they had kept that same play-house under the tree. They were playing there a few minutes ago when Mammy came out and sat down on the doorstep. She called Sarah to her and took her on her lap. He sat down beside her while she sang to Sarah. When Sarah's eyes went shut she took her into the house and laid her on the bed, then sat down on the step again. As she sat down she drew her breath in sharp and put her hand in under her apron and felt her stomach like it was sore.

He said, "What's the matter, Mammy?" But she didn't answer and he didn't say anything else.

He was looking off towards the bottom. He could see his father moving about there, axe in hand. He and Sarah had followed him down right after dinner and had watched when he felled the big beech. It burst open at the heart and red dust flew through the air and springing through the dust was a squirrel that had its nest in the rotten heart of the tree. Malcolm was running after the squirrel when his father called to him and said that he would whale the living daylights out of him and Sarah, too, if they didn't keep away when he was falling trees; so they had gone back to the house and started playing under the hickory tree again. But now Sarah was asleep and would be asleep for a long time and there was nothing to do.

He looked over at the sugar tree. The shuck doll was fallen over on her face. The pen that was to be her house needed more sticks but he didn't feel like working on it by himself. And Sarah always slept a long time.

That sound came again from his mother. She suddenly put her arms up over her face and then laid her head down on her knees. Her arms were clasped about her head. On the arm nearest him he could see the tips of the fingers dug into the flesh just above the elbow. He laid his hand on her arm and felt her shiver but she didn't say anything or raise her head, and he walked off into the yard.

There was nobody in sight anywhere. He walked over to the sugar tree, brought his palm up against the trunk and said "Hell!" He had heard Rufus Dunham say that in the fort. Somebody had told him he was wanted at the blockhouse. "Aw, tell 'em to go to hell," Rufus had said. He himself had never said that word before, and now his voice was louder than he had thought, but the sound died quickly from the air. There was left only the feeling of his hand lying up against the wood.

He took his hand down from the cool wood and walked back into the middle of the yard. One of the dung-hill hens came towards him, around the corner of the house. He called her name. "Birdie, Birdie," he called, his voice lower than when he had spoken there beside the tree. Birdie cocked an eye at him and turned and went back the way she had come. He followed her a few steps; he stopped, realizing that he was on the path to the spring where he went every day to fill the buckets with water. He looked off to the right. The cane grew thick there, right up into the yard. He and Sarah sometimes went into it a little way, pretending it was woods they were lost in, but their mother always called them back before they got to the creek. There were pools deep enough to drown Sarah in, she said.

He looked over his shoulder but nobody was coming. He left the yard and walked into the cane.

It was thick, but he got through and stood on the bank of the

creek. It was wider than he had thought but it was not deep enough
to drown Sarah in. The water flowed over a big flat rock. The rock
was green everywhere except at the edge where the water broke.
He stepped down into that place and the white water rushed up
against his knees and flowed on past. He stood in it until his feet
and legs were cool through, then stepped up on the ledge and started
upstream. The rock was slippery. He fell and got wet all over. After
that he did not go so carefully. The willows closed in, making the
stream seem narrower. In one place he had to crawl under the
branches and when he straightened up it was a round, deep pool,
the branches going up on both sides to make a little house.

The water was clear over a white sand bottom. A few pebbles
shone in the sand like pretties fallen on the cabin floor. One,
shaped a little like an arrow, was as clear as the glass tumbler
that Mammy kept on the high shelf. Another was a beautiful dark
red. He reached down through the clear water and picked them up
and while he was stooping he was minded to stay here and play in the
green-house with the pretties, but when he straightened up and the
green willow boughs were all around him he knew it would be lonesome, so he pushed through the branches and went on.

All the bottom was sandy now. In some places it was soft and
your feet sank 'way in. He stood in one place and let the sand squish
between his toes. He stepped up and dried his feet on a bank
of moss. He was turning back to the stream when he saw through
a break in the willows the big rocks like grey horses there on the
side of the hill.

Clutching his pebbles he went towards them. There were little
rocks scattered down near the stream but they got bigger as you
went in among them. Saplings grew out from under them so that
the whole place was in shade. They were grey where they were not
covered with dark, dried-up moss. One rock in the middle was the
biggest of all. It shelved out on one side so that he could not climb
it, but he went around to the side and found a place where he could
get up. There were patches of the old dried-up moss all over the
top. Lying on the grey moss was a bright something. He picked it
up. A yellow feather with a fleck of red across the tip. A parakeet
must have flown over this rock. He wondered if they ever stopped
here to play. He went over to the edge of the rock and sat down.
There was a little basin hollowed out there on the side. He put his

pebbles down in this hollow, along with the feather, and for a few minutes he played with them, the two pebbles horses that moved through the woods, the feather a bird that kept flying over them. But that was lonesome and after a little he stopped and just sat looking down at the rocks.

A sassafras bush was within reach of his hand. He broke off a piece and chewed it. The grey rocks crouched below him. They were horses, resting in the shade but he was on the high seat of a wagon. In a minute he would drive off through the woods. No, they were people kneeling with their heads on the ground. He was king. Old King Cole. Uncle Frank sang about Old King Cole. He sat on a throne and called for his fiddlers three. Mammy said that when you came to where the King was you bowed down till your head touched the ground and you kept it there till he told you to take it up. When he asked where the King was, she said over the water, and the water was so wide you couldn't see across it, and so deep that it would cover Bays' Mountain. She had been on that wide, deep water, in a boat that had a roof like a house.

Spots of sunshine broke on the grey rock as the leaves above his head shifted. Off in the woods you could hear the wind running through the leaves but you could hear something under that. Something that went on all the time. It was not varmints or anything moving through the woods but it was there all the time. This time of day when Sarah was asleep was when it was loudest. This time of day. If you stopped playing then or the people in the cabin were not talking or moving around it would leave the woods and come a little way up into the clearing.

He slid from the rock. His feet had hit the ground, he was stepping quietly around a clump of saplings when he heard a sound behind him and turned his head. A long, grey shape broke from the dark woods and sped down the slope. He stood still until the noise of its passing had died, then he started running towards the stream. He had reached the willows before he remembered that he had left his pretties there on the rock. But he did not go back. He broke through the willows and was in the stream. The water splashed higher than his head as he went through. He slipped once and would have gone down if he had not held on to a branch. He was off the bank and into the cane. Green stalks all around, but beyond them the logs of the cabin shone in the afternoon sun. He stumbled over a twisted root and was out of the thicket and standing on the hard clay of the yard. Birdie was dusting herself in a place that the chickens had made between the roots of a tree. He shooed at her as he went around the side of the house. His father and his uncle were there. His father sat on the doorstep. He was leaning a little forward, his hands on his knees. There was sweat on his forehead. He heard Malcolm come around the side of the house but he did not look at him. Uncle Frank said, "Ho, Boy" and reached over and pulled Malcolm to him. He took hold of his top-knot and shook it the way he was always doing, and then he pulled on it so hard that the boy's face turned up to his. "Did you know you had a baby brother?" he asked.

Malcolm looked at his uncle, then looked away to the woods he had just come out of.

The words just spoken said themselves on in his head as he scuttled away from the two men around the corner of the house. *Brother*. Baby now, but when he got big he would be a boy. They'd go together to that place where he'd been today. Go back and play all day long, the two of them together. Nothing would come out of the woods then.

CHAPTER 54

JANE STOOD UP. "Sun's most down. I better be getting home."

"Don't you hurry," Cassy murmured. Rion got up from the rock where he had been sitting and going to the spring dipped up a gourd full of water. "You better have a drink before you start up that hill," he said.

She shook her head, gazing past him to where the three children were playing on the slope. "Now ain't that sweet?" she said.

Rion and Cassy looked up at the children. Polly, the wild girl whom they had seen first in the fort stood under a beech tree, her body bent a little forward, a smile upon her stolid features. Malcolm was advancing towards her, dragging Sarah by the hand. Polly went to meet them. Cassy recognized the expression on her face as the one she herself must have had yesterday when she was showing them how to play "Lady Come to See." She laughed. "When I's young didn't anybody have to teach me how to play," she said, "but these young ones are wild as rabbits, living off here in the woods."

"Polly's learning fast," Jane said softly. "She plays out there by herself half a day at a time." A tender note came into her voice. "You know sometimes I want that young one to fetch me a bucket of water or brush the dooryard or something and I'll look out there and she's playing so sweet I ain't got the heart to call her."

Rion laughed. "You'll ruin her," he said. "Ain't nothing spoils as quick as a child."

"No, she won't," Cassy said quickly. She turned to Jane, "Heard anything of that man?"

The corners of Jane's mouth twitched. "Ain't nobody seen hair nor hide of him since he walked out of the fort. Amos, he says he looks for him to walk in some day. But I don't. Way I reason if he'd wanted Polly he'd taken her with him. He ain't coming back to get her."

"He ain't coming back here," Rion said with a hard grin.

"What makes you say that?" Cassy asked.

"Well, he's a kind of a timid feller and there's too many folks here want to see him."

"What you mean?" Cassy asked suspiciously.

"He's kind of timid but he's hoggish too. Went off that field with over a dozen scalps in his pocket. That's a little more'n his share any way you look at it . . . Come to think of it I never saw that man while the battle was going on."

Cassy shivered. "I don't think they ought to scalp a man after he's dead, even if he ain't anything but an Indian."

"An Indian ain't hardly a man," Rion said. "He's sort of like a nigger . . . Naw, he's worse 'n a nigger. I ain't got nothing against a nigger, long as he behaves himself but I can't even look at one of them red bastards without having my gorge rise. . . . I wish I'd been as quick as that wild feller. I'd just about be coming back from Charleston now, with money in my pocket. Seventy-five pounds I could a had for every one I took down there." He walked around the edge of the rock and looked down at the baby where he lay in his split basket. "This here one's the brightest of all," he said. "He noticed me then. I vow he did."

Cassy and Jane exchanged glances. Cassy laughed. "He ain't going to notice you or anything else for three or four months . . . I'm glad you didn't know about the scalps in time. I'd a got no pleasure out of such money. I tell you that for a fact."

"Well, you don't have to worry, thanks to Polly's dad."

"Hush," she said. "Here she comes."

The girl was coming towards them, holding Malcolm and Sarah by a hand. The gown Jane had made for her was a little too tight in the bodice—under it the budding breasts stood out as round and as hard as little melons—but it was of newly woven cloth and clean. Her face and hands, too, were clean, scrubbed so hard that they shone rosy, and her hair, new-washed, had the white sheen of milk-weed down.

Jane went to her and laid a hand on her shoulder. "We going home," she said in a low voice. "Now you say 'goodbye' to Miss Cassy and Mast' Rion."

The girl fixed her eyes on the ground and did not speak. Jane gave her shoulder a little shake. "Tell 'em you had a nice time."

Cassy lifted Sarah on to her lap. She smiled at Polly over the child's head, at the same time raising Sarah's fat hand and waving it back and forth. "Sarah says 'You all come again,'" she said.

Polly looked up at Jane quickly. "Can we come tomorrow?" she asked in a low, hoarse voice. "I don't know," Jane said irritably. "What's the use of taking you visiting if you ain't got no manners?"

"Tell Miss Jane to quit worrying you," Rion said. "Tell her cat's got your tongue."

Polly thrust the tip of her tongue out between her lips, then quickly withdrew it.

Rion laughed and Jane laughed too and gave Polly another little tap on the shoulder. "Come. Never get home if we don't start."

Sarah slid from Cassy's lap and went over to Malcolm, who was wading in the branch. Rion dropped down on the rock beside Cassy. They watched the two figures ascending the wooded hill. "I declare," Cassy said, "I wish Jane'd got that child when she was younger."

"So she could have more trouble raising her?" Rion asked.

"No, but Jane, she's so crazy to raise a young one and this girl's most grown now."

"Well, Jane can work double on her. Looks to me like she could take a sight more raising."

Cassy laughed. They sat there, watching the children's legs move through the sun-spotted water. "Isn't it funny the way children love to play in water?" Cassy said. She leaned forward suddenly. "Rion, you know what he's doing?"

Rion looked at Malcolm, squatting in the middle of the stream, picking up rocks from one place to lay down in another.

"Getting his hunkers wet," he said.

"He's building him a dam . . . when I was little, warn't anything I liked better'n building a dam . . ."

She was off the rock and down by the water. Tucking her skirts up under her waistband she knelt on the bank and began showing Malcolm how to lay one flat rock upon another to form a wall.

"It'll wash away, come the first freshet," Rion said. Malcolm looked up at him solemnly, then down at the rocks, but Cassy turned around and made a face at him.

"Who's building this dam, Master Aleck?"

Rion leaned over and looked at the baby, Frank. His eyes were blue, like the eyes of both the other children, like the eyes of most young things, but there was a brownish tinge to the blue. Both Cassy and Jane declared that the child's eyes would turn brown by the time he was a year old. He wondered if it would be the reddish brown of his own eyes or the darker brown that was more common. Well, anyway, the boy wouldn't have red hair. What little hair he had, showing now in duck tails at the nape of his neck, was a clear, soft yellow. The child had been staring straight ahead of him. Suddenly he closed his eyes and fell asleep. With the eyes closed the little face became doll-like, devoid of expression. Rion turned away from the basket.

He leaned back on his elbow on the flat rock and felt the cool of the stone strike agreeably against his bare thighs. He was wearing only a breech clout and leggings and one legging had been half ripped off by some briars that morning. It had been hot as hell in the field today. He had drunk up all the water in his gourd while the sun was still high and had come up here half an hour ago to find the women and the children idling by the spring. He had intended to return to the field as soon as he had had a drink, but they had got to talking and before he knew it an hour had slipped by. It would hardly pay him to go back to the field now. It would be dark before he got his grubbing hoe in hand. He had been grubbing roots for a month, ever since he laid his crop by. Another day would finish that west field. Then he would have twenty acres cleared. The thought animated him. He sat up, his hands clasped about his knees, and looked towards the west woods where a brightening through the trees showed that there was a clearing on the other side. Twenty acres cleared in five years—he had come here in seventy-one—and the other room built on to the house, besides the outbuildings that he had put up. Smokehouse, corncrib, and henhouse, not to mention a stout pigpen and the milk-house built there over the spring. There wasn't a man in the neighborhood better fixed than he was, not even James Robertson, who had got there a year ahead of him, or Amos Eaton who had found his house already built. Well, there wasn't a man on the Holston who had worked harder, and in the last few months with nobody to help him, now that Frank was abed most of the time.

Cassy had left the water and was moving along the bank towards the spring. She went up above the milk-house and came back, carrying a medium-sized flat rock. He watched her scooping out gravel and then settling the rock in the wall of the little dam. That rock was left from the pile that had been beside the spring when they settled here. He had used a lot of them for his chimney but there were a few still left. He remembered the day he had come down here with the Indians to look at the land, and the big chief, Dragging Canoe, had said that that cairn marked a warrior's grave and then he and his men had each gone into the bushes to find another rock to throw on the cairn.

When he was out with Christian he had camped on the island that Dragging Canoe was chief of. In the Little Tennessee. Flat as the Long Island here in the Holston but not as heavily wooded. The town was on a wooded knoll above the river. Rows of neat log houses and not a living soul in the place, not even any cattle, only a few prowling dogs and hogs rooting for mast.

The chief's house was on a rise at the far end of the town, beside a fine spring. It was bigger than the others and so old that its logs were all mossed over. There was an elm in the front yard with a trunk twice the size of a tobacco hogshead.

They had camped there because of the spring. A trader had come in that night with a flag from the Indians. Christian had taken him through the camp and had shown him how many men there were—nearly two thousand, counting the scouts—and had told him that if the Indians did not come to terms pretty quick they would burn this town as they had already burned three others. The trader acted almost like an Indian, not saying anything, just delivering his message. When he got up to go he asked Christian if he was going to burn this town. Christian said frankly that he did not know—it depended on the temper of the men. The trader asked then if he could go inside the chief's house and get something. When Christian asked what it was, he said it was a chungke stone that the chief's wife had asked him to get for her. It had belonged to her father and she wanted it saved. He had broken the door in and Rion and some other men had followed him inside and stood around while he rummaged through some chests. The chungke stone was a piece of polished quartz with its middle hollowed out. He had taken a stick and with a cottonwood ball had showed how the Indians played their game of chungke. Some of the men laughed at the idea of going through everything in a house and saving a rock, but Robertson said that the Indians thought as much of their chungke stones as anything they had—a man would polish on his at odd hours through a lifetime, and when he died would leave it to his son. The chief's wife wanted this stone for her son, the young Dragging Canoe.

Well, he hoped the boy's father, the old Dragging Canoe, was dead. Colonel Christian thought that he was the biggest mischiefmaker of the lot and they were offering twenty-five pounds more for his scalp and Alexander Cameron's than for any of the others. He wondered if the scalp would ever be brought in. It was more likely that the fellow was dead. His bullet had plowed right through his thigh and must have gone into his stomach. But a man could take a lot of lead in his stomach, if it was empty . . .

His eyes left the hollow and went to the hillside. If he were not so busy clearing the bottom land he would grub off some of that hillside. All that scrub pine and higher up the laurel thickets. The Indians couldn't ask better cover if they wanted to slip up on the house. But he didn't believe there was going to be any more trouble. They had licked them once in a fair fight and then burned out the hornets' nests. The Indians were feeling it, too. The leading chiefs had been as meek as Moses when they came to the Long Island in July to sign that treaty.

Cassy was calling out to him: the dam was finished. It was not raising the water level so much as an inch—but it curved, fully a foot high, clear across the stream. Sarah was paddling farther down the stream but Cassy and Malcolm were standing with muddy hands hanging at their sides, looking at their dam. They raised their heads at the same time and he felt like laughing. The woman looked as wondering, as pleased as the child. There was a childish streak in all grown people. For a minute he himself had had an impulse to help build the dam but the muscles in his back, that the grubbing hoe had been getting at all day, had kept him sitting down. Maybe grown people would keep on playing like children if they didn't have to work. Work was what took it out of you . . . Cassy, marrying young like she had, had always had a lot of work to do . . . He would milk the cows for her this evening. He got up and without speaking started for the house.

He was about to take the bucket down from its peg when he thought about Frank, who must be on his pallet out in the front dooryard. It had been over a year since that battle and Frank still wasn't up and around. They had probed for the bullet but never found it. It must still be lodged somewhere near the spine. When Frank stood up a pain would take him in the small of the back and he would have to lie down. It had got so that he was abed most of the time. These warm days they made him a pallet out under the shellbark tree. He kept a cow-bell beside him and rang it when he needed anything. But Frank was shy of asking people to wait on him, so both Rion and Cassy made a point of going often to see if there was anything he wanted.

Rion walked around the side of the house. As he went he heard a strange voice and then another voice that was not Frank's, answering. Frank was propped against the tree trunk and beside his pallet on stools they had brought out of the house sat two men Rion had never seen before. One of them had got up and was coming towards him: a big, serious looking fellow with a shock of black hair and blue eyes set deep under bristling brows. He was holding his hand out.

"Friend, my name is Murrow. Jonathan Murrow. I am travelling on the Lord's work."

Rion shook his hand heartily. "I'm glad to hear it," he said. "Ain't no man of God come this way since I settled here."

Frank gestured with a long, pale hand. "Rion, this is Master James Adair, but lately returned from England."

The fellow jumped up. Hazel eyes in an aging brown face. A suit of doeskin. Moccasins that hadn't been made by Cherokee. The other fellow was a man of God, all right, but this one looked more like a trapper or a trader. He was returning to his stool after shaking hands.

Rion sat down near them. It had been a long time since he had seen a strange face. He looked from one to the other, wondering. "Which way you headed, gentlemen?" he asked.

The preacher looked perplexed as if he hardly knew how to answer. "I have a letter," he said, "to the Reverend Gideon Doak."

"He lives up above here," Rion said. "At Wolf Hills."

The preacher nodded. "I hardly knew whether to present my letter, and while I was trying to make up my mind I must have strayed from the path." He laughed awkwardly. "When I fell in with this gentleman he told me I was going in the wrong direction and might have got back to Philadelphia if I had kept on."

"And might not," Rion said. He looked at Adair. "You come up from Charleston. How was things down that end of the trail?"

In Adair's hazel eyes, mottled like the sides of a trout, something stirred a second, then was gone. "I came through the Chickasaw nation," he said. "They are much distressed over the recent occurrences."

Rion laughed. "So are the Cherokee." He jerked his thumb over his shoulder. "We had a battle about six miles from here. Buried a lot of 'em out there."

"I did not come through Chota," Adair said quietly. He added: "I have been a trader to the Chickasaw for nearly forty years."

Frank leaned forward. "They'll stay the night, Rion," he said eagerly.

Rion got up. "I'll go call my wife," he said. "She's down at the branch, playing with the chaps." He laughed out of sheer lightheartedness. "She'll be wanting to come up and start your supper."

He went around to the back of the house and making a trumpet of his hands called:

"Cassy! Cassy! Strangers here. Come get supper."

CHAPTER 55

WHILE CASSY was in the straw Rion had fallen into the habit of bringing all the water that was used by the household. He continued to bring it even after she was up and about. But tonight in the excitement of having company he had forgotten all about the water. After supper he took the two biggest piggins and set off for the spring. As he came back up the hill he saw the house suddenly blossom with light. Cassy was setting another dip on the table where two already burned.

He laughed to himself. "She's sure putting the big pot in the little one," he thought, remembering the supper table that had been graced by two kinds of preserves and the last ham out of the smoke-house.

He set his piggins on the bench and stepped up inside the house. The two visitors sat on stools before the hearth. Frank was in his bed over in the corner, propped up on pillows. The table had been drawn over near the bed. The three candles blazed upon it. Frank was turning over the leaves of a book. He looked up as Rion entered.

" 'Tis a book written by our visitor," he said excitedly.

Rion crossed the room and standing behind him looked over his shoulder. Frank turned back to the title page and read aloud:

"A History of the American Indians
Particularly
Those Nations Adjoining to the Mississippi, East and West Florida,
Georgia, North and South Carolina and Virginia
Containing
An Account of Their Origin, Language, Manners, Religious and Civil Customs, Laws, Form of Government, Punishments, Conduct in War and Domestic Life, Their Habits, Diet, Agriculture, Manufactures, Diseases and Method of Cure, And Other Particulars Sufficient to Render It

A Complete Indian System
with
Observations on Former Historians, The Conduct of Our Colony
Governors, Superintendents, Missionaries Etc.
Also
AN APPENDIX
Containing
A Description of the Floridas and The Mississippi Lands, With
Their Productions, The Benefits of Colonizing Georgia And Civil-
izing the Indians; And the Way to Make All the Colonies More
Valuable to the Mother Country
With a New Map of the Country Referred To in the History
By JAMES ADAIR, Esquire,
A Trader with the Indians, And Resident in the Country For Forty
Years."

Rion looked over at Adair. The fellow sat with his hands on his
knees, his eyes, bright as a squirrel's, fixed on Frank's face. Rion
glanced back at the calf-bound volume. He shook his head.

"It takes a sight of learning now to write a book, don't it? . . .
Forty years . . . You lived among them Indians forty years?"

Adair straightened up. "Among the Choctaws first and later the
Cherokee and Chickasaw." He paused, his lively, brown face clouded.
"It was I who won the Choctaw away from the French. But the
governor of South Carolina does not believe in giving merit its due
reward. Rather he pursues and cuts it down. I, who planned the
Choctaw rebellion, I, who with Red Shoes, led the attack on the
French, am now a bankrupt and a wanderer. If I cannot win back
to my brave, cheerful Chickasaw, I am like to fall in the woods and
no man know where James Adair's bones lie."

Frank leaned forward, his mouth twitching with the pain. "What
do you care where your bones lie? James Adair's grave is here,"—
he held the book up—"and all men will visit it."

Adair laughed and throwing his head back gazed at the ceiling.
With his wide grin and his eyes shining he looked like a man drunk
on wine. "Aye," he said, "printed for Edward and Charles Dilly, in
the Poultry, London, in the year of Our Lord Seventeen Hundred
and Seventy-Five."

The book fell from Frank's hand on to the coverlet. He reached down and touched it. His long fingers caressed the calfskin, gently, as if it still covered a living beast. After a moment he spoke reflectively. "We quit the Yadkin in a flurry. My collection of plants was left behind. But I brought a sack of books with me." He pointed to the little shelf beside the door. "Galen, Pliny, Lucretius, I've not lacked for authority or a field for observation—there are plants in this very dooryard not dreamed of in the old world. When I first crossed the mountains I was on fire with ambition, but of late," he shook his head, "it has gone from me, I know not how."

"The grey-eyed one is fickle," Adair said. "Times she will not sit on the rooftree."

Frank smiled. "I deluded myself with that thought once but now I know 't'is a matter of a man's own genius. What he is to do he will do. . . . Tell me, when you landed in this country had you already mastered the Hebrew?"

Adair pulled his stool nearer to the bed. "I learned it in the woods whilst living with the Chickasaw," he said. "A pack load of hides it took to get the books across the water and landed at Charleston, but 'twas worth it. Man, you've only to read to be convinced." He got up and took the book from Frank's hands; he turned several pages then handed it back. "Read there, Man, how they call some of their tribes by the names of the cherubimical figures . . ."

Rion had been standing against the wall all this time. He went over and sat down by the other visitor. "Where might you be travelling to, sir?" he asked politely.

Murrow looked down at his clasped hands which swung between his knees. "From Philadelphia," he said. He looked up. A spasm contorted his strong, ugly mouth. "I wish to preach the word of God here on the western waters," he said, "if there be any to hear the word I bring."

"There's plenty to hear, right in this neighborhood," Rion told him. "There's a preacher at Wolf Hills, Reverend Doak, but there ain't been a sermon preached here on South Holston to my knowledge." He turned to Cassy. "We'll put out the word. Have a bush arbor meeting here on the creek come Sunday, if the Reverend here'll tarry with us . . . What might be your faith?"

Murrow suddenly took his great shock head in his hands and

bending over groaned. "I was within a day's journey of Wolf Hills. I could not bring myself to go to Doak's house."

"Why?" Cassy asked.

He raised his head. "I left Philadelphia a Calvinist. I am now a follower of Arminius."

Echoes of talk he had heard around the fire at night woke in Rion's memory. "You mean a Baptist?" he asked. "What's wrong with that? There's plenty of them around here."

The man kept his great grey-blue eyes fixed on Cassy's face. "I was educated at Edinburgh," he said. "Three years ago I came to this country on the invitation of Witherspoon. The Cynthia was driven out of her course. We were two months late. When I arrived in December the chair had been filled."

"That's too bad now," Rion said.

He shook his head impatiently, "It was God's providence." His voice rose. "I was to teach moral philosophy and divinity!"

"And you couldn't do that after your faith changed," Cassy said softly.

"At that time it had not changed. I arrived at Princetown a follower of the Genevan. I left there staunch to him. It was on the journey through the wilderness that my faith changed." He shook his head until a lock of his bristling hair fell down into his eyes. "I can no longer subscribe to the doctrine of salvation by election. To fallen Cain it was said, 'If thou doest well shalt thou not be accepted? If thou doest not well sin lieth at the door.'" He paused and looked from one to the other. "You are Calvinists?"

"I was raised one," Rion said, "but I come from Baptist country."

"Why, Rion," Cassy interrupted, "there were as many Quakers on the Yadkin as there was Calvinists."

"They'd come there Quakers but they didn't last. Take the Boones. They was all Quakers when they come there twenty years ago. Now all Boones worship at Trading Ford chapel . . . But seems like folks change their religion these days more'n they used to. Take my wife there. She was raised Church of England. Father was a parson."

"You are still an Anglican?" Murrow asked.

"I don't know," Cassy said faintly. "Been so long since I thought about those things."

The visitor brooded, his eyes on the floor. "It is a dread thought," he said. "According to Calvin the condition of one not elected from the foundation of the world is as changeless and hopeless as if he were already in the pit." He raised his head. His eyes flashed grey light. "But if you are one of the elect not your own wrongdoing nor all the powers of darkness can prevent your salvation! How can a rational man subscribe to such a doctrine?"

"I used to wonder about infant damnation," Cassy said. "Don't seem reasonable now, does it?"

Rion sat silent. It was like it used to be at the old place on the Yadkin, his father and Andrew Wallace in front of the fire at night, arguing. Andrew Wallace held that infants are neither saved through baptism nor lost through it. His father said that was Arminianism. It was listening to them had got him as a boy to wondering whether he would be damned for causing his sister, Nanny, to be burned . . . Well, sin was something he had never understood very well and hadn't worried about much, of late years anyhow. When a man battled the wilderness he had enough on his hands without pondering the future life. Was that what made the people here on the Holston so godless, for godless they certainly were, with the exception of a man here and there like James or Charles Robertson . . .

He got up and moved his stool nearer to the table. Adair was reading from his book. "The name of a wife is A-wah, which written in Hebrew makes הוה . . ." He looked up. "Eve, Man! They give woman the name of our first mother!"

Frank nodded. "The use of serviles in place of prepositions is to me of even greater significance."

"They also prefix the substantive to the adjective as the Hebrews do," Adair answered. He leaned forward. "But there are other more striking instances. The rabbins tell us that the Hebrew is so chaste a tongue as to have no proper name for the parts of generation. The Cherokee call a corn house '*watohre*'. They call the penis of any creature by the same name . . ."

"Intimating," Frank said thoughtfully, "that the sun and the moon have conspired to ripen the fruits stored therein."

"Exactly," Adair said. "*Sine Cerere et Baccho friget Venus.*"

Rion sat up straighter. He stared. "Say that again."

The trader laughed. "Without grain and wine Venus lies cold."

"Latin," Rion said. "Say some more."

The trader shot a laughing glance at Frank. He declaimed:

"Aenadum genetrix, hominum divomque voluptas,
alma Venus, caeli subter labentia signa
quae mare navigerum, quae terras frugiferentis
concelebras . . ."

Rion nodded. "I've heard you talk before," he said, "and I've seen you too."

The hazel eyes darted a quick look at him. "Where?" the trader asked. "Among the Chickasaw?"

Rion shook his head. "It was a long time ago," he said, "and a far way from here. You come to our place on the Yadkin and you stayed awhile and set around the fire nights talking about the Hebrews and the Indians. I was just a chap then."

"The Yadkin?" the trader repeated.

Rion nodded. "At the Trading Ford."

"You had a brother a little younger than you and two sisters. One of 'em was scar-faced." He walked over and clapped Rion on the shoulder. "You're Malcolm's boy!"

"That's right," Rion said, "Malcolm Outlaw."

The trader looked at him curiously and laughed.

"What you laughing at?" Rion asked.

"Nothing, just thinking how I ought to have known you."

Rion studied the man's face. "No, you warn't. You was laughing at something about the old man. Him and me never got along none too well but ain't nobody going to laugh at him while I'm around."

"Hush, Rion," Cassy said. "Master Adair didn't mean anything."

"I ain't going to hush." He stood up. "What was it now?"

Adair made Cassy a little bow and looked back at Rion. His eyes lighted. He laughed again. "Man, 'tis comical, you not knowing your own name, and standing there every inch a MacGregor."

"MacGregor. . . ." Rion said. "You mean the old man changed his name?"

"You might say 'twas changed for him. 'Tis a proscribed clan. Since the Lennox no man's allowed to bear the name."

"I always knew the old man was into some trouble in the old country," Rion said.

"Didn't you know he was out in the 'fifteen?"

"I never heard him say anything about it but I never heard him talk about anything in the old country."

"Aye," Adair said, "he'd not want to talk after what happened." He came over to the hearth and took a seat. "I was in Edinburgh when Lord Mar raised the Chevalier's standard. The Chevalier didn't land till December, but the work went forward all fall." He looked up at them and grinned. "I wear leather breeches but I'm cousin to the great. Where should I be but supping with my cousin, the Lord Deputy-Governor, when the attack was made on the castle? 'Twas a mad venture of my Lord Drummond's and he had down a hundred MacGregors, to carry it through."

"What was the venture?" Rion asked impatiently.

"To scale the castle walls, man and—we found later—to shoot off three rounds which were to be the signal for Lord Mar to march on the town."

"But it didn't come off?"

Adair shook his head. "I was with my cousin when the alarm came. Mrs. Arthur had sent a letter! A hundred wild Highlandmen gathered at the west sally port.

" 'Twas late in the evening. I had to help my cousin up. But he was a man ready to fight, drunk or sober! 'The clan MacGregor can gather and not carry this fortress,' " says he.

" 'Aye,' the man said, 'but there's treason in your guard. Willy Ainslie is to drop them a rope.'

"My cousin called for another bottle and said he would nail William Ainslie's liver to the east gate and his. . . ." He stopped with a glance at Cassy. "Well, no more of that. I was young then and had a head for the *usquebaugh*. 'You'd best see what's happening at the gate,' I told him.

"They called the guard out. We went with them. We could see the poor *widdiefows* huddled at the foot of the wall. They had a rope ladder half way up but 'twas too short. And then they heard the shots and knew the game was up and made off. But they left four wounded behind them."

"They ought to a seen to the ladder beforehand," Rion said.

"Aye, but a few turns of rope would have mended that. 'Twas the time. They'd stayed at the tavern two hours after the time appointed."

"That don't sound like the old man," Rion said. "He was ever for doing things on time."

The trader laughed. "They'd not heed his advice. He was but a breekless boy. I went down with my cousin next morning to view the prisoners and I saw this boy mother-naked and wild as a cat-amount. They were taking the prisoners' names. They were all Campbells or Drummonds or Eliots—'twas worth a man's head to bear the name MacGregor then. They came to this boy. He looked at the governor and he said, ' 'Tis MacGregor, and Man, yours is Stewart.' "

"The governor ought to been a Jacobite then?" Rion asked.

" 'Twas a touch. Some said Mrs. Arthur's message was not the only one reached my cousin that night, some said he wanted William Ainslie's tongue nailed up before his parts. However that be, William and the wild Highland lad were lodged on the other side of the castle from the others."

"How'd the old man get away?" Rion asked.

"I couldn't be saying. I went down that afternoon and I saw him lying in the straw, a different lad from the morning. They'd been at him in the night, to find out the names of the leaders. 'Twas Lord Drummond's doing. Everybody knew that. But they wanted the names of the chieftains.

"I called on MacGregor: 'Come, lad, or they'll have you crawling for the rest of your life.' He raised up as well as he could. 'A curse on you,' he says, 'and a curse on every Stewart, be he King or ghillie, and the blackest curse of all on James Mhor that left me lying at the foot of yon wall!' "

"Who was Big James?" Cassy asked.

"His cousin that was at the head of the band and left him wounded."

"He turned against his King!" Rion said. "I reckon there's some things a man goes through he ain't ever the same afterwards. . . . What did they use on him, Master?"

" 'The Boot!' "

"That's why he always walked so slow," Rion said. "I remember once I was surprised—I was about fifteen—when I put him on his back."

"Aye. . . . I looked at all the prisoners that afternoon. Two were dead and a third would be dead by morning. But the boy could walk. There was a bit gate on that side of the castle kept by an old *bodach* called Hugh. I gave him a bottle of brandy with the gov-ernor's compliments and told him to have a special care for the wild lad. . . . We were at table and there was a great hue and cry, the boy was gone. My cousin called for another bottle. ' 'T'is a fine night,' he said, 'for a run in the heather.' I told him, 'Foxes are better off in the hills,' but I aye wondered. . . . There was a ship in port that night and her master was from the Lewis."

"That was in 'fifteen, warn't it?" Rion said, "I always thought he came to this country sooner than he'd allow he did."

"When did he say he came?"

"He wouldn't say exactly. . . . I mind he never liked to have any black Scotch come around him. . . . How did you know him after all them years?"

"The scar on his forehead," Adair said. "Poor lad. He did well to cross the water."

"Aye. . . . did you see any more of the 'fifteen?"

"No, I was back in Dublin before the Chevalier landed. But I was not surprised at the outcome. He was not the man for such a rising and he had not proper men around him. When he made his public entry into Dundee they kept him on horseback an hour with the crowd kissing his hand. But they say that many that kissed turned away asking was he wax doll or man, so frigid was his demeanor. . . ."

"They liked the young prince better?"

"Aye, but no good came of that either. . . . There were MacGregors in that rising, too, and fared no better than in the 'fifteen."

Cassy had been speaking in a low tone to the preacher in the corner. She came towards them now. "Rion, we're going to have prayers. The Reverend is willing."

Rion and Adair both stood up. Rion glanced around uncertainly. What would the preacher use for a pulpit and would he want them to keep their same places? But Murrow stood up where he was and bending his head slightly and clenching his big hands at his sides began at once to pray: "Almighty God, thou who hast wrestled with Satan, thou who wast taken up into the high place and shown the kingdoms of the earth. . . ."

Rion tried to keep his mind on what the Reverend was saying but never since he was a small boy had he been able to follow a prayer through to the end. He kept thinking of his father, of his ways that did not seem so strange to him now. . . . That day in the

stable lot when he had stood there and laughed at him. He had
thought it was just an old man's meanness but it looked now as if the
old man was wanting to say something to him and yet knew he
couldn't. What was it he had wanted to say? That in the end no
uprising did any good? He had joined the Regulators in the same
way his father had joined the Jacobites but neither time had it done
any good, just landed one across the water and the other across the
mountains. . . . He wished he could see the old man again and
maybe sit down and talk with him but it was not likely now that he
ever would.

CHAPTER 56

THE TRADER GOT UP to go as soon as he had had his breakfast. The preacher said he would travel along with him.

"I thought you were going to stay a while," Rion said. "What about that bush arbor meeting?"

"On Sunday," Cassy said. "Have a big crowd." She took a step towards the men. "We could get word to the neighbors in time, couldn't we, Rion?"

"I wish the Robertsons weren't so far away," Rion said. "I tell you. I could ride down as far as John Washburn's. He's got three boys. Any one of 'em'd be glad to step down to Doe Creek. On the way back I could stop at Bullochs' and Grundys'. They'd git the word to the people back of them. . . . Master Adair'll pass by Mulroons' on his way to the Island. . . ."

"They're godless people," Cassy said absently. "No use telling them."

"They got tongues in their heads like everybody else," Rion said. "They can pass the word on." He looked at Adair. "You'll tell 'em?"

The trader bowed. "I'll be proud to carry the message and I'll tell any others I meet on the way."

"That's right," Rion said. "Well, we better be starting. The Reverend here can ride along with me. Give him a chance to meet the neighbors."

The preacher had been standing a little apart, his head bowed, his eyes fixed on the ground. Suddenly he looked up. "I will preach Sunday," he said in a loud, strong voice. "I will take my text from John 1, 4: 'Whosoever shall confess that Jesus is the Son of God, God dwelleth in him and he in God.' "

"Well," Rion said again. "We better be starting." He looked at Cassy. "I'll stop by Jacob's and ask him and Sarah to come up."

She shook her head. "It ain't any need. You ain't going to be gone long."

"I'll be back long before dark," Rion said. "I don't aim to go farther than Washburn's. His boys can take the word on from there."

He came over and kissed her. It was a way he had, to kiss her goodbye when he left the house. He didn't care who saw him do it. If they were going to be separated as much as an hour he came over and kissed her goodbye.

After the men rode off she stood on in the dooryard enjoying the morning cool. Here in front of the house the ground was dusty but over in the woods you could see dew glistening. She walked to the edge of the clearing. There was a little path there that the children had made. She took a few steps along it. A big mullein came up beside the path. Its high-headed stalk was yellow with the tiny flowers, the broad, hairy leaves at the base of the stalk looked as if they had been brushed with dew. She pulled a leaf; it was velvet between her fingers. When she was little they always used mullein for dolls' blankets, but her children had it for cabbages. . . . She looked up. Over her head rose the black branches of the sugar trees and above them layer on layer of green. The leaves had broadened and darkened just in the last few days. It was full summer. The season had turned without her noticing it. It was full summer now! She looked along the path and would have walked a little farther into the woods and then she remembered that she had stopped in the midst of straining the milk to tell the men goodbye. Cream would start rising if she let it set much longer.

She went back into the house. The children were playing over by the hearth, and Frank had come up from the lower room and was rocking the baby's crib.

"You want to stay indoors or out this morning?" she asked him.

He said that he thought it would be cooler out under the trees.

"You better get in the back then," she told him. "The sun'll be in the dooryard now directly."

She made up his pallet under the sugar tree and settled him there with the baby and a book to read, then finished straining the milk. When she had finished she went out into the garden and gathered two cabbages and a mess of snaps, then made the fire up and put them to boil, with a piece of side meat in each pot.

The baby was crying for her. She took him from Frank and nursed him, then washed his face and hands and changed his hippens. When she had finished she glanced up at the sun. It would be a good two hours before dinner time. She had a piece of cloth in the loom. She would spend the time weaving.

She put the baby back in his crib and moved the crib into the room where the loom was. Rion had finished building that room last fall after they got back from the fort. It was a step down from the old room and darker. Rion had cut only one window and that was on the north wall next to the door. He had not had time to make any furniture, and there was nothing in it except the loom and Frank's pallet and a three-legged stool. She set the baby's crib over in the corner where it was cool and dark and as she worked she looked around the room, imagining how it would look when there was a bed in the corner and a table and stools to sit up to the table. Rion said he was going to get at the table the first thing after his fall work eased up.

The baby cried for a few minutes, then dropped off to sleep. He always went to sleep quick when you put him in here—the sound of the loom soothed him. But he didn't cry much any time. That was because he was so healthy. Yes, all her children had been healthy. Even Sally had never been sick except that one spell with her bowels when they were cooped up in the fort so long and couldn't get any greens to eat.

She glanced out through the open door. Frank had put his book down and lay turned over on his side, sound asleep. She could not see the children but she could hear their voices over by the garden. They had a play-house there under a big elder-bush.

She went back to her weaving. As she moved to and fro her eyes dwelt on the bit of yard framed in the doorway. There was a bare, open space between the two big sugar trees. They would put the tables there—if they had the bush arbor meeting Sunday. But they would have it! The preacher had said he would stay and Rion would stop at three or four places before he came home. If each of those families got word to even one other family the noration would get out for ten miles around. Fifty to a hundred people gathered here under the trees! Every woman would bring her basket, but she and Jane and Elsa would have to cook a sight of victuals too. She wished now that they hadn't started on that ham last night—the trader and the preacher had made a big hole in it. But they had plenty of deer hams hanging in the smokehouse and a whole round of dried beef. She would cook the hams tomorrow and have all day Saturday to make the pies and puddings. There was still pie plant in the garden and she was getting ten or twelve eggs a day. It would take every one of them to make the pies and custards. But what matter? It would be a day to remember, the first church meeting ever held on South Holston.

The baby stirred in his sleep and whimpered. He would be waking any minute. The fire in the other room must be getting low. She had better go out and get some wood. She laid the shuttle down and was stepping to the door when she heard the cry from the yard.

She ran to the door. An Indian was standing over Frank. Feathers stuck up in his hair. He had an axe in one hand. A scalp was dangling from the other.

He saw her and looked into her eyes and smiled. She looked down. There was blood on Frank but the cry had not come from him but from Sally over by the garden: "*Mammy!*"

She turned her head and was free of the eyes. She gave him her back, passed the loom, stumbled on the one step and was in the big room. She took a step to the right before she remembered that Rion's gun was gone. But Frank's was over the east door. She had it down with her right hand while her left hand pulled the powder horn off its peg. It was half full. She spilled a little pouring it into the pan; she pulled the hammer back, and was at the back door with the gun raised.

There was no Indian in the yard, no Indian in sight anywhere. Then she heard a whoop from over back of the garden and saw the brown legs moving off through the ravine.

She gave Frank one look as she passed him. He lay still, blood all over his back. She ran on, past the smokehouse, past the big beech, and was at the garden fence. Malcolm lay in the middle of the path. He was hacked near in two. She could not find Sally and then something told her to look over the fence and she saw her lying on some honeysuckle vines, scalped, with a hole in her side.

She said to herself: "*She's dead*," and then she was running back towards the house. There was no Indian outside, no Indian in the room. The baby came up into her arms, warm, with a gulp that turned into a cry. She held him to her with her left arm and still grasping the musket went up the one step into the other room and out into the front dooryard. For a second the bare ground was white under her feet, then there were brown leaves. She was on the path.

The baby was crying. She held him tighter and ran on. There was no sound except his crying and her own feet slapping on the path. Her left arm ached with his weight. She brought the musket up and pressed it against her bosom but it was harder to run that way, and after a little she let it trail again. She was out of the woods and running through the corn. A waving blade nicked her forehead and blood ran down over her eyelid. She winked it away. The path veered and made for the branch. She slipped on the bank and was down in the water, jerked herself up and made for the house.

Elsa was off the doorstep and coming towards her.

"Cassy! You hurt!"

Cassy felt the baby leaving her arms. She let the gun fall.

"It's Malcolm and Sally. Been killed."

CHAPTER 57

RION PUT THE AWL DOWN. It showed a spot of red as big as his thumb nail near the tip.

"I reckon that's enough," he said.

Elsa, holding the child on her lap, let out a long, shuddering sigh. Rion looked down at the child's head. It was crusted and dark all over with yesterday's blood and now the fresh blood he had drawn when he punctured the skull was welling up in four bright crimson spots.

He picked the awl up again. "That's the way he said. Make four holes and don't stop till it shows blood. . . ." He saw the surgeon's face: the beefy jowls lapping over his red soldier's collar, his little blue eyes that lighted as he talked. "He kept using words," he muttered, "said 'induce granulation,' and when I pinned him down that was what he said: bore four holes and don't stop till it shows blood." His face twisted. He flung the awl from him. "Boring holes in a little child's skull when it's sick enough to die!"

Elsa had drawn her knees up and was holding the child against her bosom as if she thought he might try to repeat the operation, but Cassy behind him spoke steadily. "Doctor Vance is a real surgeon or he wouldn't a been there with those soldiers. We was lucky to get him before he left the fort."

"Yes," Rion mumbled. "He was on his horse and ready to leave when I rode up. Said he'd a come himself but he'd got orders and had to ride. . . ."

He felt sick at his stomach. He walked over and sat down on the doorstep.

Behind him the women moved about in the room. There was the splash of water being thrown from a basin out the back door; then the floor creaked as Elsa got up clumsily from her chair and walked over and laid Sally down on the bed. He turned around and looked at the child. Blood was still oozing from her head but not as fast as it had been. He closed his eyes, then opened them again quick. It was like last night. Towards morning they had lain down to try to get some rest but whenever he shut his eyes he saw Sally as they had seen her coming towards them from around the corner of the smokehouse.

He had not got back to Jacob's till around four o'clock. Elsa was down at the gate to break it to him. "The children been hurt." He looked into her eyes. "No, they ain't. They're dead." "The baby's here," she said, "and Cassy."

He tried to make Cassy stay at Wagners' but she would go up to the house with him. "Let her go," Elsa said. "She wants to see her children's bodies. . . . And you got to have help with the burying." It ended by their all going.

Frank looked the worst, scalped and his back bone hacked in two. He must not even have known what hit him, asleep there on his face and the Indian creeping out on him from behind the tree.

But Frank was grown, not a little child. He almost broke down when he saw Malcolm and he turned off and started digging the grave, but Cassy kept saying she couldn't find Sally and then all of a sudden they saw Sally, rising up out of the grass like a wounded bird.

She looked at them like she thought they might be somebody else and then she started towards them, her face white as paper and her head all bloody and the blood all on her gown. He thought for a second that she was coming from the other side and he prayed for the Lord to turn her back. Then she stretched her hands out and called "Mammy!" and he knew that she was alive.

"Oh God!" Cassy said. "Oh, God! I thought you was dead!"

She ran to Sally and caught her in her arms. Sally laid her head back on her mother's shoulder and shut her eyes. She slept about an hour before she talked.

She and Malcolm were playing by the fence when they saw the Indians rise up at the far end of the garden. They didn't say anything and the Indians didn't say anything either, just tipped along the path. The one in front caught hold of Malcolm and then another one came from behind him and put his hand over her mouth and grabbed her by the neck. He hurt her head real bad and stuck his knife in her side and then she must have gone to sleep, for she woke up in some honeysuckle vines on the other side of the fence, with blood coming from her head and her side. She lay real still till she thought the Indians had gone and then she got up and went towards the gate. But while she was trying to unlatch it she went to sleep again.

When she woke up Sir'us was digging a hole at the gate. She crawled through the hole and went on to the house. Uncle Frank was lying there under the tree with blood all over him and would not answer, and Mammy was gone from the house. She stayed behind the door until she heard somebody coming; then she ran out and hid in the grass. . . .

He felt something brush his shoulder, and Cassy stepped over the sill and sat down beside him on the doorstep. He glanced back into the house. Elsa had drawn a stool up beside the bed. Sally's limbs were stretched out quiet under the sheet but she was talking again, saying over some of the things she had just told them.

"We ought not to let her talk," Cassy said. "We ought not to have asked her anything."

He reached over and laid his hand on top of hers where it lay in her lap. It fluttered in his for a second, then was still.

Inside the house the thin, feverish voice went on. Cassy suddenly began speaking: "I went to the door and he was standing over Frank. We looked at each other, and I thought I better go get the gun before I try to do anything. . . . It took me such a long time. They were gone when I got back to the door. I run on past Frank. I saw Malcolm first and I knew he was dead, and then I found Sally and she looked to be dead too, and it shot through me that the baby was in the house, and I got him and run to Wagners'. . . ."

"You did right," he said, "trying to save the one that was alive."

"If I'd known she was living I couldn't a run to the baby. I'd a had to stop and drag her out of the garden. . . ."

"But you thought she was dead. . . ."

"I wish now I hadn't gone back for the gun. It didn't do me any good. I wish I'd come on out and grappled with 'em. . . ."

"You couldn't done no good, one woman against them savages. . . ."

She began again: "If Frank hadn't been asleep when they come. . . ."

"I can't stand it!" he said and put his head down in her lap, shaking it with his sobs. She clasped both arms tight around his head and bent over him.

"Don't cry. Don't cry now. Don't cry no more."

PART FOUR

Je porte en moi la mélancholie des races barbares, avec ses instincts de migrations et ses dégoûts innés de la vie qui leur faisaient quitter leur pays comme pour se quitter eux-mêmes.

GUSTAVE FLAUBERT TO LOUISE COLET

CHAPTER 58

IN THE SUMMER of 1778 Dragging Canoe sent Archy to Fort Dearborn on a mission to the British General Hamilton. He and his two companions stayed in the north for a month. The trip back down the Great Warpath took them twenty days and after that they had to make their way through the wild mountain country to Chickamauga creek where the Cherokees who had followed Dragging Canoe were now settled.

The moon was full. They slept by day and travelled by night, all except the last day. They were anxious to get home and travelled all of that day with no sleep except an hour snatched at noon in a cane brake.

It was dusk when they came around the base of the long ridge and saw the great plain with the river coiling through it and the mountain, Chat-a-nu-ga, towering in the distance.

They left the woods, crossed a meadow and entered the secret path through the cane. Fireflies flitted before them. The Otter Lifter beckoned to them. "Come, cousin and carry me home."

Doublehead laughed. He had been examining the trail. "There have been no *Hoobuk Waske* along here." He looked up at the mountain and shook his head. "I had forgotten how that fellow dominates the landscape. Everywhere you look," he turned his head rapidly from side to side, "he is there and frowning at you. But perhaps you differ from me," he added politely. "Do you find his expression friendly, Bear Killer?"

Archy did not answer. He was thinking of the words Doublehead had just uttered: *Hoobuk Waske*. The Indians out of delicacy did not often use that expression before him. But Doublehead and Otter Lifter, travelling with him day after day, had forgotten that he was not one of themselves. The British general had allowed his amazement to show in his face when the three ambassadors had been brought in and he saw that one of them was a white man. And after he had dismissed them he had Archy brought back to him for private conversation. He had wanted to know to what extent he could rely on Dragging Canoe. "As on yourself," Archy told him.

Hamilton had stared out of his pale eyes, seeming for a moment to think his loyalty impugned, and then had changed the subject, wanting to know how long Archy had lived with the Cherokees and if he knew any of the other tribes. "I am blood brother to the chief of the Chickamaugas and know no other tribe," Archy said.

They were at the end of the brake. Before them lay a wide meadow. At the top of the slope fires flickered. The town house showed in the middle of the square and beyond it in a grove of oaks twenty or thirty new houses.

The tired horses broke into a gallop. They rattled up to the square, dismounted and, pulling the ropes from the horses' necks, turned them loose on the range.

Some men standing around a fire turned and saw them. A cry rose. "The ambassadors have returned!"

Noonday was the first to reach Archy. He took him by the arm, laughing. "You are back in time for the dance," he said and pointed to a rack made of willow withes that came up beside the fire.

Archy walked, stiff-legged, over to the rack. Ten scalps were suspended on hoops thrust through the netted withes. Eight were the scalps of grown people. The two small scalps were those of children.

"Where'd you take 'em?" he asked.

"Three days ago on the Watauga," Noonday said. He looked up at the moon, murmuring under his breath the ritual greeting. "Ten scalps we have taken since the first showed there between the trees."

Archy laughed. "They will not think so much of the Raven's talk now."

Noonday nodded. "They know now that there are men in the Nation who do not follow the Raven or any other coward." He spat on the ground, then looked up slyly. "The Long Knives have found out the name of our river. I heard them call it over on the Watauga. I heard a boy call: 'The Chickamaugas are coming!'"

Archy looked around him, at the new town house, almost as large as the one at Chota, as well placed here among its fertile fields. He thought of the meaning of the Creek word: "The dwelling place of the chief." "It's a good name," he said.

He was walking up towards the houses. Noonday kept beside him. "Where do you go now?"

"To see the chief. As soon as I have gone to water and drawn the briars from my feet."

On the sanded ground in front of the houses some boys were playing *Toli*. One boy was leading the field, the ball flying before his long, forked stick. But an antagonist came up behind him and sent the ball flying towards the opposite goal.

The others dashed after it. The boy who had had the ball stood scowling, his fists clenched.

"Yo!" Archy cried.

The Fox saw his father and ran and leaped off the ground into his arms. Archy put him down, laughing. "Thou hast not forgotten me?"

The Fox shook his head. "We have looked for thee every night since the full moon came."

He had dropped his *Toli* stick and was running along beside his father. Archy went back and picked up the stick and handed it to him.

"They will make a goal if you do not hurry."

The child ran off. Archy crossed the street and entered his house. She was not there. He stood in the middle of the room, observing the improvements that had been made during his absence: a new chest and three new stools carved of poplar.

There were steps outside. She came through the doorway, bearing a water jug. She set the jug down. "It is you," she said in a calm voice. "I heard the news on the street." And then she was kissing him the way he had taught her, and beating him on the shoulders with her little, clenched fists.

"If I had known what awaited me here I would have hid all night in the cane brake," he said, laughing.

Her hands came up and clasped about his neck. "I could not have lived another moon without you," she whispered. "If another moon had come and you were not here I would have thrown myself into the river."

He put his hand under her chin and forced her head back until he could see her eyes. "Thou talkest like a child."

In the moonlight her eyes glittered with tears. Her lower lip went wry. She caught it between her teeth. "Why does he have to send you?" she cried. "Why cannot some other man be his ambassador and go north, south, east, west?" Behind his neck she snapped her fingers in the air. "You run the forest like a deer."

Archy saw over her shoulder a shadow darken the doorway. He set his hands on her waist, gave it a quick pressure before he dislodged her arms, and stepped forward.

"I was coming to your house as soon as I had drawn the briars from my feet," he said.

Dragging Canoe stooped. "I will draw the briars from your feet."

Archy put out a hand. "You do me too much honor."

The woman stood back. They walked out of the house and sat down on a bench that was placed against the wall. The chief held a *chungke* stone in his hand. He sat quietly, turning it round and round.

Archy considered a moment, then began speaking: "The British general is a heavy man, swollen with importance and with the eyes of a pig, but he is brave. I bring a good talk from him. The King's men will come in the hungry month.*. . ."

Dragging Canoe stirred impatiently. "They will wait that long?"

"He says he needs time to prepare his plans. In the meantime he wants you to call a council of all the chiefs."

"They will come," Dragging Canoe said softly. "They will be afraid not to come now. . . . Does he promise the Chickamaugas the place of honor in the battle?"

"Yes."

"Where does he plan the attack?"

"On the whole frontier."

Dragging Canoe rose and paced up and down. His giant shadow fell across the sanded ground. As Archy watched the gigantic arm rose. The *chungke* stone was a boulder large enough to crush a man. The giant had his lips parted as if in the heat of battle.

He resumed his pacing back and forth, his head lowered in meditation. Suddenly he raised his head again and turned his dark eyes steadily on Archy. He said in a low tone, "It is our last chance, Bear Killer."

* February.

CHAPTER 59

RION MADE A GOOD CORN CROP that year. He began gathering on the last day of October and finished three days later. It was early in the afternoon when he drove the sled up from the bottom for the last time. He unhooked the horses and turned them out to range, then loaded the corn into the crib. He had kept his own seed this year. Bloody Butcher. Hardly a nubbin in the lot. He picked out a bushel of the choicest ears and put them in a sack. He would take them down to mill this afternoon. Cassy had said last night that she was almost out of meal. But first he would go up to the house for a few minutes.

He threw the sack over his shoulder and started along the path. Off to the west somebody must be firing a crop of tobacco. There was a blue haze under the trees and the air smelled of burning wood. He emerged from the path and was in the open, sun-lit yard. There was nobody in sight. The door of the house was closed.

He dropped his sack of corn beside the step and opened the door. The baby was crawling around on the floor. There was a bright fire leaping on the hearth and in front of it sat Cassy and the Reverend Murrow, he talking, she shelling black-eyed peas.

The room seemed warm and close after the bright out-of-doors. "God's sake," Rion said. "You don't need a fire a day like this," and he left the door open behind him.

Cassy glanced at the sunshine streaming in through the open door, then back at the fire. "I'd have to make my fire up anyway in a few minutes to get supper," she said quietly.

Rion picked the baby up and drawing a stool up between them dandled the baby on his knee. The baby squirmed for a little, then springing up on his toes began pulling at his father's beard. Rion laughed and put him down on the floor. "Little more and I wouldn't have a hair in my head," he said.

Cassy got up and taking a small copper pan from the wall gave it to the baby. "He can chew on that a while," she said. She looked at the preacher and smiled faintly. "When they're that age they've either got to be sucking something or crawling."

Rion turned to Murrow. "How'd you come on in the grove this morning?"

The preacher tossed the wandering lock of hair out of his eyes. "I smote them hip and thigh, Brother Outlaw. Five oaks and three poplars fell before my axe."

"I'd a made it all oak," Rion said. "You don't want poplar in your house if you can get oak."

"When you going to roll the logs, Rion?" Cassy asked.

"Well, we'll have to split 'em first. I can't get to it before the middle of next week but it ought not to take more'n two days to notch 'em. Maybe Amos'll lend a hand. . . ." He laughed. "You could get a lot out of Amos, Reverend, if you'd set there on a log and talk to him whilst he worked."

"If you could give me a brief preparatory lesson I could start splitting the logs myself on Monday," the preacher said. "That is," he added, "if I derived as much profit as from your last lesson." He smiled and for a moment his gaunt face took on a boyish, winning expression. "I find that I am able to fell the trees with much less effort since you showed me the proper method of attack."

Rion looked at Cassy. "The Reverend held his axe too low. I was feared he'd chop his leg off before he got e'er tree down." He looked back at the preacher in wonder. "And you mean to say you never set out to fell a tree till you struck the wilderness?"

Murrow was apologetic. "I came up in Glasgow . . . the fires were of coal."

He shook his head. "I begin to fear my education has been neglected. A man must have many trades in order to battle the wilderness."

"Well, there's always somebody around that's proud to show you how to do," Rion said.

They were all silent for a few minutes. The preacher was staring into the fire. There was no sound in the room except the baby's grunts and the rustling of the dried pods that Cassy kept throwing down into the basket at her feet. Rion raised his eyes stealthily to her face.

It had been two months since she had cut her hair off. He had not got used to seeing her with it cut short. It made her look younger in a way and in a way older. No, it wasn't her hair, it was her face that had changed. It kept the same downcast, brooding expression, even when she laughed. He had seen her the same as take it into her hands and pull it into the shape of laughing, and had looked away, wanting to tell her not to do it, not to try.

At first she had kept going over and over things, saying how if she hadn't stopped to get the gun or if he had been at home or if they hadn't thought about having the bush arbor meeting. . . . But she didn't break down until after Sarah died. It would have been better if Sarah had been killed right off, better for her and for everybody else, than to linger the way she did. Cassy had sat by her bed day after day, not able to do much for her, just sitting there waiting.

It was then that the idea of sin had taken hold of her. She had worked it out that it was all her fault. She knew just where she did wrong, when she looked over the garden fence, and instead of going to help Sally said—out loud she told it now—"She's dead," and ran to the house. It was Satan spoke then, she said, not her. Satan whispered, "Run to the house. Save the baby," but what he was really saying was "Save yourself." She had minded him instead of doing what was right. It was wrong to leave a little child lying wounded without doing anything for her, even if you were trying to save another child's life. It was wrong to look ahead. You had to leave consequences to God and just always do what you knew was right.

"How do you know what's right?" he said once.

"There's something in here tells you," she said, and laid her hand on her breast. "All the time I was running towards the house my feet were like lead. Satan was pulling me forward but God was pulling me back."

"Why don't you ask the Reverend what he thinks about it?"

She had asked the Reverend, all right, but it was hard to get a straight answer out of the Reverend. He was like Frank, couldn't express himself without using big words. This world, he said, was one of trial and discipline. God often sent afflictions on purpose to try you. *Cast away from ye all your transgressions whereby ye have transgressed and make you a new heart and a new spirit.* . . . When he wasn't working on the piece of land that Rion and Jacob had given him to settle here he was sitting in front of the fire, talking religion with Cassy. It was the only thing seemed to ease her these days. . . .

Rion's mouth twisted. He himself had asked the Reverend's advice once. It was while the Reverend was staying with the Wagners. When he got up to go that night he had got up too, saying he would walk part of the way with him. On the path he had put his question to him. What was he to do about Cassy? "She don't want to have nothing to do with me—at night, you know."

The Reverend had thrown his head back and thundered out quite a piece, standing there on the path. "The disposition to regard the body as intrinsically evil and all natural impulses as worthy only to be trampled on, is a Manichaean heresy . . ."

"That may well be," Rion said, "but it don't help me none."

The preacher came to himself with a start. He put his big hand on Rion's shoulder. "My brother, you have been sorely tried. . . . I pray for you. . . . I wake sometimes in the night and pray for you."

"Much obliged," Rion told him. "Well, there ain't nothing to do but wear through it, I reckon." And he said good night and went back to the house.

That had been a month ago. Here lately, in the last few days, since the season had turned and the blue haze of fall was drifting through the valley a change had come over him. He would wake in the morning and for a while it would be as if it hadn't happened and then he would get up and stir around and it would all come over him again. But at different times through the day that feeling would come back over him, that none of it had ever been, that there was nothing to keep him from being happy.

Yesterday this feeling had come over him so strong that he had quit work in the middle of the morning and come up to the house. Cassy was in the loom room, weaving, the baby was playing on the floor. He asked her to come into the other room with him—she wouldn't ever do it if the children were anywhere around. "You can bar the outside door and leave him playing there by himself just a minute," he said. She argued but finally came. . . . Afterwards he wished he hadn't made her. It wasn't the same and hadn't been since the children and Frank went.

He thought of the three graves. They had buried them, deep, in the woods just east of the clearing, near some big rocks that Malcolm used to play around. He had started a wall around the place, bringing rocks up from the branch every time he went over there, but he had not had time to work on it as much as a whole day. The wall wouldn't be finished before spring.

The first few days after they were buried he felt them out there and in the mornings he couldn't rest until he had gone and stood a minute at the graves. But now it was different. When he went now he didn't feel them there. The three graves were just mounds of earth and they were gone somewhere else. He didn't know whether Cassy felt the same way he did. She went to the graveyard every day, he knew, and she had planted a root of yellow jasmine on each grave.

He thought of Malcolm, the solemn way he had of raising his head and looking at you and then tucking his chin in quick. He used to wonder what he would be like when he was grown. But he would never be grown.

They were talking again, about a man the preacher often mentioned, named Tertullian. He stood up and pushed his stool back. "I'll take my corn on down to the mill," he said.

"Tell Elsa I got plenty of late beans left in the garden if she wants some," Cassy said.

"All right," he called from the door and was out of the house and into the yard.

The sun was still high. He picked up his sack of corn and struck into the woods. The smell of burning wood was stronger. He came out of the woods and saw the whole bottom filled with the drifting blue haze. From up the river came a sound he had never heard before, in these woods, at least: a high, sweet piping. He was puzzled to account for it and stood in the field for a moment, listening; then went on down to the mill.

There was nobody before him. Jacob took the sack of corn and Rion sat there and watched the white meal pour down the chute.

It was strange the different ways men took through the world. He had worked, rain or shine, almost every day since he came to the Holston. Jacob had not worked half as hard but he had set this mill up and it had worked for him. That first day the old coot had looked across the river and picked this for a likely mill site while he, Rion, had stood there, figuring how many trees he could cut down. Jacob had been here seven years and did not have two acres of land cleared. Still he wouldn't work them if he had them cleared—as long as the wheel kept turning and everybody in the neighbourhood brought him their corn to grind. He didn't know, though, that he'd like a miller's life for himself. Made a man lazy. Days when nobody brought any corn Jacob just sat there on his butt or maybe fished a little. But he was getting old and of course with just him and Elsa there wasn't much to do around the place.

He raised his head, turning it a little to the right. "What's that sound up the river?"

"It's Mulroon's flute," Jacob said. "Ain't you ever heard it before? Times he'll play all afternoon."

"I ain't ever stopped there," Rion said, "and him and his wife ain't ever stopped at our house either. No hard feelings, just happened not to be passing."

"It ain't his wife," Jacob said. "It's his sister. She comes down here and sets with Elsa sometimes. Fine figger of a woman," and he grinned and winked a bleared blue eye.

"You old scoundrel," Rion said. "One foot in the grave and still worrying over the women!"

The sack was full. Rion leaned over and tied the sack with a piece of hemp, then hoisted it over his shoulder.

"I better be getting along," he called to Jacob and started off.

He crossed the creek and was about to take the path home when he heard the flute again. What little wind there had been had died. He could hear the flute plain now, could even distinguish the tune: "The Soldier and the Lady."

> One morning, one morning, one morning in May
> I saw a fair lady a-wending her way. . . .

Joe Lovelatty used to play that on his fiddle and Kate would sing and they would all come in on the chorus:

> And if ever I return,
> It will be in the spring,
> For to see the waters flowing,
> Hear the nightingale sing. . . .

He dropped his sack behind a bush and went towards the music. It came from Mulroon's, all right. He had never stopped there but he knew where the clearing was, on the other side of the river, just below the island. A little patch of ground, not more than two acres, right at the foot of Bays' Mountain. He came to the river, walked along the bank for a while and finally found the ford he was seeking, a deep one. He was wet to the waist when he came up on the other side.

The path was narrow and hedged with laurel. He looked about him with disfavor. Mulroon ought to bring a grubbing axe down here one morning and fix it so that his neighbors could get through to see him. The path ended. He was in the clearing.

The house was a one-room shack, with one window and a stubby cat-and-clay chimney. A woman sat on the doorstep, her chin resting in her cupped hands. In the patch of sunlight in front of the house a man sat on a stump, playing his flute.

He raised a red face in which little grey pig's eyes twinkled merrily, and took the flute from his lips long enough to say, "Set down, neighbor," and gesture towards a stump, then began playing again.

Rion touched his forelock to the woman and sat down, eyeing the fellow curiously. He had a schoolmasterish look to him. That was from his coat of bottle-green store cloth or perhaps it was the way he wore his hair. At first glance it looked like a wig but if you looked close enough you saw that the thick, brown hair, coming down almost to the cheekbone on each side, was his own.

Mulroon gave a final flourish, then took the flute from his lips. "It's a pretty tune now, ain't it?"

"I used to hear it when I was a boy over across the mountains," Rion said.

Mulroon nodded. "It's a queer thing now the travels a tune'll be taking. I brought this one all the way from the old country."

"It's likely you brought a pack of others," Rion said with a smile.

"Aye, I'm never without a tune in my head. Did ye ever hear this?" and he lifted the flute to his lips and played a jig.

"Is it 'Tullochgorum'?" Rion asked.

He shook his head. "It's 'Will Ye Gang To the Baugy Burn?'" He glanced at the woman. "Ann here can jig it when she's a mind to."

The woman smiled lazily and looked over the two men's heads into the trees.

"Can you make the music too?" Rion asked.

She shook her head, hardly withdrawing her gaze from the forest.

Seeing her so abstracted Rion eyed her up and down. She was younger than Mulroon but she was no chicken. A bit plump, too,

with curling, taffy-colored hair and a mouth the color of the wild
strawberries that crushed under your foot when you walked along
the river bank. She was tanned for a cabiner. Well, she probably
did all the work that was done around here. Mulroon more than
likely took his flute to the field with him. He smiled at the thought:
Mulroon lying in the shade and playing while the woman broke the
clods; then he realized that she had turned her blue, sleepy-looking
eyes on him.

"You'll know me next time you see me, I reckon."

He grinned cheerfully. "Well, I ought to see a lot of you. We're
about the nearest neighbors you got, ain't we?"

"Mrs. Wagner's our nearest neighbor," she said primly.

"Well, we ain't a whoop from the mill. Just keep on up the path
instead of turning off to the river and you'll come to our clearing."

"I was by there once," Mulroon said, "but you warn't at home.
I came by with Master Grundy and Master Bulloch. . . ." He
cleared his throat. "I settled here with the idea of establishing a
school but the settlement appears too young. Grundy's boys and
Bulloch's was the only ones that was promised. Three Grundys and
three Bullochs. I says: 'Gentlemen, it ain't enough, by a long shot!'
. . . I aimed to go on up above the Island after that but the winter
set in and here we be. . . ." His voice trailed off. He lifted the flute
to his lips as if from force of habit, then laid it down. "Ann," he said
suddenly in a loud, firm voice, "ain't you going to offer Master
Outlaw nothing?"

The woman rose silently, went into the house and brought a stone
jug and three horns out and set them down beside him on the stump.

He poured a horn full and offered it to Rion. Rion lifted it to his
lips, expecting to taste persimmon or wild cherry wine but it was
whiskey, raw, full-bodied corn whiskey.

He drank it off at one draught. "Well, now," he said, "it's been a
long time since I had a drink of whiskey. Where'd you get it?"

Mulroon gestured at the ragged corn stalks in the clearing. "Out
of that field."

"You got a still?" Rion asked. "You know how to set one up?"

Mulroon nodded. "In the old country whiskey was all we'd drink,
poor folks, that is." He lifted the jug hospitably. Rion let him fill
his horn again. "I mind the first whiskey I ever saw," he said musingly. "An old man brought it to an infare once. In a square bottle."

"I was knee high to a duck when I first looked on it," Mulroon said. "As soon as I was high enough I used to turn the tap for my old uncle that raised me, God save his soul, in county Kerry."

"You going to make any more?" Rion asked.

"Aye . . . as long as the corn lasts. It's better'n journey cake. I tell Ann, as long as ye git the corn inside ye what difference the shape it comes in?"

The woman laughed, suddenly, scornfully.

Rion grinned at her and looked back at Mulroon. "Well, I'd not mind having some to warm me of winter nights. . . . If I bring a load of corn over could ye make me a run? I don't know the art and mystery of it myself, so I'll pay ye—in kind or cut money as ye prefer."

Mulroon waved his hand. "There'll be no quarrel over the payment. I'll be proud to make a run for a neighbour." He laughed with a hiccup; "the nearest neighbor I got."

"If you don't take that corn on down to the mill we ain't going to have any supper,' the woman said in a cold tone. "Three days now I been scraping the bottom of the barrel."

Mulroon laid his flute down with exaggerated care and got to his feet. The woman was dragging a sack of corn over the doorstep. Mulroon took it from her, then looked at Rion. "Will ye walk along, neighbor?"

Rion saw the woman smiling to herself and realized that she thought that he was tipsy enough to walk out of his way for company. "No," he said with dignity. "It's getting late. I'd best take the short cut home."

Mulroon had started down the path, the sack over his shoulder. The woman went back to her seat on the doorstep. Rion yawned and stretched himself. "Well, I better be getting along," he said.

The woman did not answer. But she was not looking over his head the way she had when he first came into the clearing. She was looking straight at him. There was a peculiar glint in her eyes. Her lips were parted. From where he sat he could hear her hard breathing.

It had been a long time since any woman had given him the eye like that. He sat there a second, wondering if he could be mistaken and then she spoke in a low, husky voice, "You got any pole beans at home?"

"No."

"Will you come with me while I gather you some?"

"Aye," he said and got up and followed her around the corner of the house. He walked close beside her but not touching her until they were around the corner. She stopped there beside the rain barrel that was set under the eaves. He drew close to her then and let his fingers close on her firm, warm arm.

"Where'll we go?" he whispered.

CHAPTER 60

CASSY CAME SLOWLY up the path through the corn field, holding the baby on one arm while the other hand grasped the split basket which she had carried to Elsa full of turnips. The baby was heavy, and the day which had been chill in the early morning had turned off hot. She had to stop twice to rest while she was crossing the corn field. It was cooler when she got into the woods. She shifted the baby to her hip and went more slowly. Rion had said that he would be working here in the west woods most of the afternoon. But she had not heard his axe for some time. She wondered whether he had quit work and gone to the house.

She looked off into the woods. A little way from the path some big trees had been felled to make timbers for the house. A thicket of May-pops had sprung up around the stumps. Under the broad leaves the fruit showed yellow.

She went over into the grove and setting the baby down on the ground began to fill her basket. He stretched out his hands and said "Pop." That and "Mammy" and "Daddy" were the only words he could say—he was slower to talk than the other children. She took the seeds out of one and fed it to him slowly, then wiped the juice from his mouth with one of the big leaves. "There," she said, "that's all you're going to get now."

She had her basket full and was reaching down to pick him up when she heard a voice speak over in the woods:

"I told you not to be coming up here."

Rion's voice. A woman's voice answered. "I just wanted to bring her some beans. . . . She said you all didn't have any."

Cassy's hands came away from the baby's shoulders. She straightened up slowly.

Rion's voice came again. "Don't you be bringing nothing up here."

There was silence, then the woman's voice: "You coming down tonight?"

"I don't know. Don't know whether I can get off. . . . You better go on home now."

The woman laughed, then there was the brush of feet over the leaves.

Cassy's hands went in and pressed tight against her stomach. She turned her head, slowly, as if her neck were in a vise, and stared through the trees with bright eyes.

There were more of the brushing sounds, then the woman laughed again, lower this time and softer. . . .

Cassy looked at the baby. He was smiling, holding a broken branch in one hand while with the other hand he ripped the leaves from it.

Bending her head and shoulders so as not to brush against the leaves she tip-toed off between the slender trunks. The small growth that came up at the other side of the grove was hung thick with honeysuckle. The green leaves were edged with light. She took a few more steps then stopped behind a mat of vines and looked over the speckled bough of a wild cherry tree into the clearing.

The pale yellow stump, the great, grey trunk of the fallen beech. Silver leaves still on the boughs, silver leaves on all the ground. Rion stood up there against the boughs and the woman pressing against him. His face, hanging over hers, was dark with blood that looked like it might burst out of the veins. He looked over his shoulder once then pulled her by the arm, around the boughs, into the cloud of leaves.

The bough he had been leaning against sprang up, trembling, into the air. Cassy stood motionless, and watched the leaves jerk back and forth. One spray among them was withered. She watched until that withered spray hung quiet then turned and tip-toed back into the grove.

The baby was crawling towards her. She picked him up and walked slowly, carefully out of the grove. When she was halfway out she remembered that she had left the basket sitting there under the trees. She went back and got it, then went up the path to the house.

The door was ajar. She pushed it open and set the baby down on the floor. He grasped the leg of a stool and tried to stand up. She gave him a big pewter spoon to play with, and went out into the backyard.

The chickens had come up to be fed. There were some ears of corn piled on the high shelf beside the door. She got half a dozen down and shelled the grains and flung them a handful at a time to the chickens.

The corn was all gone. The chickens were moving off to their roosts in the trees. She turned back to the house. The baby had quit playing with his spoon and was crying. She got him a cup full of morning's milk and a piece of cold journey cake, and kneeling beside him held the cup to his lips until he had drunk all the milk. He clutched at her as she was rising from the floor. She swung him up into her arms and carried him over to his crib. His body, resting against hers for a moment, was warm and soft. She shuddered as she laid him in his crib and put the piece of corn bread in his hand.

She was outdoors again. There was no living thing in sight except one old rooster who fixed her with a cold, red-rimmed eye as he stalked past. She began walking to and fro, slowly at first and then faster, until she could see her shadow spin on the ground as she turned. Suddenly something—her whirling shadow or some motion of the leaves over her head—made her feel that she was not alone. She dodged into the house. But there was no one there. She came out into the yard again. As she came she pressed her hand to her throat. It felt sore and now she realized that her whole body felt sore, as if it had been beaten with whips. She tried to remember whether she had run against a branch or fallen over anything when she was coming out of the woods, but it seemed a long time ago and she could not remember very clearly.

She looked up at the sun. When she had left Elsa's house she had said that she must get home to do her night chores. She had thought then that she hardly had time for them and yet the sun was still high in the sky. She stared at it until her eyes blurred from the brightness and she had to close them. She opened them and it danced before her in smoky light. She thought of what a long time it would be before it slipped behind the western rim and then she thought of all of the rest of her life to get through and she sank down, whimpering, on the doorstep.

CHAPTER 61

RION WORKED on after Ann had gone. It was almost dark when he came up the path. There was no one in the yard. He stepped up into the house. He thought at first that there was no one there and then he saw Cassy sitting on the back doorstep. He set his axe in the corner and went towards her. She drew to the side. He passed through the door and looking up on the shelf saw the two milk buckets still standing there.

"Ain't you milked yet?" he asked.

She looked up. "No," she said in a tone of surprise. "No, I ain't milked yet!"

Rion turned and in the dim light made out the forms of the two cows standing under the trees. "It's a wonder they didn't call to you," he said and laughed.

But she was already gone down the path. He took the other bucket and followed her to the cowpen. She was sitting on the three-legged stool he had made for her, her head pushed into the hollow of Old Suke's flank while her hands steadily rained the white milk down into the bucket. He squatted down beside the heifer and had begun to fill his bucket when he heard Cassy's voice behind him: "Let me finish her."

He went on milking. "I thought I'd milk her for you long as it's so dark."

Her voice came again, strained and with an underlying note of harshness. "You'll ruin her bag. She ain't used to your hands."

"I ain't ever ruined a cow's bag yet," he said, but he got up and stood aside while she squatted down beside the heifer. When he would have brought her the milking stool she shook her head; so he took it over and set it down under the trees. She was rising up, the bucket in her hand. He picked up the other bucket and followed her to the house.

There were a few coals smoldering on the hearth. He fanned them to flames then laid on fresh wood. Cassy was moving about in the lower room. They had moved the big table there and ate in

442

there now. When he had the fire going he went down. A tallow dip burned on the table. She had set out meat and bread and a dish of cold greens. As he entered she was pouring out a bowl of milk. He noticed that there was only one bowl set out.

"Ain't you going to eat anything?" he asked.

"No," she said in the same low, strained voice and walked away from him and stood in the open doorway with her back turned.

Rion sat down at the table. He pulled the platter over. He cut himself a slice of venison and helped himself to greens and broke off a piece of journey cake.

Cassy turned around suddenly. "Would you like some plum butter?"

"No," he said. "I don't want any."

She had turned her back again and stood looking out into the twilight. Rion slowly lowered the hand that had been raising a piece of corn bread to his mouth. He had had a glimpse of her face when she had turned around, the eyes sunk back in the head and darker than usual, the mouth withered. She looked like a person who had suddenly been taken ill or had just had some kind of shock. A coldness settled at the pit of his stomach. His throat felt dry. He laid the piece of bread carefully on the side of his plate and sat staring into the candle flame. It had come then. He had always known that it would, when he stopped to think about it, and yet he had always felt safe, minute by minute. . . .

There was a little sound from the doorway as she shifted her foot on the sill. He pushed his stool back and stood up. No use waiting. He might as well get it over with.

He walked over to within a few feet of her. "What's the matter, Cassy?" he asked in a low voice.

She turned her head and looked at him, her eyes bright with tears, then she had turned around again. "Nothing," she said in a harsh, unsteady voice. "There ain't nothing the matter—that can be helped."

"Is it the children?" he asked.

She did not answer.

He went back to the table and sat down again. The candle flame eddied in a little gust from the door. He watched it turn from greenish-yellow back to pure blue. He ought not to have said that about the children. She was right not to answer. But her not answering meant something. She must know, not just suspect. Could she have seen anything this afternoon? He had told Ann he would break her neck if she came up there again but he ought not to have let her stay, even for a minute, that near the house. . . . Well, there was no help for it.

He got up again and went towards Cassy. "Was you down in the new ground this evening?"

"Yes," she said without turning around.

He was silent a moment, then he said: "I reckon you saw that Mulroon woman. She came up there, said she had some beans she wanted me to bring up here." He laughed awkwardly. "She ain't no better'n' she should be, that woman. I spoke to her rough, told her not to come around no more."

Cassy had whirled about in the doorway. Her eyes, still bright with tears, were wide open and fixed on his face. Something seemed to have happened to her throat. She put her hand up and clutched at it. When words came they were so guttural and harsh he hardly understood them. ". . . Woman . . ." she panted. ". . . spoke rough!"

"Well, I did," he said boldly.

She shook her head from side to side as if in that way she could dislodge the thing that clogged her throat, then her voice came, high and thin: "I saw you . . . standing there by the beech tree. . . . I saw you go around and hide in the leaves. . . ."

He had a vision of the great, fallen tree and remembered how as he and Ann dived in among the leaves he had thought that it was as good a hiding place as could be found, but now it was as if that great spread of bough and all those yellow leaves had been torn away and he left lying there on the ground naked. He shook his head doggedly. "You might have seen me go in there but there wasn't anything else to see."

She was coming towards him, her eyes as bright, as venomous as a snake's in the grass. "I didn't see you mount her. I went away from there, soon as I knew what you were up to."

He stared at her while his face flushed deep crimson. "I never thought to hear you talk like that," he said.

She stopped still. The muscles on the sides of her neck sprang out like cords. Her chin came up between them, the mouth above it a taut, open square. She screamed, the kind of scream he had heard a horse give once when it was trapped by high water and knew it couldn't get out.

CHAPTER 62

THAT WAS ON MONDAY NIGHT. The next day it turned off rainy and it rained for a week. If things had been different at the house Rion would have been glad of the chance for a little rest. As it was he kept on working through the bad weather. He put in three days shucking corn and when the corn was all shucked he went back to felling trees, working sometimes in a driving rain. He worked in the clearing all Saturday morning. After dinner he took his axe and started out as if he were going back to the clearing. But he did not stop in the clearing. He went on to Mulroon's. He stayed there only an hour and around three o'clock came on back to the clearing. The rain had let up but the wind was still blowing and clouds were piling up in the south.

He worked a while but the wind kept rising, tearing the leaves from the trees so fast that once he was blinded by a drift of them and almost cut his leg. Finally he stopped work and went to the house.

The fire was low in the upper room. He made it up, then drew a stool up to the hearth and sat there drying off. The baby was asleep in his crib in the corner. Cassy kept moving about back there. She had had a bad cold and every now and then she coughed. Once she spoke to him in a formal, constrained tone:

"Ain't you going to change your clothes?"

"No," he said absently. "I'll dry out here in a minute."

She did not say anything else and he stared into the fire. It had been a week since Cassy had found him out. She had stood that night, screaming, and then she went all to pieces, falling on the floor, striking her hand so hard on the corner of the chest that blood came. When she got up she was calm. "I hurt my hand," she said. She let him bandage it and let him take off her clothes—she let him help her all through it as if he were somebody else, somebody she didn't have anything against. And after they were in bed she had caught hold of him, shivering and crying like a child. Lying there, holding her tight in his arms, even with that cry of hers ringing in both their ears it

445

had seemed to him that there was some hope, that things might yet be all right. But in the morning, up and dressed and going about his work, he heard her voice, cold and strange, and his heart closed up. He knew that it would never be the same again between them and all that day he had gone about feeling an immense weariness, as if somewhere far off, so that he only heard her faintly, she was still screaming that terrible scream.

But even then, even after all that, if he just hadn't gone back to Mulroon's! He put his hand up over his mouth. When he took it down it was damp from the sweat that still beaded his upper lip. It was over an hour since he had come from Mulroon's and yet he still felt that shaking about his mouth. He glanced behind him, then hunched his shoulders and drew his stool closer to the fire. He ought not to have come in here in the shape he was in. But a man had to be somewhere and he couldn't stay outdoors a day like this.

After he had stayed away from Mulroons' for three days he got to thinking. Suppose Ann should come here to the house. She had threatened once to do that and he had told her what he would do to her if she did. But he could beat her half to death and the mischief would still be done. He got to worrying and did what he had never thought to do—went back again. Tom, by ill luck, was gone and Ann was sitting there alone. He didn't tell her what had happened, just told her he wouldn't be coming there again. She didn't say anything, just went on shelling corn. He ought to have gone away after that but he sat on for a few minutes and then she put the basket down and came up and put her hands on him. . . . He had been back twice since then . . . and then this afternoon.

They had been there in bed together when they heard Tom coming up the path. Ann was quick, out of the bed, and with her clothes on before you could say Jack Robinson. He was slower but even then he had plenty of time, for Tom stopped just as he came to the doorstep and stood a little time before he opened the door and came in.

There was something about it, his stopping just long enough to give them time and the quiet way he came in that made Rion angry. Had Tom known all along? He did not say anything—what was there he could say?—and yet he couldn't go home without knowing.

They sat by the fire. Tom was talking, about something that had happened at the Wagners', and then he leaned over to straighten a log and his thick hair slipped out of place and Rion saw his ear.

Tom was straightening up, not knowing that anything had happened.

Rion got to his feet. "Is the other one like that?" he asked and looked him straight in the eye.

Tom did not know what he meant for a second, then his hand flew to his hair. It was in place, the ear covered. He looked at Rion, and smiled his finagling smile. "I don't know what you mean, Neighbor."

All of a sudden Rion knew that he was not going to let them stay here in this house any longer. He walked over and lifted the man's hair. The ear was cut off square just above the place where it sprang from the cheek.

"Where'd you get it?"

"In Anson county . . . it war'n't a thing, Neighbor . . . a dispute over a pig and they sided against me."

Rion walked slowly around and lifted the hair from the other ear. It was mutilated in the same way.

He spoke slowly: "You might as well get out of here now—if you don't want to be up before court. It's meeting Monday."

Tom stared. "I've nothing to fear," he began and then the woman came up behind him and spoke in a dead-sounding voice: "Ain't no use, Tom. He wants to get rid of us."

"We ain't done nothing to him," Mulroon said, "and as for what happened in Anson . . ."

"It ain't no use," the woman said again.

She looked at Rion over the man's shoulder and she turned away. There were some gowns hanging on pegs behind the bed. She got them down and began stuffing them into an elkhide bag.

The man stood staring at her; then he looked back at Rion. His face had changed, all his cozening ways had suddenly dropped from him. He nodded his head up and down but carefully—you saw now that he always moved his head carefully, probably never quite forgetting what that greasy mat of hair covered.

"We'll be out of here directly, Neighbor. Up the river. . . . There ain't much to pack. . . . We'll be out of here in a jiffy. Up the river."

"You don't need to push," Rion said sullenly, "long as you're gone by morning."

He started towards the door. The woman was taking quilts off the bed and folding them. She dropped the quilt she was holding and ran towards him. He saw her coming and put his hand out to fend her off but she ducked in under his arm.

"Come away with me," she whispered. "You come with me."

He looked at her, his face stiff with distaste. Her hands were tearing at his collar. He caught her wrists and extending his arms pushed her slowly back from him. Her wrists went limp in his grasp. He let her go. She sank to the floor and was turning up the hem of her gown. Something gold showed where she was ripping the stitches. She looked up and a fatuous, desperate smile played on her face. "Three sovereigns," she whispered. "We could go a fur piece on that."

He had left her there on the floor, still scrabbling in the tail of her gown . . . but he kept seeing the poor bitch's face. It would be a long time before he got the taste of what had happened out of his mouth. Maybe he ought not to have been so hasty, ought to have given them more time to pack up. . . . No, he couldn't have done it at all if he'd stopped to wait. It had come over him all of a sudden and he had to do it then or never. And they were better off, up above the Island where the country was still rough. Down here the settlements were thick. Somebody would have caught on to the fact that Mulroon was a thief and sooner or later he would have been run out of the neighborhood. He wondered what it was the man had stolen in Anson and whether there had been many thefts or just one. It looked like he had been run out of more places than Anson, the way he was ready to pack and be off at a moment's notice. . . .

There was a knock at the door. He got up wearily and opened it. The Reverend Murrow came in. He had on his riding cloak. His horse was hitched under the trees.

Rion shut the door and bade him in to the fire but he would not sit down. Then Rion saw Cassy coming up from the lower room. She had on her cloak and an old scarf was tied over her head. She looked a little to the side of him and spoke in a low voice:

"You'll have to milk tonight. . . . And will you feed my late chickens?" She let her eyes rest briefly on his face and gestured towards the lower room. "Your supper's set out . . ." She gestured to the mantel shelf. "When the baby wakes up give him that bowl of milk that's setting there. It's got bread already crumbled in it."

He started at her. "Where you going?"

"Mistress Honeycutt is ill of a fever," Murrow said. "I am going over to pray with her and read the Scripture. Sister Outlaw told me yesterday that she would accompany me there. I have borrowed Amos Eaton's pillion so that she may make the journey in comfort."

Rion looked at him a moment in silence and he got up and went to the door. The whole west was black. As he stood there the sky lightened and a clap of thunder came.

"You can't go to Honeycutts'," he said, "it's going to storm."

Cassy had come up and was standing beside him in the doorway. "We can get there before the storm," she said.

"It's coming any minute," he told her. "Look at that horse."

Murrow's horse had flung his head up and was whinnying. From the range came an answering whinny. Gal and the colt felt the storm coming too.

She passed him and was in the dooryard. Murrow came after her. He was beside the horse, bending to offer his cupped hand.

She was up on the pillion, looking down at him.

"If I don't get back by noon tomorrow, don't worry."

He looked into her eyes. They were brilliant and hard. She was saying that he didn't care enough about her to worry but saying it in a way that would sound right before the preacher. Everything she said lately seemed to have a double meaning. His brain was tired, trying to get at her meanings.

He gave her back her look but did not answer. The horse wheeled and made for the bridle path. Rion watched until the horse and riders had disappeared into the woods, then went back into the house.

CHAPTER 63

HE GOT the buckets down from the shelf and went to the cowpen and milked the cows, and afterwards scattered corn for the chickens. The whole sky was overcast. The storm broke just as he got back to the house. The room was as dark as night. He had brought wood in earlier in the afternoon and he threw on fresh logs and let the fire blaze up bright. The thunder had waked the baby. He was howling in his crib. Rion took him up and pulled his wet hippens off and let him crawl around on the floor. The lightning was coming every few minutes and the thunder shook the cabin. Frank was frightened and cried at every crash. Rion took him on his knee and held him until the thunder and lightning stopped.

He was not hungry and had forgotten all about giving the child any supper until the baby himself saw his bowl sitting on the mantel shelf and stretched his hands to it and cried. Rion got the bowl of pap and fed it to him spoonful by spoonful, then put him back down on the floor.

There was a scratching at the door. He opened it and Sir'us came in. Rion let him run past him to the fire as he stood in the open doorway looking out.

The rain was still coming down but the wind had died and the sky was getting lighter. A hard storm. The dooryard was littered with blown leaves and a big bough had been torn from one of the sugar trees.

He was about to turn back into the house when he heard hoofbeats on the path and the sound of voices. A few minutes later two men rode into the clearing.

They rode across the yard and up to the doorstep. One of them was the boy who had brought the news of the Indian rising. The other was a lithe, dark man whom Rion had never seen before.

Rion stared at the boy. "Indians coming?"

The boy shook his head. The other man spoke. "This boy's John Lea. He's all that's left of his family. They got 'em all. Last Saturday."

"Where was that?"

"On Reedy creek," the boy said in a hoarse voice. "It ain't far from here."

"Light and rest," Rion said.

The boy shook his head. "I'd rather ride on."

But the older man was already dismounting. He came to Rion and shook hands. "I'm Joe Hubbard, from Wolf Hills." He looked up at the boy who still sat his horse. "Light, John. We got to get something to eat if we're going to ride all night."

"Where you going?"

The man lifted a dark, smiling face. "Against the Chickamoggies," he said. "There's nigh a thousand men gathering up here at Big Creek on the Clinch."

Rion stepped down into the yard. "You go on in," he said. "I'll throw these horses some corn and they can be eating while we're getting ready."

He fed the two strange horses and whistled his own horse up and bridled him; he threw him ten big ears of corn, and went back into the house.

The strangers were standing in front of the fire, drying their steaming clothes. He got a pitcher of milk and set out bread and milk and cold greens. "Come and get it," he said.

Hubbard stepped over at once but the boy did not turn from the fire until Hubbard spoke to him sharply: "Come on, John!"

The boy was startled; then he came forward. As he stepped into the light Rion saw his face. He looked as if he had blundered into a hornet's nest, the lips swollen, the eyes bloodshot under puffy lids. He sat down heavily. Rion pushed the platter towards him. He cut himself a big slice of side meat and helped himself to greens and began eating, talking between mouthfuls in the thick, toneless voice of one who has wept a long time:

"It was early in the morning. Pa called me and then he went out to the woodpile. I was just coming down the ladder and I heard him holler: '*John*'." His jaws stopped revolving. He fixed dull eyes on Rion's face. "I never went to him! Ma come at me. Said for me to slip out the back door and get Hubbard. Arthur was right behind me, and him and Ma started barring the doors." He took another mouthful of greens and chewed abstractedly. "I never even seen those savages. When I come back, with Joe and the rest, they was gone . . ."

"And the house burned down," Hubbard said.

The boy shook his head. "Warn't anything left but the hearthstone. The hearthstone," he repeated in a wondering voice. "Warn't any way to know what become of them."

"They were burned up," Hubbard said.

"Maybe. Maybe they tomahawked 'em before they burned 'em."

"What's the difference how they killed 'em?" Hubbard said gruffly.

"Your Pa never even got back to the house?" Rion asked.

The boy shook his head again. "They got him when they first slipped out of the woods. He was still laying there when I got back, so full of arrows he looked plumb ridiculous." He gave a hoarse laugh and sat staring at the candle flame. He had stopped eating but he held his knife in his hand. His swollen lips were parted. He did not seem to know that a trickle of greenish juice ran from between them down on to his chin.

Rion looked away from him at Hubbard who had left the table and was standing on the hearthstone. He was not a tall man and not very broad but he was put together as neat as a cat. He had an air of gayety as if he had a secret that he liked to think about. His eyes met Rion's now and he smiled. Rion got up and went over and stood beside him. Hubbard reached a hand up to the mantel shelf and thrust his moccasined foot farther in towards the flames.

"I hear you lost your children," he said after a moment.

"Two," Rion said, "and my brother-in-law."

"You know which ones did it?"

"No. I was away from home."

Hubbard looked into the flames, the smile still touching his lips. "I'll never forget the day I found my old daddy, lying at the spring with his head bashed in."

"How long ago was that?"

"Must have been five years ago. I'd just turned twenty and I'm twenty-five now." He raised his head. His brown eyes lighted. "I had the advantage of you. I knew which one did it. Feller they called Slim Tom."

"D'you get him?"

"Took me a year and a half. But I kept laying for him at different places along that Island road and one day he came along by himself. He wasn't quite dead when I got to him and I told him who I was, and then I put a rope around his heels and dragged him three miles to our house." He shook his head. An indulgent smile came on his face. "I wished afterwards I hadn't done that."

"Why?"

"Spoiled the skin. Still, it wasn't broke in many places."

"What did you do with it?"

"Tanned it in the smoke house 'longside of the hams. He was a big Indian. I got me a shot pouch out of him and a saddle seat that I'm still using." He laughed.

Rion looked into the warm, brown eyes and laughed too. "Maybe we'll all have us saddle seats this time next week."

Hubbard nodded and glanced back at the boy. "You ever run into a big chief named Dragging Canoe? Got a lot of pockmarks on his face. Son to the Old Carpenter."

"Yes," Rion said.

"He was leading this band. They passed by Tom Rogers' house before they got to Leas'. One of the Rogers boys was hid in the woods and got a good sight of them as they passed. Said it was the Canoe, all right, big as life. Most folks thought he was killed in that battle on the Flats here."

"I put a bullet in him that day," Rion said.

"Seems you didn't shoot sharp enough. . . . Well, he's drawn off from the others and started him a new town. There's a fellow in our neighborhood named Duncan got over into it once trading. Says the Canoe is the great man there. Got nigh a thousand warriors."

"When'd you get up this expedition?" Rion asked. "I never heard anything about it till tonight."

"I was there when it started, you might say. At Rogers' store. This fellow, Duncan, was there and young Colonel Shelby. They hadn't heard about the Lea massacre till I rode up with this boy—now his folks are gone he's living with us. Evan Shelby, he looked at this boy and then he looked at that fellow, and he says, 'By God, Duncan, if you can guide us to the towns I'll recruit the men!'

"We started out riding that afternoon and by night we had

passed the word to five hundred men. . . . That was day before yesterday. I met Jim Lyles at the crossroads just before I turned in here and he says he rounded up another hundred today."

"Big Creek!" Rion said, "It'll take two days to get there."

He went out to the smokehouse and got down a side of meat and filled a sack with meal and laid the meat on top and tied the sack up and took it back to the house.

"Well," he said, "we better be starting."

Hubbard was looking down at the baby who had crawled over and was playing with the lace of his moccasin. "What you going to do with the young one?"

But Rion was already stooping to pick him up. "We'll drop him at Jacob Wagner's. Jacob's too old to fight but he'll tend to my stock till I get back."

The creeks were high everywhere and some of the currents were so swift they could not be forded. They had to go many miles out of their way. It was well past midnight on the second day when they arrived at the banks of the Clinch. The encampment was on a low bluff between the river and the mouth of the creek. Although it was so late the camp was still in motion. Fires were burning high and men went to and fro between them. As they rode up they heard off in the woods the crash of a falling tree.

"I reckon they ain't got all the flatboats built yet," Hubbard said.

They dismounted beside the first campfire. A long pit had been dug at one side and men were raking red coals into it. A long way off a man knelt on the ground, cutting up the carcass of a deer. He saw Hubbard and swung his bloody knife high in the air. "Evening, Major!"

The men came from the pit and took the collops he had cut and spitted them on their ramrods. Hubbard looked down at the haunch from which the collops had been cut. "You going to have any of that left for us, Bill?"

Bill reached around behind him and dragged a shoulder forward. "I'll start this broiling for you now."

"Much obliged," Hubbard said, "I want to go over here and speak to the colonel."

"What we going to do with these horses?" Rion asked.

Hubbard put two fingers to his mouth and whistled. A boy came running. "Here's some more horses for you, Bud," Hubbard said.

"Where's the range?" Rion asked as he threw his bridle to the boy.

" 'Tain't a quarter of a mile from here," the boy said. "You want me to hobble 'em?"

"Yes. . . . Is the pea vine plentiful?"

The boy laid his thin hand against his waist. "Up to here. And there's clover too."

"How many horses you got now?" Hubbard asked.

"I done quit counting." He sidled up to Hubbard. "Listen, Bro' Joe. That old man lives over there by the branch says he and his boys'll look after the horses."

Hubbard shook his head. "I don't much like that old man's looks."

As they walked off he laughed. "That's my baby brother. I been teasing him, saying he'll have to stay here to look after the horses."

"You going to take him, ain't you?" Lea asked suddenly in his hoarse voice.

"Sure, I'm going to take him. Boy that age, it'd kill him to miss the fight."

They walked on. The fires made a continuous line of light. Over where the bluff sloped the flatboats lay end to end. Some men were knocking the last boards into place on one. A heavy-set, fair-haired young fellow put down his hammer and came towards them.

"Well, Joe, how many did you round up?"

"Fifty to seventy," Hubbard said easily. "Colonel, this here's the Lea boy and here's Lieutenant Outlaw from over near the Island."

Evan Shelby stepped over and shook John Lea's hand, then turned to Rion. "You must have been at the battle at the Flats."

"That's right," Rion said.

"The Canoe was leading them there?"

"I got a shot at him," Rion said. "I thought for a while I'd finished him off."

Shelby shook his head. He looked off at the glittering water. "Well, this time day after tomorrow you'll get another shot at him."

"You figure on starting in the morning?" Hubbard asked quietly.

Shelby nodded. "The sooner the better, the river's already

started falling. And we've got enough men now." He jerked a thumb over his shoulder. "A hundred and fifty of Clark's men just came in under Colonel Montgomery."

"That makes around nine hundred," Hubbard said. He stood there smiling, head bent down, swaying lightly from foot to foot, then suddenly said, "I'll see you around light," and turned on his heel.

"That's old Master Isaac Shelby's son, ain't it?" Rion asked as they walked off.

"Aye, and he's a one now, I tell you! Those Shelbys are all good Indian fighters. . . . And they'll go out on a limb, too, if there's need. Old man Shelby raised the money for the men's pay on his own guarantee. . . ."

They were back inside the pit. The deer flesh, nicely broiled, was lifted on a ramrod and carried over to a stump and cut into three pieces. Hubbard had some salt in his pocket. They ate the flesh and washed it down with brandy from Bill Kirk's jug.

As soon as he had eaten, the Lea boy lay down in the shadow of a log with his eyes shut. The others sat around the fire talking for a few minutes until Rion yawned and glanced up at the sky. No color in the east yet. They could get in two or three hours' sleep before day broke. He stretched out beside Kirk near the fire.

Hubbard had gone off into the bushes. He came back in a few minutes, carrying his saddle. Kirk laughed.

"Got to have ye a pillow, Joe?"

Hubbard was settling down with his head on the saddle. He looked over at Rion and smiled. "I think a lot of this saddle," he said and suddenly put his hand up and touched the skin. Rion looked at the skin where it showed between his cheek and his fingers. Like pigskin, only not as coarse-grained, and darker, and yet not as dark as you'd expect it to be. Did a man's skin wear lighter as time went on, like a beast's?

He looked away to the river rushing tumultously past. In a few hours he would be on that rushing water, moving to the Chicka-mauga towns.

CHAPTER 64

THE COFFIN had come to rest with a thud. The four men were clambering up out of the grave. Cassy looked down at the slabs of glistening oak. They rested in a pool of water and water was oozing out of the sides of the freshly dug grave.

"I wish they didn't have to bury her now," she thought.

Murrow was reading from the Scriptures: "And as Moses lifted up the serpent in the wilderness even so must the Son of Man be lifted up. That whosoever believeth on him shall not perish but have eternal life. . . ."

She closed her eyes and for a second it was as if she were back in the storm. She had not been off the place since the rainy spell began. She had not realized that there was a flood until she came out of the woods and saw the water covering the cornfield. She was afraid that Murrow would want to turn back when he saw the water in the field, but he did not seem worried and they rode on the bridle path past Jacob's house. It was lightening then. They were several miles on their way before the storm broke. There was a great clap of thunder and the woods for miles around were lit with the flash. An oak beside the path showed a white streak down its trunk where the bark had been peeled off. The branches tossed wildly across the path as the wind rose. The downpour came, so hard that the horse stopped in his tracks, trembling. Ahead she could see the creek rushing yellow. "He'll turn around when he sees that," she thought and reached up and broke a switch from a tossing bough.

Murrow turned his head. "Sister Outlaw, do you think we can get across?"

She did not answer, only cut the horse with the switch. He bounded forward, was down the slippery bank and into the water. Black twigs hurled past in a nest of foam. The horse was swimming; they had been swept past the ford. She felt his haunches gathering under her and then he was scrambling up a shelving bank. A hoof slipped. He was down. She jumped free, staggered and rolled back into the water.

When she came up she was headed downstream. She struck out as best she could but she could not make any headway against that current and would have been carried on downstream if a sycamore root had not thrust out into the water. She caught hold of it and hauled herself up on to the bank.

Murrow was running towards her. He stopped, pale as a ghost, his big hands outstretched. "I thought you'd be drowned!"

She laughed. "I wasn't feared."

He had closed his eyes and seemed to be praying. She touched him on the arm. "Where's Tom?" But even as she spoke she saw the horse making off through the woods on the other side of the creek.

Murrow opened his eyes. "He didn't stand! I thought he'd stand a minute." He stared at the raging water. "We can't go back."

"No," she said fiercely, "we can't go back."

Standing there with the water streaming off her, she looked across the creek and through the trees. The house was four miles away through those woods. But it seemed farther than that. And it seemed a long time ago that she had left it. She might never go back.

Murrow had started off. She ran and caught up with him. Trudging along beside him, her head bent against the slanting rain, seeing only the black trunks go by one after another, she thought about what had happened. That first night, after she had screamed out like that and then had fallen and cut her hand, a feeling of calm had come over her. She had told herself that she could forgive, that she could make it be as if it had never happened. She told herself that and had been glad to feel his arms about her and had finally gone to sleep. In the night she had waked from a dream that he was gone forever and had pressed closer to him. Lying there, feeling him warm against her she had been overcome with pity for him. Those people. She remembered the first time she had ever seen them when they came up to the house with some beans that they wanted to trade for potatoes. The man, dirty, greasy, always faintly smiling. "What is it he is hiding?" she had thought. When the woman was handing her the basket of beans their hands had touched. The flesh of that hand was firm and cool and yet she had not liked to touch it. Lying there beside him, thinking of that woman, she had gone cold as a stone and all the next day that moment kept coming back as if the woman walked behind her and now and then put out a hand and touched hers. She tried to drive it away by working but it kept coming back. And with the memory came the knowledge that Rion had endured the touch of that flesh, had sought it out, had gone to it again and again. "Like a dog to his vomit," she whispered to herself and standing at the churn, her arms still going up and down while her lashes beat off the tears she had whispered, "No, it was what he wanted . . . more than me. . . . She was what he wanted." And she saw herself a creature of such poor account that a man would hardly go out of his way to avoid stepping on it and yet a creature that went on living its desperate life, like a rattlesnake that she had seen once that some boys had caught and were teasing with Seneca root. The thing kept turning its head from side to side, loathing what was offered, and yet it had to go on, and every time it turned the boys would be there, holding the loathsome root up before it. She whispered, "There's no chance," and staggered away from the churn, feeling all faint within, and as she sat down on the doorstep, bringing her knees up against her forehead, she felt a shuddering go all through her and thought that now she must never have a child again or it would be such a monster as she herself had become.

That afternoon he had come up to the house early—no wonder with the wind rising so outside. He had come in, looked at her wildly, and then had gone to sit down by the hearth. She had thought "What have they done to him?" And then she knew that she could not stay in that house any longer and was about to slip out the back way when the Reverend's knock came at the door. . . .

The grave was almost filled. They were raising the hymn:

> The day is past and gone,
> The evening shades appear
> Oh may we all remember well
> The night of death is here. . . .

She tried to sing with the others but when she took a deep breath the pain stabbed through her side and she fell silent. She knew the moment when that pain had settled there, when they came into the Honeycutt clearing and the wild cry rang out from the house. Murrow had turned his sodden, streaming face towards hers. "I fear we are too late, Sister." "Yes," she said and felt the breath flutter in her throat like a bird beating against a pane. "Yes. It's Death. Left her and come to me." She shivered, feeling her wet clothes cold against her skin, and then the lightness came over her and she walked by his side, as if she were floating, up the hill and into the house.

Joe Honeycutt had been at the foot of the bed and the women all standing around it. Joe was crying. You could hear him through all the talk. She went into the other room where his sister, Rena Duncan, was keeping the children. She sat down on a stool by the fire and took the five-year-old on her lap. He sat there a second and then he turned around and looked up into her face and twisted off her lap and was gone to the other side of the hearth.

Rena Duncan had raised a face soiled with tears. "You mean you walked here by yourself in this storm?"

"The parson came with me," she told her. "He's in there now." Rena got up and went to look at him.

She could remember that moment when, seeing Rena's broad back in the doorway, she had felt herself alone in the room, and smiling had held her hands out to the flames, but she could not remember everything that had happened last night. There had been a wake. A man had fallen down drunk on the floor and had been rolled out like a log, and once a woman, carrying a pitcher of milk, had stopped to lay a hand against her cheek. "You got fever," she said and was gone through the crowd.

The song was done. They were turning away from the grave. Joe Honeycutt walked between his brother and the parson, his eyes bent on the ground, his hands clasped before him. Behind him came the five children and after them Rena, holding the baby in her arms. Charlotte Robertson stepped up beside Cassy. They walked out of the graveyard toward the house.

Charlotte was talking about the children. Rena was going to take the three little ones home with her but the oldest girl and the two boys would stay with their father.

Cassy put her hand against her side. The pain had settled in one place now. It would be all right if she did not have to breathe, but when she took air into her lungs it seemed to turn to fire.

She suddenly staggered off the path and sat down on a stump. Charlotte ran to her. "*Cassy!* You're sick?"

Cassy looked straight ahead and did not answer. The other woman, bending over her, noticed for the first time that her cheeks were darkly flushed, her lips livid. She slipped her arm about her waist. "Come on. Let me help you to the house."

Cassy stood up. Holding herself rigid she drew in shallow breaths, and started walking, as carefully as an old woman, along the path.

CHAPTER 65

By DAWN the flotilla was in motion: over a hundred scows, and behind them dug-outs and canoes—some men who came in during the night did not want to take time to knock a flatboat together and followed in their own vessels. Rion, through his friendship with Hubbard, got a place in the lead boat, with Colonel Shelby and the guide.

The river fell slowly all that day. But the current still raced, full of snags and drifts. The boats hugged the banks as much as they could. There were bad jams when somebody took pike hold without warning—it had been agreed that they would not call out once they got started—but nobody was hurt except Tom Bulloch who fell backwards off a flatboat and was picked up by a dug-out.

The descent was easier after they turned into the Tennessee. Thursday night was fair, with stars showing. The river was still swollen but calm. They floated on all night, half the men sleeping while the others kept watch. Rion had taken his turn at the swivel during the earlier part of the night and after midnight lay down to sleep. When he woke the sky was grey. A canoe was drawing up alongside the boat.

Two men climbed out: Evan Shelby and Ed Duncan. Rion worked his way to them over the bodies of sleeping men. They had been scouting. The creek they were hunting for emptied into the river about a mile below. It was swollen far out of its banks but Duncan had identified it by a peculiar rock formation near the mouth. The town was two miles up this creek.

"But you'll have to purty nigh swim to get to it," Duncan said. "There's low ground all the way between here and there."

"That's all the better," Shelby told him. "They won't look for us to come that way."

He went to the side of the scow and told the men waiting in the dug-outs to paddle back up the line with the word.

An hour later the whole force had landed, in water, on the north bank of the river. They pushed around some drift and through some

461

willows and were on the edge of a tall cane brake. The water was waist deep. They had slung their powder horns and shot pouches over the muzzles of their guns and waded on, holding the guns high over their heads. The cane grew thick: you could hear it popping as the men broke their way through and the sloshing of the feet was like the sound of cattle crossing a ford. Shelby was worried about the noise they were making and wanted to turn back and try some other way, but Duncan said they had better go on; this brake was the best cover anywhere near the town.

It was not so dark now. A man could see where he was going. Rion looked up over the tops of the cane. The huge mountain that they had first seen through mist late yesterday afternoon towered up not a mile away. Thick woods stretched away from its base. The town must be this side of those woods. He looked to the east. Above the long wooded ridge the sky glowed red. They had not much time to lose if they were going to attack before day.

They were coming to the end of the cane. Beyond, on rising ground, lay a cornfield, and beyond that the houses: twenty or thirty of them standing in a grove of oaks. A meadow sloped from the grove down to the creek. At the far end of it, just out of the high water, stood the town house.

Rion heard hard breathing behind him. He looked back into the forest of green stalks. Everywhere dark forms showed. There was a click as the man next to him drew his ramrod out. He made his own gun ready.

Evan Shelby standing beside him gave an exclamation.

"What's the matter?" Rion whispered.

Shelby pointed silently. Rion saw a figure coming up the slope from the creek. It moved forward slowly through the pearly light, passed the sleeping houses and came to the one at the end. A woman. The first rays of the sun struck on her as she walked over to a hominy mortar that stood under a big willow, and taking up the mall began to pound it up and down.

Shelby swore under his breath. "Why couldn't she have stayed asleep!"

"There's somebody else," Rion said.

A young man had come out of the end cabin. He yawned and stretched himself, then going over to where the woman stood put his arms about her and catching hold of the mall began to work it up and down.

The yellow feather in his hair jerked to and fro as his arms moved. The woman struggled a little in his embrace, then stood still. Their laughter floated thinly across the meadow.

From the cane behind them came a shot. Evan Shelby turned his head. "The fool!"

He was off across the cornfield. Rion ran after him.

The young warrior lay face downwards on the ground. The woman threw her head back and screamed, then bent and slipped her arms about the upper part of his body. As she was straightening up with her burden Rion brought his gun up and fired. Her hands fell away from the man's shoulders. She grasped at the air and fell slowly backward.

Evan halted, looked over his shoulder and made a circling motion with his hand. "Go around to the back," he called. "Tell some of 'em to go around to the back!"

Some of the men were already deploying across the cornfield. Rion stopped where he was, poured a charge from his horn, laid the patch on and rammed the bullet home, then ran on, priming as he went. Behind him the woman's scream still beat the air. Down at the end of the row shadowy figures bobbed. Up here there was no one and then a man was standing in a doorway, musket in hand.

He looked at Rion, sleep still in his eyes, and threw the gun from him and sprang forward. Rion fired. The bullet struck the Indian in the shoulder. He spun around and fell on his face.

Rion stood over him and loaded again. White men poured past. Down under the trees the fighting had started, the Indians backed up there against the town house. White men were coming on them from all sides. He ran up, fired once, then shifting his gun to his left hand, drew his tomahawk and went in. The fighting was close. It was hard to tell white men from Indians, and then suddenly it was all over and Evan Shelby was yelling out men's names, throwing a guard around the prisoners.

Rion stepped back and felt of the cut on his arm. He looked towards the creek. They were still fighting there. He loaded and went over. Indians were racing down the bank and escaping into the woods on the other side. A canoe was moving down the stream.

Empty. No, an arm crooked up over the side moved like an oar. He was about to take aim when somebody called to him to hold his fire. A head bobbed through the water. A hand reached up and grasped the side of the canoe.

The Indian sat up squealing: "I Cherokee, not Chickamauga!"

"What are you doing here?" John Lea said and, holding on to the side of the canoe, swung at him with his tomahawk. He had to strike three times before the canoe spun around and shot down the stream, the dark arm still trailing over the side. Lea was swimming back. Rion saw his face as he started up the bank, the dull look gone, the pale eyes gleaming.

There was a yell from over near the town house, white men, not Indians. It came again, a prolonged, hoarse shouting from many throats.

Rion ran over to where men were milling about a big oak tree. An Indian lay sprawled at the foot of the oak, bleeding from a wound in the chest. Joe Hubbard was kneeling beside him.

As Rion approached he lifted the flap that covered the man's loins. The left thigh was revealed, scarred and bitten by an old wound.

Joe straightened up and looked around the circle. "It's him!"

Evan Shelby was pushing through the crowd. Joe got to his feet. "I was standing there by him and he made a break. . . . I thought I might as well finish him off."

Shelby was looking down at the Indian. "It's the Canoe, all right," he said.

Hubbard was leaning over, his knife out, his hand on the man's head, when Shelby spoke: "Don't! Let's take him like he is."

"He ain't dead yet," a voice said from the crowd.

Shelby bent and, lugging the man by the shoulders, propped him against the tree trunk.

He was even bigger than Rion had thought he was, about fifty, barrel-chested and long-legged. His eyes were closed. His head hung limp to one side but you could see breath flutter in the chest. The motion had brought fresh blood spilling from the wound and blood ran between the slack lips down over the chin. Suddenly the cords of the neck tightened. The lips closed. The head went back against the tree trunk. The black eyes opened and he glared around the circle of watching men; the lids sank, slowly, but did not close.

The glare shone on from behind the slitted lids after the blood had found its way between the closed lips and his neck went slack and he slumped to the ground.

The cries had died down. The men were moving away. Rion walked off towards the cabins. Hubbard was beside him wiping his knife on a twist of grass.

He turned shining eyes on Rion: ". . . I came out there between the cabins and there wasn't an Indian in sight and then I saw this fellow come hobbling and knew it was the Canoe. I missed my shot at him but I worked in through the crowd and I was right by him when they gave in. He kept yelling for 'em not to. I knew all along he'd make a break for it. . . ."

They had come to the end of the street. Under the greyish plumes of the willow a woman's flung skirt was a scarlet blur on green grass. They walked over and stood beside her. Her eyes, wide open, gazed past them across the meadow. The red upper lip, drawn back, showed her white teeth. Her hands were clenched at her sides.

Hubbard had put his foot out and was turning the man's body over. He gave a whistle. "White man!"

Rion looked down. The bullet had entered the back and must have found the lungs; there was a froth of blood on the mouth and chin. Otherwise the face was unscarred. Hubbard took his foot away. Archy rolled over on his back and lay, one arm upflung, the other crumpled under him. His brown eyes stared up into the trees. His bloody lips were parted in a kind of surprise.

Rion became aware of lively eyes fixed on his face.

"You know the feller?"

"I knew him once," Rion said. He leaned over and pulled the arm out from under the body and straightened it at the side. "I knew him a long time ago."

CHAPTER 66

ELSA GOT up and tied a cloth over her head. "I'm going to feed the chickens."

Rion did not answer. She picked up the bucket of shelled corn and went out.

When the door had closed behind her he tiptoed over to the foot of the bed. Cassy had a sheet drawn over her. Under it she lay on her side, her knees raised high. One hand was slipped under the pillow, the other lay on top of the sheet and rested against her side, just under the breast.

When they had brought her back from Honeycutt's a week ago —the two stout Honeycutt boys bearing the litter—her face had been as dark they said as a negro's, with the lips grey. Her lips were still swollen and cracked from the fever but her cheeks were pale. The flesh of the forehead glistened a little where the hair was turned back. Was it sweat? He did not dare go any closer and after a moment he tiptoed back to his stool and sat down.

Through the window came the sound of subdued voices. They had moved around to that side of the house early in the afternoon to get out of the sun and still sat on into the dusk. James Robertson and his wife had come this morning and Joe Hubbard and Amos Eaton had come with him last night. Jane, of course, had been there all along.

He stretched the muscles of his back. He had slept ill last night because his arm had bothered him, and then there had been the breathing. After a while it did not seem to come from Cassy but from some creature that crouched beside the bed. Towards morning he had fallen into a doze and dreamed that he and Cassy, walking through the woods, came on a cave and they knew from the harsh breathing that a monster lived inside. He had been waked by the sound of Jane crying softly to herself. "We've got good neighbors," he thought, "good neighbors." And then he thought how it would be if Cassy died, and his lips trembled and he felt sweat starting out in the palms of his hands.

He rose and going softly to the window pushed the shutter open and looked out. Polly and the baby were off in the grass playing. The others sat on stools, dim in the round shadow of the sugar tree. The two women stared at the ground but the men were talking. Hubbard had slid off his stool and lounged on his back, looking up at Jim. His voice came clearly through the stillness of the falling light:

"I'm going. I've made up my mind to that."

Jim Robertson raised his head and looked off towards the mountains in the west; then his eyes came back to Hubbard's face. He nodded his head slightly. "I'll go with you, to look the land over anyhow."

"If you do you won't ever come back," Hubbard said. He threw his hand out towards Bays Mountain. "None of these little fifty acre coves. It's all level. . . . A man can get him a thousand acres and all of it flat as the palm of your hand. . . ."

All level, as far as the eye can see. The last time Daniel Boone had been in this house he had been talking about a new land. This one was called Cumber Land, down below the Kentuck road. Judge Henderson had transferred his operations there and was trying to start a new commonwealth.

Cassy moved in the bed. He turned around. Her eyes were open. She was looking at him. He went quickly to her side and knelt down.

She put out her hand and touched his. "Where you been?" He gripped her hand.

"On the Tennessee, fighting Indians."

Her eyes were on his bandaged arm. She was trying to sit up. Still holding her hand, he pressed her gently back on the bed with his other hand. "It's nothing." He bent closer. "Cassy. . . ."

She lay back flat on the pillow, her eyes on his face. Her breath came hard but at last she got enough to speak.

"I was a fool to go off like that."

"It was me," she said. "I've been a fool . . . all my life, always trying to run away from something."

She was smiling, looking away from him up at the ceiling. "I remember the first time you ever paid any attention to me," she whispered.

"At the infare," he said. "Kate Lovelatty's wedding. They were caging the bird. You stood on a chair and held the candle and I thought then. . . ."

Her eyes came slowly back to his face. "Thought what?"

"That you were the one I wanted."

Tears came into her eyes. He bent closer and kissed her and slipped his arm under her back and put his other arm around her waist. She cried out with the pain of being moved. He was about to let her down but she nodded her head to him to keep on holding her like that.

"Does it hurt?" he asked, his lips close to her face.

"Not so much . . . now."

She lay back against his arm. Her eyes were closed and her breath was coming a little harder. He wished that Elsa would come back and then he was glad that she was gone from the room.

Her eyes fluttered open and her hand came up. The fingers closed on his arm. At first he did not know what she wanted and then he slipped his arm out from under her back and let her lie flat.

She lay with her head thrown back, her mouth stretched wide to take in the rasping breath. There was something inside her chest that fought to keep the breath out. A pulse beat in her throat. In the fading light it seemed to him that her face had gone greyer. He leaned over her. "Cassy," he said. "Cassy, you want me to get you anything?"

Her eyes opened and stared at the wall. There was no sound in the room except her hard breathing. He thought: It can't be long. He went over to the bench and dipped a gourd full of water and took a cloth in his hand; then noticing that his hand was shaking he steadied the other hand on the window sill and leaned against it.

They were still sitting under the trees. He raised his eyes to the black rim of western woods. Those stars that Frank used to point out to him were showing. They made a picture: Orion, the mighty hunter. He had been beloved by Diana. One day he was wading through the sea and the goddess' brother, jealous, had showed the dark thing in the water to his sister. The archer-goddess discharged her shaft with fatal aim. The waves rolled the dead body to the land and Diana, weeping, placed him among the stars.

When he was a boy on the Yadkin he used to like to think that he took his name from the mighty hunter, and out in the woods at night or coming home from a frolic he would look up and pick out the stars: the hunter's foot, his club, his girdle, the red eye of the bull that he pursued ever westward. . . . His father had come west across the ocean, leaving all that he cared about behind. And he himself as soon as he had grown to manhood had looked at the mountains and could not rest until he knew what lay beyond them. But it seemed that a man had to flee farther each time and leave more behind him and when he got to the new place he looked up and saw Orion fixed upon his burning wheel, always pursuing the bull but never making the kill. Did Orion will any longer the westward chase? No more than himself. Like the mighty hunter he had lost himself in the turning. Before him lay the empty west, behind him the loved things of which he was made. Those old tales of Frank's! Were not men raised into the westward turning stars only after they had destroyed themselves?

He walked back to the bed. He could not hear her breathing. Fearfully he lifted her wrist and held it in the dark. There was no pulse. He got a candle and lit it and held it over her face, and knew that she was dead.

The candlestick rattled on the boards as the light went out. In the yard the voices murmured composedly. Standing alone beside the bed until the walls closed in, he stumbled out of the room to where the others sat under the dark trees.

Greensboro, North Carolina, October 27, 1938.
Princeton, New Jersey, June 11, 1941.

ACKNOWLEDGMENTS

If I should be fortunate enough to number any local historians among my readers I wish to ask their indulgence for a liberty taken with historical fact. I have reported Dragging Canoe as being killed on Evan Shelby's expedition of 1779, but historians agree that he died some time between March 1, 1792, when he is known to have attended a dance at Lookout Town, and June 26, 1792, when Chief Black Fox announced at the Cherokee National Council at Ustanali that "the Dragging Canoe has left this world."

For this and other liberties taken with historical fact I have to plead the exigencies of the fictional form which impose limitations on history as well as fancy.

Anyone reading pioneer American history even casually must be struck by the original and exhaustive research that has been done by local historians. Like all students of the period I have profited by the lifelong labors of Judge Samuel C. Williams and A. V. Goodpasture. I am particularly indebted to John P. Brown, whose definitive history of the Cherokees, *Old Frontiers*, was published privately in 1938. For quotations from certain old ballads I am indebted to Professor Fletcher Collins, of Elon College, North Carolina.

I would like to thank Professor Paul Counce of the Kingsport, Tennessee, High School who has located the sites of the Battle of Island Flats, Amos Eaton's Station and other landmarks.

C. G.

CAROLINE GORDON (1895–1981), a native of Kentucky, began her literary career in the 1920's after her marriage to poet Allen Tate. In 1929 her first story appeared. In 1931 her first novel, *Penhally*, was published. This was followed by three volumes of short fiction and eight more novels, of which *Green Centuries* (1941) is considered the finest. With her husband she co-authored the influential *The House of Fiction*.

THOMAS H. LANDESS is editor of *The Short Fiction of Caroline Gordon* and a widely published poet and critic of Southern letters. He formerly taught with Caroline Gordon at the University of Dallas and is currently employed by the Federal Government. He holds a Ph.D. in English from the University of South Carolina.